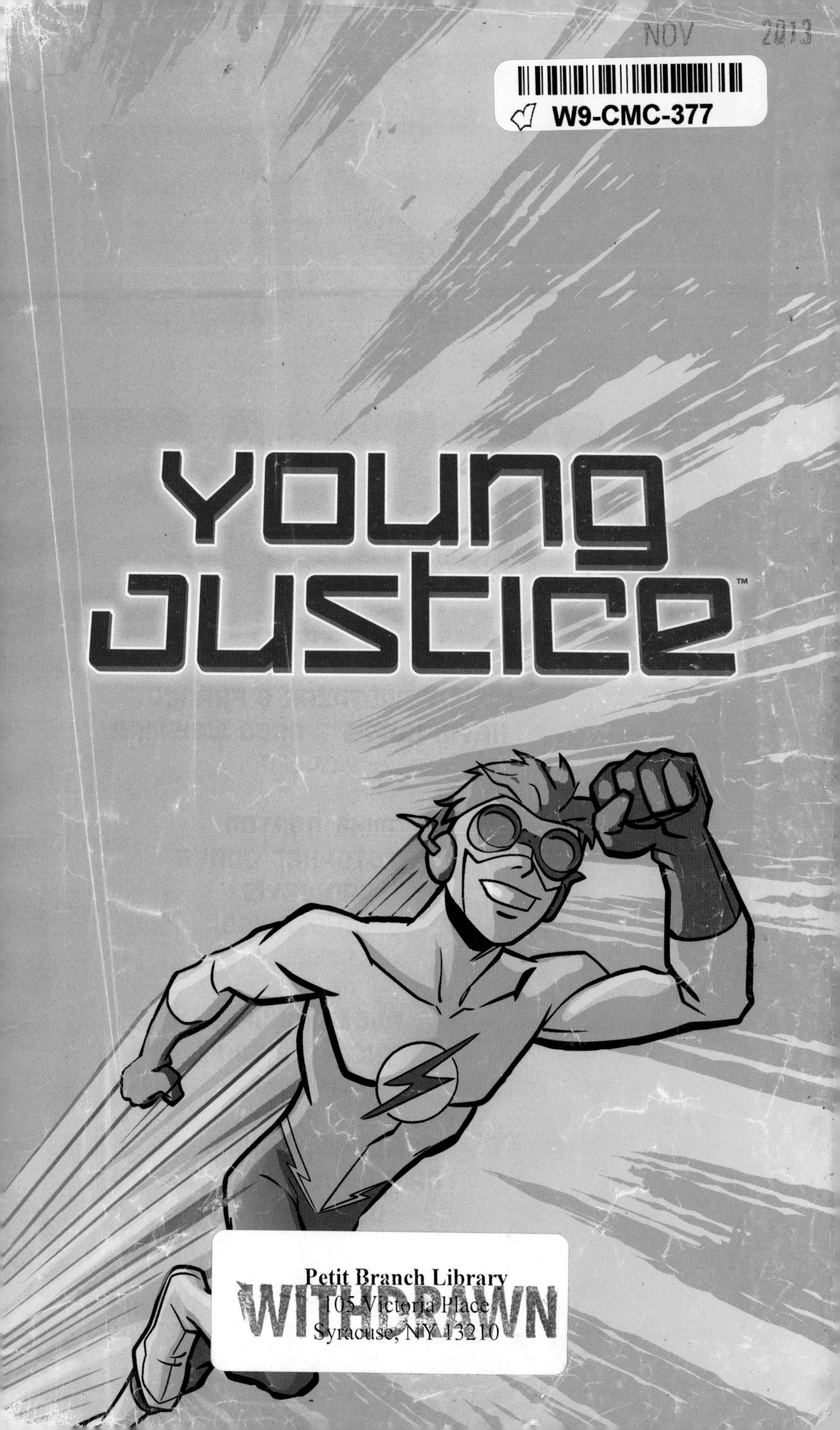
YOUNG
JUSTICE™

YOU

JUS

ART BALTAZAR & FRANCO
KEVIN HOPPS & GREG WEISMAN
Writers

MIKE NORTON
CHRISTOPHER JONES
DAN DAVIS
JOHN STANISCI
Artists

ALEX SINCLAIR
ZAC ATKINSON
Colorists

TRAVIS LANHAM
CARLOS M. MANGUAL
DEZI SIENTY
Letterers

MIKE NORTON & ALEX SINCLAIR
Cover

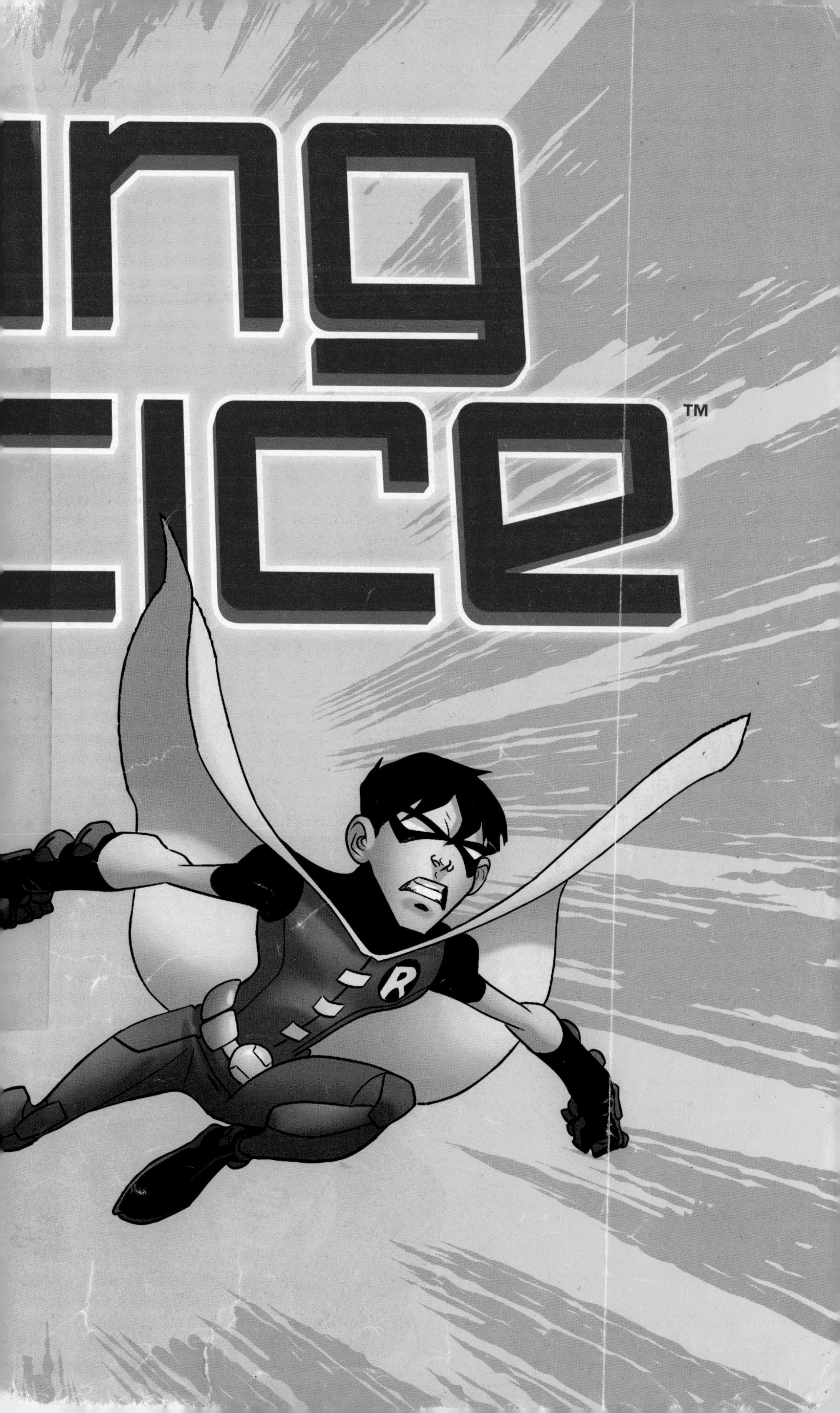

Jim Chadwick Scott Peterson Editors – Original Series
Michael McCalister Assistant Editor – Original Series
Ian Sattler Editor
Robbin Brosterman Design Director – Books
Bob Harras VP – Editor-in-Chief
Diane Nelson President
Dan DiDio and **Jim Lee** Co-Publishers
Geoff Johns Chief Creative Officer
John Rood Executive VP – Sales, Marketing and Business Development
Amy Genkins Senior VP – Business and Legal Affairs
Nairi Gardiner Senior VP – Finance
Jeff Boison VP – Publishing Operations
Mark Chiarello VP – Art Direction and Design
John Cunningham VP – Marketing
Terri Cunningham VP – Talent Relations and Services
Alison Gill Senior VP – Manufacturing and Operations
Hank Kanalz Senior VP – Digital
Jay Kogan VP – Business and Legal Affairs, Publishing
Jack Mahan VP – Business Affairs, Talent
Nick Napolitano VP – Manufacturing Administration
Sue Pohja VP – Book Sales
Courtney Simmons Senior VP – Publicity
Bob Wayne Senior VP – Sales

YOUNG JUSTICE

DC Comics, 1700 Broadway, New York, NY 10019
A Warner Bros. Entertainment Company.
Printed by RR Donnelley, Salem, VA, USA. 3/29/13. Third Printing.
ISBN: 978-1-4012-3357-0

Library of Congress Cataloging-in-Publication Data

Baltazar, Art.
  Young justice / Art Baltazar & Franco Kevin Hopps & Greg Weisman
    p. cm.
  Summary: "Your favorite cartoon teen heroes are back in action! The Justice
League needed a covert team that could operate on the sly, so who better than
experienced crime fighters Robin, Kid Flash and Aqualad? Together with
Superboy, recently rescued from the top-secret Project Cadmus, and the
crush-worthy shape-shifting alien Miss Martian, these teens are ready to stop
being sidekicks and start taking down villains—like the League of Shadows and
the Joker—all on their own. But Superboy may have a secret mission of his own
to complete—destroying Superman!"—P. [4] of cover.
  ISBN 978-1-4012-3357-0 (pbk.)
  [1. Graphic novels.] I. Baltazar, Art. II. Hopps, Kevin. III. Jones, Christopher,
1969- IV. Young justice (Television program; V. Title.
  741.5'973–dc23

                                    2011287684

SUSTAINABLE
FORESTRY
INITIATIVE
Certified Chain of Custody
At Least 20% Certified Forest Content
www.sfiprogram.org
SFI-01042
APPLIES TO TEXT STOCK ONLY

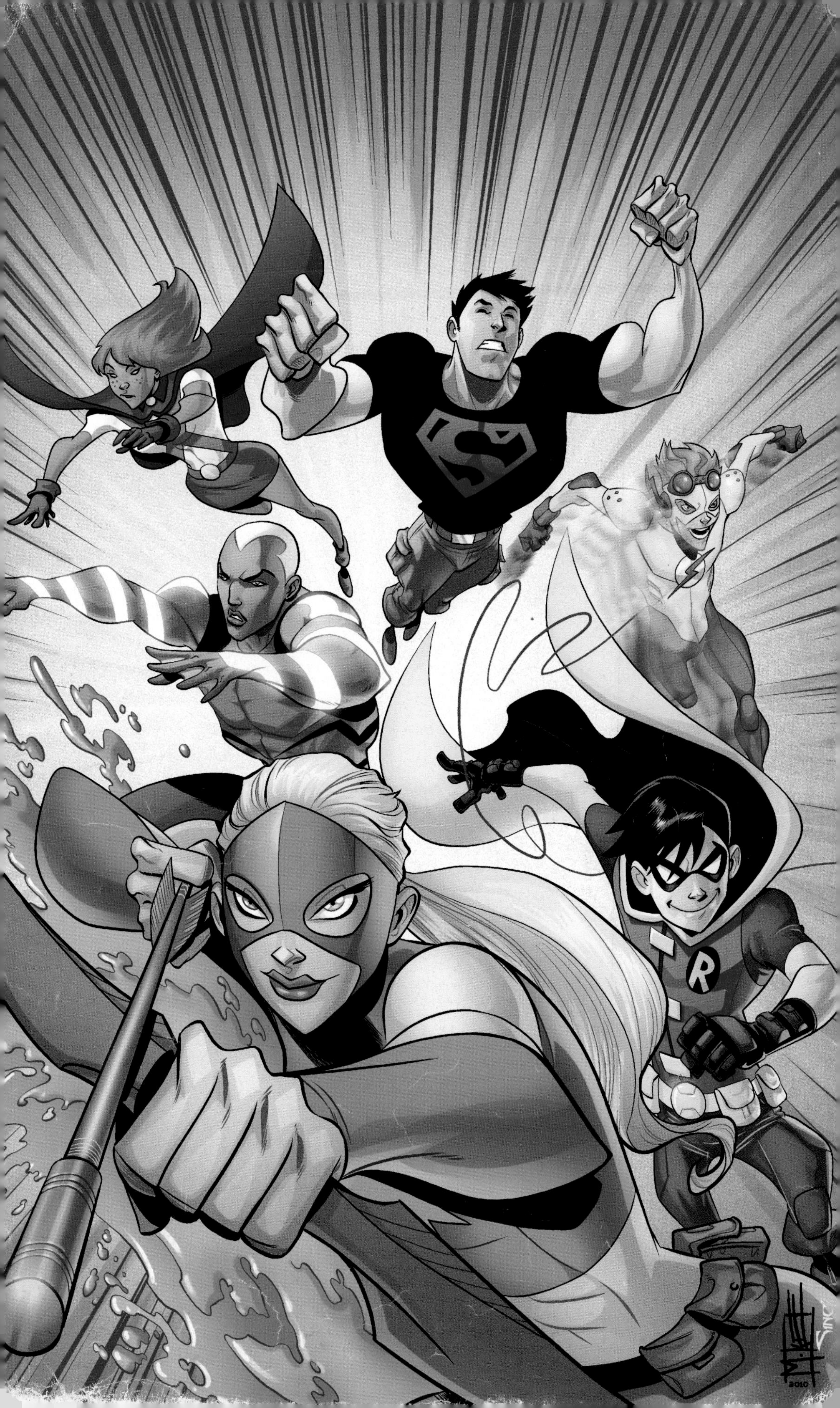

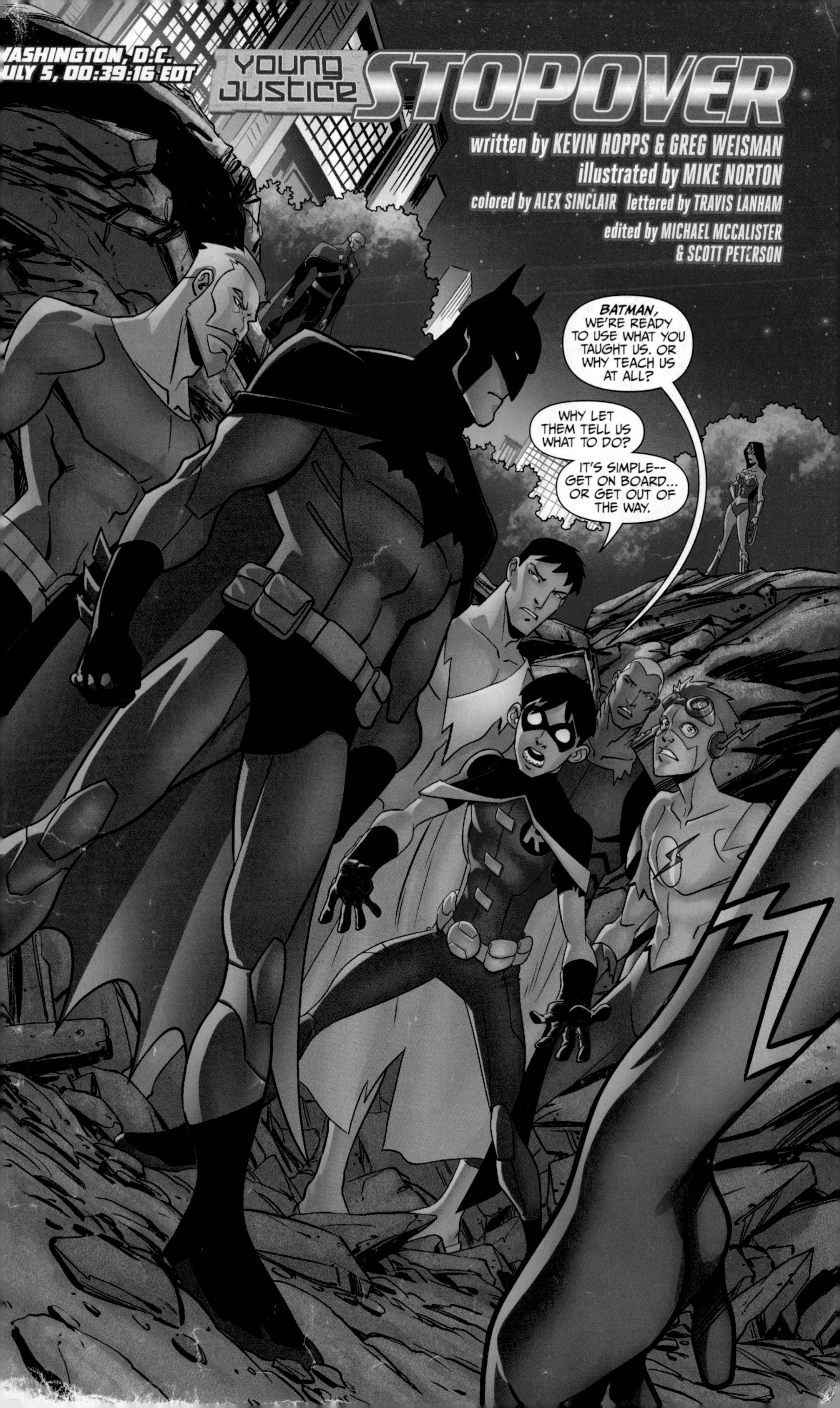

WASHINGTON, D.C.
JULY 5, 00:39:16 EDT
YOUNG JUSTICE
STOPOVER
written by KEVIN HOPPS & GREG WEISMAN
illustrated by MIKE NORTON
colored by ALEX SINCLAIR lettered by TRAVIS LANHAM
edited by MICHAEL MCCALISTER & SCOTT PETERSON
BATMAN, WE'RE READY TO USE WHAT YOU TAUGHT US. OR WHY TEACH US AT ALL?
WHY LET THEM TELL US WHAT TO DO?
IT'S SIMPLE-- GET ON BOARD... OR GET OUT OF THE WAY.

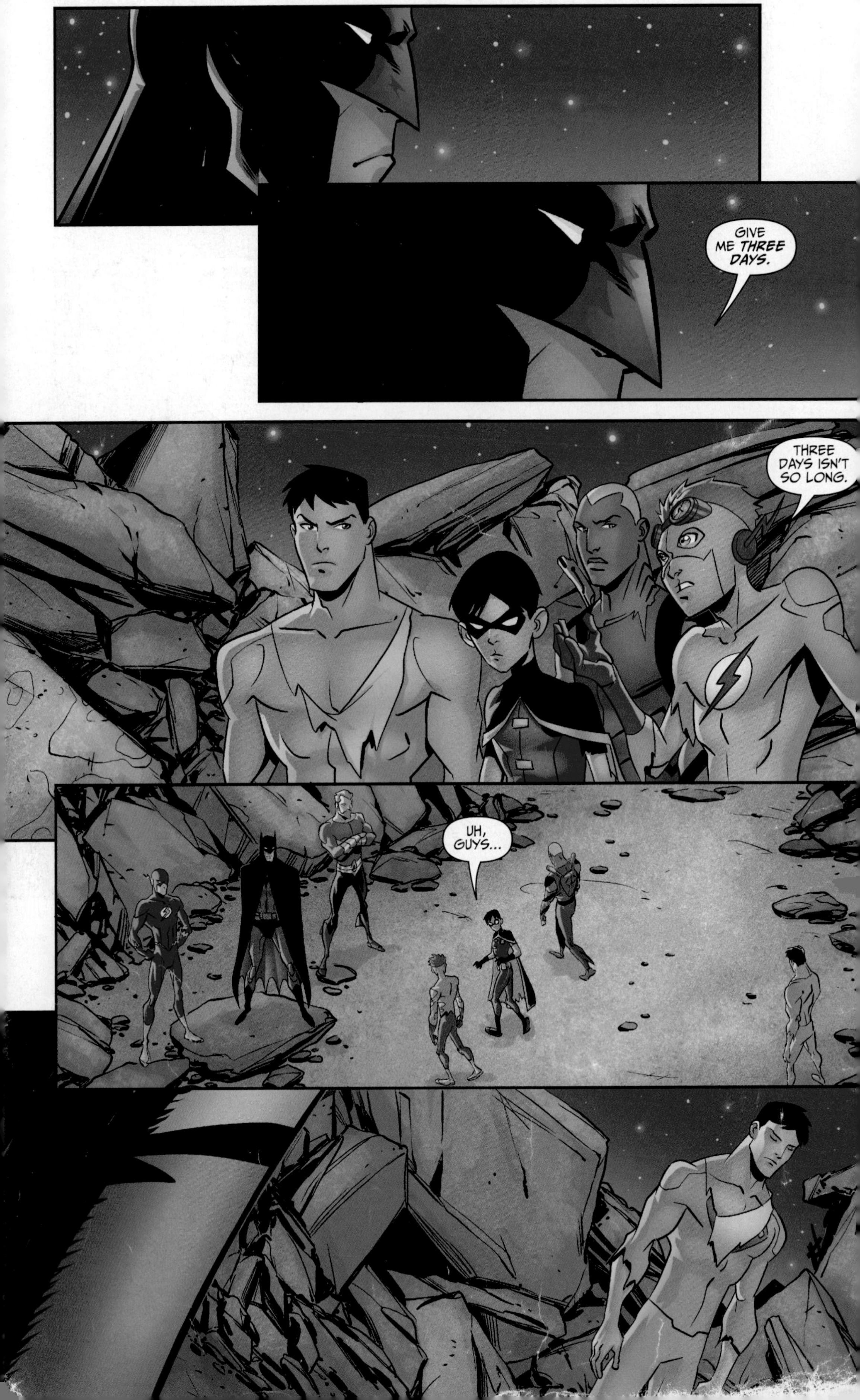
GIVE ME THREE DAYS.
THREE DAYS ISN'T SO LONG.
UH, GUYS...

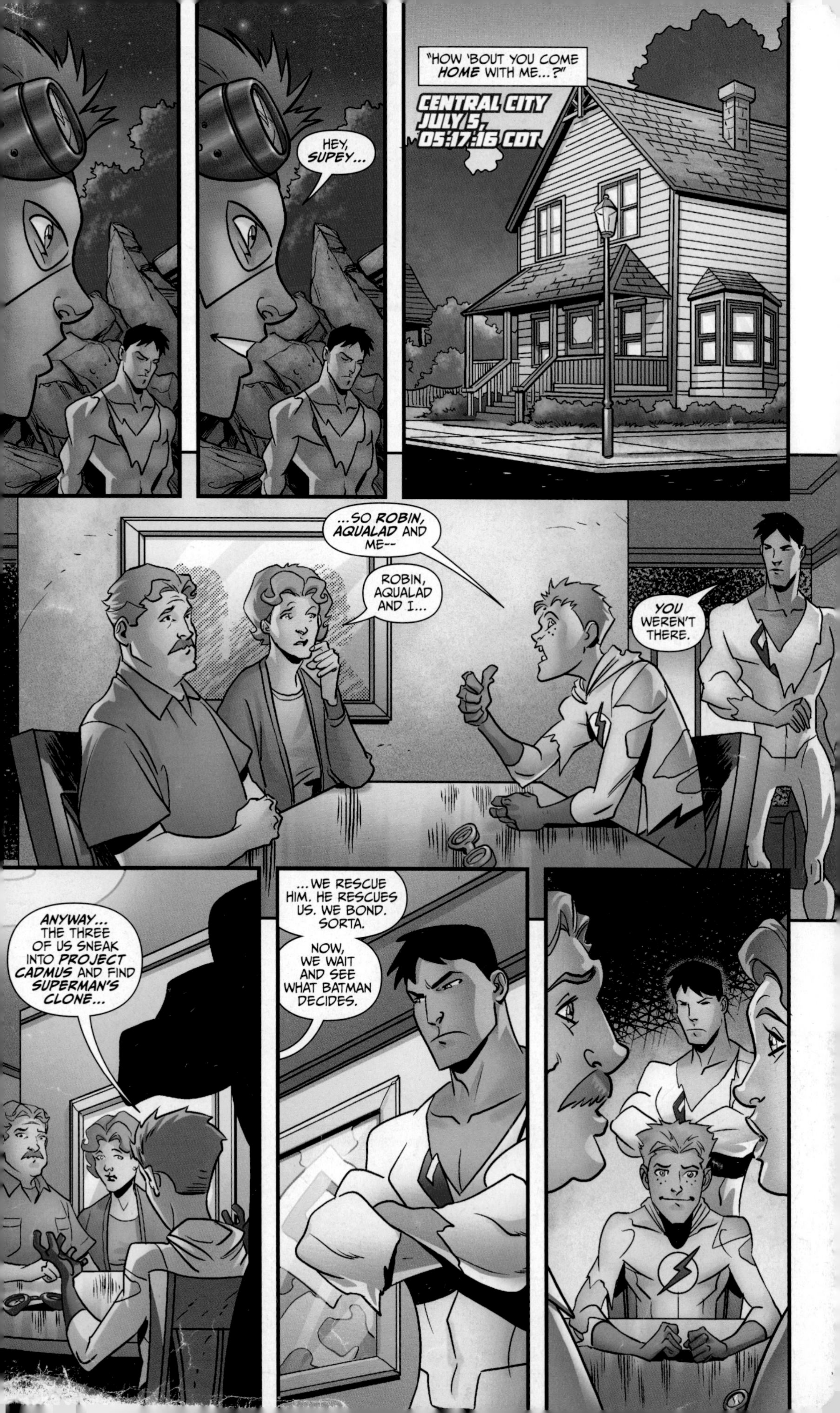
HEY, SUPEY...
"HOW 'BOUT YOU COME HOME WITH ME...?"
CENTRAL CITY JULY 5, 05:17:16 CDT
...SO ROBIN, AQUALAD AND ME--
ROBIN, AQUALAD AND I...
YOU WEREN'T THERE.
ANYWAY... THE THREE OF US SNEAK INTO PROJECT CADMUS AND FIND SUPERMAN'S CLONE...
...WE RESCUE HIM. HE RESCUES US. WE BOND. SORTA.
NOW, WE WAIT AND SEE WHAT BATMAN DECIDES.

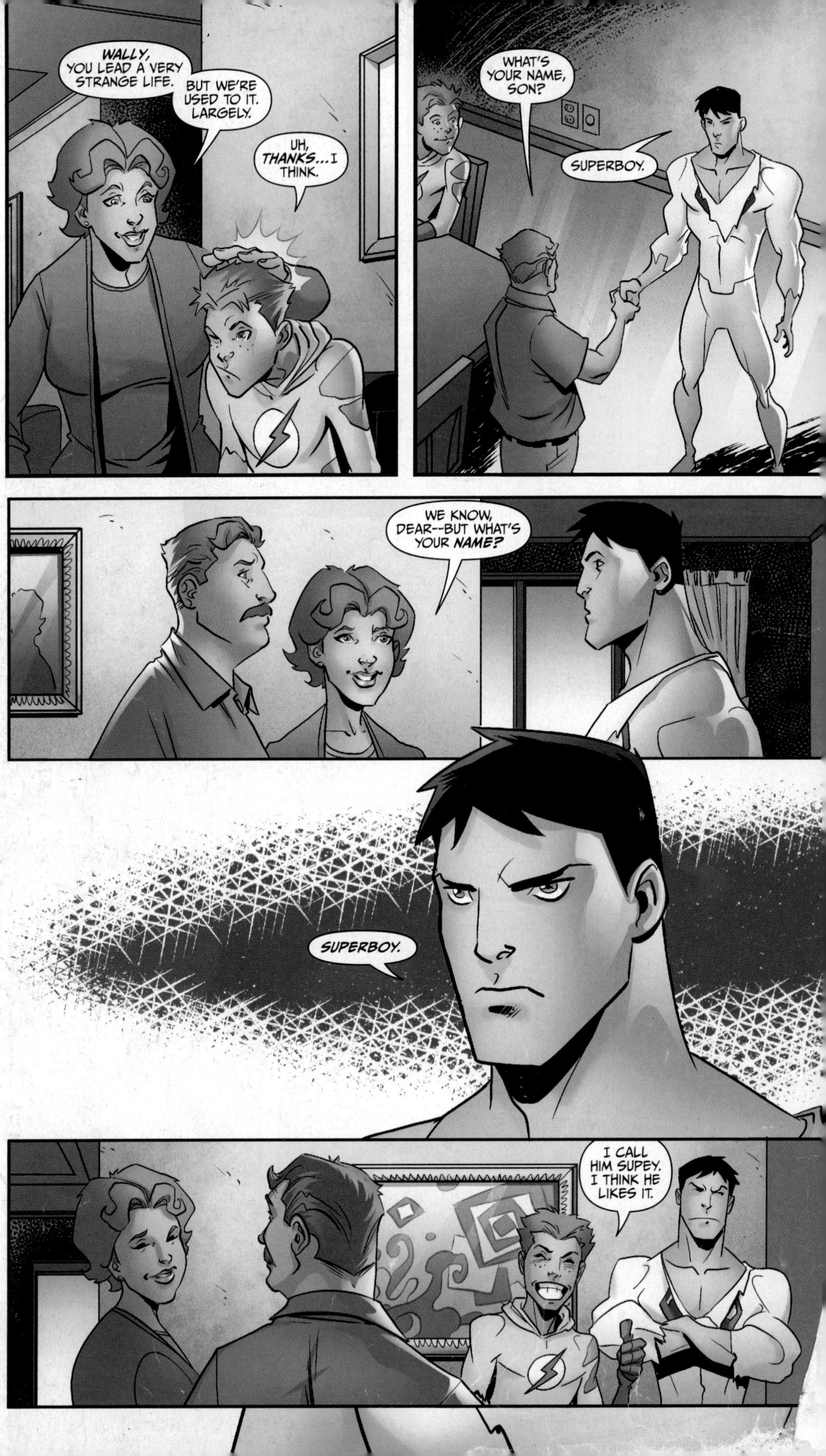
WALLY, YOU LEAD A VERY STRANGE LIFE.
BUT WE'RE USED TO IT. LARGELY.
UH, THANKS...I THINK.
WHAT'S YOUR NAME, SON?
SUPERBOY.
WE KNOW, DEAR--BUT WHAT'S YOUR NAME?
SUPERBOY.
I CALL HIM SUPEY. I THINK HE LIKES IT.

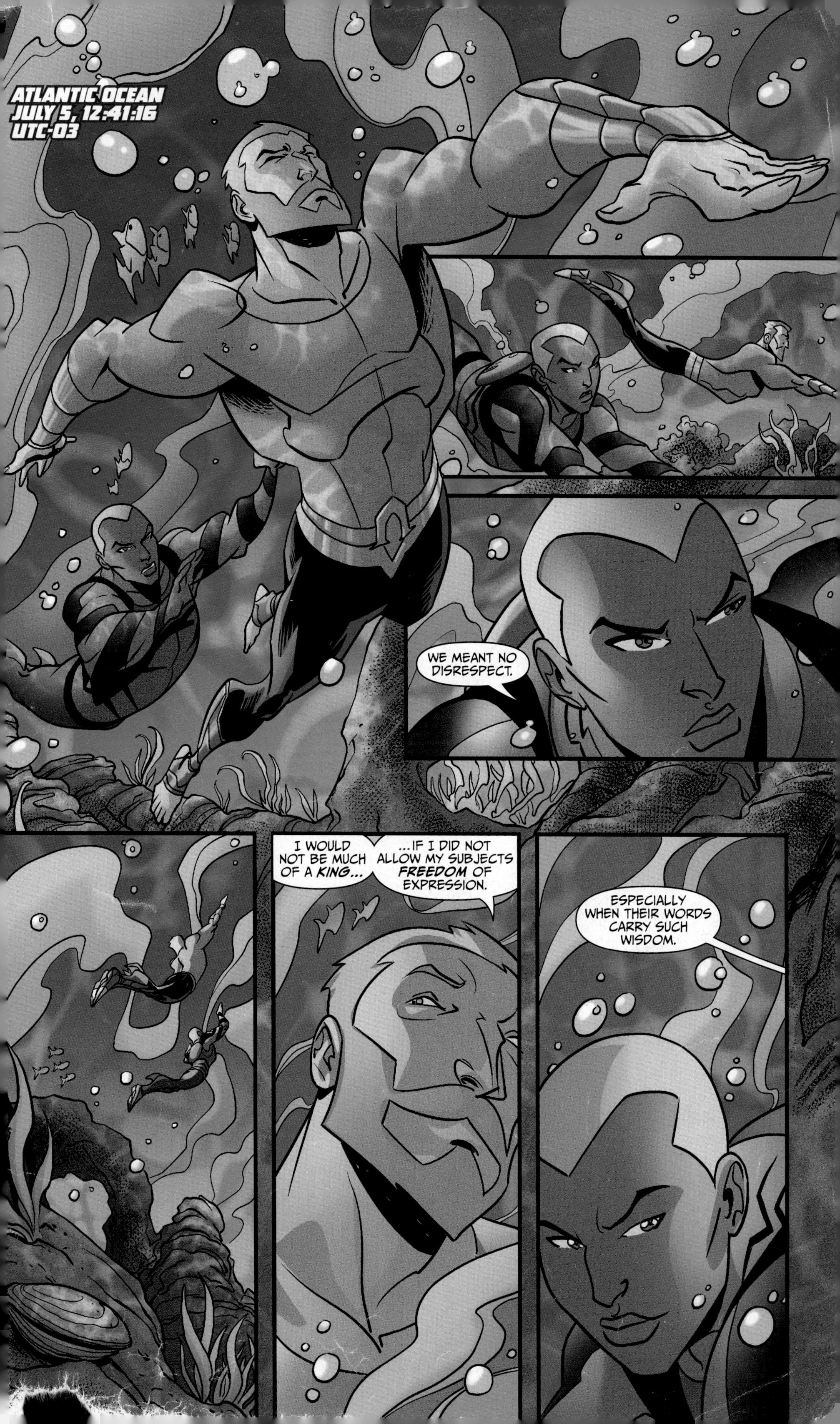
ATLANTIC OCEAN
JULY 5, 12:41:16
UTC-03
WE MEANT NO DISRESPECT.
I WOULD NOT BE MUCH OF A KING...
...IF I DID NOT ALLOW MY SUBJECTS FREEDOM OF EXPRESSION.
ESPECIALLY WHEN THEIR WORDS CARRY SUCH WISDOM.

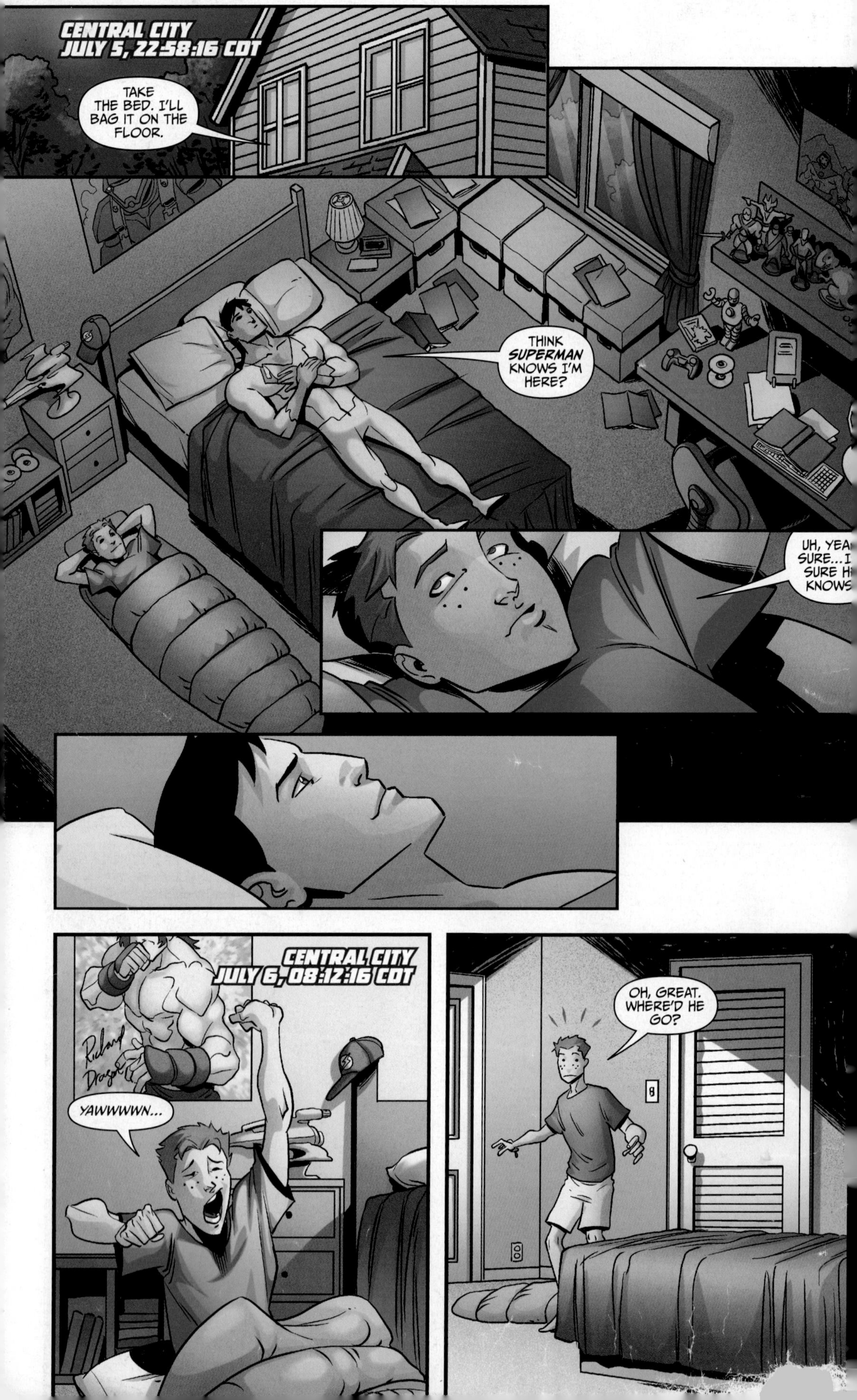
CENTRAL CITY
JULY 5, 22:58:16 CDT
TAKE THE BED. I'LL BAG IT ON THE FLOOR.
THINK SUPERMAN KNOWS I'M HERE?
UH, YEA SURE... I SURE H KNOWS
CENTRAL CITY
JULY 6, 08:12:16 CDT
YAWWWWN...
OH, GREAT. WHERE'D HE GO?

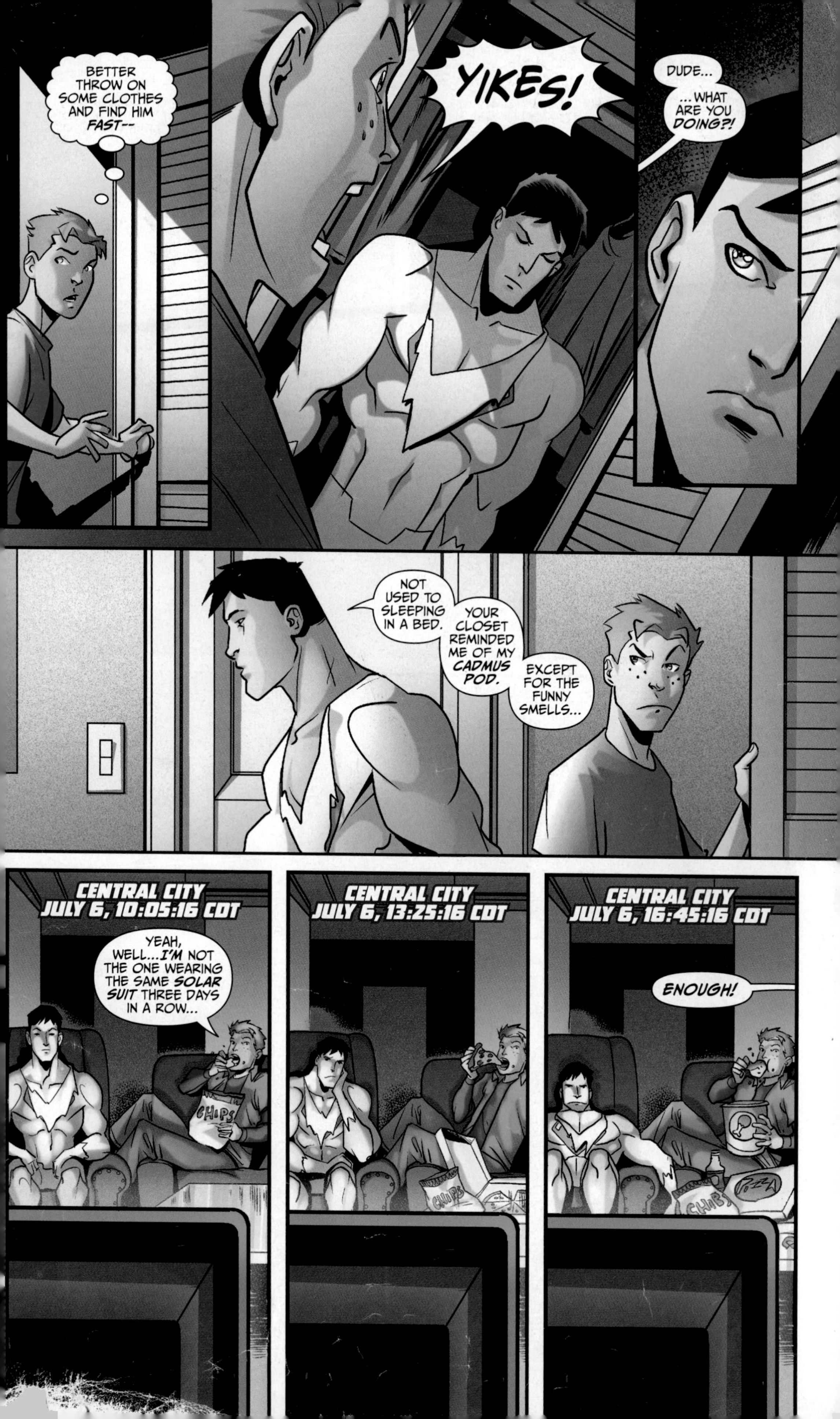
BETTER THROW ON SOME CLOTHES AND FIND HIM FAST--
YIKES!
DUDE...
...WHAT ARE YOU DOING?!
NOT USED TO SLEEPING IN A BED.
YOUR CLOSET REMINDED ME OF MY CADMUS POD.
EXCEPT FOR THE FUNNY SMELLS...
CENTRAL CITY JULY 6, 10:05:16 CDT
YEAH, WELL...I'M NOT THE ONE WEARING THE SAME SOLAR SUIT THREE DAYS IN A ROW...
CHIPS
CENTRAL CITY JULY 6, 13:25:16 CDT
CHIPS
CENTRAL CITY JULY 6, 16:45:16 CDT
ENOUGH!
CHIPS
PIZZA

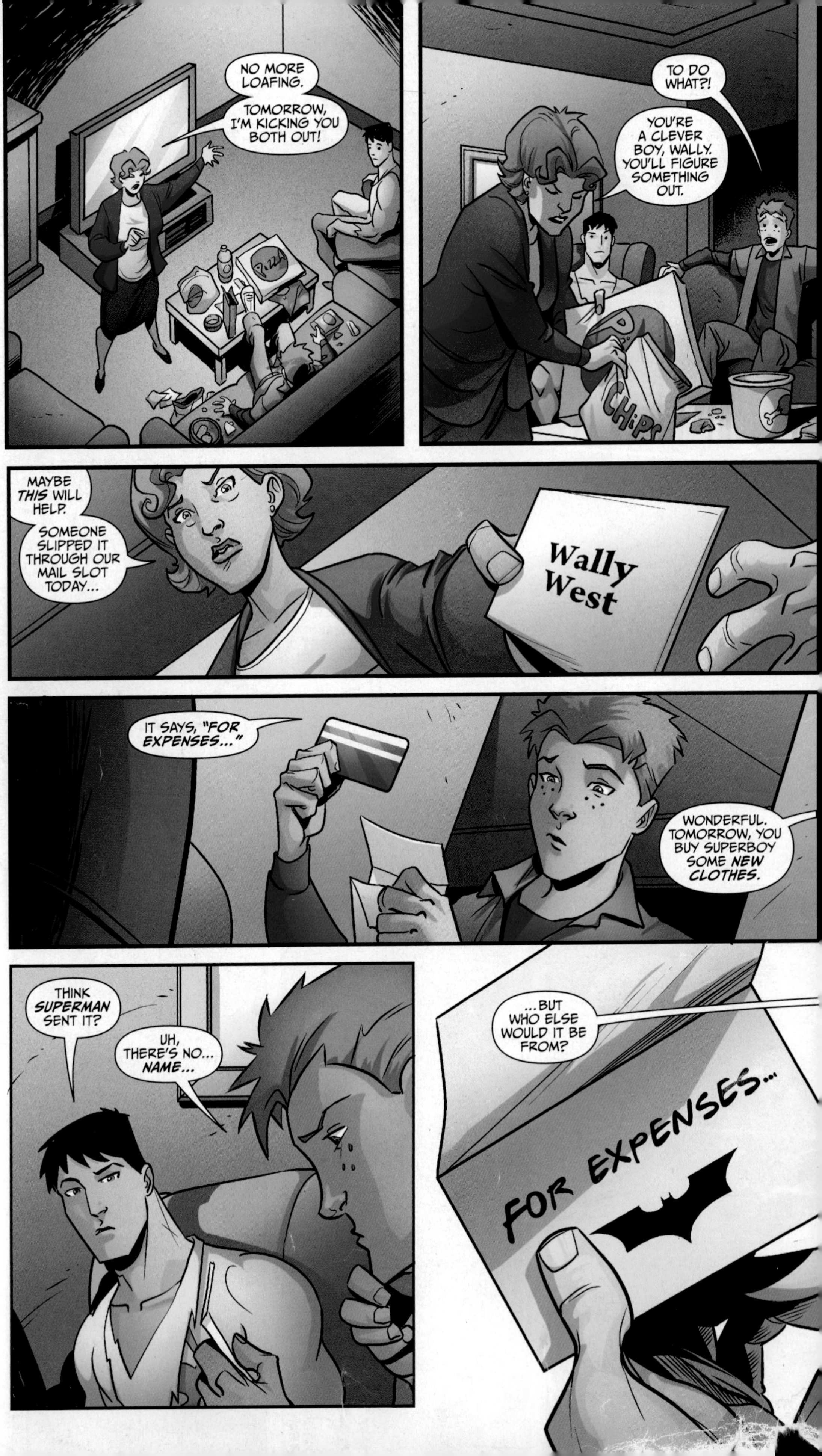
NO MORE LOAFING.
TOMORROW, I'M KICKING YOU BOTH OUT!
TO DO WHAT?!
YOU'RE A CLEVER BOY, WALLY. YOU'LL FIGURE SOMETHING OUT.
MAYBE *THIS* WILL HELP.
SOMEONE SLIPPED IT THROUGH OUR MAIL SLOT TODAY...
Wally West
IT SAYS, "*FOR EXPENSES...*"
WONDERFUL. TOMORROW, YOU BUY SUPERBOY SOME *NEW CLOTHES.*
THINK *SUPERMAN* SENT IT?
UH, THERE'S NO... *NAME*...
...BUT WHO ELSE WOULD IT BE FROM?
FOR EXPENSES...

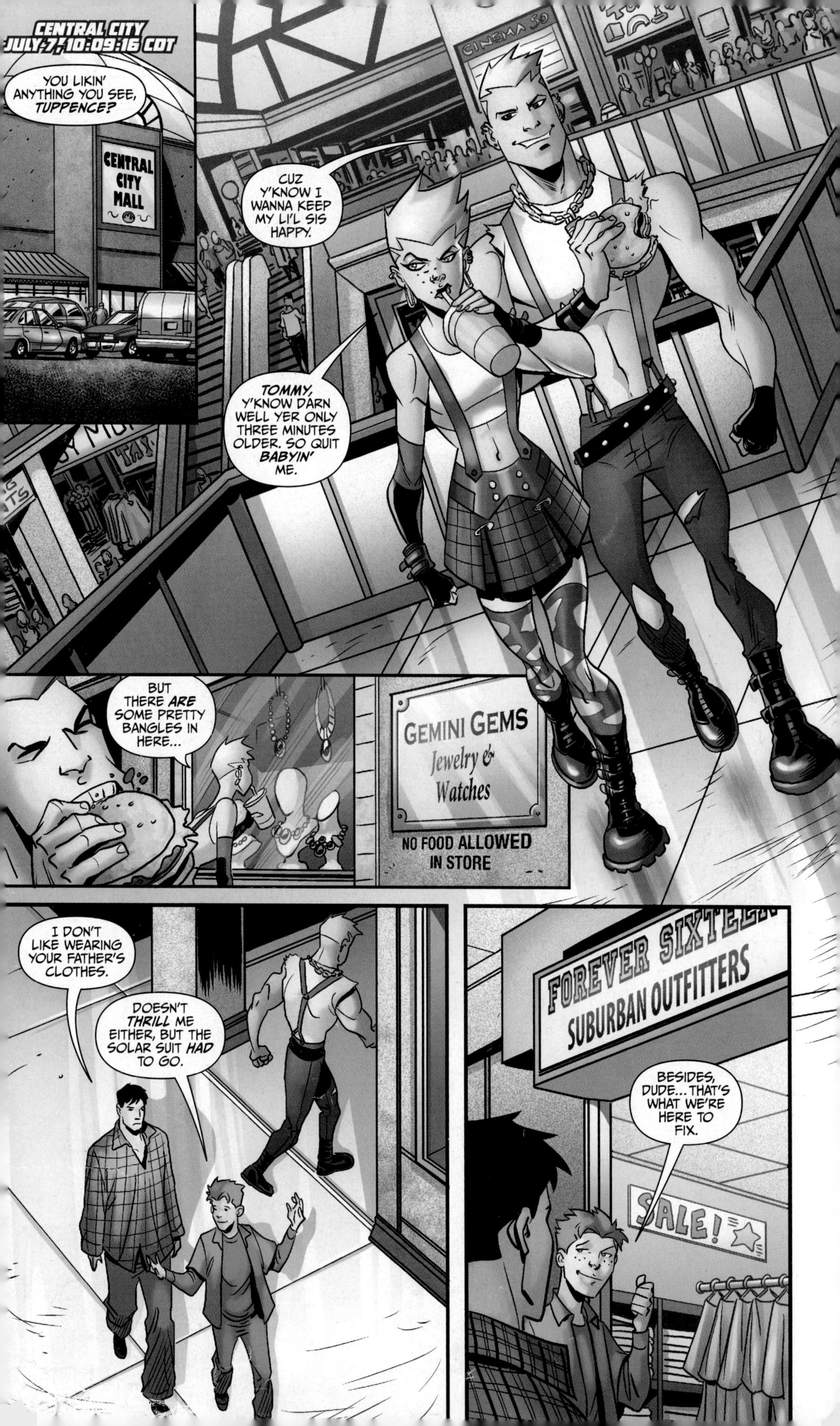
CENTRAL CITY
JULY 7, 10:09:16 CDT
YOU LIKIN' ANYTHING YOU SEE, TUPPENCE?
CENTRAL CITY MALL
CINEMA 50
CUZ Y'KNOW I WANNA KEEP MY LI'L SIS HAPPY.
TOMMY, Y'KNOW DARN WELL YER ONLY THREE MINUTES OLDER. SO QUIT BABYIN' ME.
BUT THERE ARE SOME PRETTY BANGLES IN HERE...
GEMINI GEMS
Jewelry & Watches
NO FOOD ALLOWED IN STORE
I DON'T LIKE WEARING YOUR FATHER'S CLOTHES.
DOESN'T THRILL ME EITHER, BUT THE SOLAR SUIT HAD TO GO.
SUBURBAN OUTFITTERS
BESIDES, DUDE...THAT'S WHAT WE'RE HERE TO FIX.
SALE!

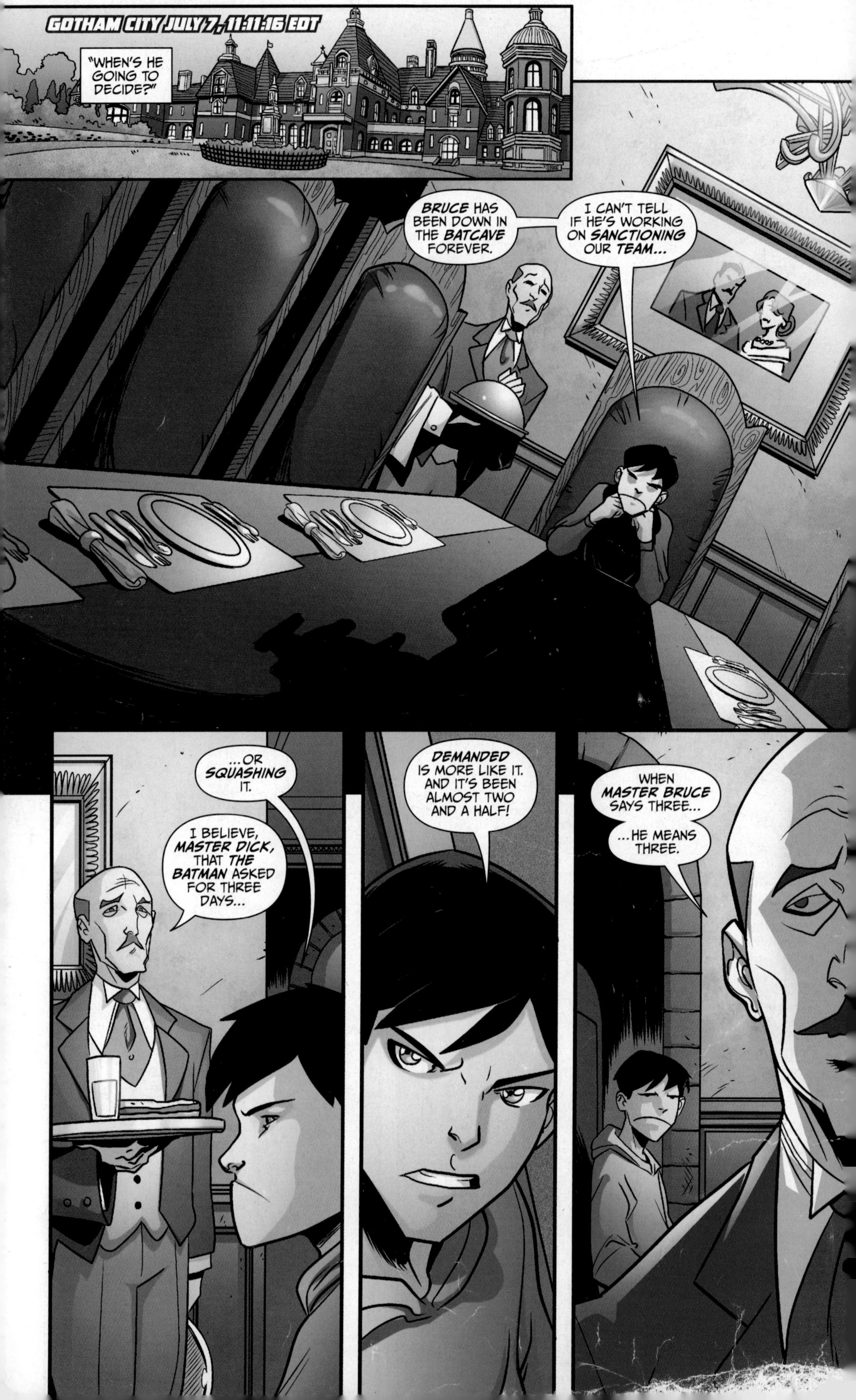
GOTHAM CITY JULY 7, 11:11:16 EDT
"WHEN'S HE GOING TO DECIDE?"
BRUCE HAS BEEN DOWN IN THE BATCAVE FOREVER.
I CAN'T TELL IF HE'S WORKING ON SANCTIONING OUR TEAM...
...OR SQUASHING IT.
I BELIEVE, MASTER DICK, THAT THE BATMAN ASKED FOR THREE DAYS...
DEMANDED IS MORE LIKE IT. AND IT'S BEEN ALMOST TWO AND A HALF!
WHEN MASTER BRUCE SAYS THREE...
...HE MEANS THREE.

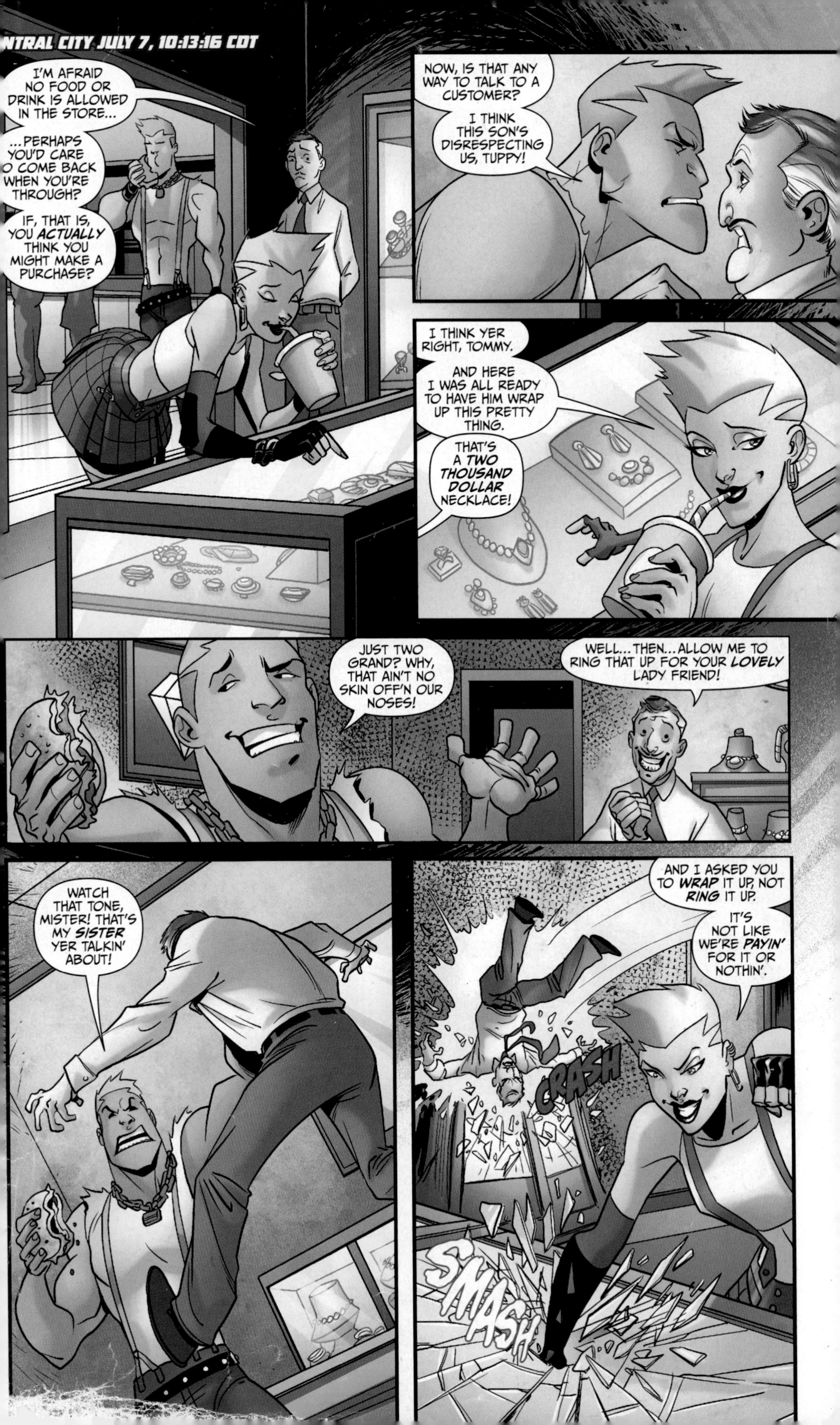
NTRAL CITY JULY 7, 10:13:16 CDT
I'M AFRAID NO FOOD OR DRINK IS ALLOWED IN THE STORE...
...PERHAPS YOU'D CARE O COME BACK WHEN YOU'RE THROUGH?
IF, THAT IS, YOU ACTUALLY THINK YOU MIGHT MAKE A PURCHASE?
NOW, IS THAT ANY WAY TO TALK TO A CUSTOMER?
I THINK THIS SON'S DISRESPECTING US, TUPPY!
I THINK YER RIGHT, TOMMY.
AND HERE I WAS ALL READY TO HAVE HIM WRAP UP THIS PRETTY THING.
THAT'S A TWO THOUSAND DOLLAR NECKLACE!
JUST TWO GRAND? WHY, THAT AIN'T NO SKIN OFF'N OUR NOSES!
WELL...THEN...ALLOW ME TO RING THAT UP FOR YOUR LOVELY LADY FRIEND!
WATCH THAT TONE, MISTER! THAT'S MY SISTER YER TALKIN' ABOUT!
AND I ASKED YOU TO WRAP IT UP, NOT RING IT UP.
IT'S NOT LIKE WE'RE PAYIN' FOR IT OR NOTHIN'.
CRASH
SMASH

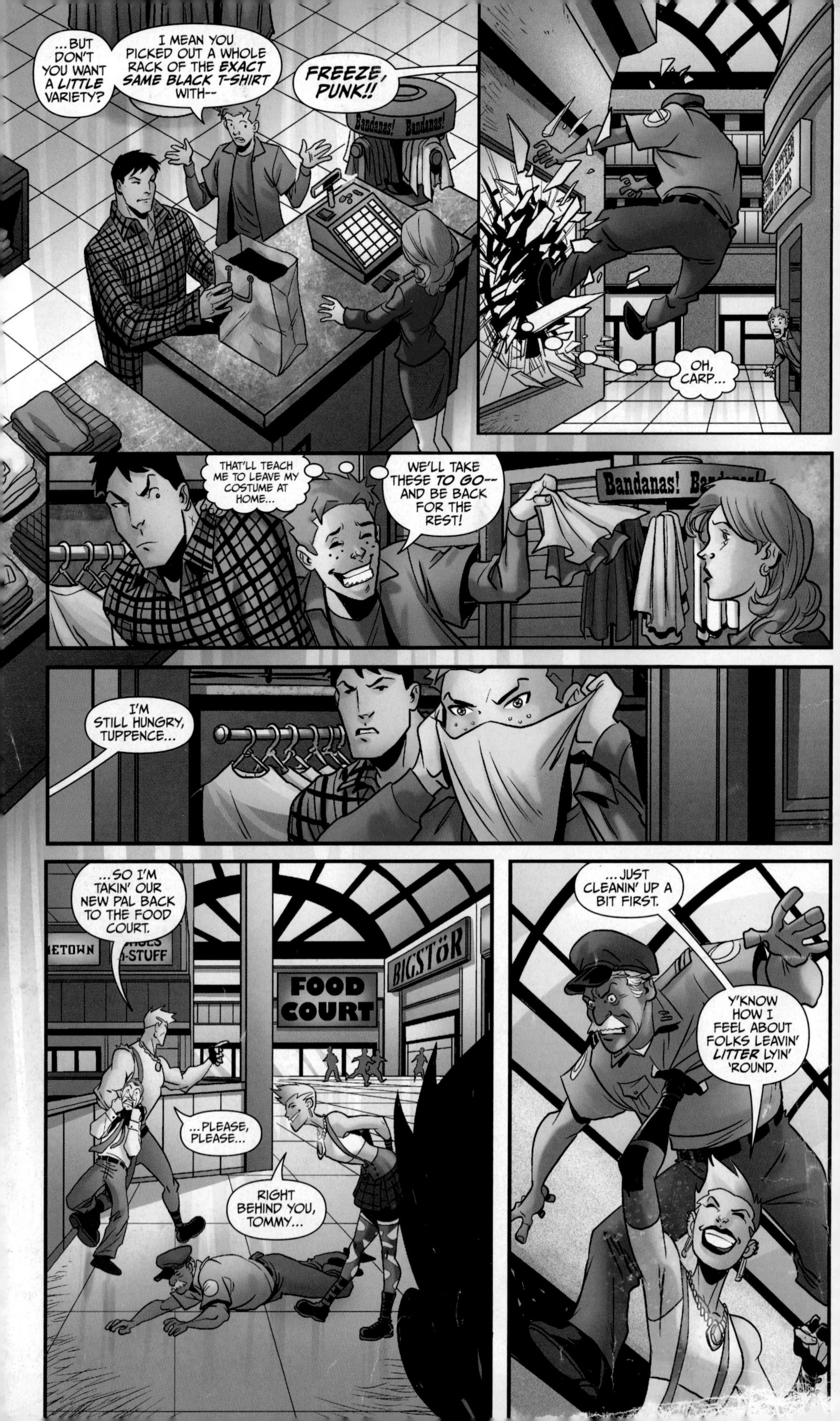
...BUT DON'T YOU WANT A LITTLE VARIETY?
I MEAN YOU PICKED OUT A WHOLE RACK OF THE EXACT SAME BLACK T-SHIRT WITH--
FREEZE, PUNK!!
Bandanas! Bandanas!
OH, CARP...
THAT'LL TEACH ME TO LEAVE MY COSTUME AT HOME...
WE'LL TAKE THESE TO GO-- AND BE BACK FOR THE REST!
I'M STILL HUNGRY, TUPPENCE...
...SO I'M TAKIN' OUR NEW PAL BACK TO THE FOOD COURT.
FOOD COURT
BIGSTöR
...PLEASE, PLEASE...
RIGHT BEHIND YOU, TOMMY...
...JUST CLEANIN' UP A BIT FIRST.
Y'KNOW HOW I FEEL ABOUT FOLKS LEAVIN' LITTER LYIN' 'ROUND.

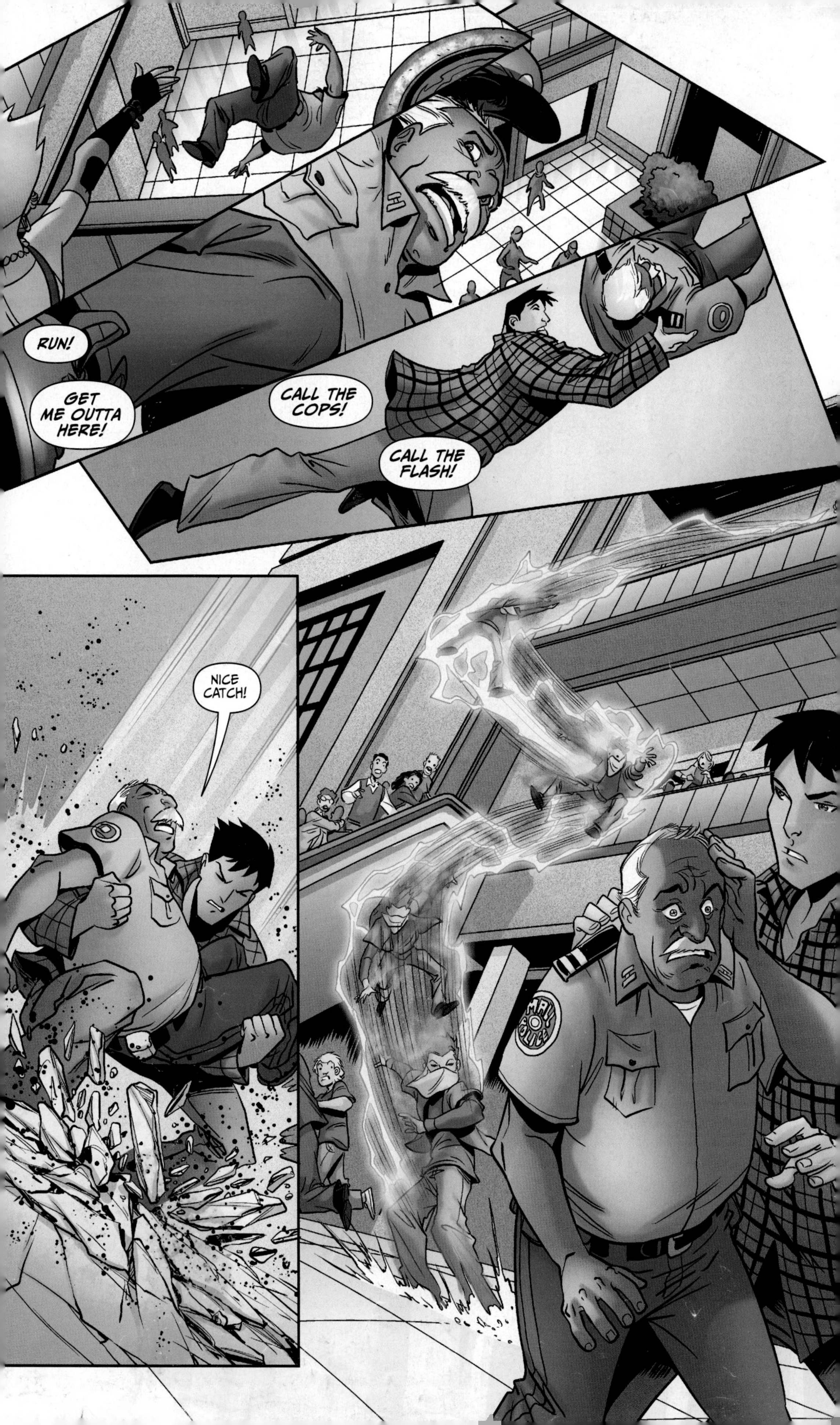
RUN!
GET ME OUTTA HERE!
CALL THE COPS!
CALL THE FLASH!
NICE CATCH!

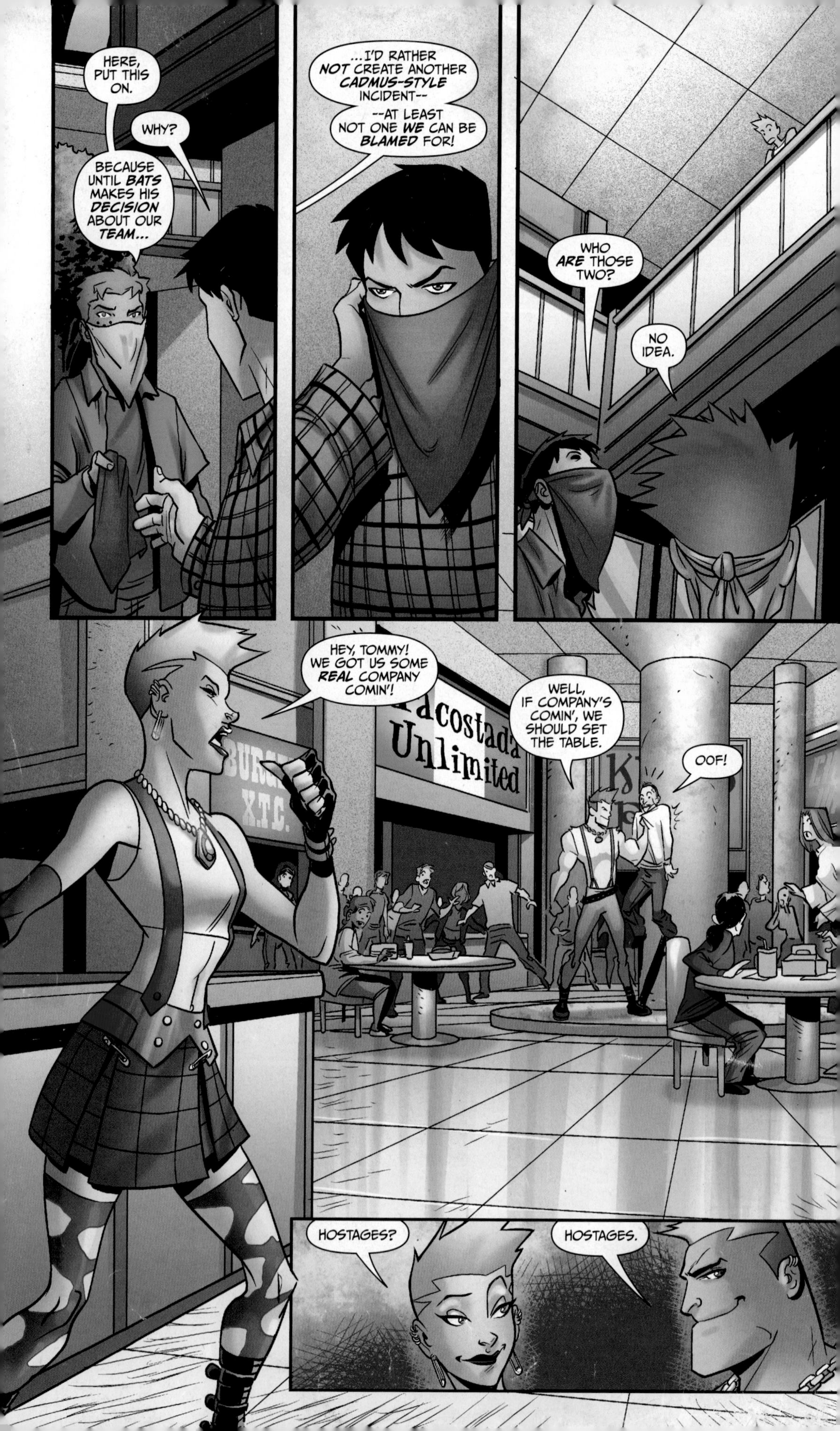
HERE, PUT THIS ON.
WHY?
BECAUSE UNTIL BATS MAKES HIS DECISION ABOUT OUR TEAM...
...I'D RATHER NOT CREATE ANOTHER CADMUS-STYLE INCIDENT--
--AT LEAST NOT ONE WE CAN BE BLAMED FOR!
WHO ARE THOSE TWO?
NO IDEA.
HEY, TOMMY! WE GOT US SOME REAL COMPANY COMIN'!
WELL, IF COMPANY'S COMIN', WE SHOULD SET THE TABLE.
OOF!
BURG
X.T.C.
Unlimited
HOSTAGES?
HOSTAGES.

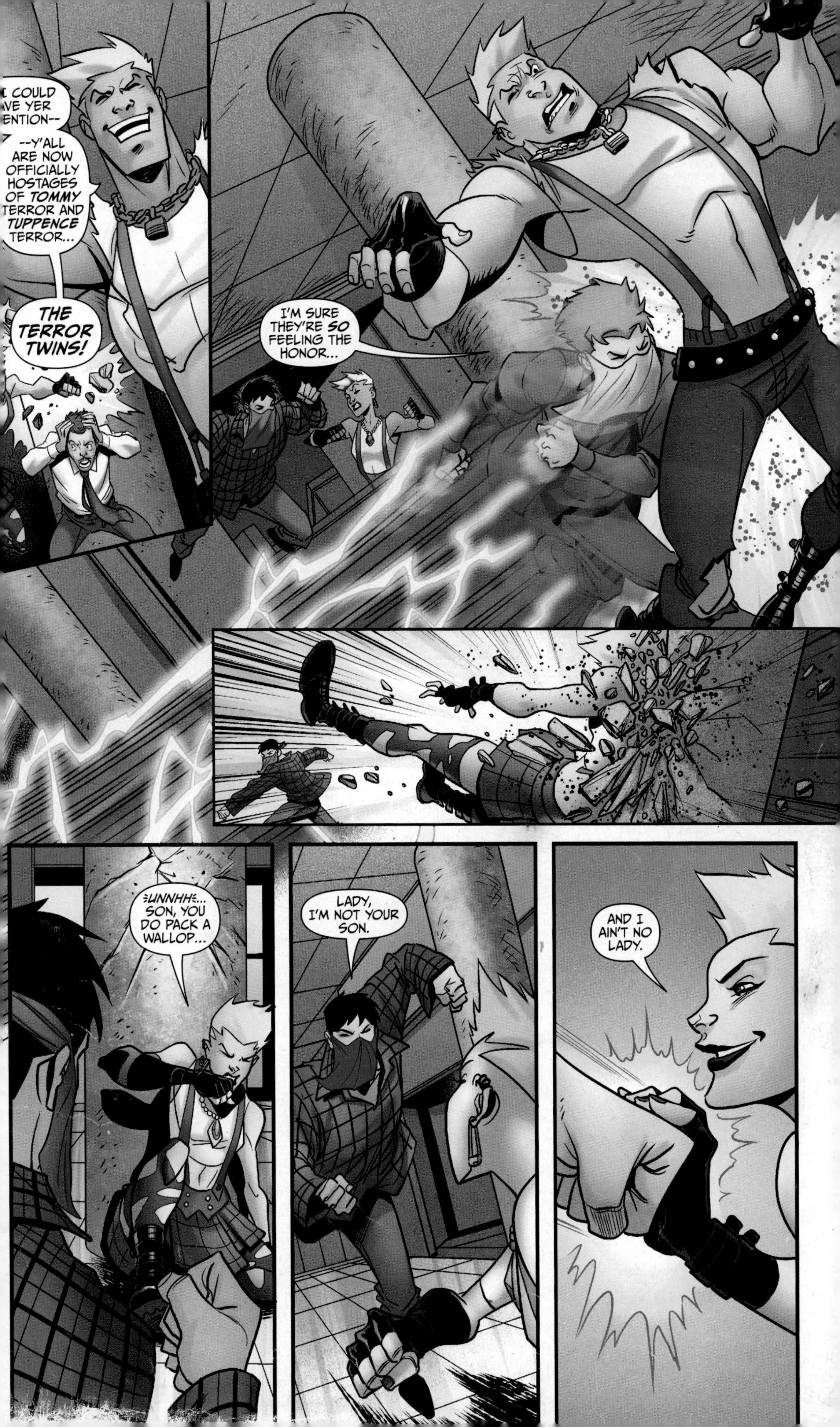
I COULD
AVE YER
ENTION--
--Y'ALL ARE NOW OFFICIALLY HOSTAGES OF *TOMMY* TERROR AND *TUPPENCE* TERROR...
THE TERROR TWINS!
I'M SURE THEY'RE *SO* FEELING THE HONOR...
UNNHH... SON, YOU DO PACK A WALLOP...
LADY, I'M NOT YOUR SON.
AND I AIN'T NO LADY.

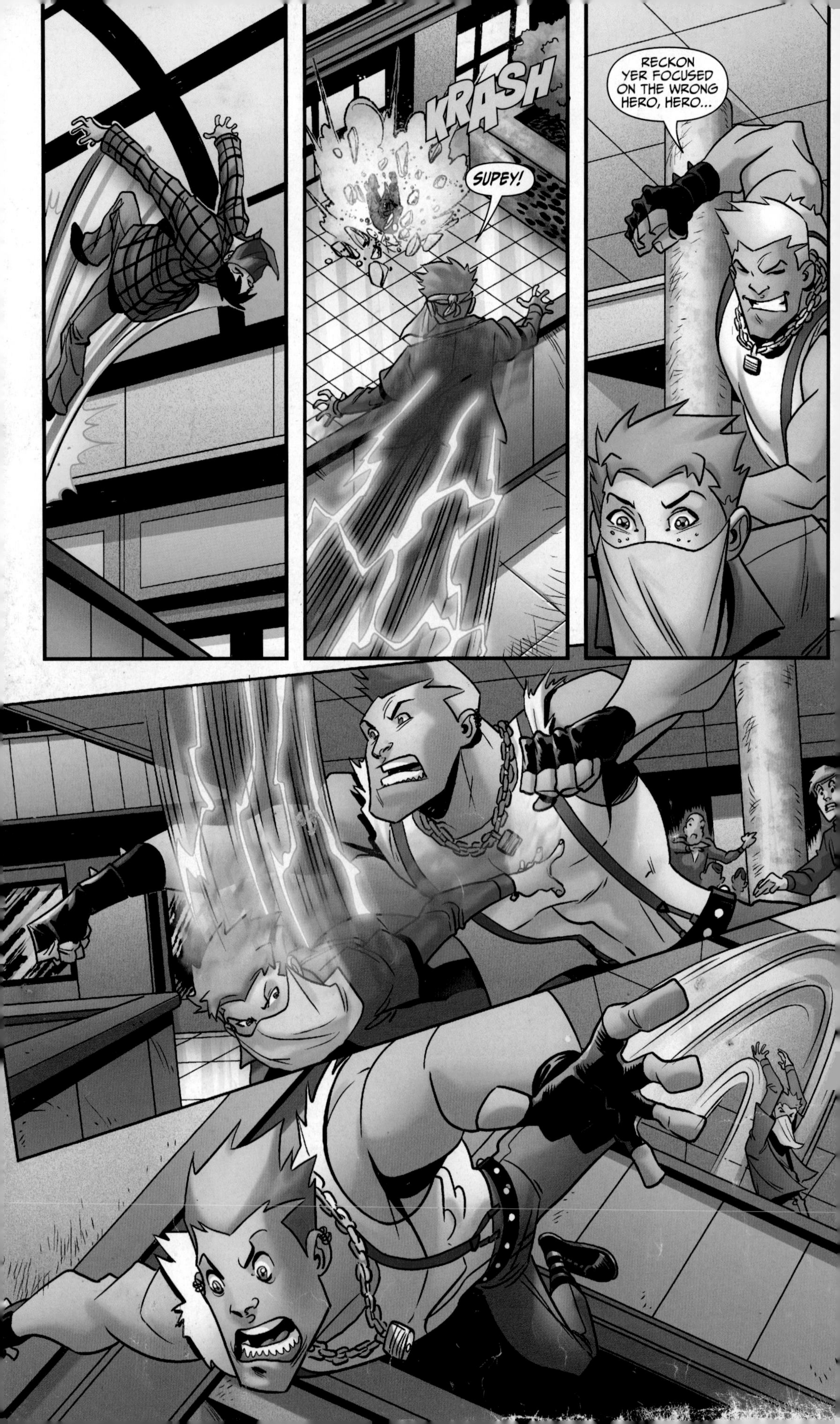
KRASH
SUPEY!
RECKON YER FOCUSED ON THE WRONG HERO, HERO...

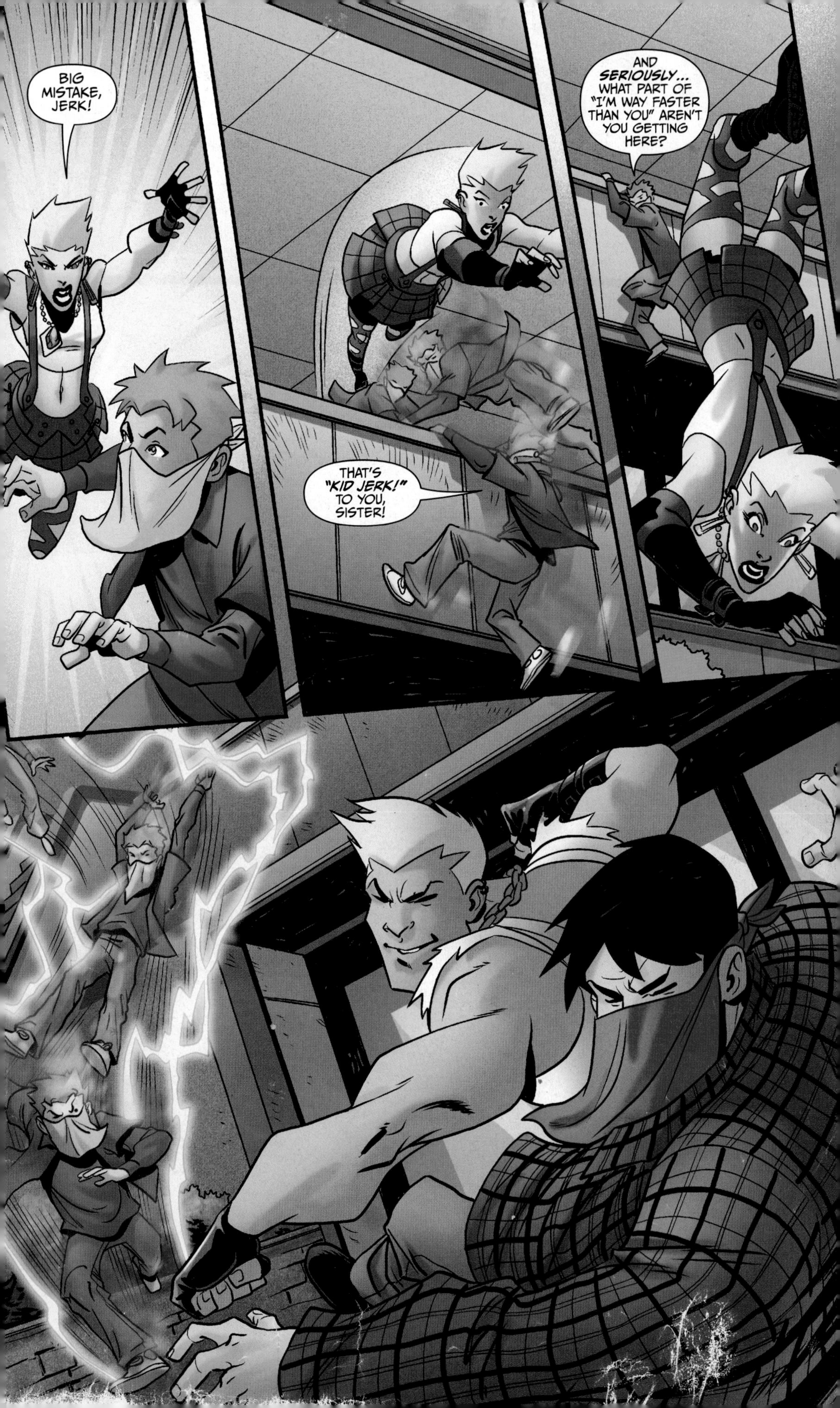
BIG MISTAKE, JERK!
THAT'S "KID JERK!" TO YOU, SISTER!
AND SERIOUSLY... WHAT PART OF "I'M WAY FASTER THAN YOU" AREN'T YOU GETTING HERE?

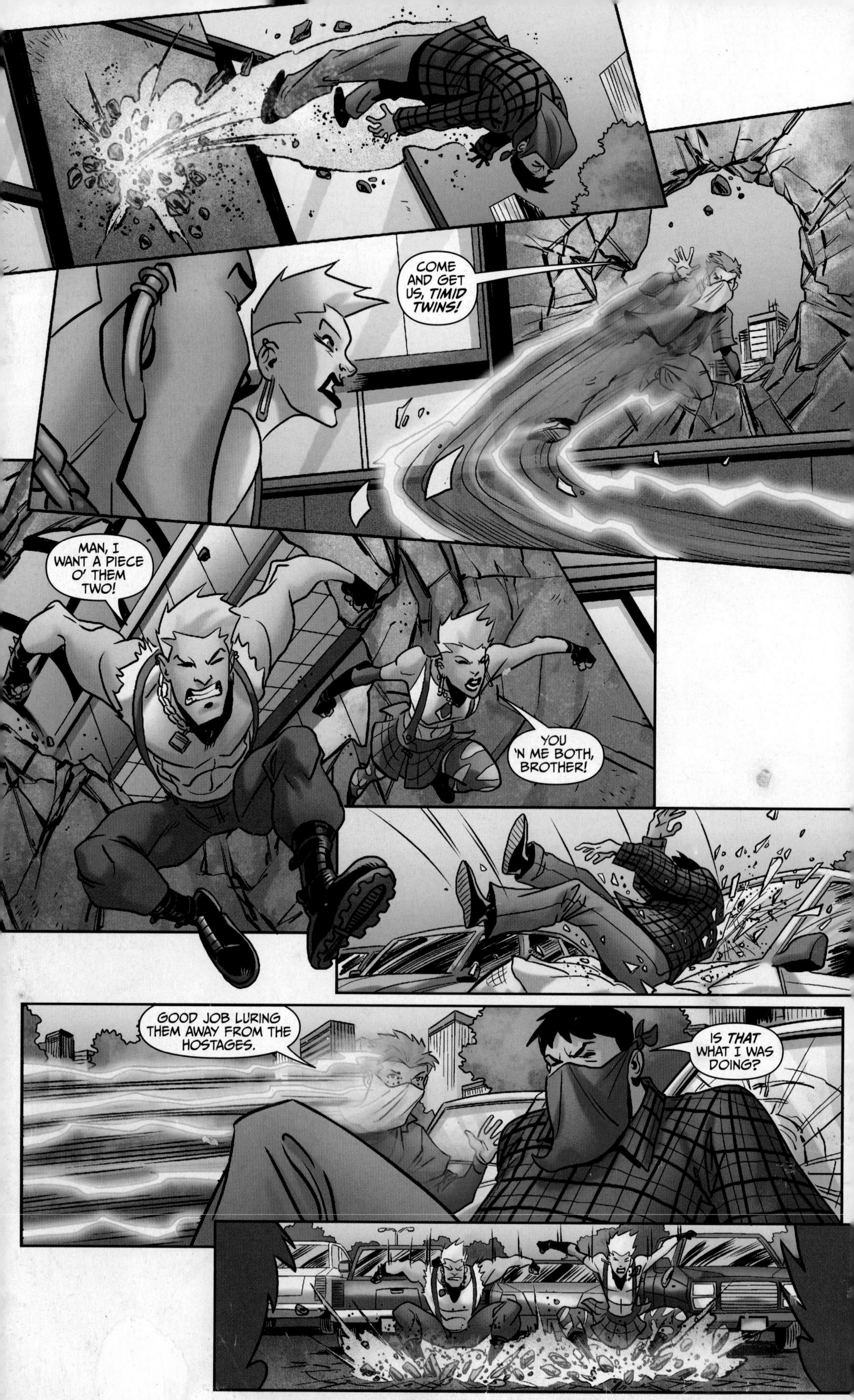
COME AND GET US, *TIMID TWINS!*
MAN, I WANT A PIECE O' THEM TWO!
YOU 'N ME BOTH, BROTHER!
GOOD JOB LURING THEM AWAY FROM THE HOSTAGES.
IS *THAT* WHAT I WAS DOING?

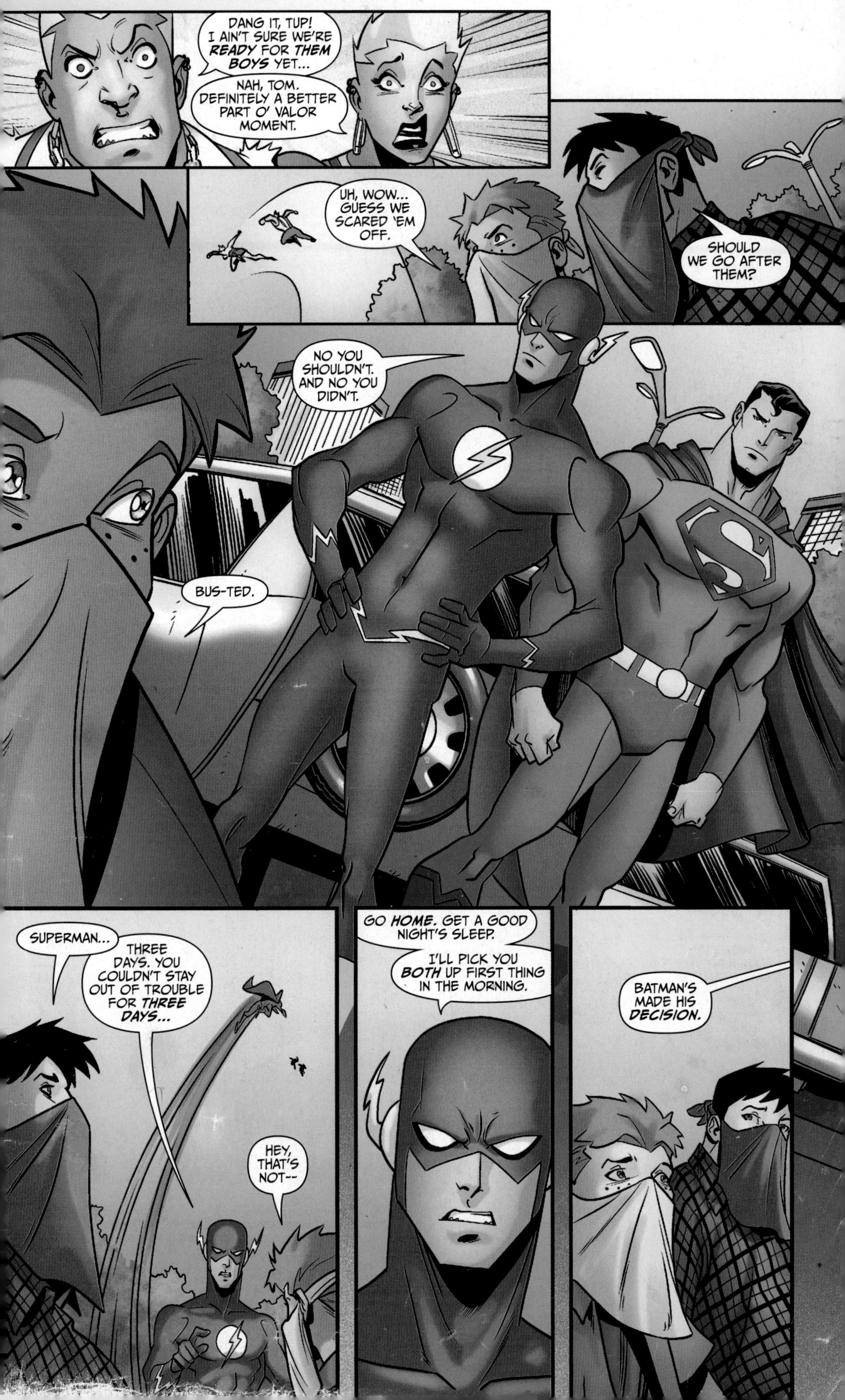
DANG IT, TUP! I AIN'T SURE WE'RE **READY** FOR **THEM BOYS** YET...
NAH, TOM. DEFINITELY A BETTER PART O' VALOR MOMENT.
UH, WOW... GUESS WE SCARED 'EM OFF.
SHOULD WE GO AFTER THEM?
NO YOU SHOULDN'T. AND NO YOU DIDN'T.
BUS-TED.
SUPERMAN...
THREE DAYS. YOU COULDN'T STAY OUT OF TROUBLE FOR **THREE DAYS...**
HEY, THAT'S NOT--
GO **HOME.** GET A GOOD NIGHT'S SLEEP.
I'LL PICK YOU **BOTH** UP FIRST THING IN THE MORNING.
BATMAN'S MADE HIS **DECISION.**

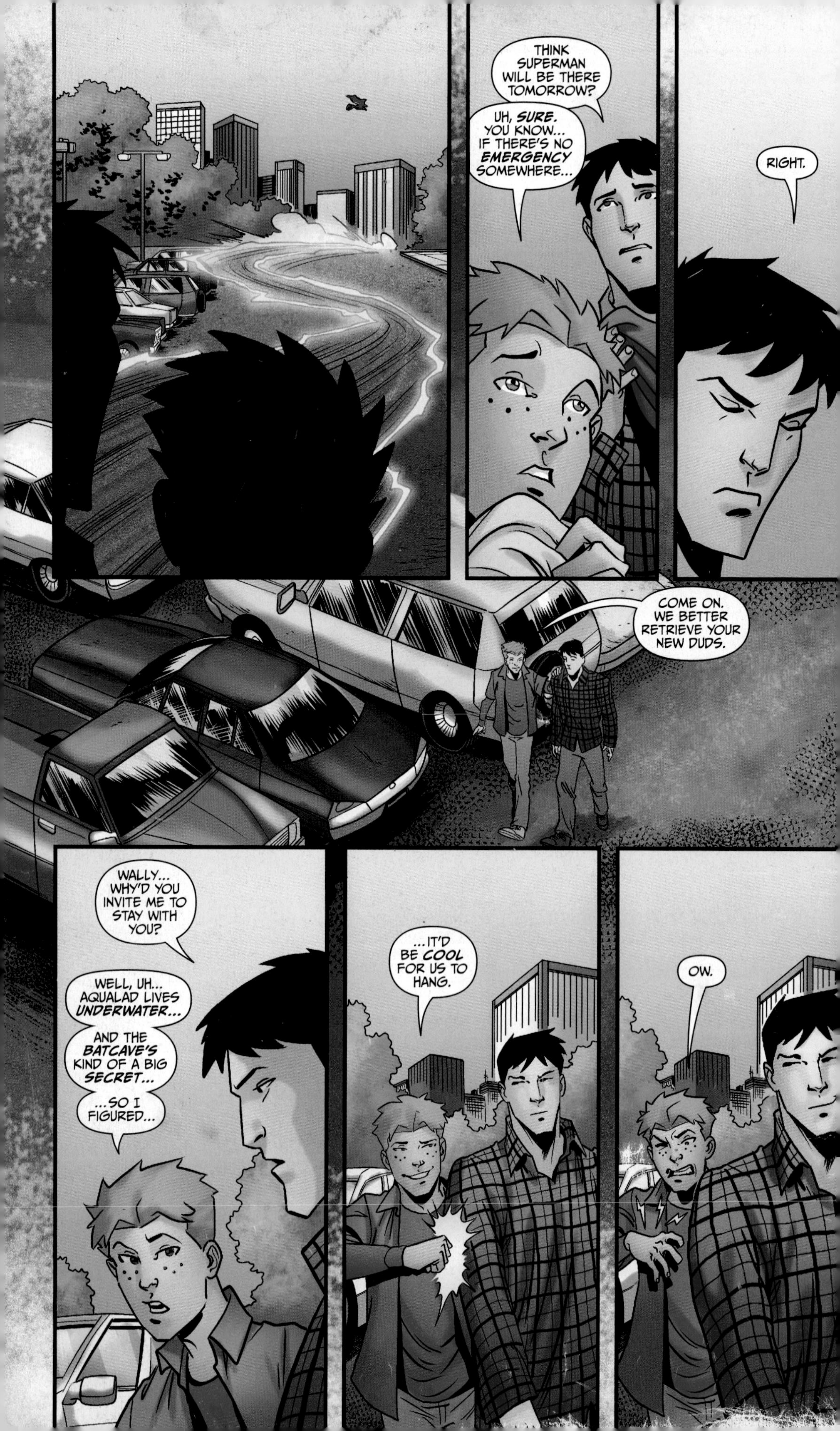
THINK SUPERMAN WILL BE THERE TOMORROW?
UH, SURE. YOU KNOW... IF THERE'S NO EMERGENCY SOMEWHERE...
RIGHT.
COME ON. WE BETTER RETRIEVE YOUR NEW DUDS.
WALLY... WHY'D YOU INVITE ME TO STAY WITH YOU?
WELL, UH... AQUALAD LIVES UNDERWATER...
AND THE BATCAVE'S KIND OF A BIG SECRET...
...SO I FIGURED...
...IT'D BE COOL FOR US TO HANG.
OW.

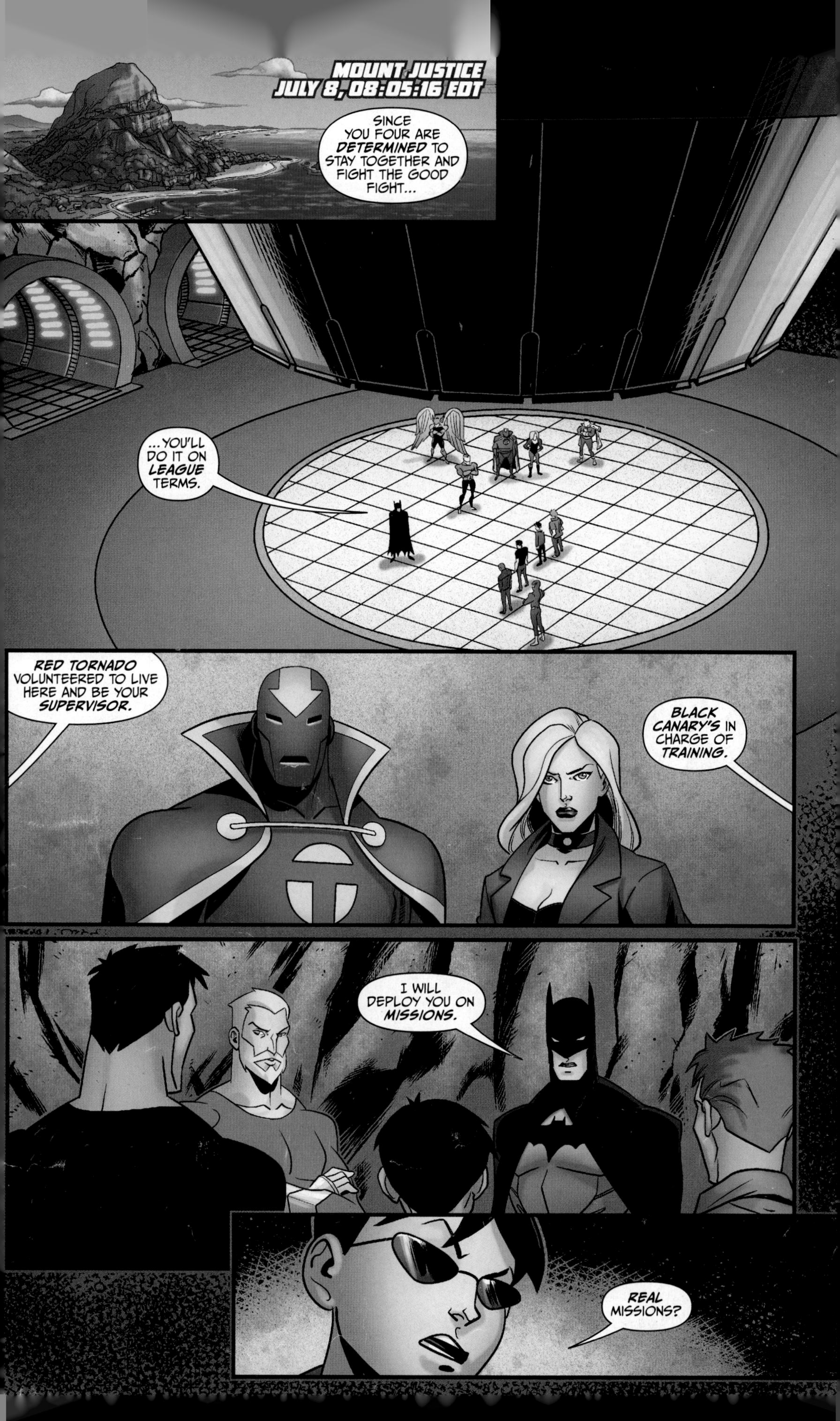
MOUNT JUSTICE
JULY 8, 08:05:16 EDT
SINCE YOU FOUR ARE DETERMINED TO STAY TOGETHER AND FIGHT THE GOOD FIGHT...
...YOU'LL DO IT ON LEAGUE TERMS.
RED TORNADO VOLUNTEERED TO LIVE HERE AND BE YOUR SUPERVISOR.
BLACK CANARY'S IN CHARGE OF TRAINING.
I WILL DEPLOY YOU ON MISSIONS.
REAL MISSIONS?

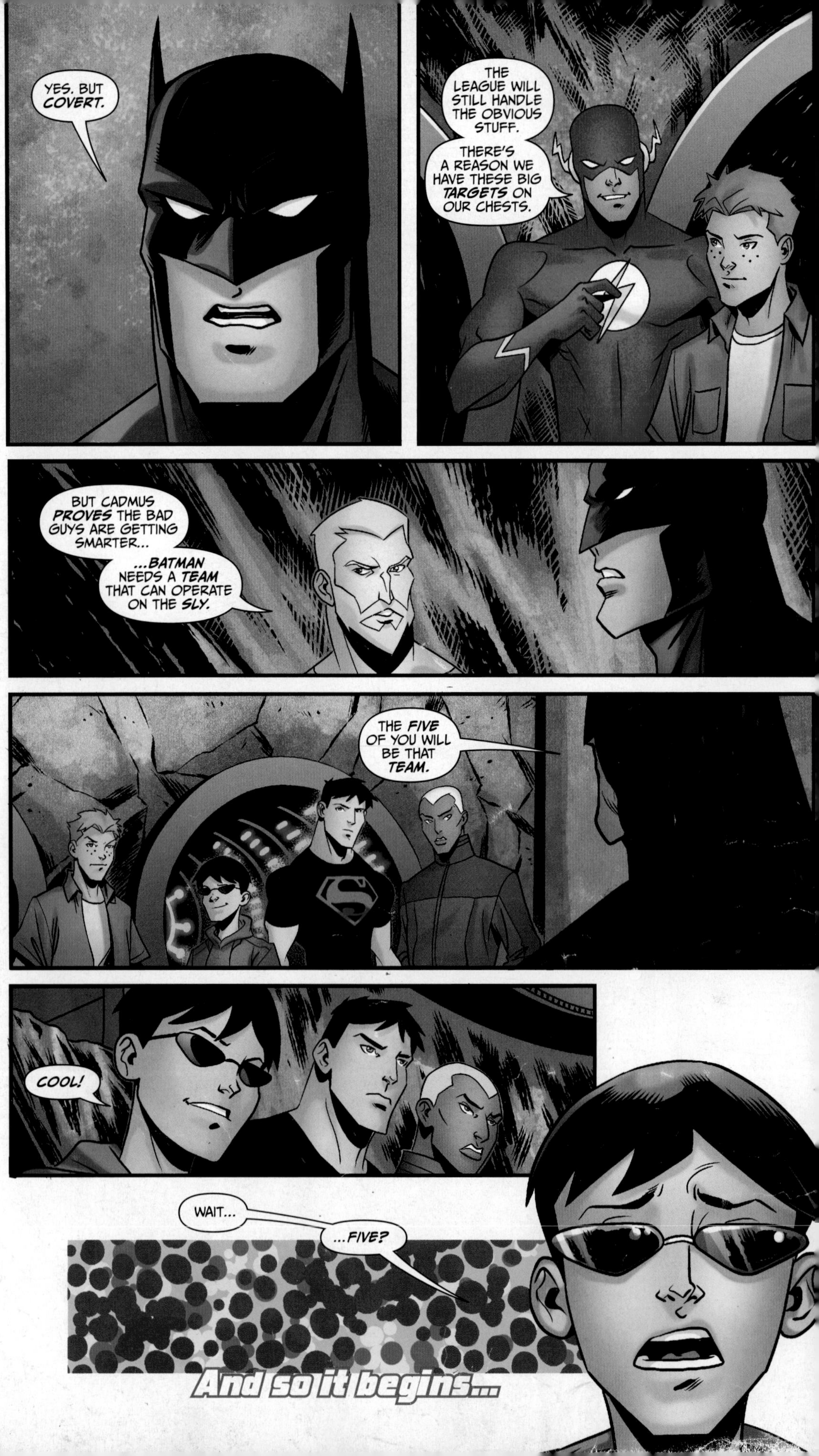
YES. BUT COVERT.
THE LEAGUE WILL STILL HANDLE THE OBVIOUS STUFF.
THERE'S A REASON WE HAVE THESE BIG TARGETS ON OUR CHESTS.
BUT CADMUS PROVES THE BAD GUYS ARE GETTING SMARTER...
...BATMAN NEEDS A TEAM THAT CAN OPERATE ON THE SLY.
THE FIVE OF YOU WILL BE THAT TEAM.
COOL!
WAIT...
...FIVE?
And so it begins...

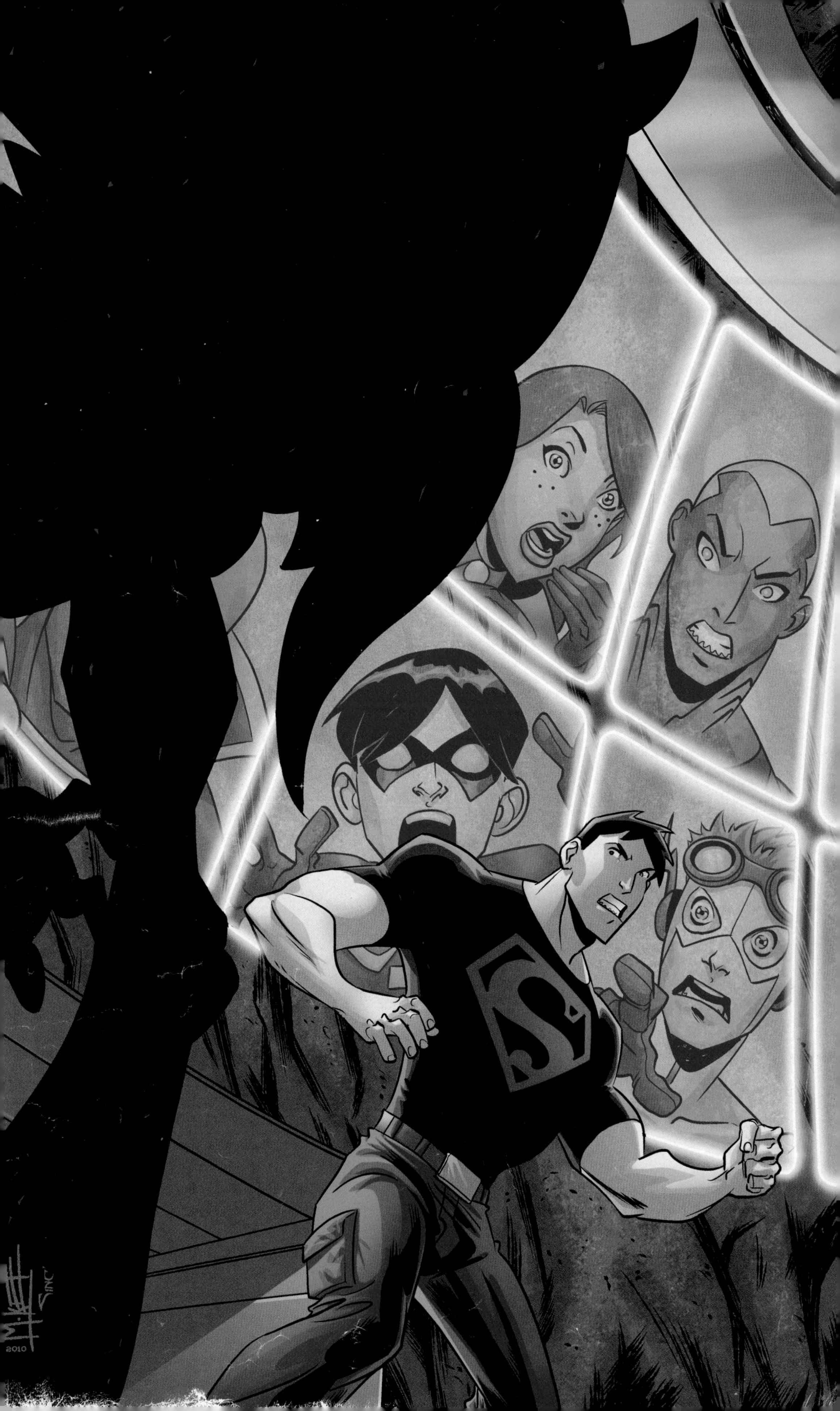

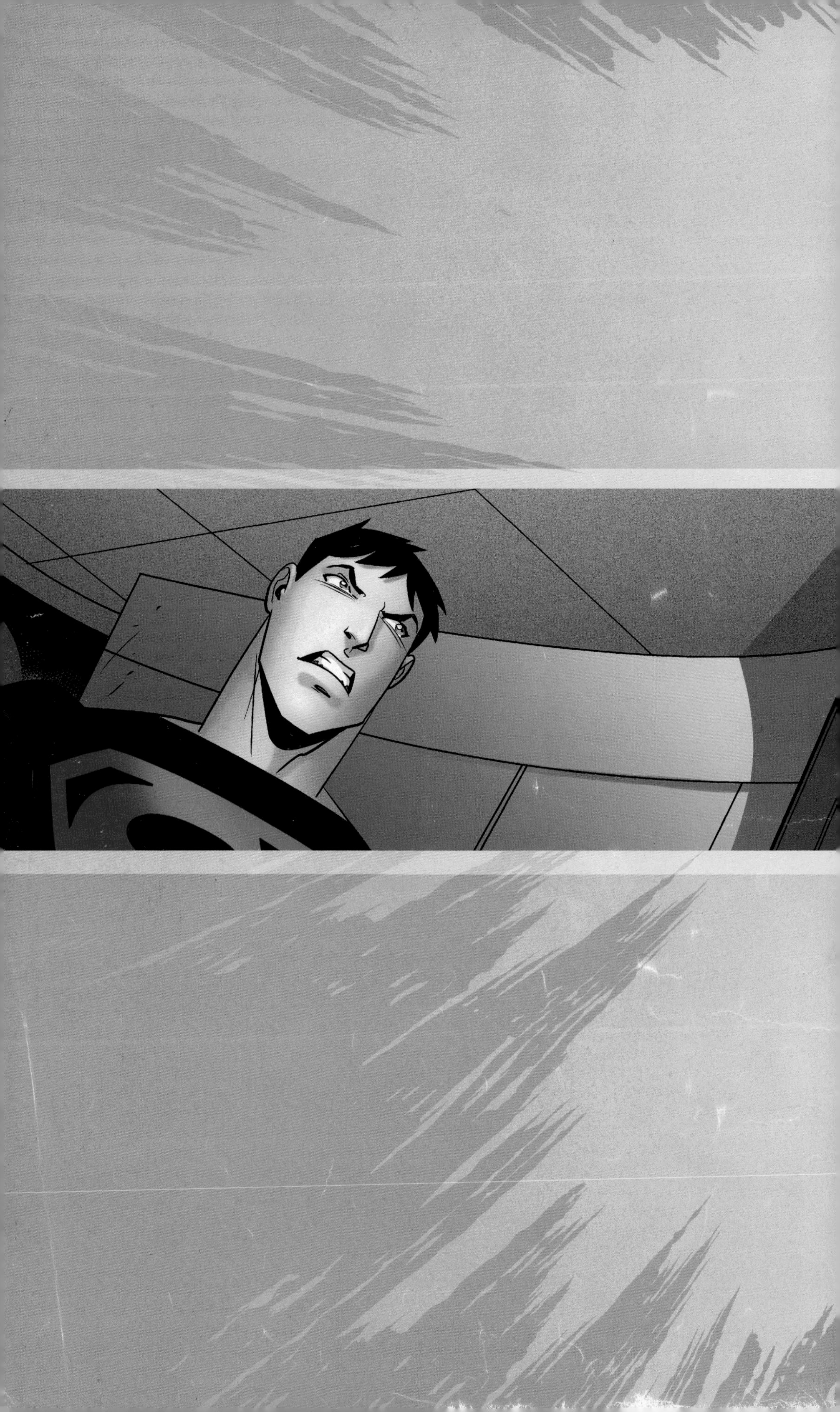

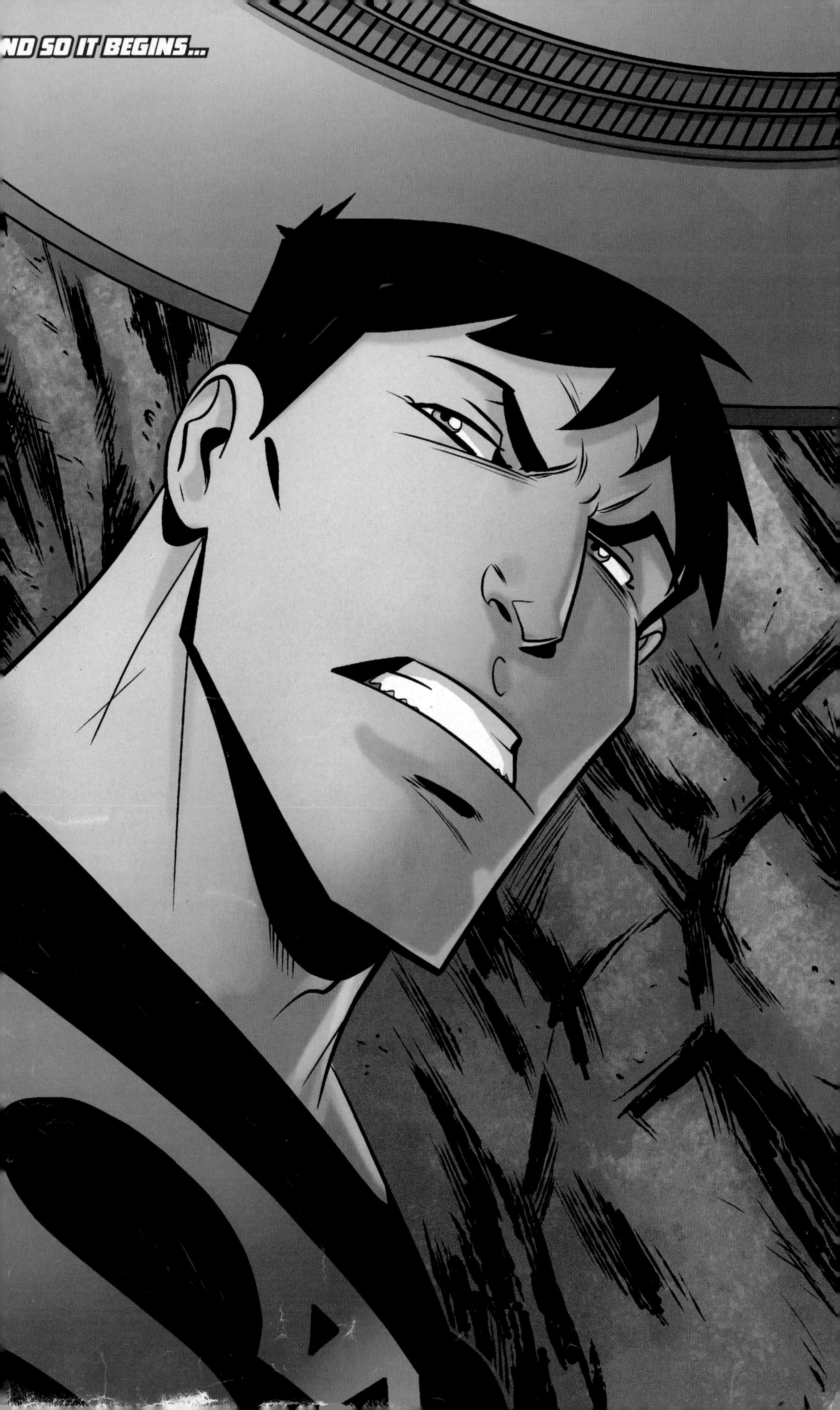
ND SO IT BEGINS...

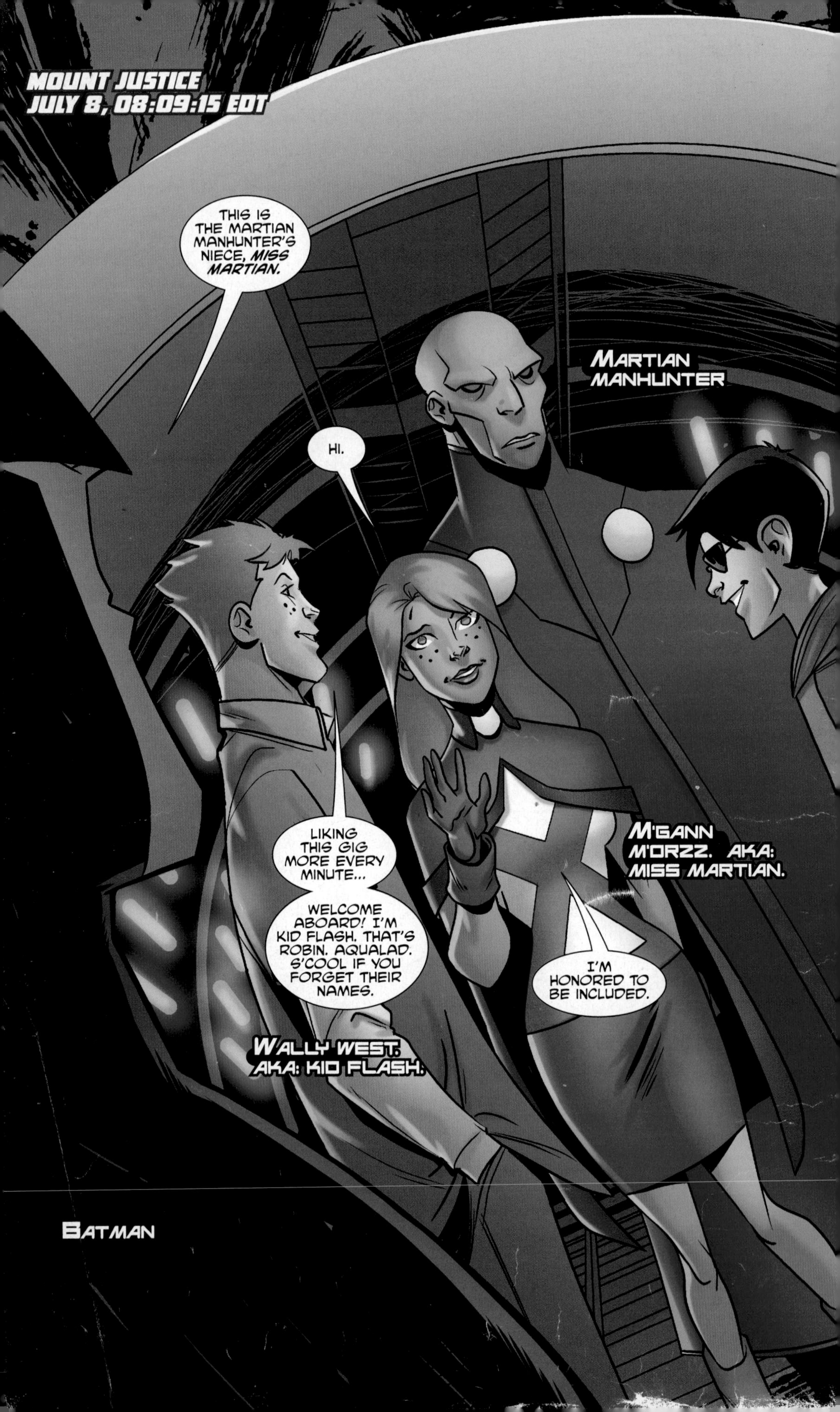
MOUNT JUSTICE
JULY 8, 08:09:15 EDT
THIS IS THE MARTIAN MANHUNTER'S NIECE, MISS MARTIAN.
MARTIAN MANHUNTER
HI.
LIKING THIS GIG MORE EVERY MINUTE...
WELCOME ABOARD! I'M KID FLASH. THAT'S ROBIN. AQUALAD. S'COOL IF YOU FORGET THEIR NAMES.
M'GANN M'ORZZ. AKA: MISS MARTIAN.
I'M HONORED TO BE INCLUDED.
WALLY WEST. AKA: KID FLASH.
BATMAN

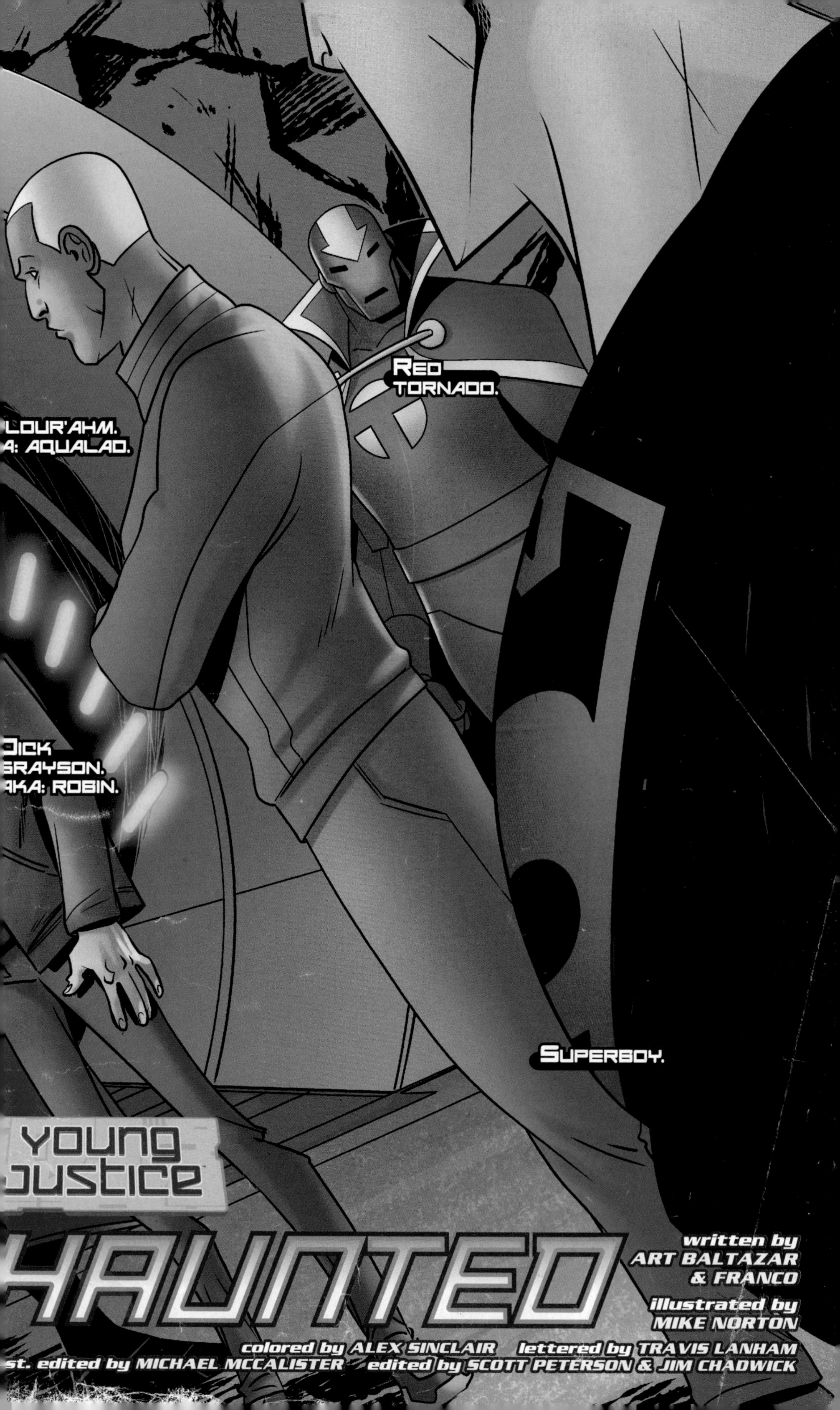

LOUR'AHM.
A: AQUALAD.
RED
TORNADO.
DICK
GRAYSON.
AKA: ROBIN.
SUPERBOY.
YOUNG JUSTICE
HAUNTED
written by
ART BALTAZAR
& FRANCO
illustrated by
MIKE NORTON
colored by ALEX SINCLAIR
lettered by TRAVIS LANHAM
st. edited by MICHAEL MCCALISTER
edited by SCOTT PETERSON & JIM CHADWICK

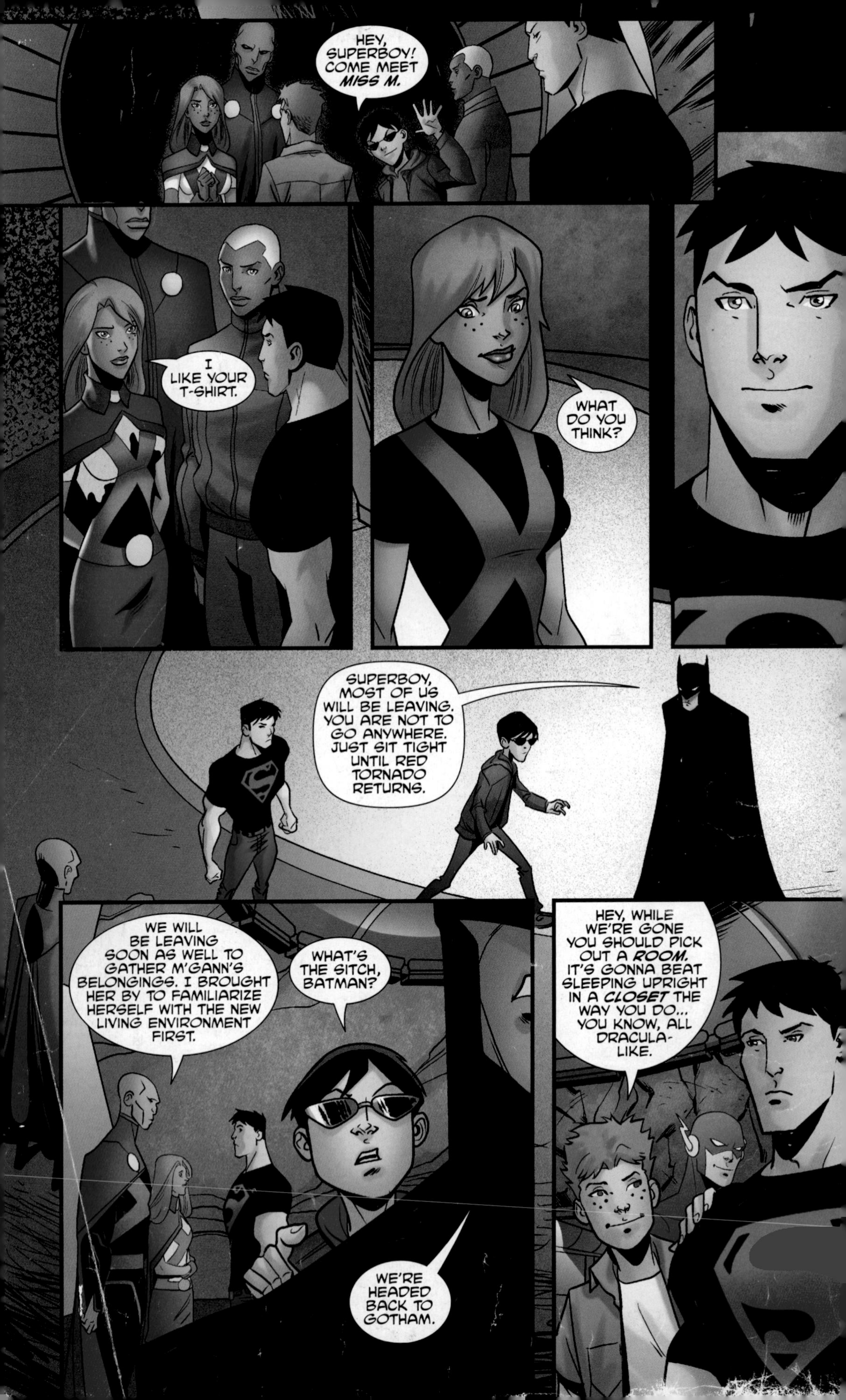
HEY, SUPERBOY! COME MEET *MISS M.*
I LIKE YOUR T-SHIRT.
WHAT DO YOU THINK?
SUPERBOY, MOST OF US WILL BE LEAVING. YOU ARE NOT TO GO ANYWHERE. JUST SIT TIGHT UNTIL RED TORNADO RETURNS.
WE WILL BE LEAVING SOON AS WELL TO GATHER M'GANN'S BELONGINGS. I BROUGHT HER BY TO FAMILIARIZE HERSELF WITH THE NEW LIVING ENVIRONMENT FIRST.
WHAT'S THE SITCH, BATMAN?
WE'RE HEADED BACK TO GOTHAM.
HEY, WHILE WE'RE GONE YOU SHOULD PICK OUT A *ROOM.* IT'S GONNA BEAT SLEEPING UPRIGHT IN A *CLOSET* THE WAY YOU DO... YOU KNOW, ALL DRACULA-LIKE.

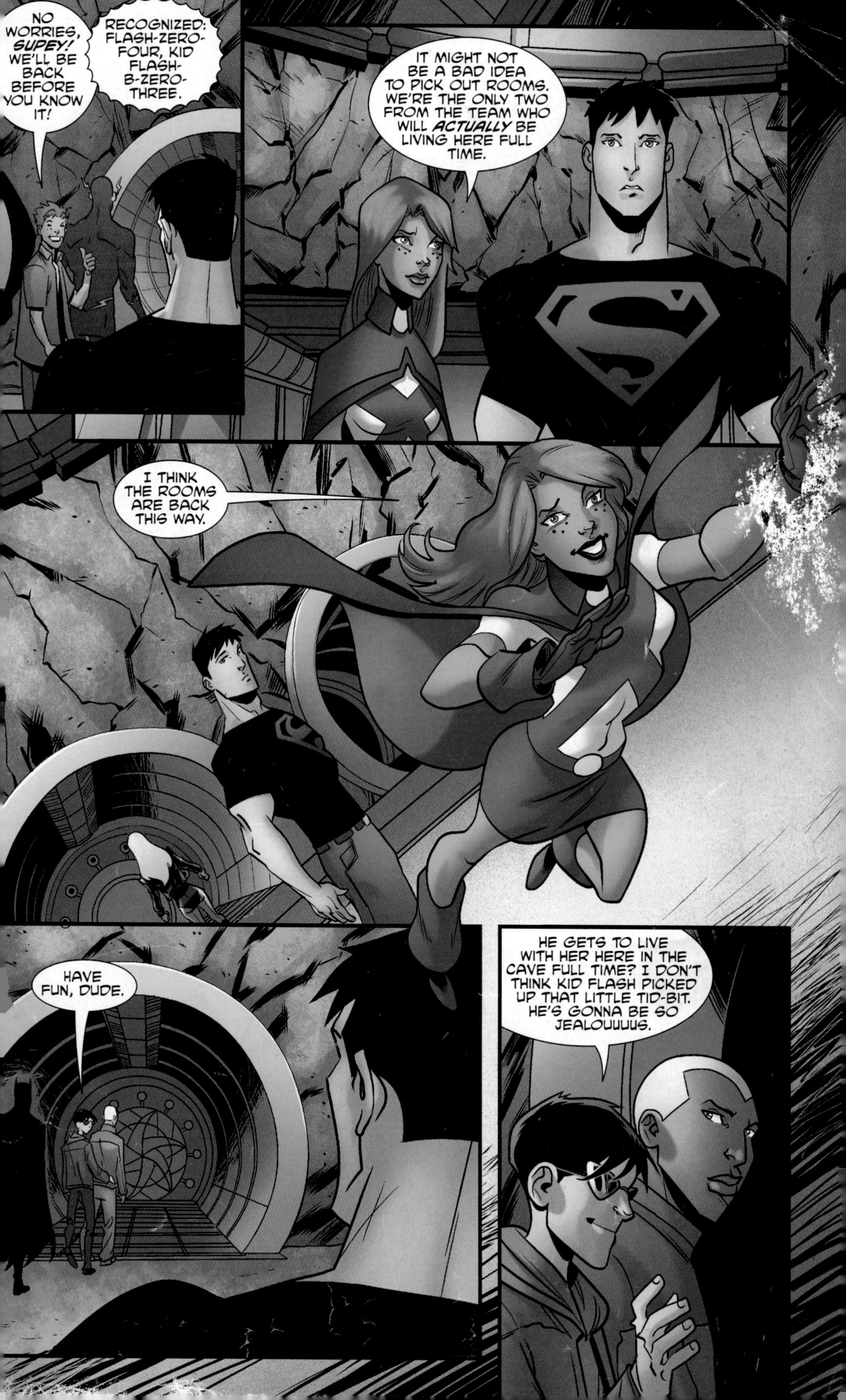
NO WORRIES, SUPEY! WE'LL BE BACK BEFORE YOU KNOW IT!
RECOGNIZED: FLASH-ZERO-FOUR, KID FLASH-B-ZERO-THREE.
IT MIGHT NOT BE A BAD IDEA TO PICK OUT ROOMS. WE'RE THE ONLY TWO FROM THE TEAM WHO WILL ACTUALLY BE LIVING HERE FULL TIME.
I THINK THE ROOMS ARE BACK THIS WAY.
HAVE FUN, DUDE.
HE GETS TO LIVE WITH HER HERE IN THE CAVE FULL TIME? I DON'T THINK KID FLASH PICKED UP THAT LITTLE TID-BIT. HE'S GONNA BE SO JEALOUUUUS.

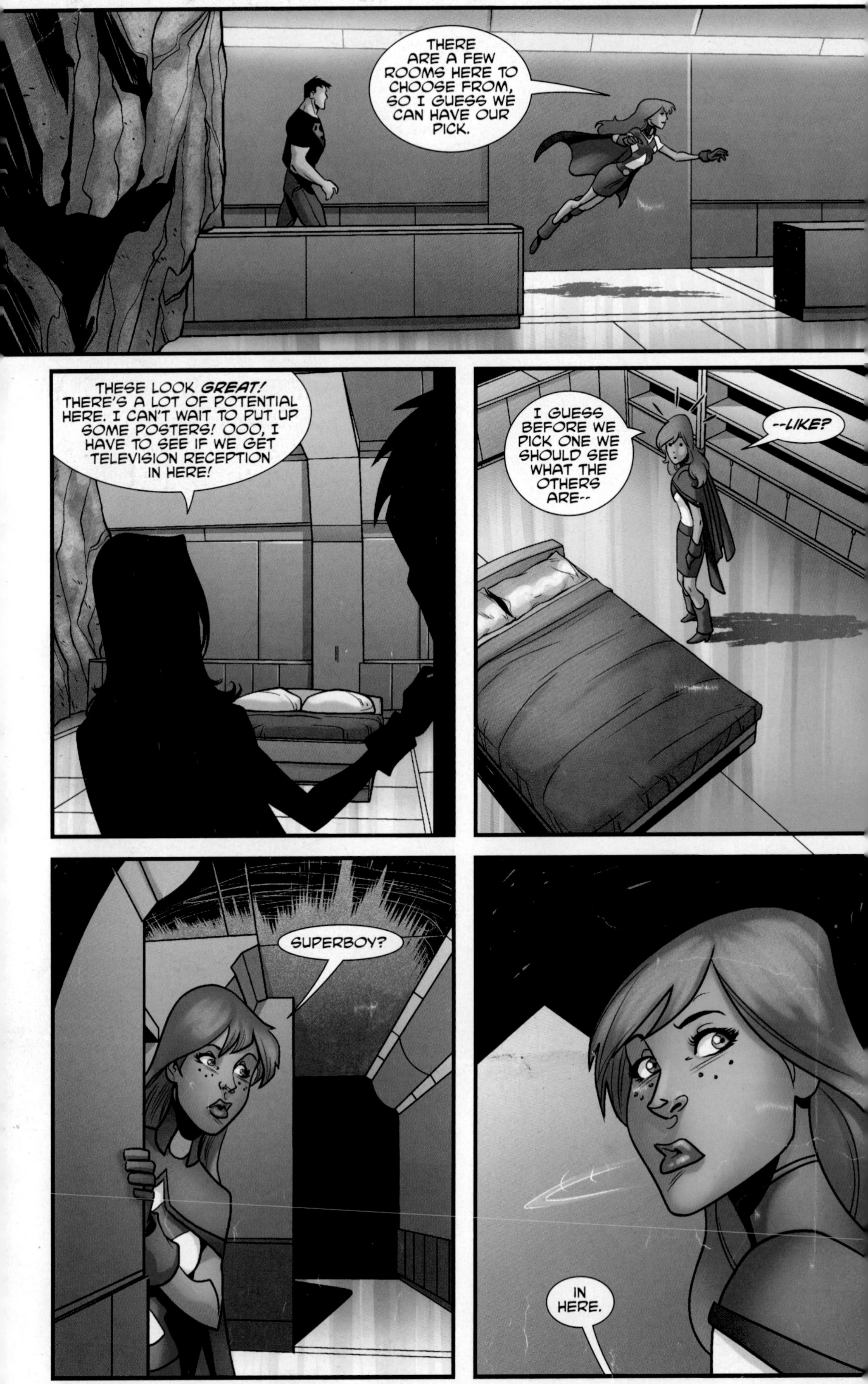
THERE ARE A FEW ROOMS HERE TO CHOOSE FROM, SO I GUESS WE CAN HAVE OUR PICK.
THESE LOOK GREAT! THERE'S A LOT OF POTENTIAL HERE. I CAN'T WAIT TO PUT UP SOME POSTERS! OOO, I HAVE TO SEE IF WE GET TELEVISION RECEPTION IN HERE!
I GUESS BEFORE WE PICK ONE WE SHOULD SEE WHAT THE OTHERS ARE--
--LIKE?
SUPERBOY?
IN HERE.

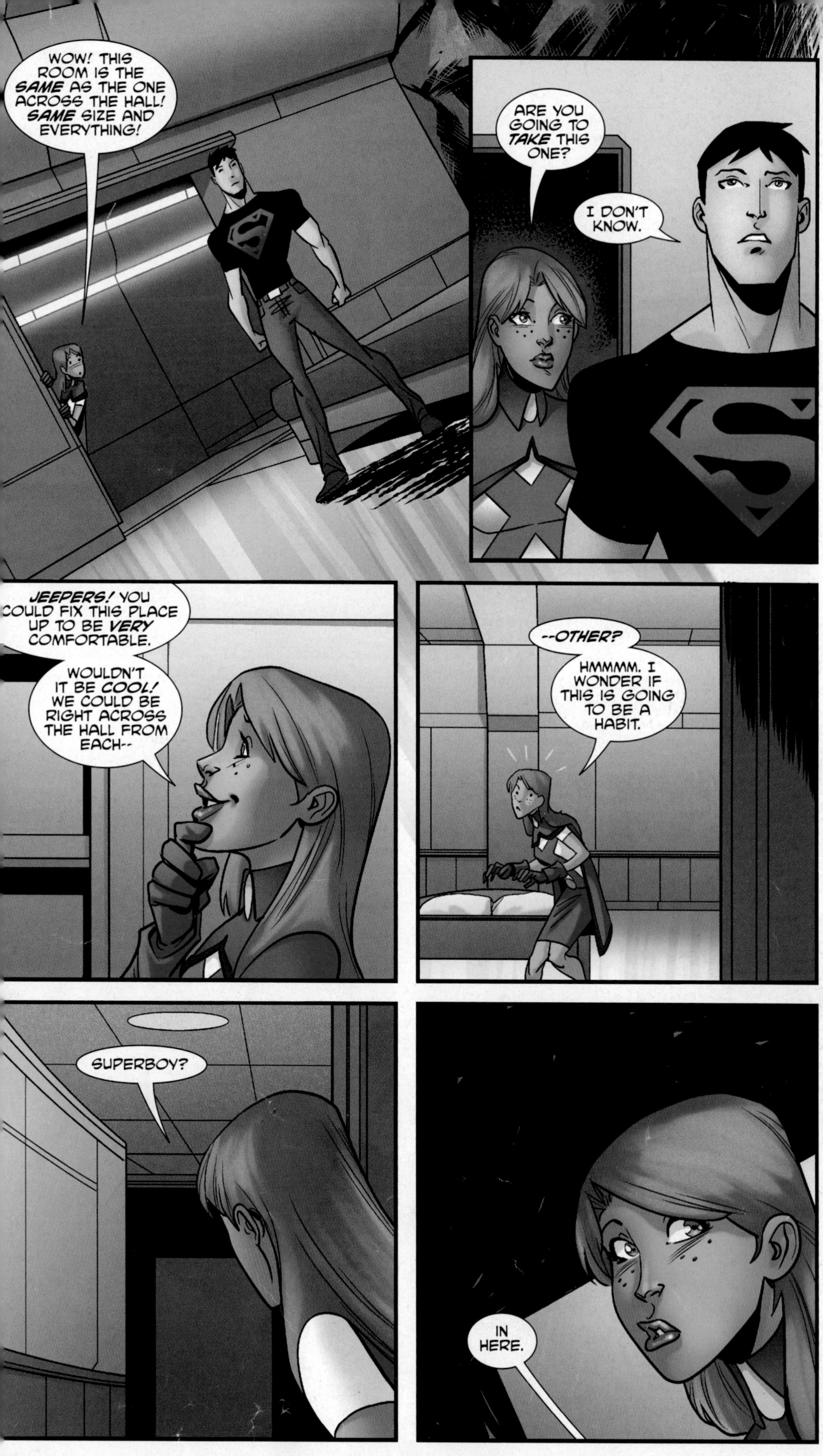
WOW! THIS ROOM IS THE *SAME* AS THE ONE ACROSS THE HALL! *SAME* SIZE AND EVERYTHING!
ARE YOU GOING TO *TAKE* THIS ONE?
I DON'T KNOW.
JEEPERS! YOU COULD FIX THIS PLACE UP TO BE *VERY* COMFORTABLE.
WOULDN'T IT BE *COOL!* WE COULD BE RIGHT ACROSS THE HALL FROM EACH--
--*OTHER?*
HMMMM. I WONDER IF THIS IS GOING TO BE A HABIT.
SUPERBOY?
IN HERE.

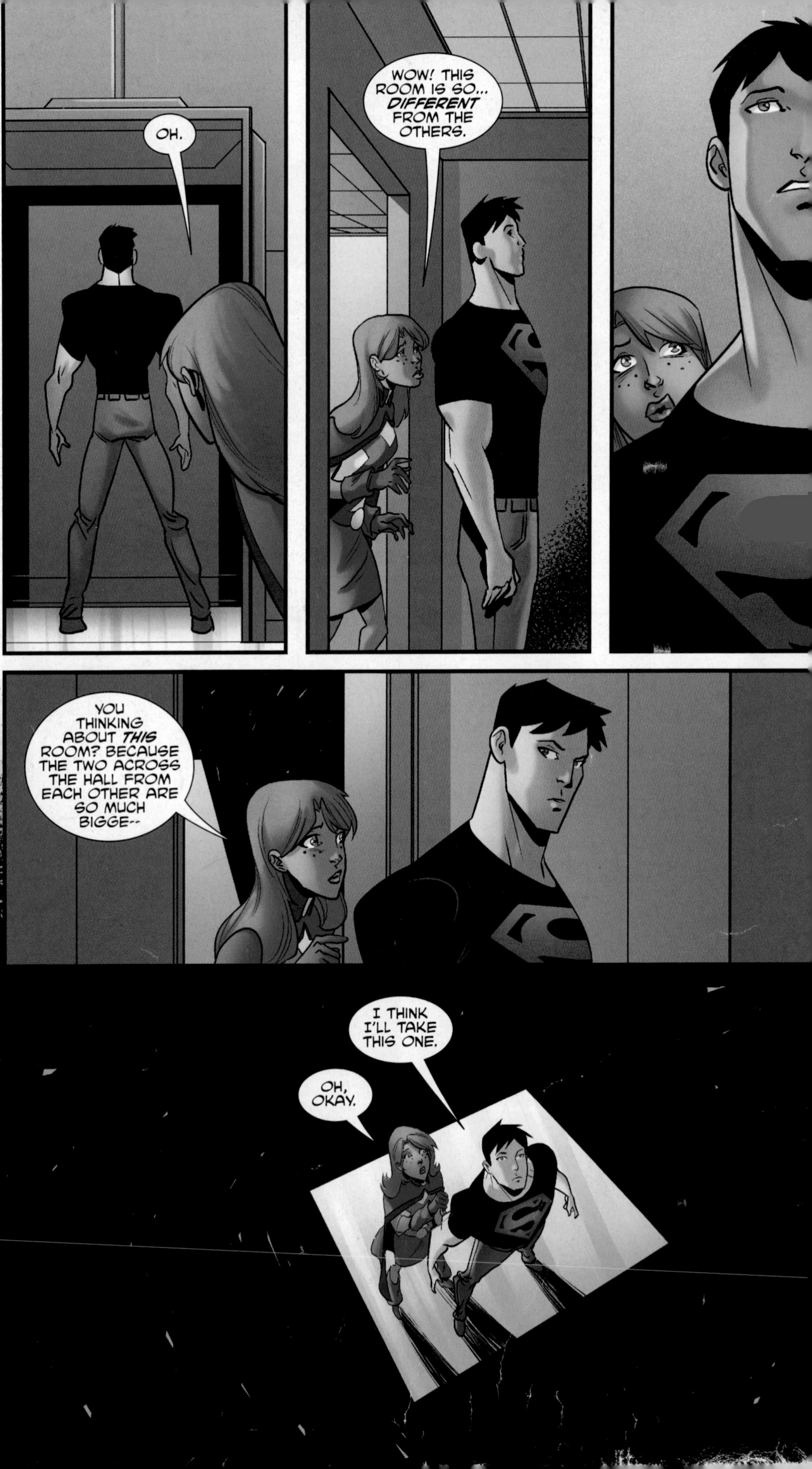
OH.
WOW! THIS ROOM IS SO... *DIFFERENT* FROM THE OTHERS.
YOU THINKING ABOUT *THIS* ROOM? BECAUSE THE TWO ACROSS THE HALL FROM EACH OTHER ARE SO MUCH BIGGE--
I THINK I'LL TAKE THIS ONE.
OH, OKAY.

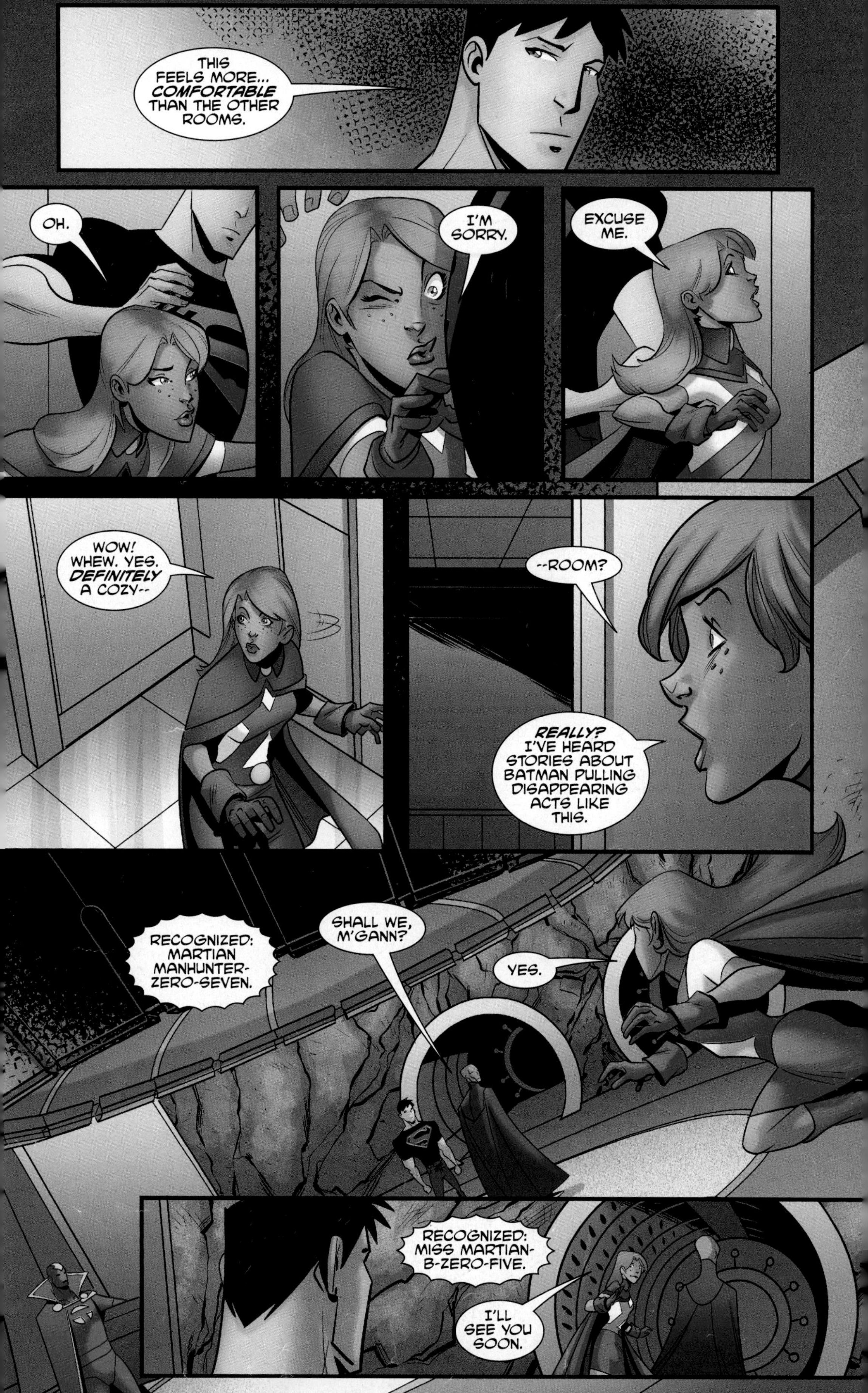
THIS FEELS MORE... COMPORTABLE THAN THE OTHER ROOMS.
OH.
I'M SORRY.
EXCUSE ME.
WOW! WHEW. YES. DEFINITELY A COZY--
--ROOM?
REALLY? I'VE HEARD STORIES ABOUT BATMAN PULLING DISAPPEARING ACTS LIKE THIS.
RECOGNIZED: MARTIAN MANHUNTER-ZERO-SEVEN.
SHALL WE, M'GANN?
YES.
RECOGNIZED: MISS MARTIAN-B-ZERO-FIVE.
I'LL SEE YOU SOON.

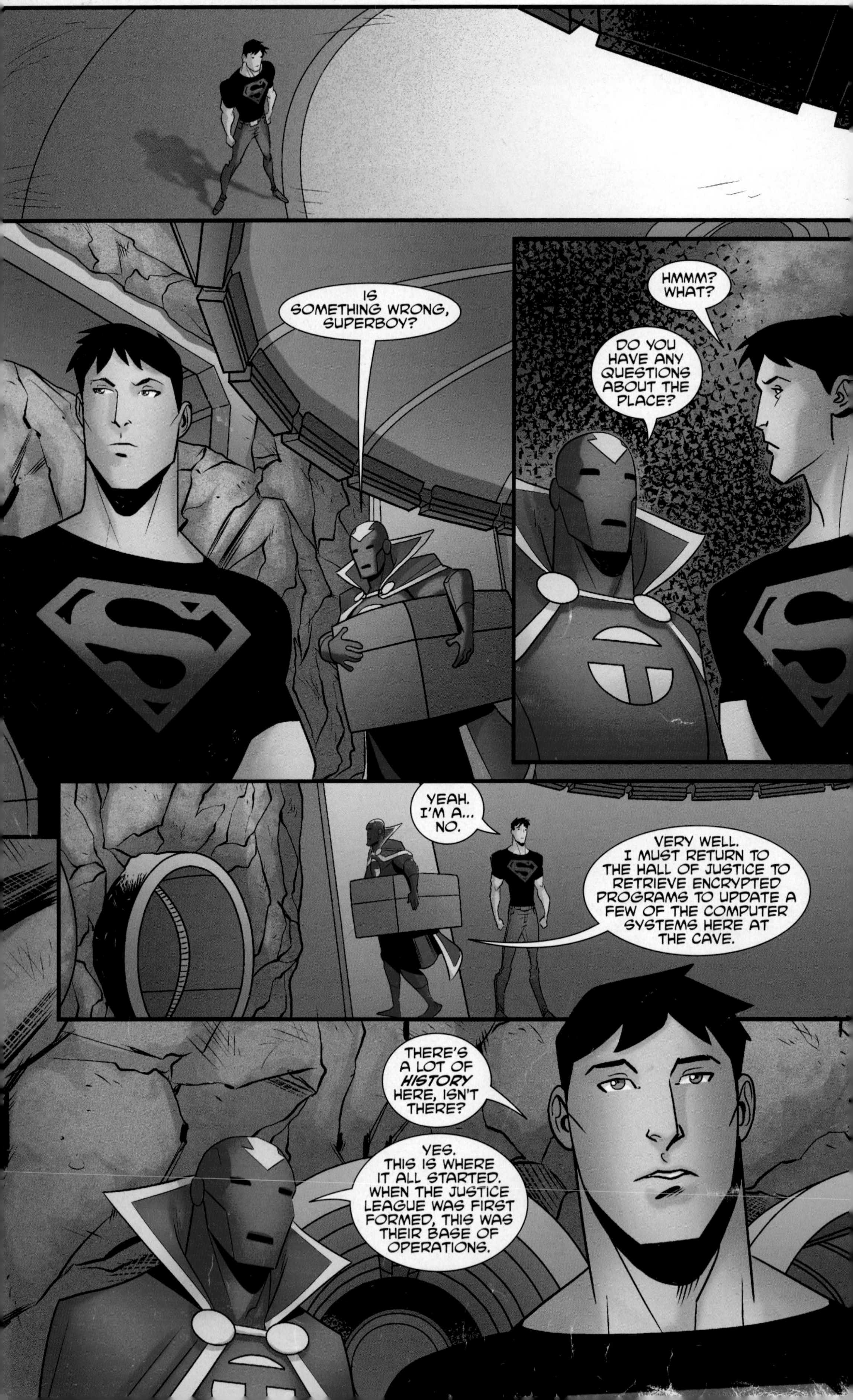
IS SOMETHING WRONG, SUPERBOY?
HMMM? WHAT?
DO YOU HAVE ANY QUESTIONS ABOUT THE PLACE?
YEAH. I'M A... NO.
VERY WELL. I MUST RETURN TO THE HALL OF JUSTICE TO RETRIEVE ENCRYPTED PROGRAMS TO UPDATE A FEW OF THE COMPUTER SYSTEMS HERE AT THE CAVE.
THERE'S A LOT OF *HISTORY* HERE, ISN'T THERE?
YES. THIS IS WHERE IT ALL STARTED. WHEN THE JUSTICE LEAGUE WAS FIRST FORMED, THIS WAS THEIR BASE OF OPERATIONS.

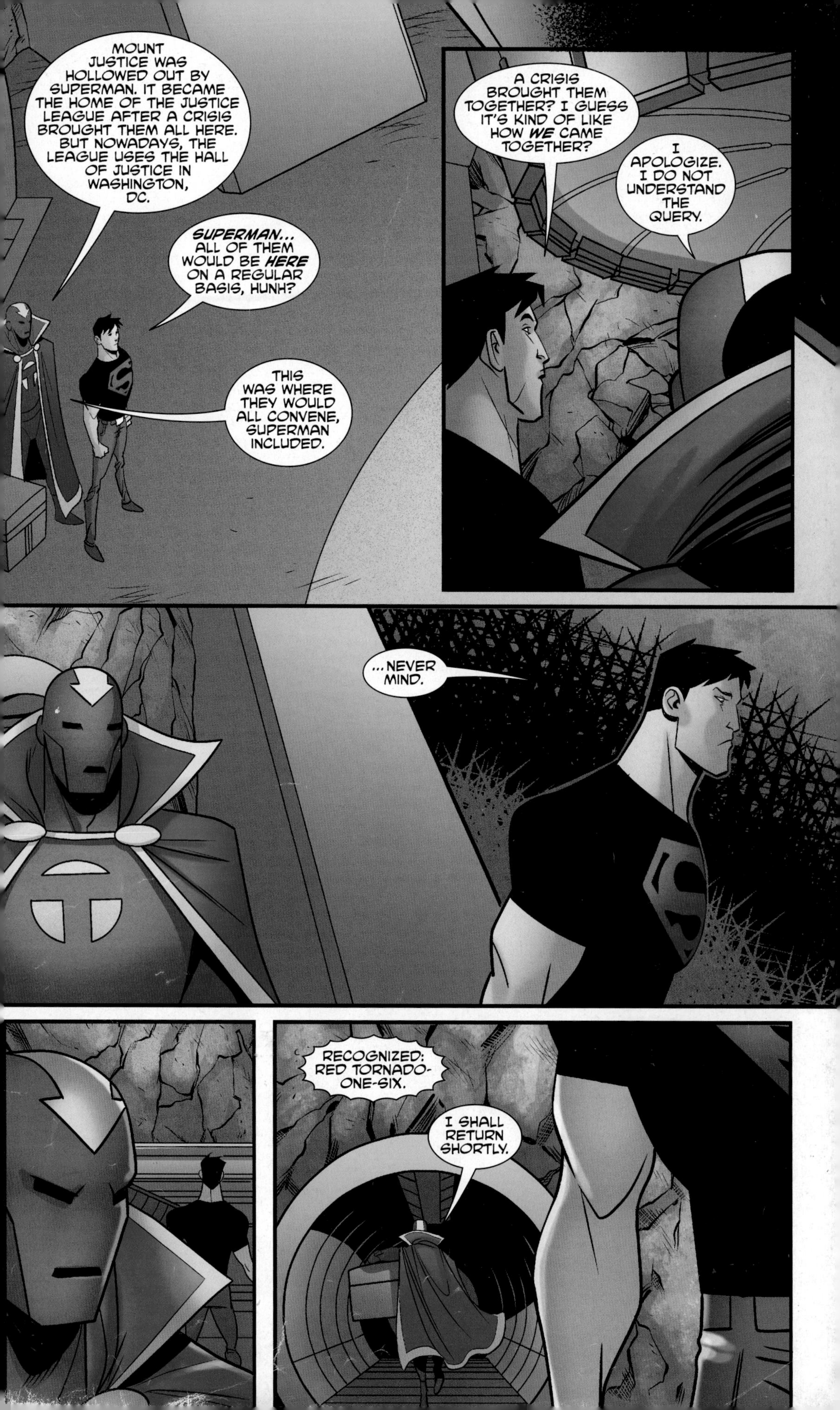
MOUNT JUSTICE WAS HOLLOWED OUT BY SUPERMAN. IT BECAME THE HOME OF THE JUSTICE LEAGUE AFTER A CRISIS BROUGHT THEM ALL HERE. BUT NOWADAYS, THE LEAGUE USES THE HALL OF JUSTICE IN WASHINGTON, DC.
SUPERMAN... ALL OF THEM WOULD BE *HERE* ON A REGULAR BASIS, HUNH?
THIS WAS WHERE THEY WOULD ALL CONVENE, SUPERMAN INCLUDED.
A CRISIS BROUGHT THEM TOGETHER? I GUESS IT'S KIND OF LIKE HOW *WE* CAME TOGETHER?
I APOLOGIZE. I DO NOT UNDERSTAND THE QUERY.
...NEVER MIND.
RECOGNIZED: RED TORNADO-ONE-SIX.
I SHALL RETURN SHORTLY.

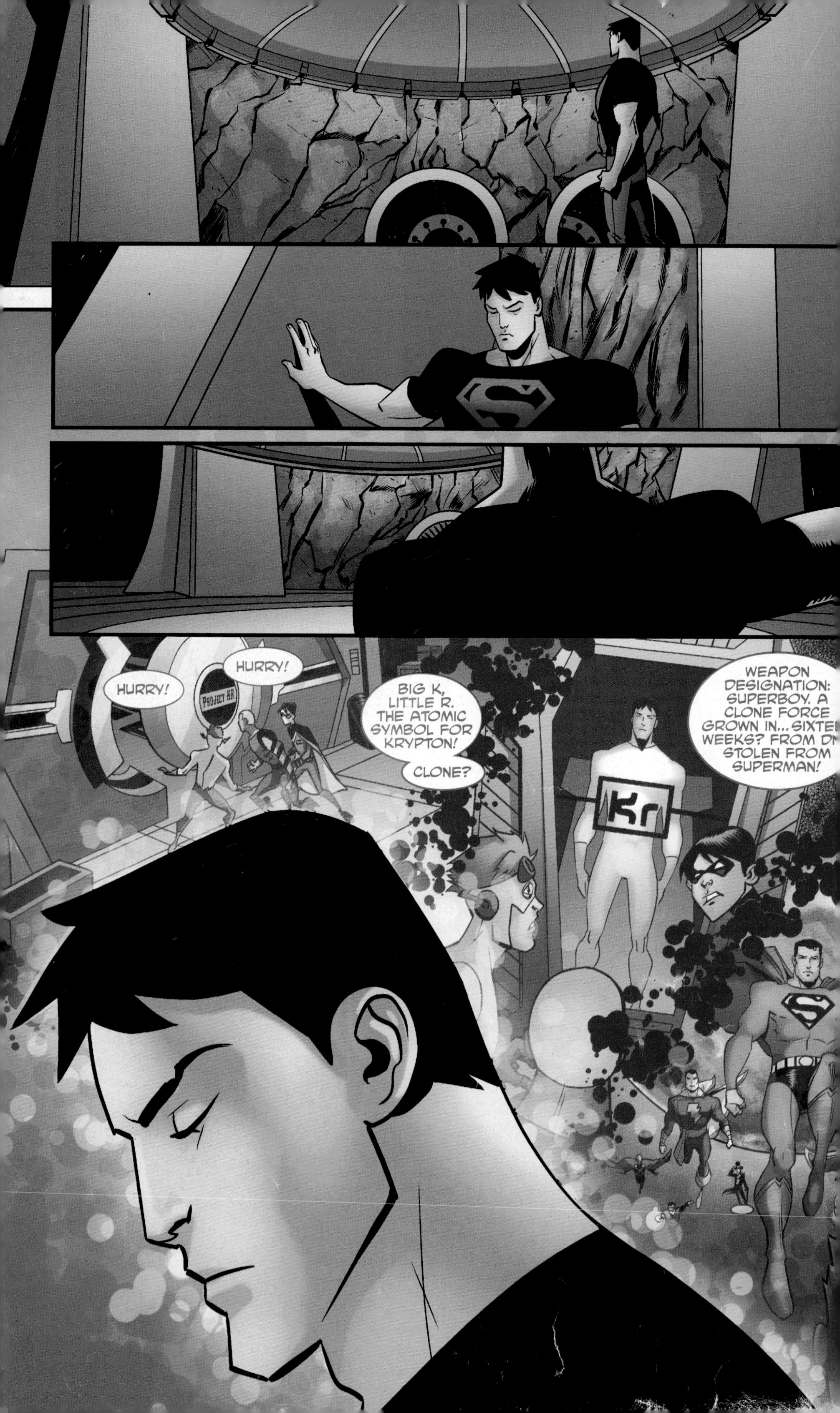
HURRY!
HURRY!
PROJECT KR
BIG K, LITTLE R. THE ATOMIC SYMBOL FOR KRYPTON!
CLONE?
WEAPON DESIGNATION: SUPERBOY. A CLONE FORCE GROWN IN... SIXTE WEEKS? FROM DN STOLEN FROM SUPERMAN!
Kr

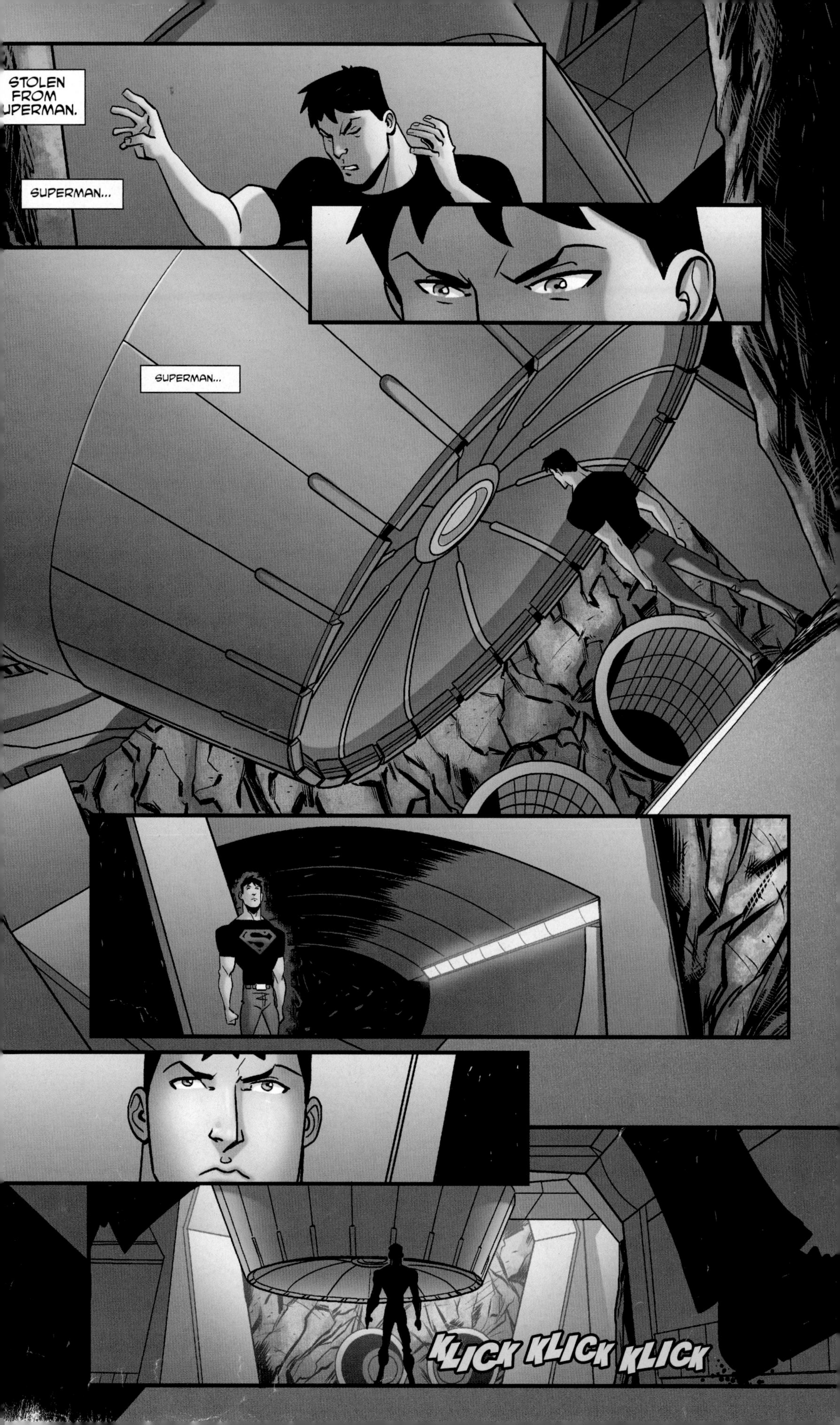

STOLEN FROM SUPERMAN.
SUPERMAN...
SUPERMAN...
KLICK KLICK KLICK

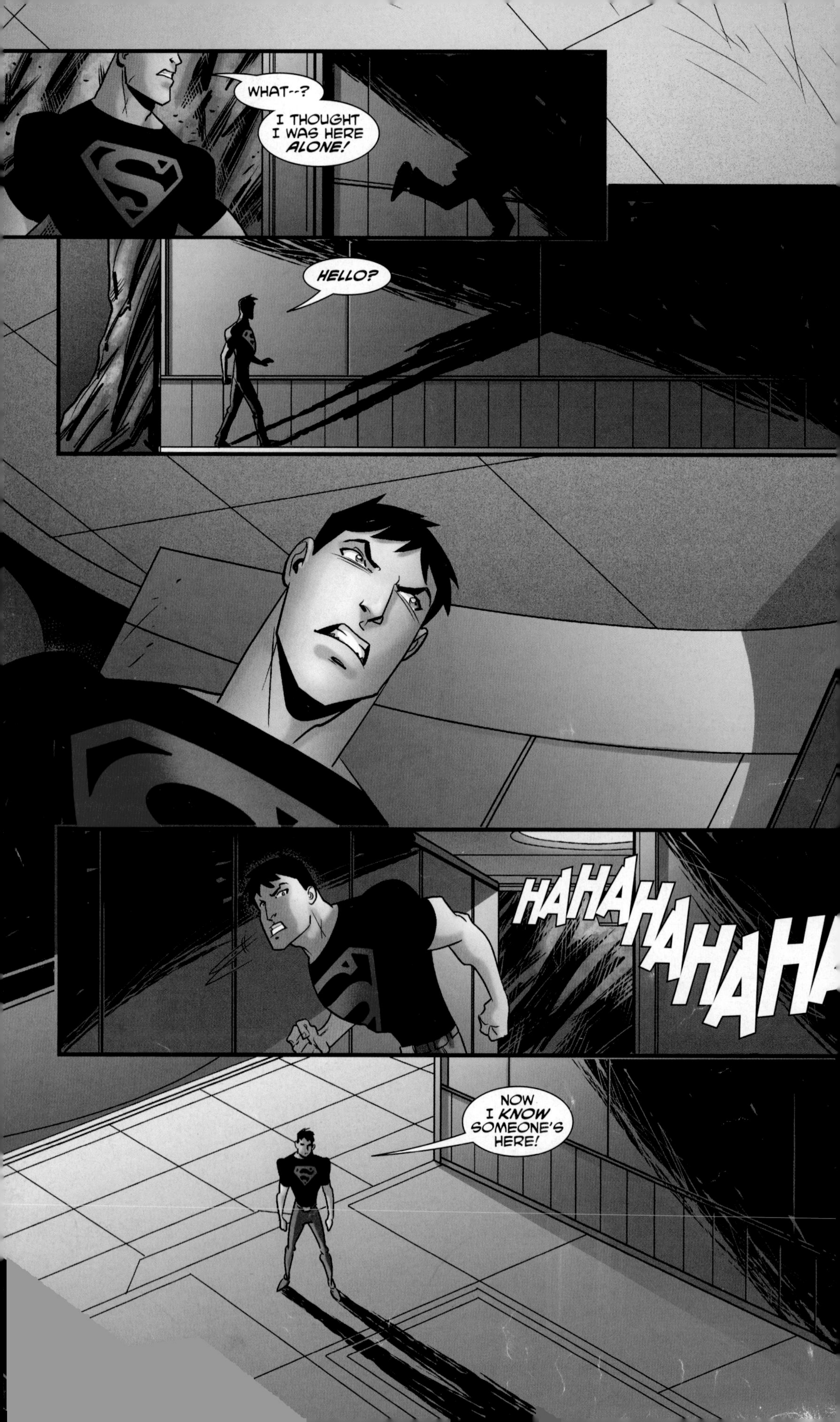
WHAT--?
I THOUGHT I WAS HERE *ALONE!*
HELLO?
HAHAHAHAHAHAHAHA
NOW I *KNOW* SOMEONE'S HERE!

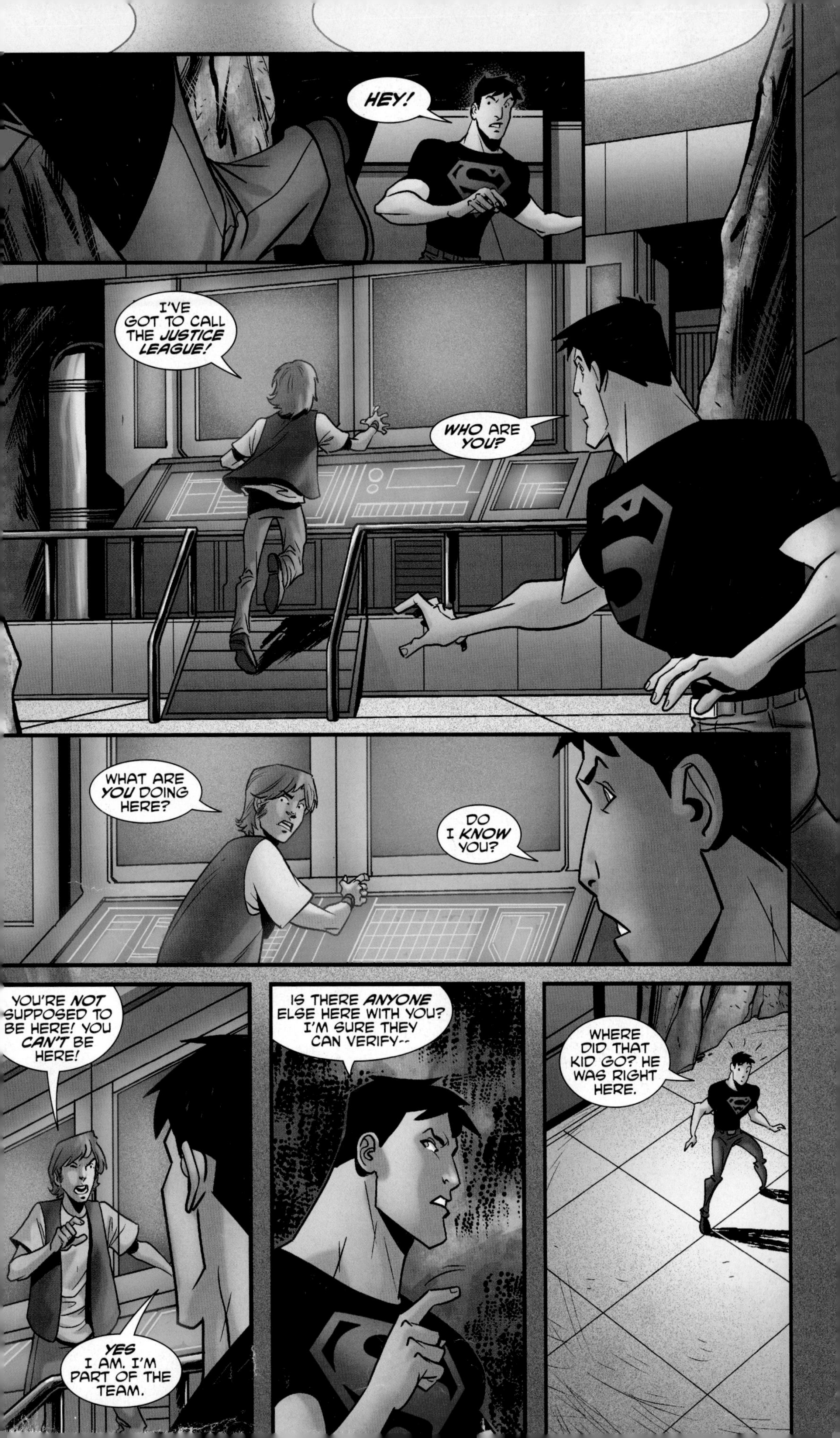
HEY!
I'VE GOT TO CALL THE JUSTICE LEAGUE!
WHO ARE YOU?
WHAT ARE YOU DOING HERE?
DO I KNOW YOU?
YOU'RE NOT SUPPOSED TO BE HERE! YOU CAN'T BE HERE!
YES I AM. I'M PART OF THE TEAM.
IS THERE ANYONE ELSE HERE WITH YOU? I'M SURE THEY CAN VERIFY--
WHERE DID THAT KID GO? HE WAS RIGHT HERE.

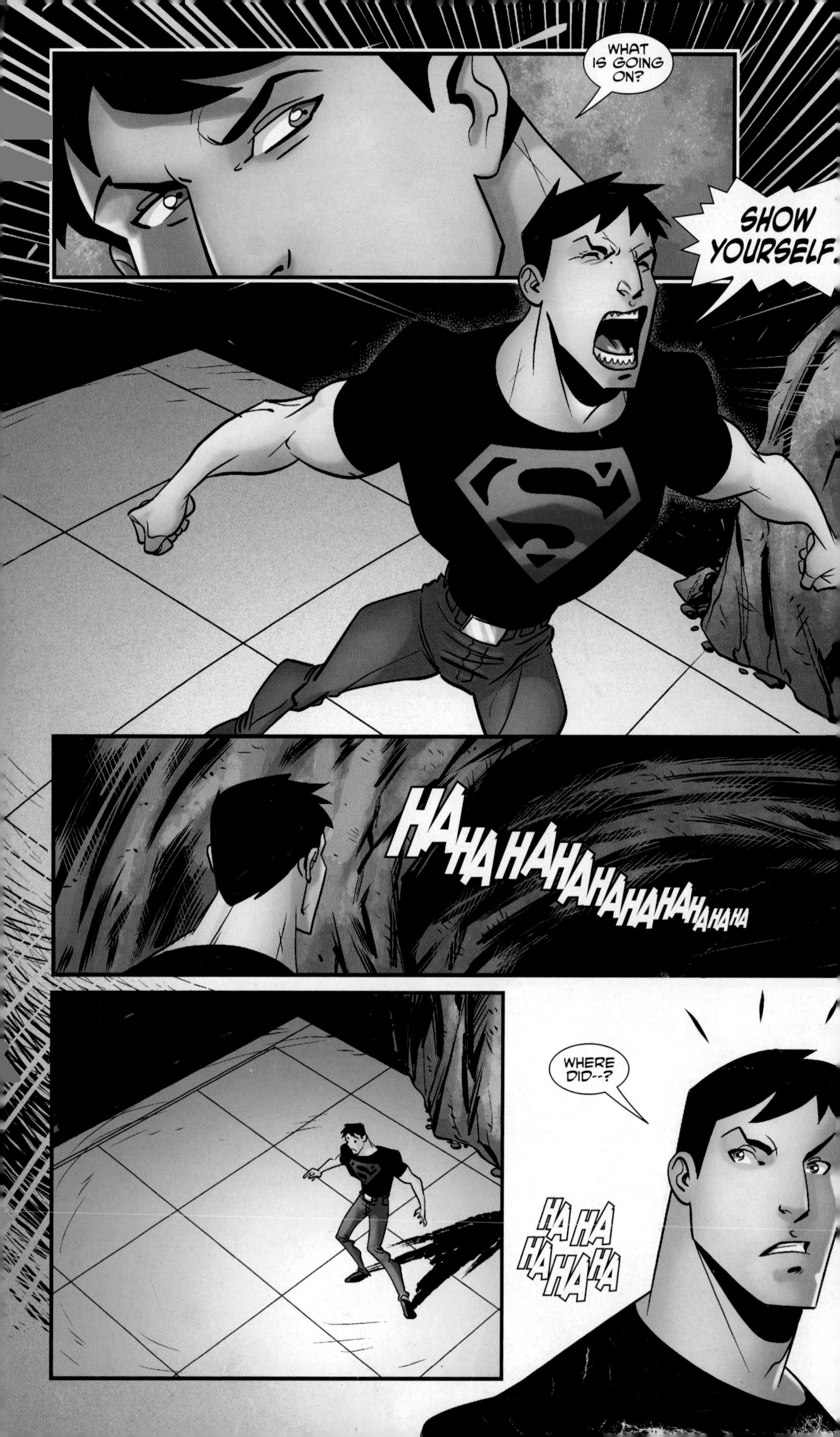
WHAT IS GOING ON?
SHOW YOURSELF.
HAHA HAHAHAHAHAHAHAHAHA
WHERE DID--?
HA HA HA HA HA HA

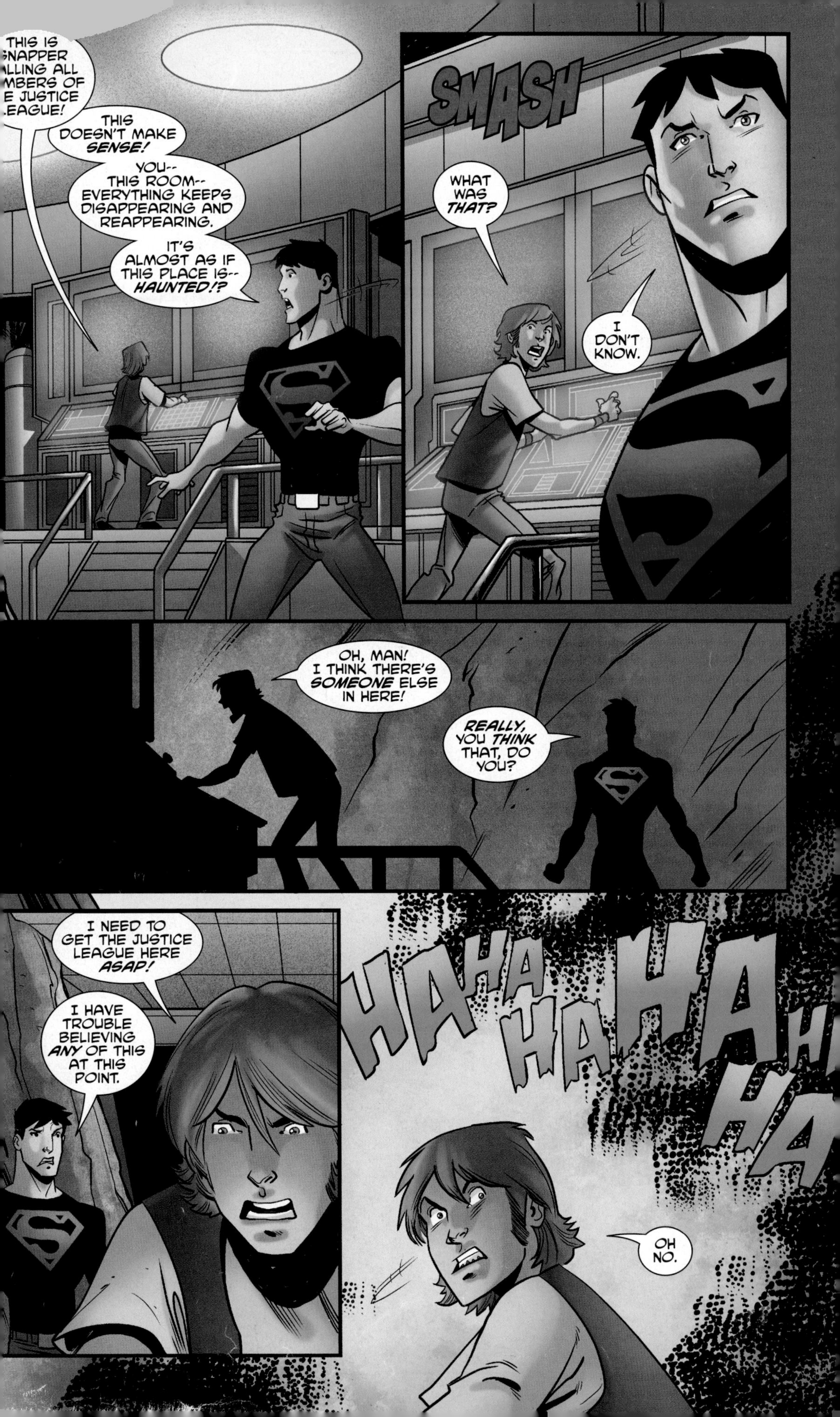
THIS IS SNAPPER CALLING ALL MEMBERS OF THE JUSTICE LEAGUE!
THIS DOESN'T MAKE SENSE!
YOU-- THIS ROOM-- EVERYTHING KEEPS DISAPPEARING AND REAPPEARING.
IT'S ALMOST AS IF THIS PLACE IS-- HAUNTED!?
SMASH
WHAT WAS THAT?
I DON'T KNOW.
OH, MAN! I THINK THERE'S SOMEONE ELSE IN HERE!
REALLY, YOU THINK THAT, DO YOU?
I NEED TO GET THE JUSTICE LEAGUE HERE ASAP!
I HAVE TROUBLE BELIEVING ANY OF THIS AT THIS POINT.
HAHA HAHA
OH NO.

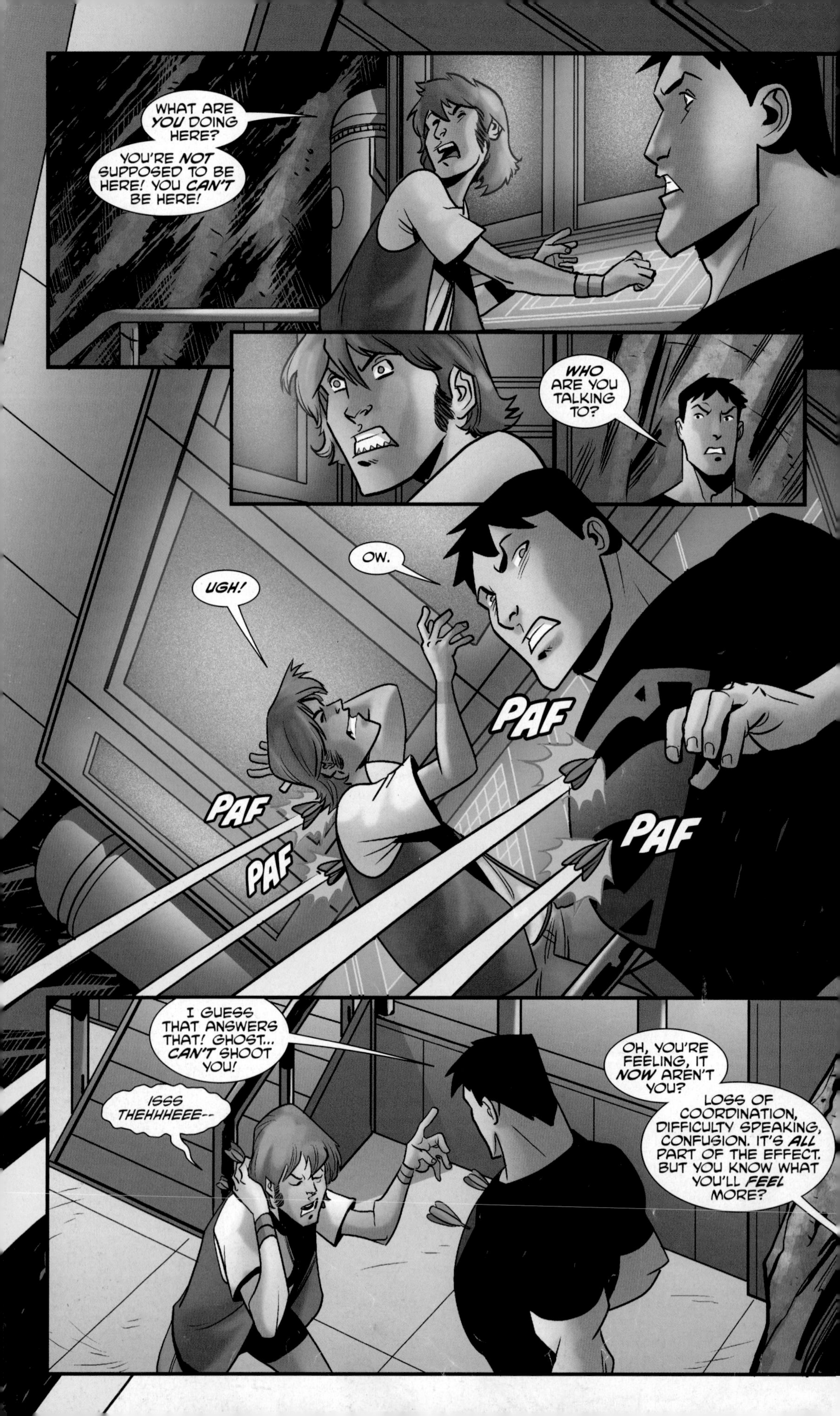
WHAT ARE YOU DOING HERE?
YOU'RE NOT SUPPOSED TO BE HERE! YOU CAN'T BE HERE!
WHO ARE YOU TALKING TO?
OW.
UGH!
PAF
PAF
PAF
PAF
I GUESS THAT ANSWERS THAT! GHOST... CAN'T SHOOT YOU!
ISSS THEHHHEEE--
OH, YOU'RE FEELING, IT NOW AREN'T YOU?
LOSS OF COORDINATION, DIFFICULTY SPEAKING, CONFUSION. IT'S ALL PART OF THE EFFECT. BUT YOU KNOW WHAT YOU'LL FEEL MORE?

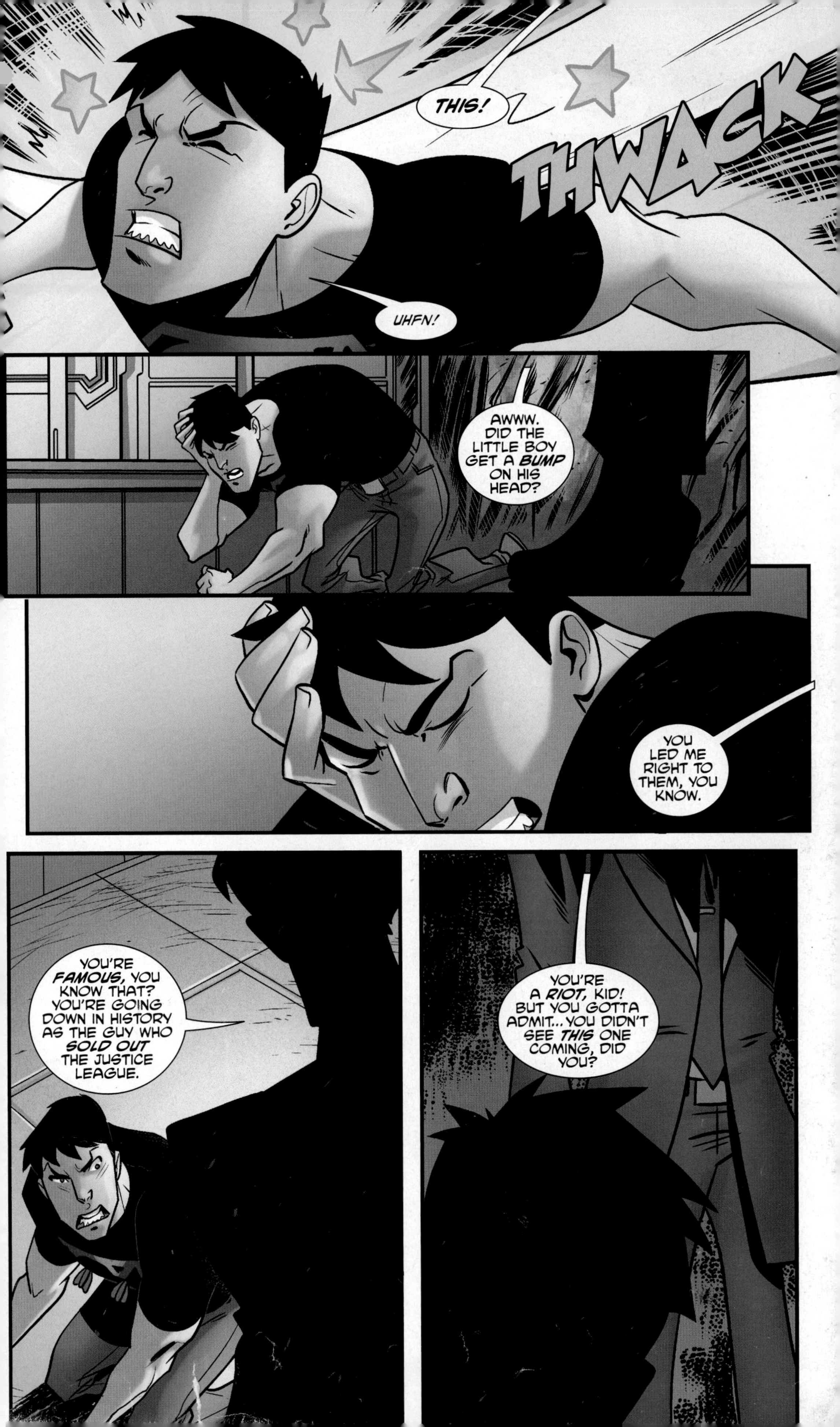
THIS!
THWACK
UHFN!
AWWW. DID THE LITTLE BOY GET A *BUMP* ON HIS HEAD?
YOU LED ME RIGHT TO THEM, YOU KNOW.
YOU'RE *FAMOUS,* YOU KNOW THAT? YOU'RE GOING DOWN IN HISTORY AS THE GUY WHO *SOLD OUT* THE JUSTICE LEAGUE.
YOU'RE A *RIOT,* KID! BUT YOU GOTTA ADMIT... YOU DIDN'T SEE *THIS* ONE COMING, DID YOU?

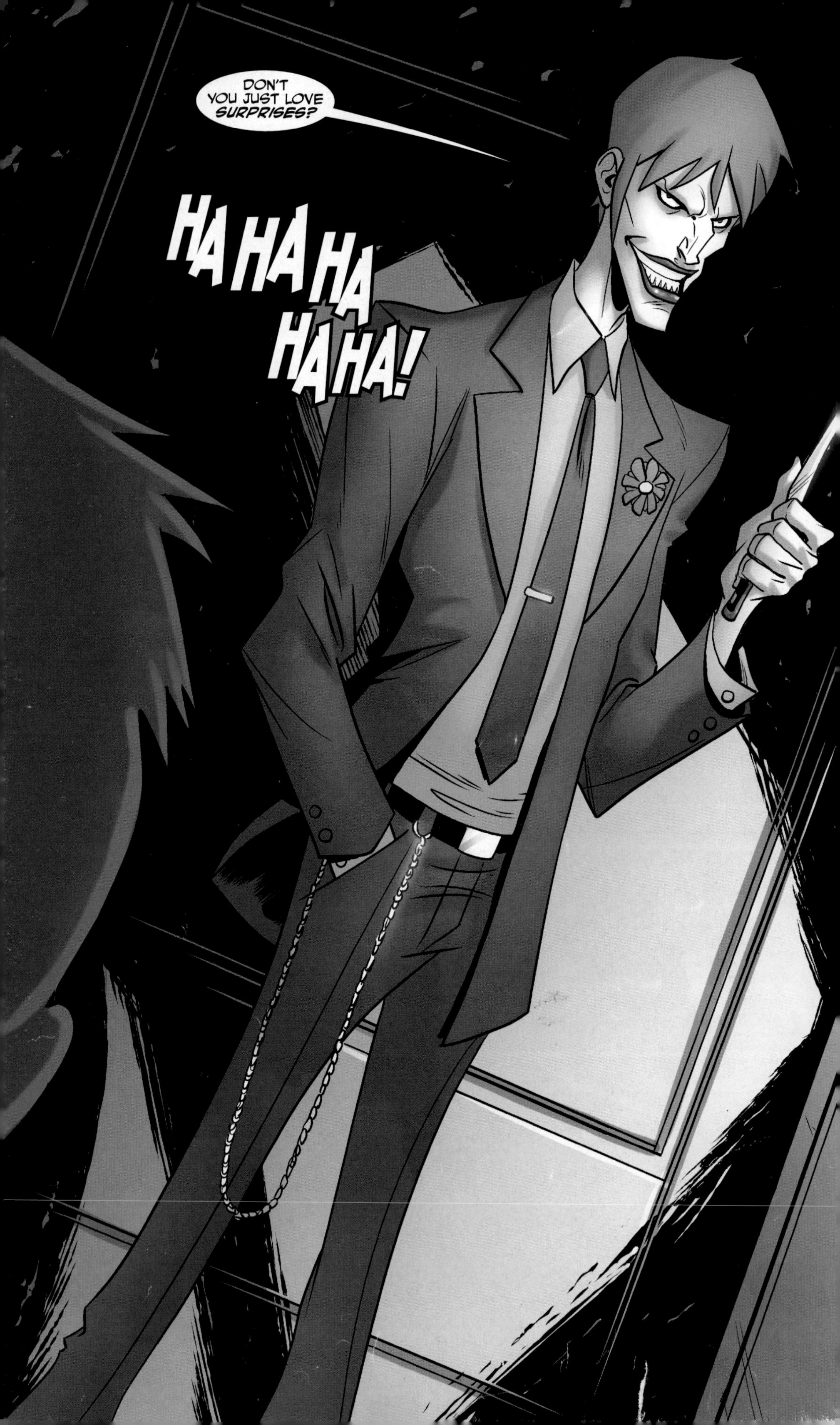
DON'T YOU JUST LOVE SURPRISES?
HA HA HA HA HA HA!

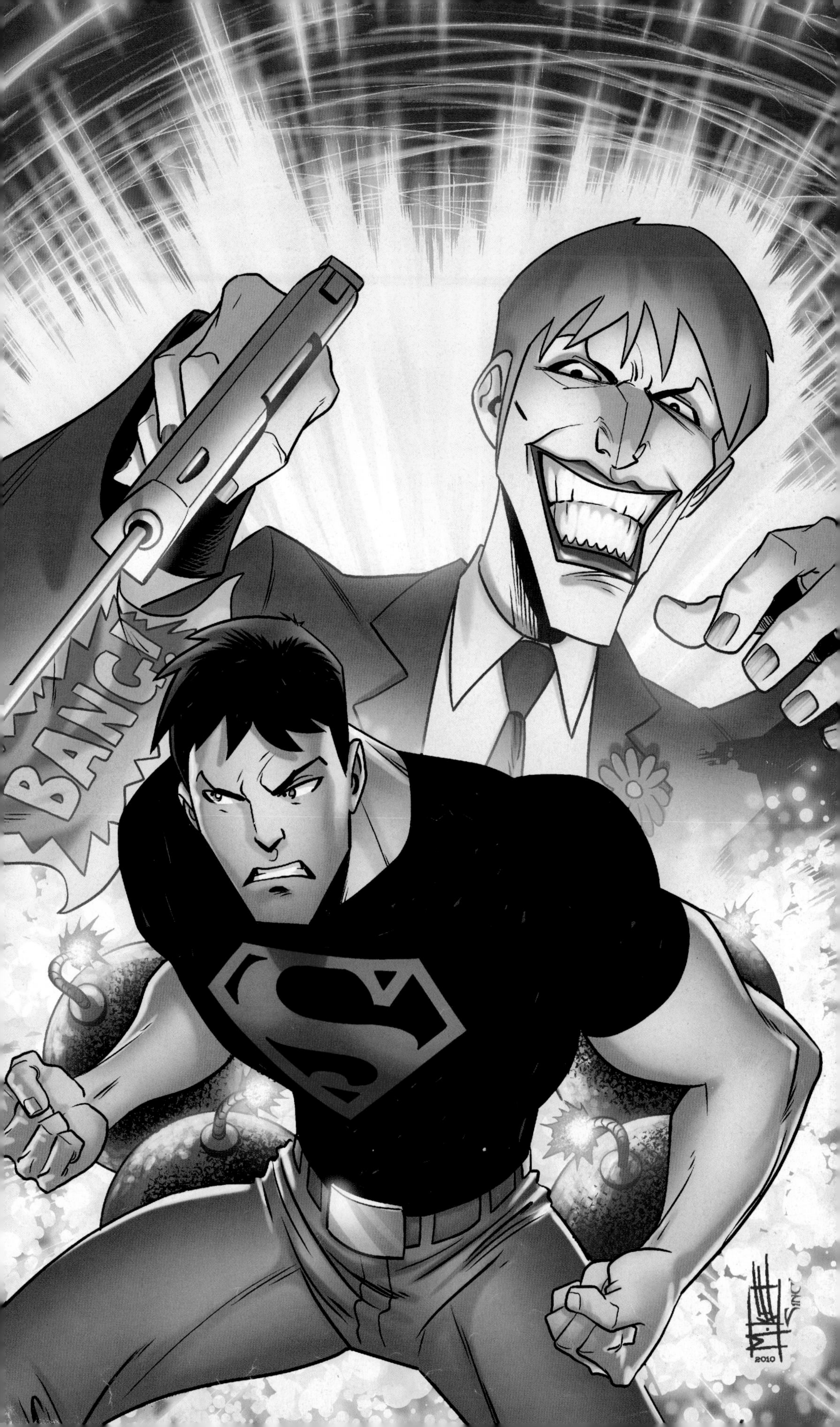
BANG!

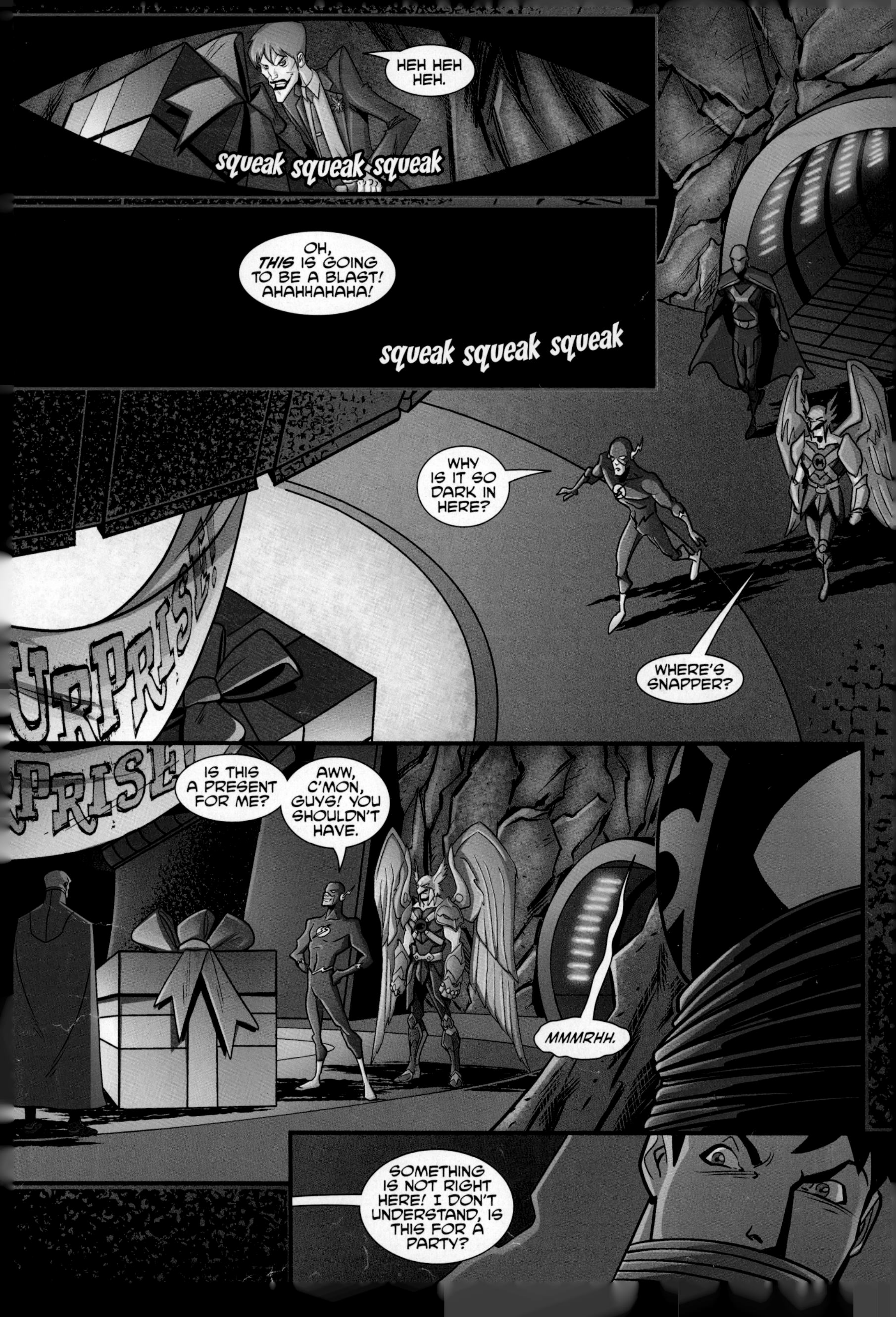
HEH HEH HEH.
squeak squeak squeak
OH, THIS IS GOING TO BE A BLAST! AHAHHAHAHA!
squeak squeak squeak
WHY IS IT SO DARK IN HERE?
WHERE'S SNAPPER?
SURPRISE!
IS THIS A PRESENT FOR ME?
AWW, C'MON, GUYS! YOU SHOULDN'T HAVE.
MMMRHH.
SOMETHING IS NOT RIGHT HERE! I DON'T UNDERSTAND, IS THIS FOR A PARTY?

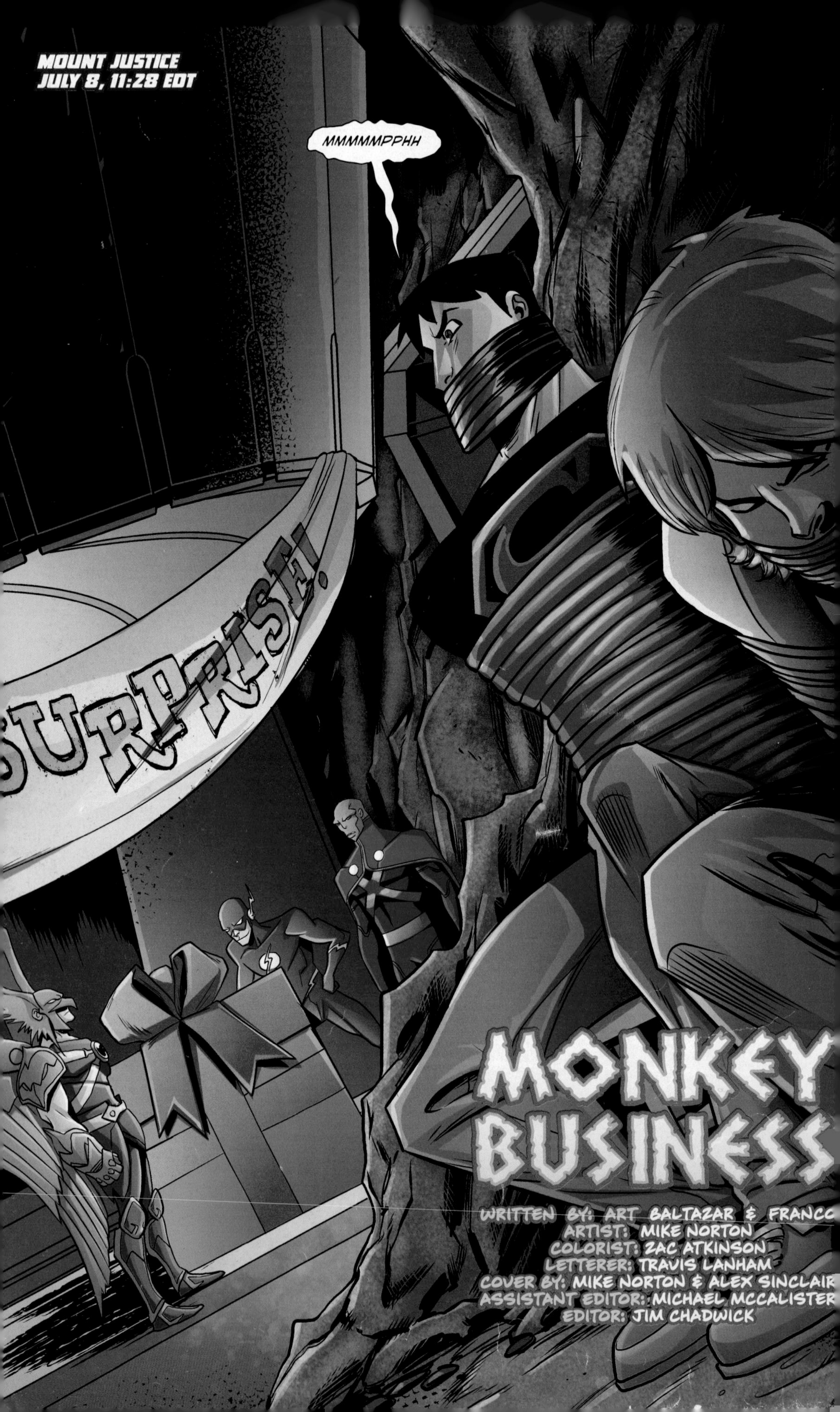
MOUNT JUSTICE
JULY 8, 11:28 EDT
MMMMMMPPHH
SURPRISE!
MONKEY BUSINESS
WRITTEN BY: ART BALTAZAR & FRANCO
ARTIST: MIKE NORTON
COLORIST: ZAC ATKINSON
LETTERER: TRAVIS LANHAM
COVER BY: MIKE NORTON & ALEX SINCLAIR
ASSISTANT EDITOR: MICHAEL MCCALISTER
EDITOR: JIM CHADWICK

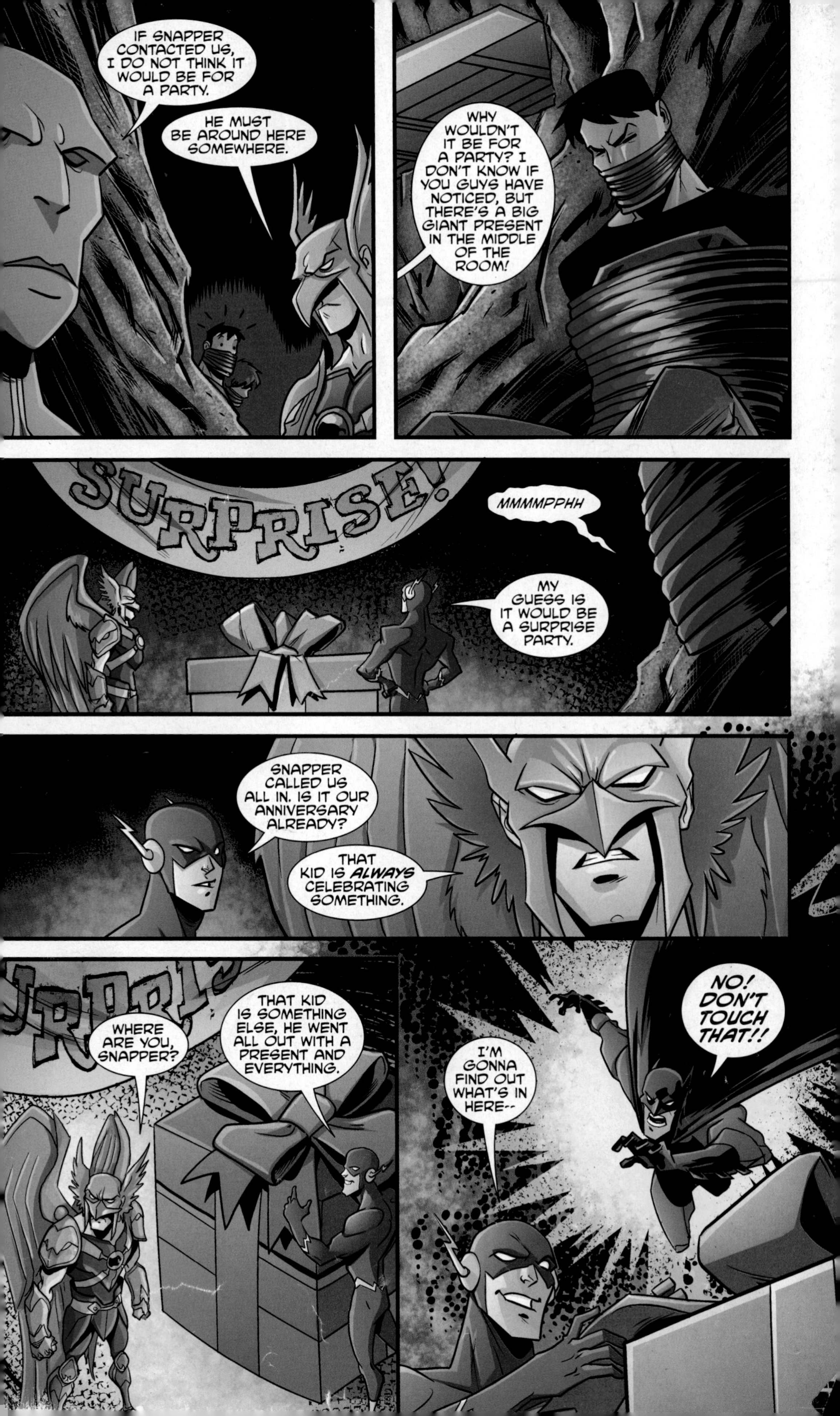
IF SNAPPER CONTACTED US, I DO NOT THINK IT WOULD BE FOR A PARTY.
HE MUST BE AROUND HERE SOMEWHERE.
WHY WOULDN'T IT BE FOR A PARTY? I DON'T KNOW IF YOU GUYS HAVE NOTICED, BUT THERE'S A BIG GIANT PRESENT IN THE MIDDLE OF THE ROOM!
SURPRISE!
MMMMPPHH
MY GUESS IS IT WOULD BE A SURPRISE PARTY.
SNAPPER CALLED US ALL IN. IS IT OUR ANNIVERSARY ALREADY?
THAT KID IS *ALWAYS* CELEBRATING SOMETHING.
WHERE ARE YOU, SNAPPER?
THAT KID IS SOMETHING ELSE, HE WENT ALL OUT WITH A PRESENT AND EVERYTHING.
I'M GONNA FIND OUT WHAT'S IN HERE--
NO! DON'T TOUCH THAT!!

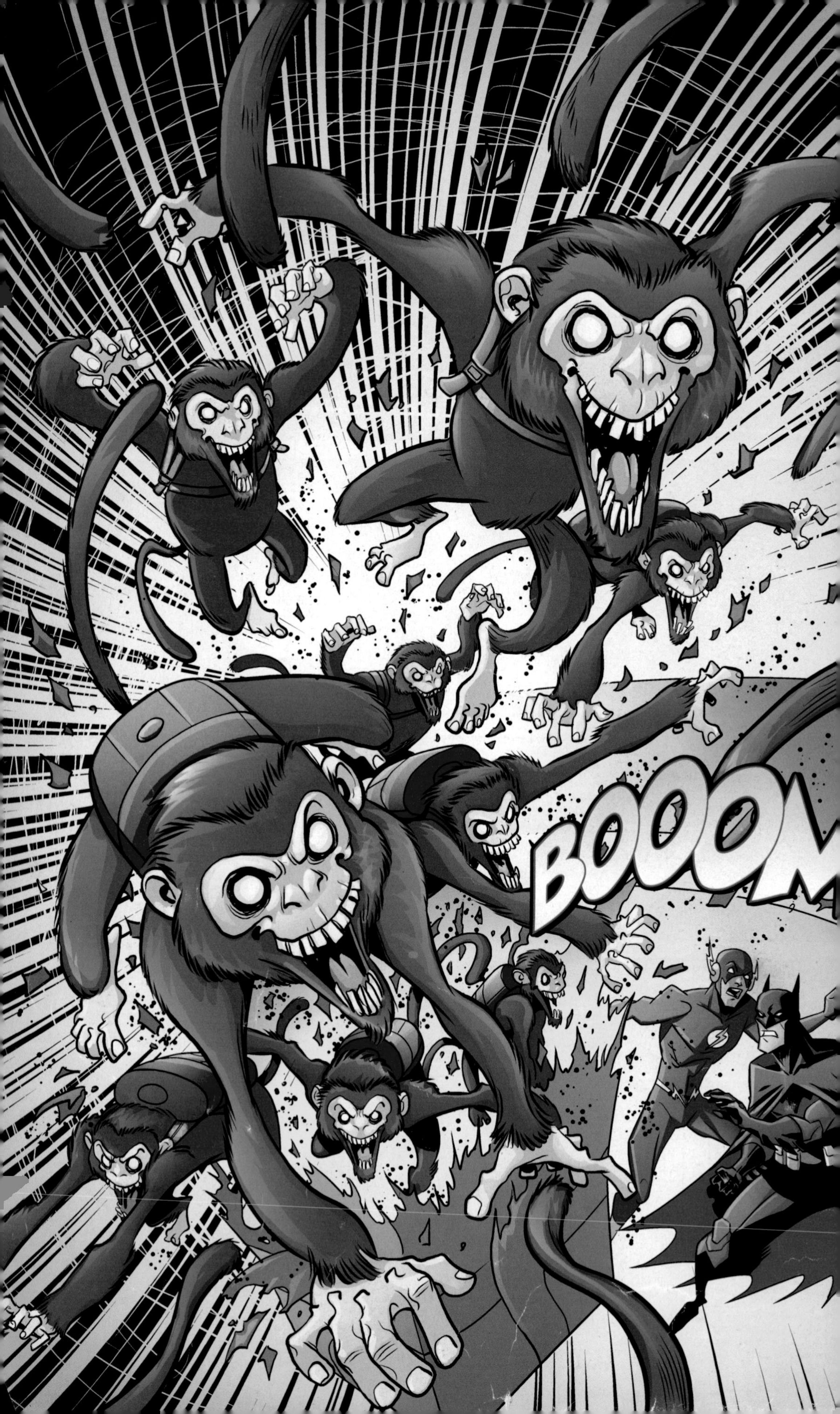
BOOO

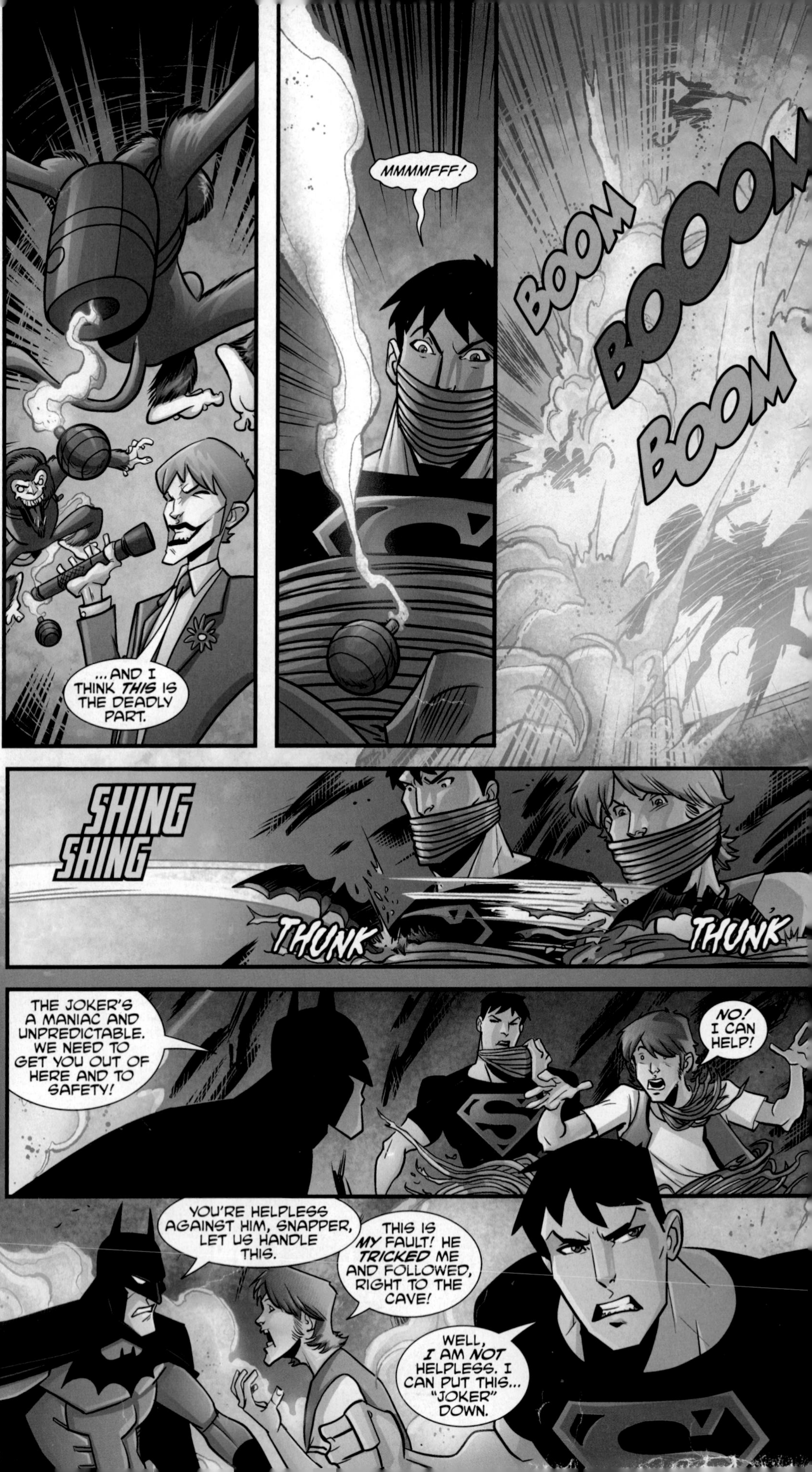
...AND I THINK THIS IS THE DEADLY PART.
MMMMFFF!
BOOM
BOOOOM
BOOM
SHING SHING
THUNK
THUNK
THE JOKER'S A MANIAC AND UNPREDICTABLE. WE NEED TO GET YOU OUT OF HERE AND TO SAFETY!
NO! I CAN HELP!
YOU'RE HELPLESS AGAINST HIM, SNAPPER, LET US HANDLE THIS.
THIS IS MY FAULT! HE TRICKED ME AND FOLLOWED, RIGHT TO THE CAVE!
WELL, I AM NOT HELPLESS. I CAN PUT THIS... "JOKER" DOWN.

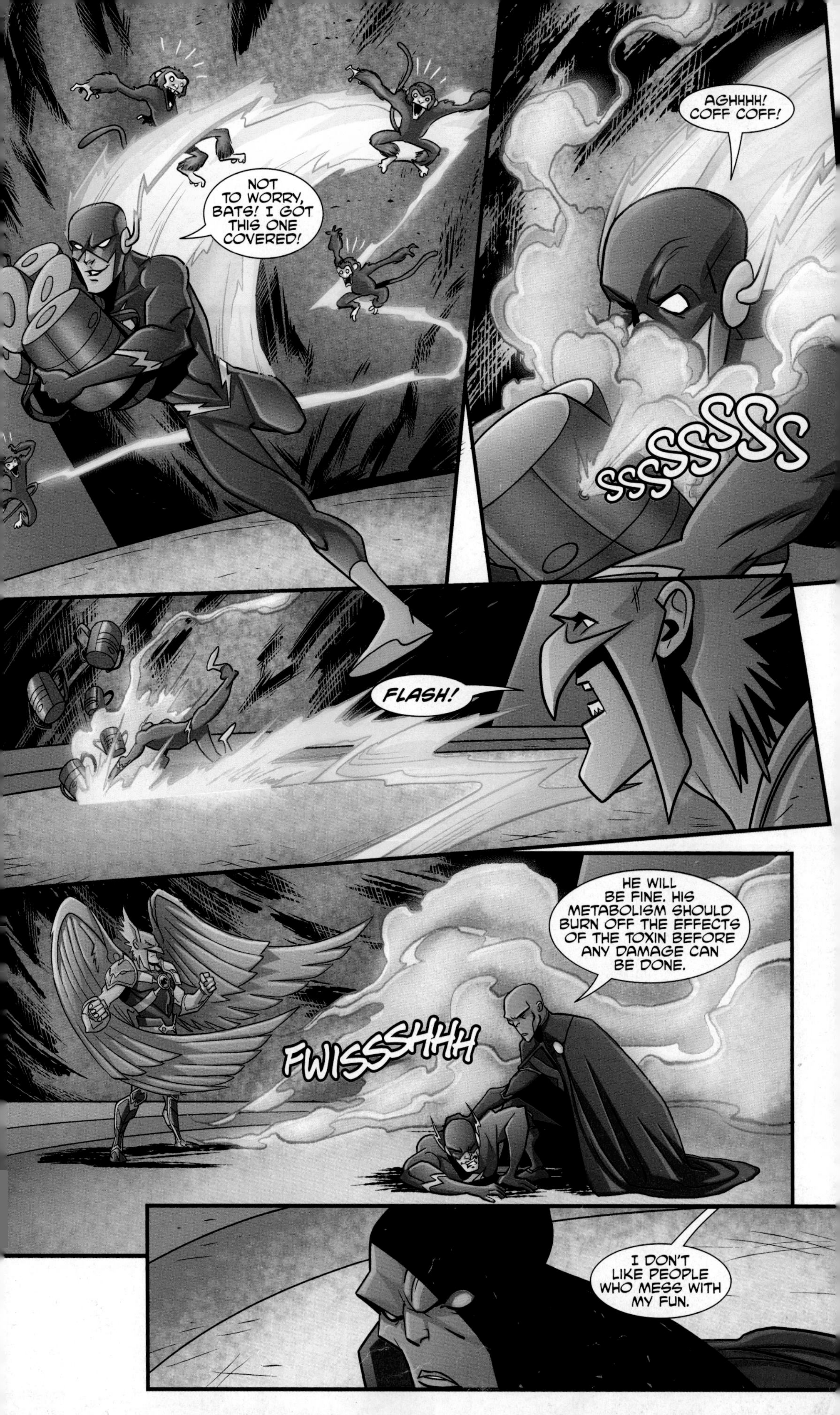

NOT TO WORRY, BATS! I GOT THIS ONE COVERED!
AGHHHH! COFF COFF!
SSSSSSSSS
FLASH!
HE WILL BE FINE. HIS METABOLISM SHOULD BURN OFF THE EFFECTS OF THE TOXIN BEFORE ANY DAMAGE CAN BE DONE.
FWISSSHHH
I DON'T LIKE PEOPLE WHO MESS WITH MY FUN.

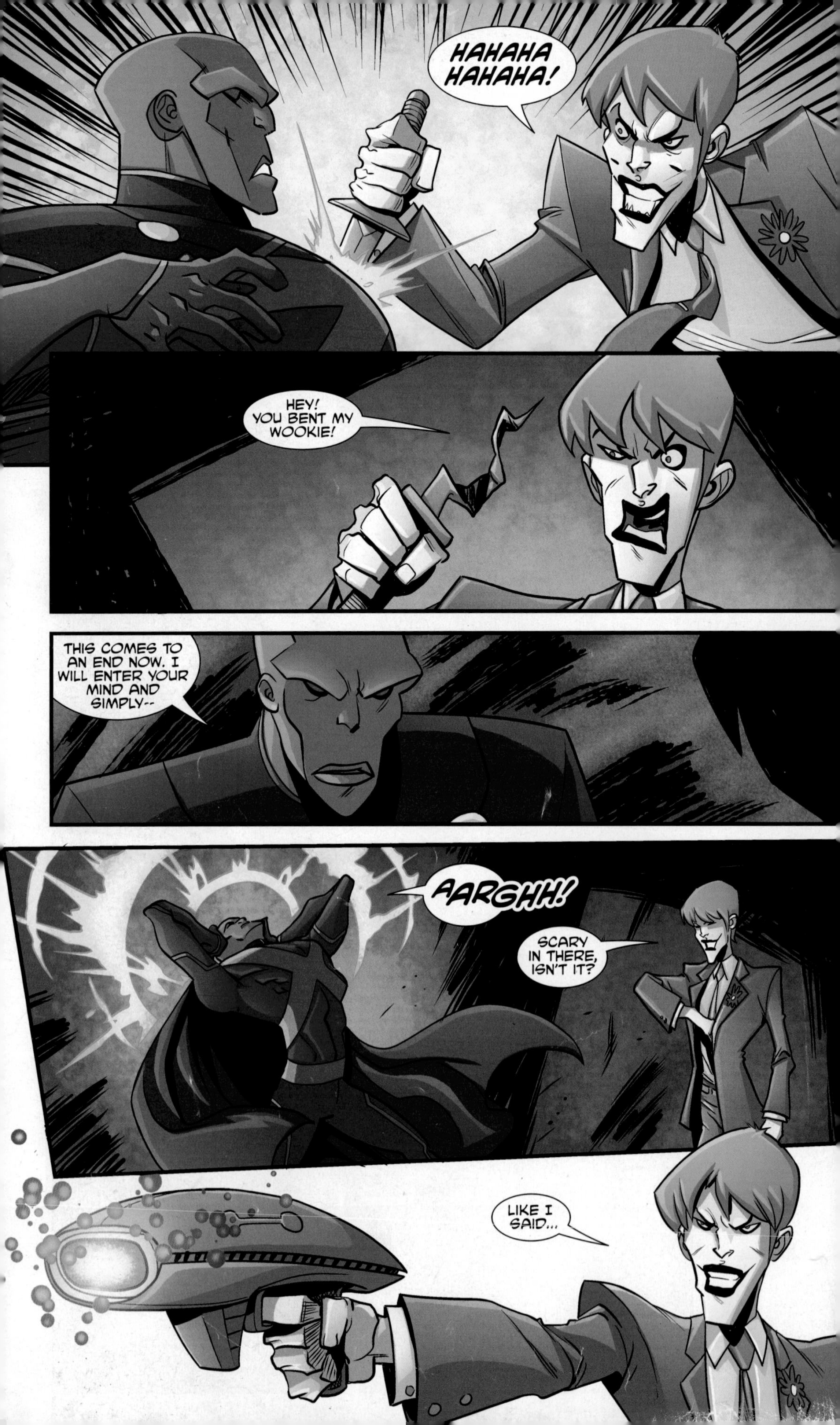
HAHAHA HAHAHA!
HEY! YOU BENT MY WOOKIE!
THIS COMES TO AN END NOW. I WILL ENTER YOUR MIND AND SIMPLY--
AARGHH!
SCARY IN THERE, ISN'T IT?
LIKE I SAID...

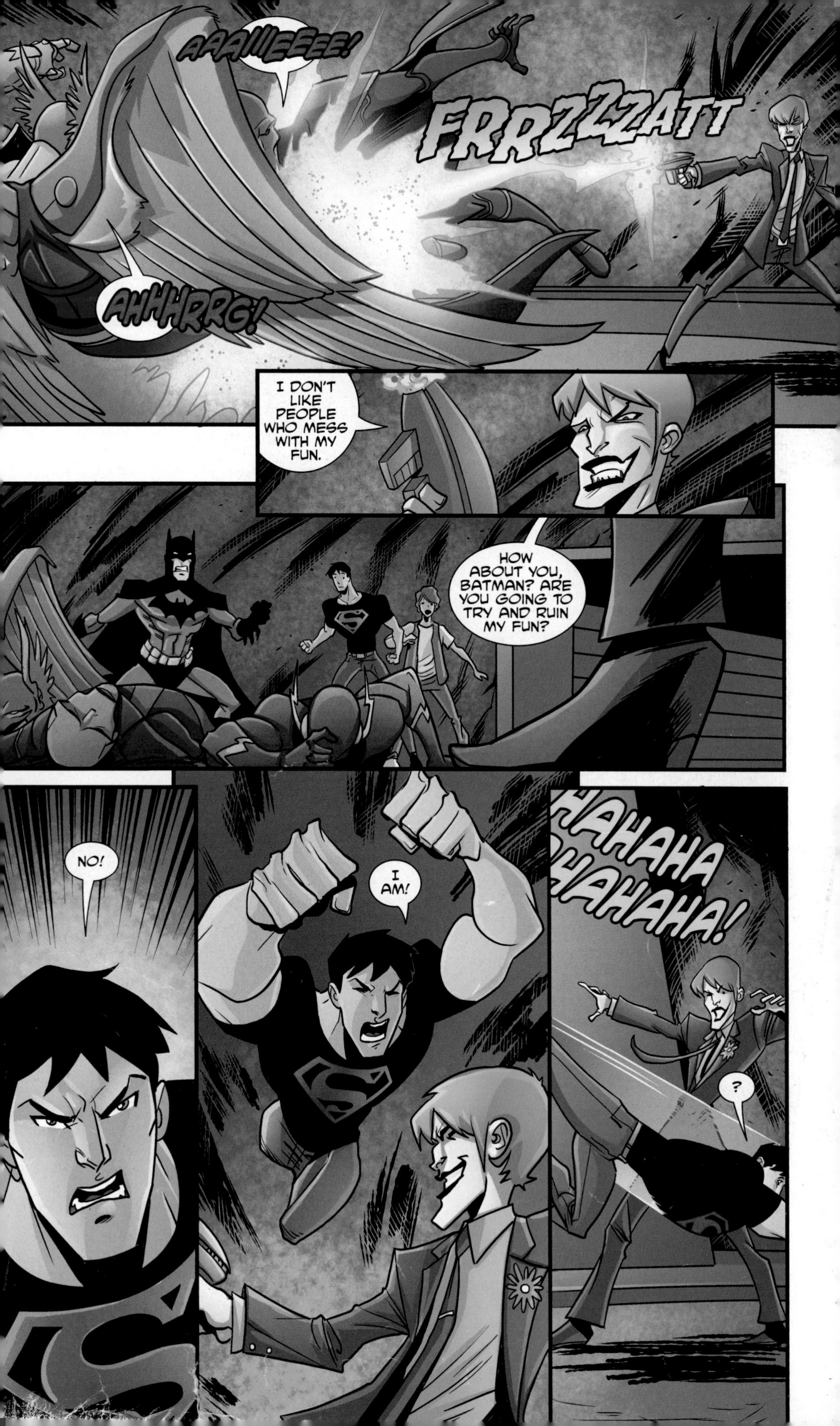
AAAIIIEEEEE!
FRRZZZZATT
AHHHRRG!
I DON'T LIKE PEOPLE WHO MESS WITH MY FUN.
HOW ABOUT YOU, BATMAN? ARE YOU GOING TO TRY AND RUIN MY FUN?
NO!
I AM!
HAHAHA HAHAHAHA!
?

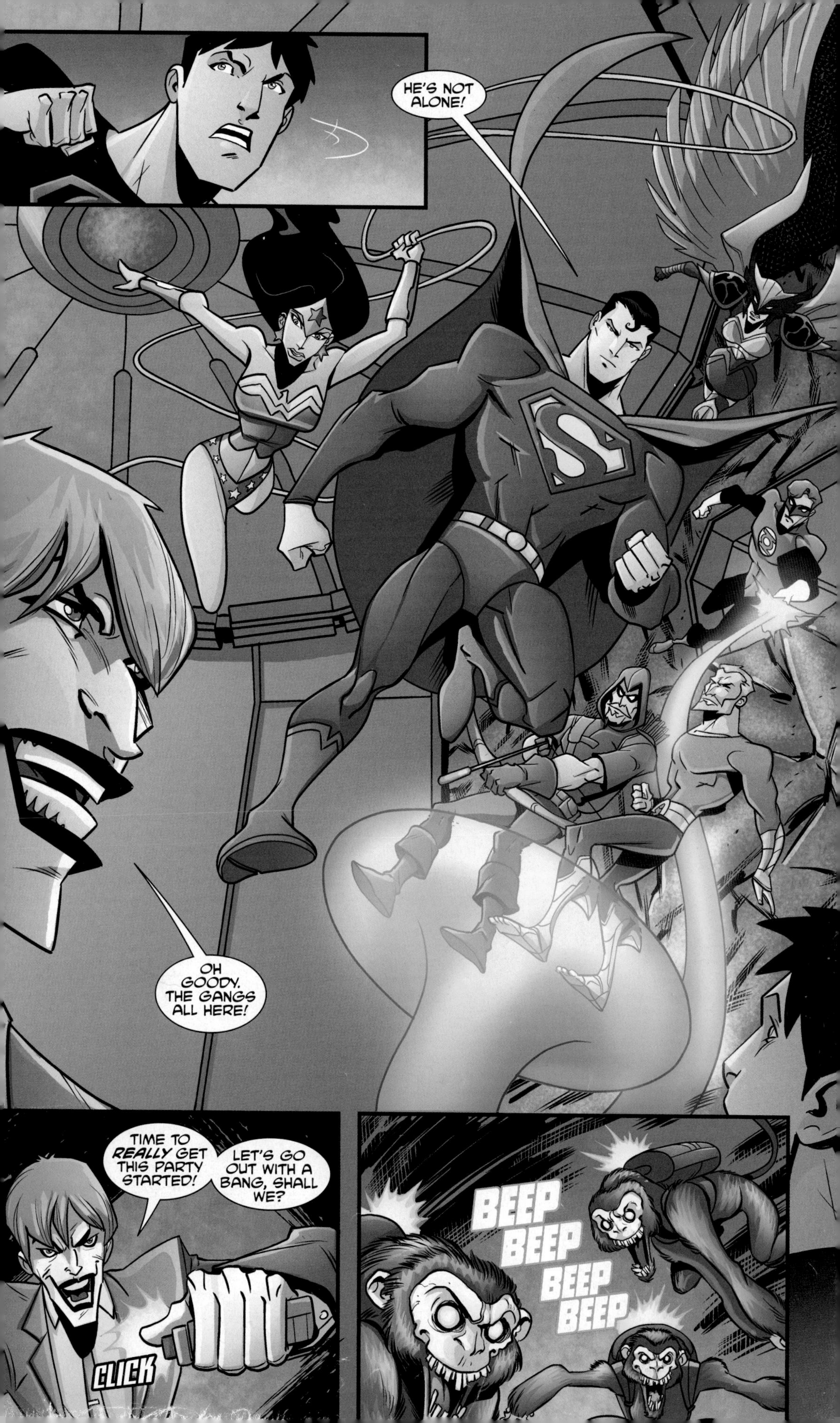
HE'S NOT ALONE!
OH GOODY. THE GANGS ALL HERE!
TIME TO *REALLY* GET THIS PARTY STARTED!
LET'S GO OUT WITH A BANG, SHALL WE?
CLICK
BEEP BEEP BEEP BEEP

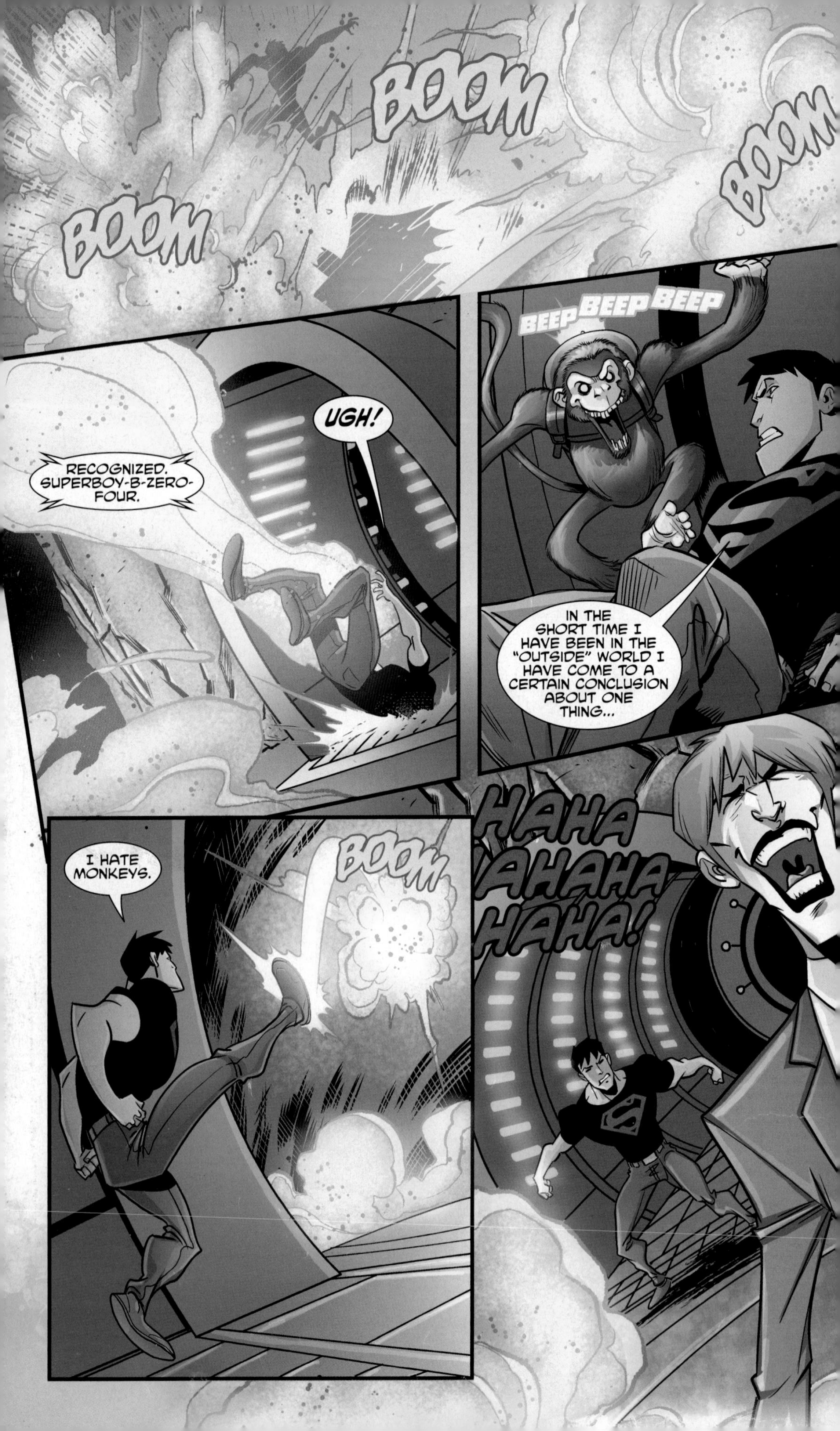
BOOM
BOOM
BOOM
BEEP BEEP BEEP
UGH!
RECOGNIZED. SUPERBOY-B-ZERO-FOUR.
IN THE SHORT TIME I HAVE BEEN IN THE "OUTSIDE" WORLD I HAVE COME TO A CERTAIN CONCLUSION ABOUT ONE THING...
I HATE MONKEYS.
BOOM
HAHA HAHAHA HAHA!

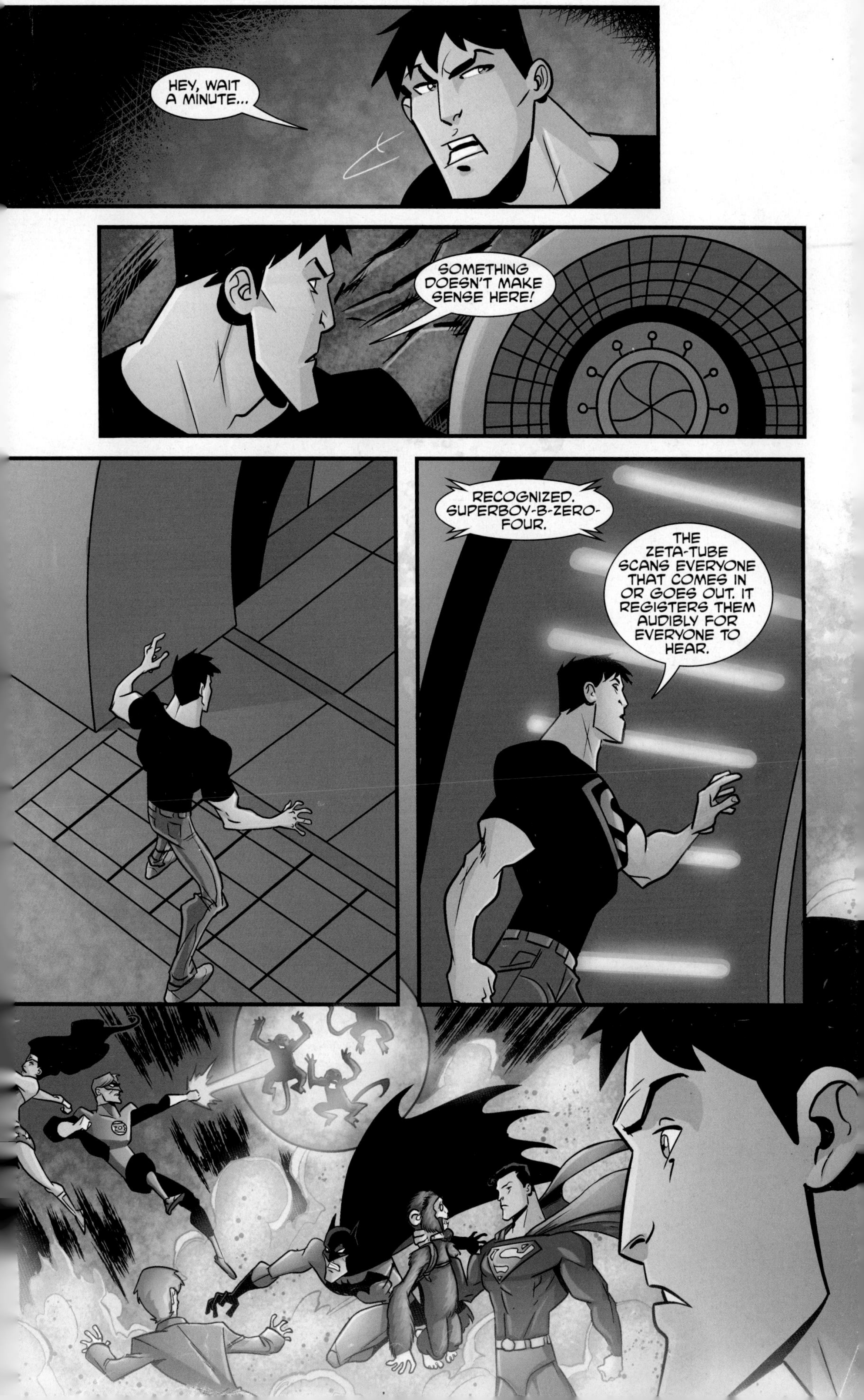
HEY, WAIT A MINUTE...
SOMETHING DOESN'T MAKE SENSE HERE!
RECOGNIZED. SUPERBOY-B-ZERO-FOUR.
THE ZETA-TUBE SCANS EVERYONE THAT COMES IN OR GOES OUT. IT REGISTERS THEM AUDIBLY FOR EVERYONE TO HEAR.

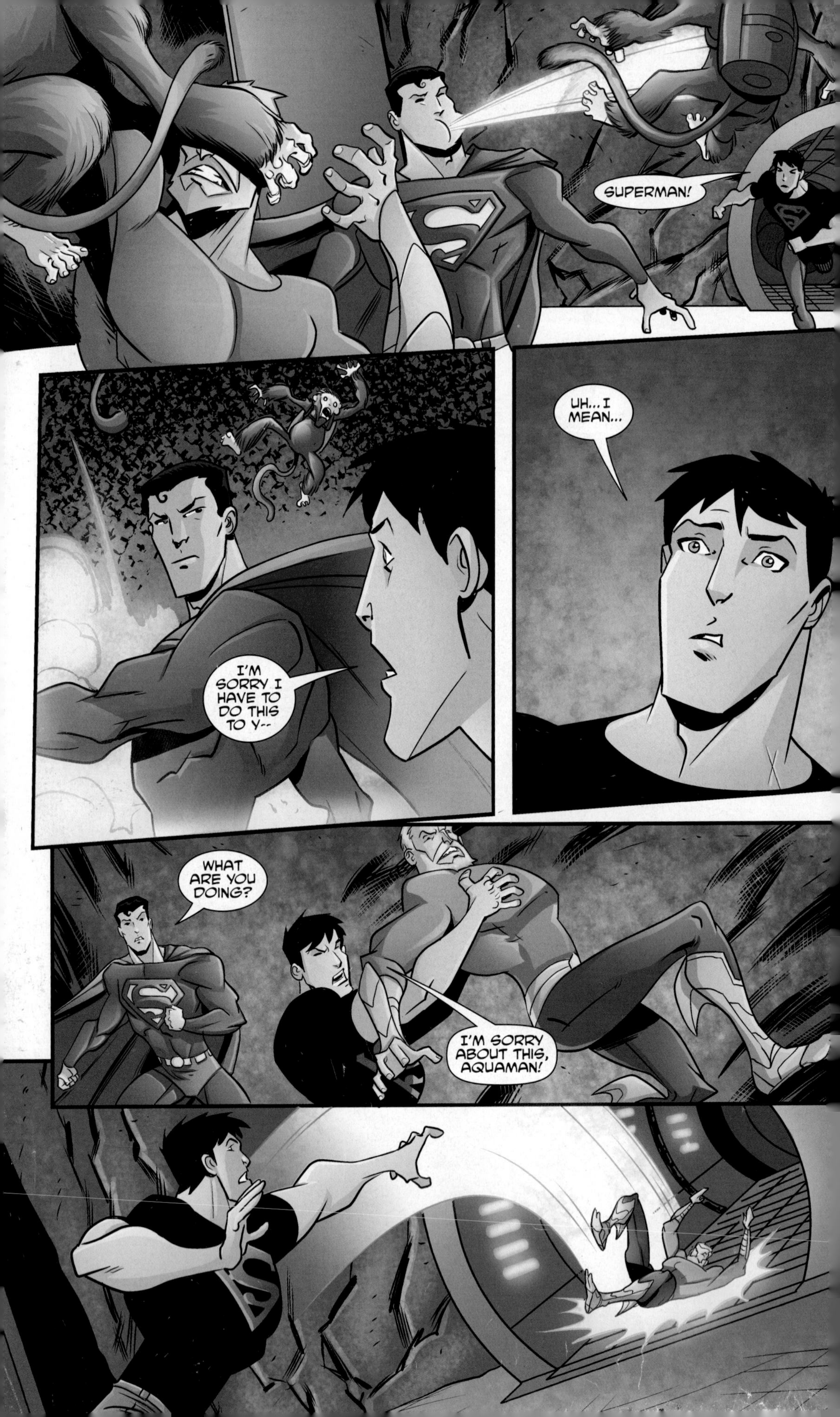

SUPERMAN!
I'M SORRY I HAVE TO DO THIS TO Y--
UH... I MEAN...
WHAT ARE YOU DOING?
I'M SORRY ABOUT THIS, AQUAMAN!

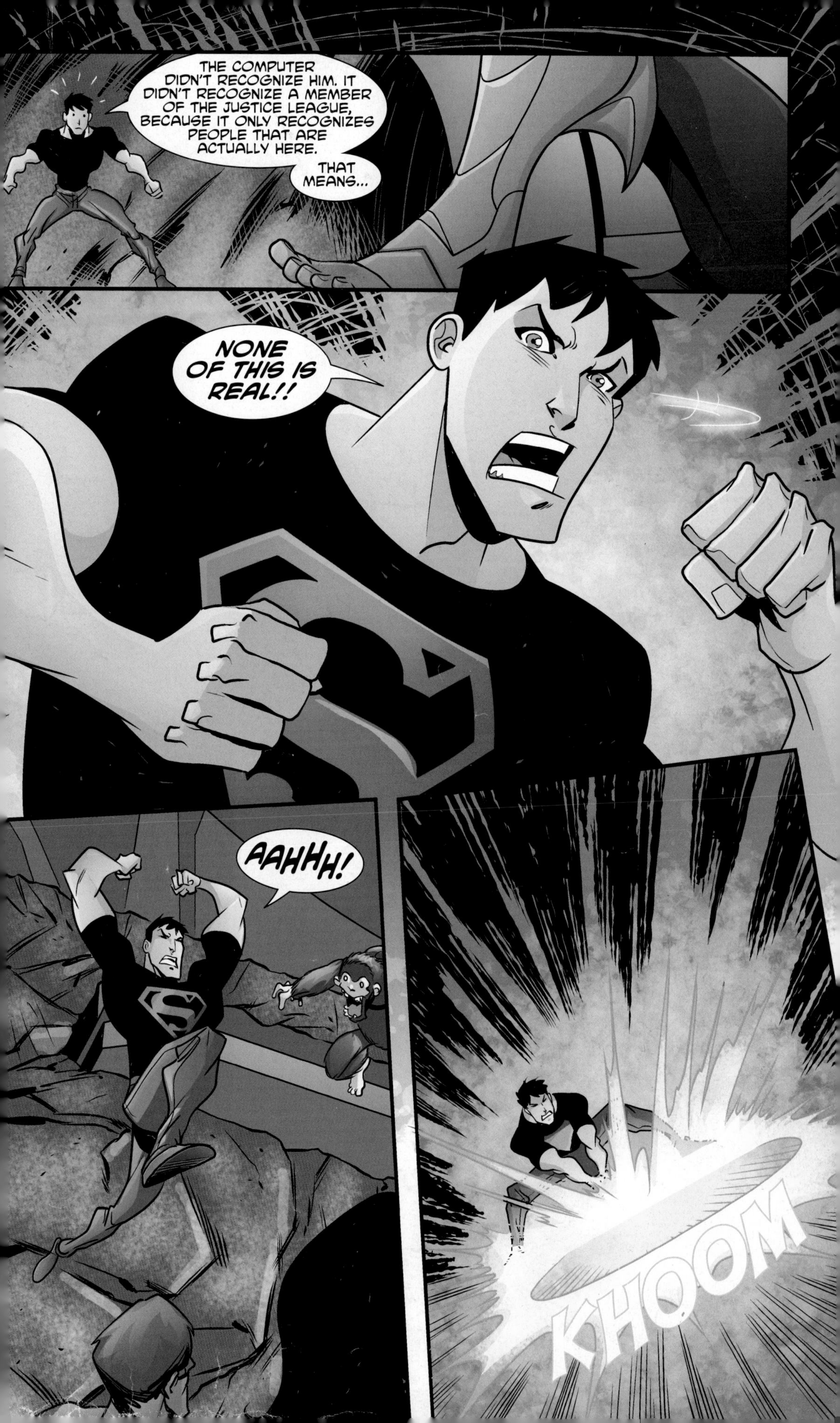
THE COMPUTER DIDN'T RECOGNIZE HIM. IT DIDN'T RECOGNIZE A MEMBER OF THE JUSTICE LEAGUE, BECAUSE IT ONLY RECOGNIZES PEOPLE THAT ARE ACTUALLY HERE.
THAT MEANS...
NONE OF THIS IS REAL!!
AAHHH!
KHOOM

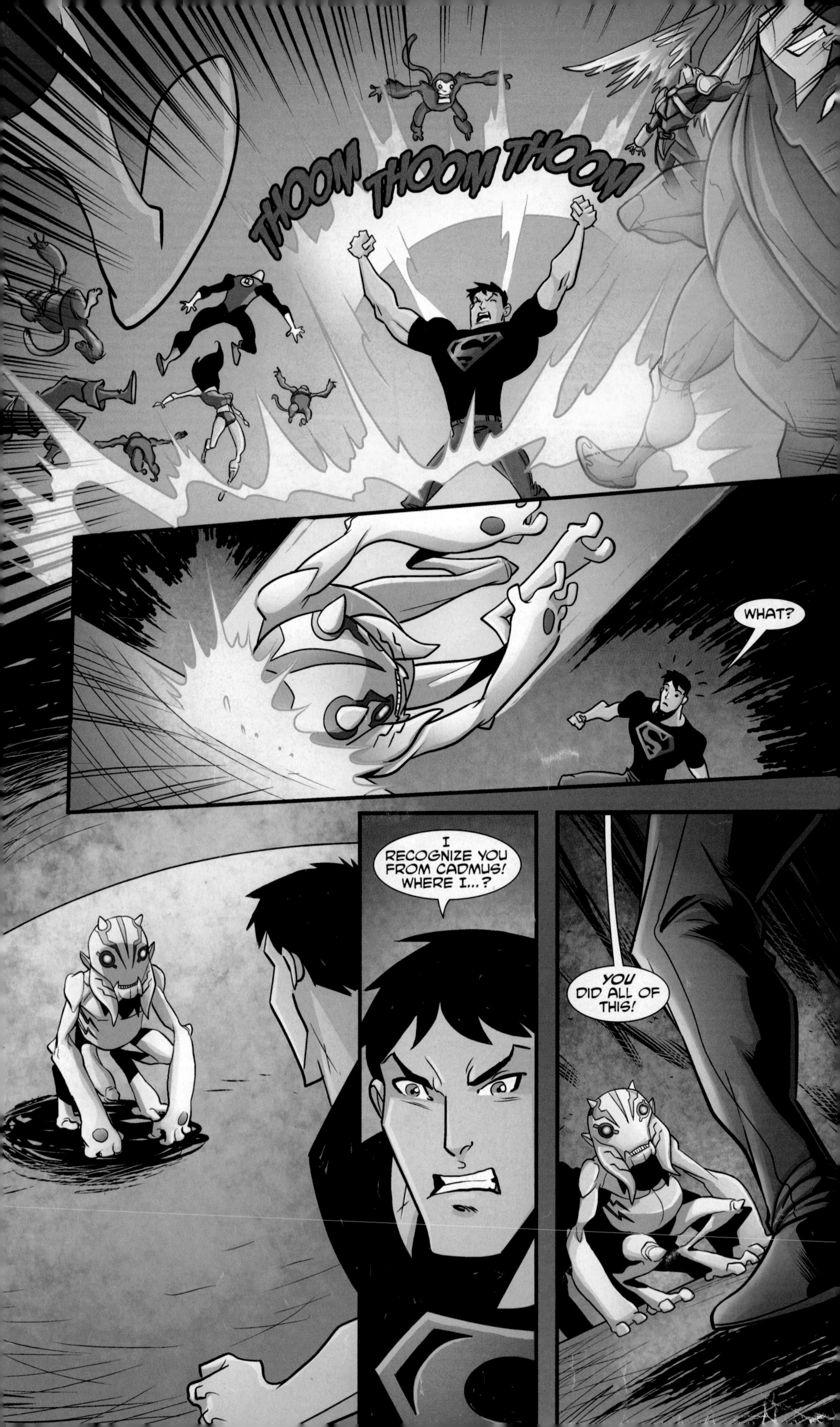
THOOM THOOM THOOM
WHAT?
I RECOGNIZE YOU FROM CADMUS! WHERE I...?
YOU DID ALL OF THIS!

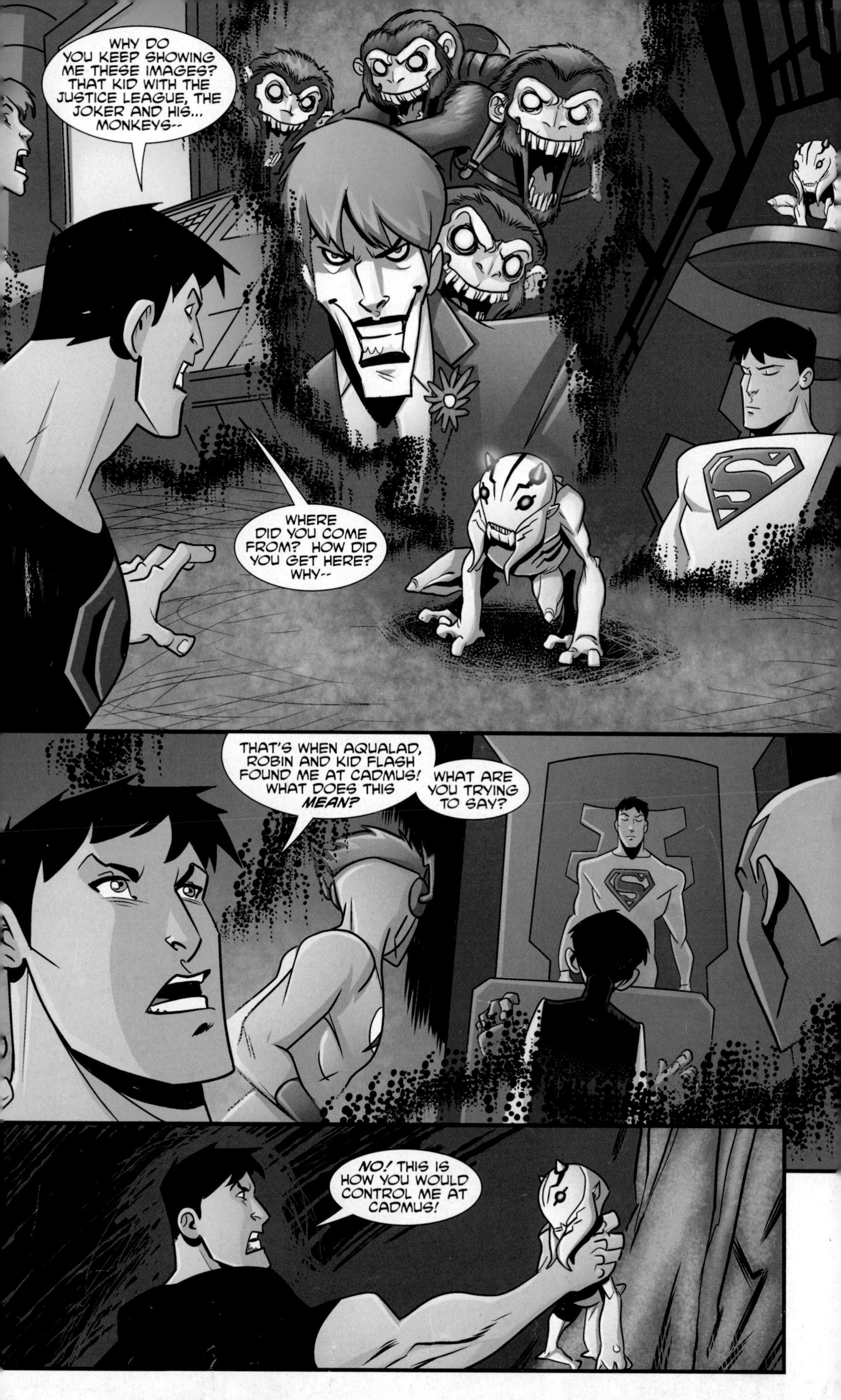
WHY DO YOU KEEP SHOWING ME THESE IMAGES? THAT KID WITH THE JUSTICE LEAGUE, THE JOKER AND HIS... MONKEYS--
WHERE DID YOU COME FROM? HOW DID YOU GET HERE? WHY--
THAT'S WHEN AQUALAD, ROBIN AND KID FLASH FOUND ME AT CADMUS! WHAT DOES THIS *MEAN?*
WHAT ARE YOU TRYING TO SAY?
NO! THIS IS HOW YOU WOULD CONTROL ME AT CADMUS!

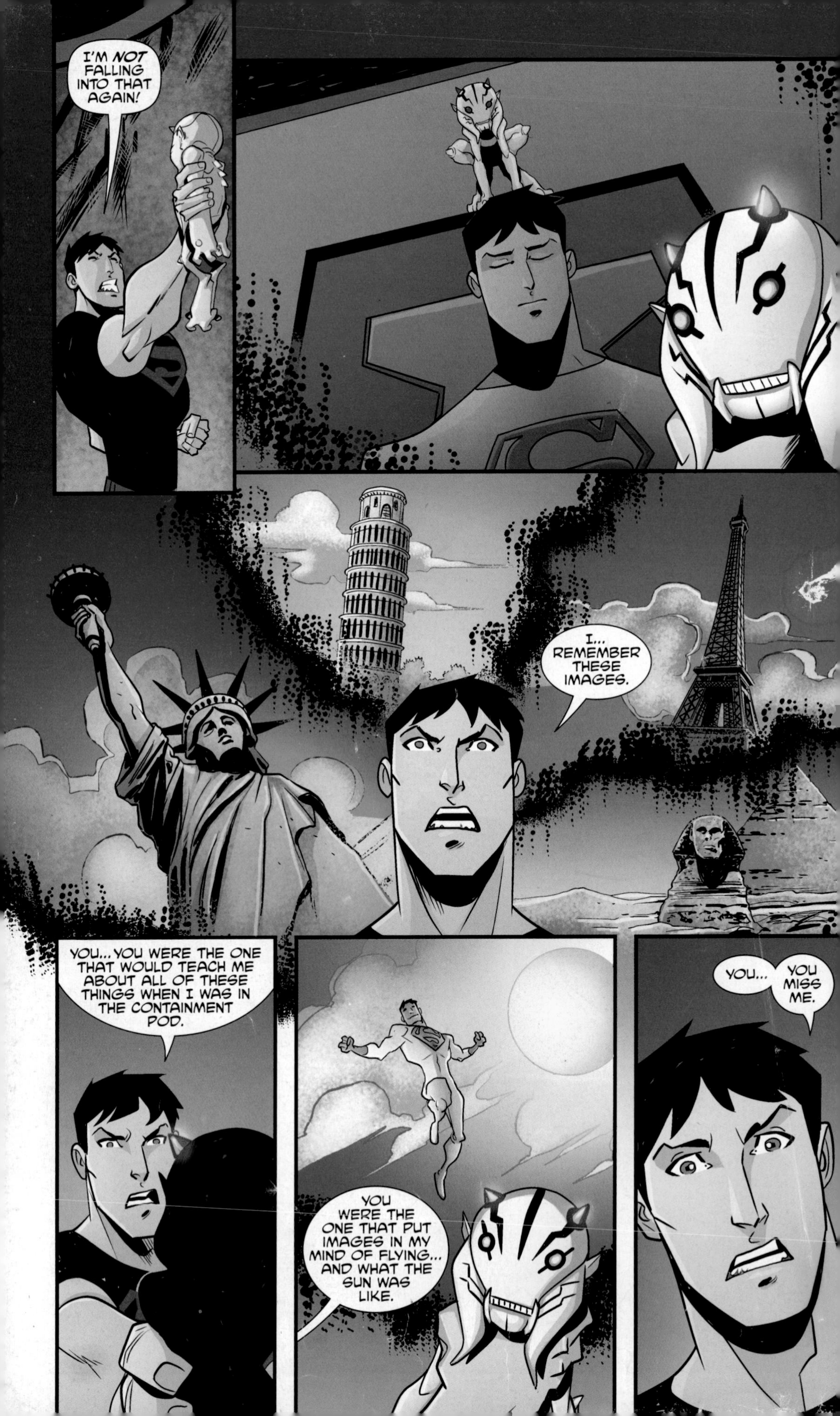

I'M NOT FALLING INTO THAT AGAIN!
I... REMEMBER THESE IMAGES.
YOU... YOU WERE THE ONE THAT WOULD TEACH ME ABOUT ALL OF THESE THINGS WHEN I WAS IN THE CONTAINMENT POD.
YOU WERE THE ONE THAT PUT IMAGES IN MY MIND OF FLYING... AND WHAT THE SUN WAS LIKE.
YOU...
YOU MISS ME.

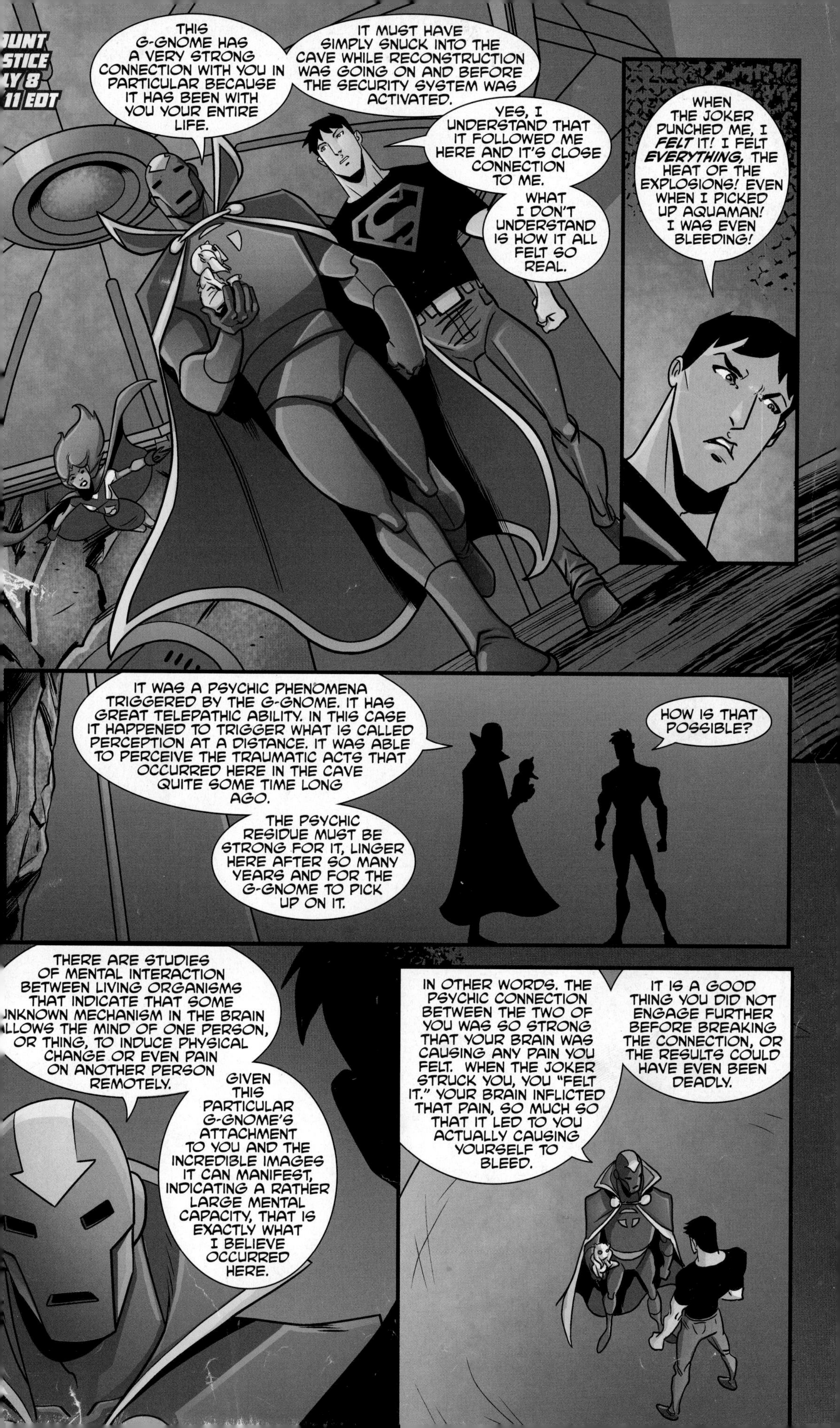
THIS G-GNOME HAS A VERY STRONG CONNECTION WITH YOU IN PARTICULAR BECAUSE IT HAS BEEN WITH YOU YOUR ENTIRE LIFE.
IT MUST HAVE SIMPLY SNUCK INTO THE CAVE WHILE RECONSTRUCTION WAS GOING ON AND BEFORE THE SECURITY SYSTEM WAS ACTIVATED.
YES, I UNDERSTAND THAT IT FOLLOWED ME HERE AND IT'S CLOSE CONNECTION TO ME.
WHAT I DON'T UNDERSTAND IS HOW IT ALL FELT SO REAL.
WHEN THE JOKER PUNCHED ME, I *FELT* IT! I FELT *EVERYTHING,* THE HEAT OF THE EXPLOSIONS! EVEN WHEN I PICKED UP AQUAMAN! I WAS EVEN BLEEDING!
IT WAS A PSYCHIC PHENOMENA TRIGGERED BY THE G-GNOME. IT HAS GREAT TELEPATHIC ABILITY. IN THIS CASE IT HAPPENED TO TRIGGER WHAT IS CALLED PERCEPTION AT A DISTANCE. IT WAS ABLE TO PERCEIVE THE TRAUMATIC ACTS THAT OCCURRED HERE IN THE CAVE QUITE SOME TIME LONG AGO.
THE PSYCHIC RESIDUE MUST BE STRONG FOR IT, LINGER HERE AFTER SO MANY YEARS AND FOR THE G-GNOME TO PICK UP ON IT.
HOW IS THAT POSSIBLE?
THERE ARE STUDIES OF MENTAL INTERACTION BETWEEN LIVING ORGANISMS THAT INDICATE THAT SOME UNKNOWN MECHANISM IN THE BRAIN ALLOWS THE MIND OF ONE PERSON, OR THING, TO INDUCE PHYSICAL CHANGE OR EVEN PAIN ON ANOTHER PERSON REMOTELY.
GIVEN THIS PARTICULAR G-GNOME'S ATTACHMENT TO YOU AND THE INCREDIBLE IMAGES IT CAN MANIFEST, INDICATING A RATHER LARGE MENTAL CAPACITY, THAT IS EXACTLY WHAT I BELIEVE OCCURRED HERE.
IN OTHER WORDS. THE PSYCHIC CONNECTION BETWEEN THE TWO OF YOU WAS SO STRONG THAT YOUR BRAIN WAS CAUSING ANY PAIN YOU FELT. WHEN THE JOKER STRUCK YOU, YOU "FELT IT." YOUR BRAIN INFLICTED THAT PAIN, SO MUCH SO THAT IT LED TO YOU ACTUALLY CAUSING YOURSELF TO BLEED.
IT IS A GOOD THING YOU DID NOT ENGAGE FURTHER BEFORE BREAKING THE CONNECTION, OR THE RESULTS COULD HAVE EVEN BEEN DEADLY.

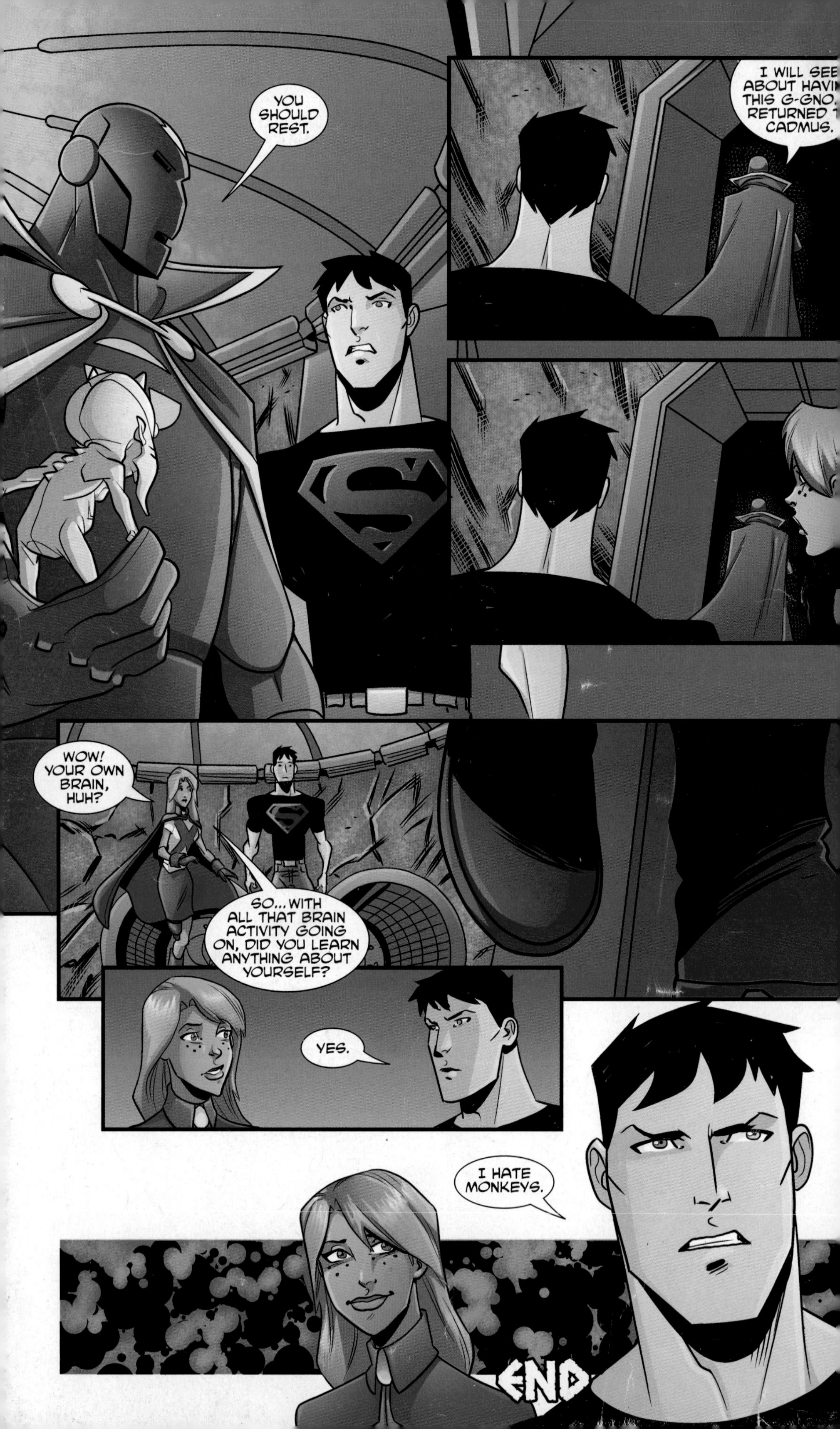
YOU SHOULD REST.
I WILL SEE ABOUT HAVIN THIS G-GNO. RETURNED T CADMUS.
WOW! YOUR OWN BRAIN, HUH?
SO...WITH ALL THAT BRAIN ACTIVITY GOING ON, DID YOU LEARN ANYTHING ABOUT YOURSELF?
YES.
I HATE MONKEYS.
END

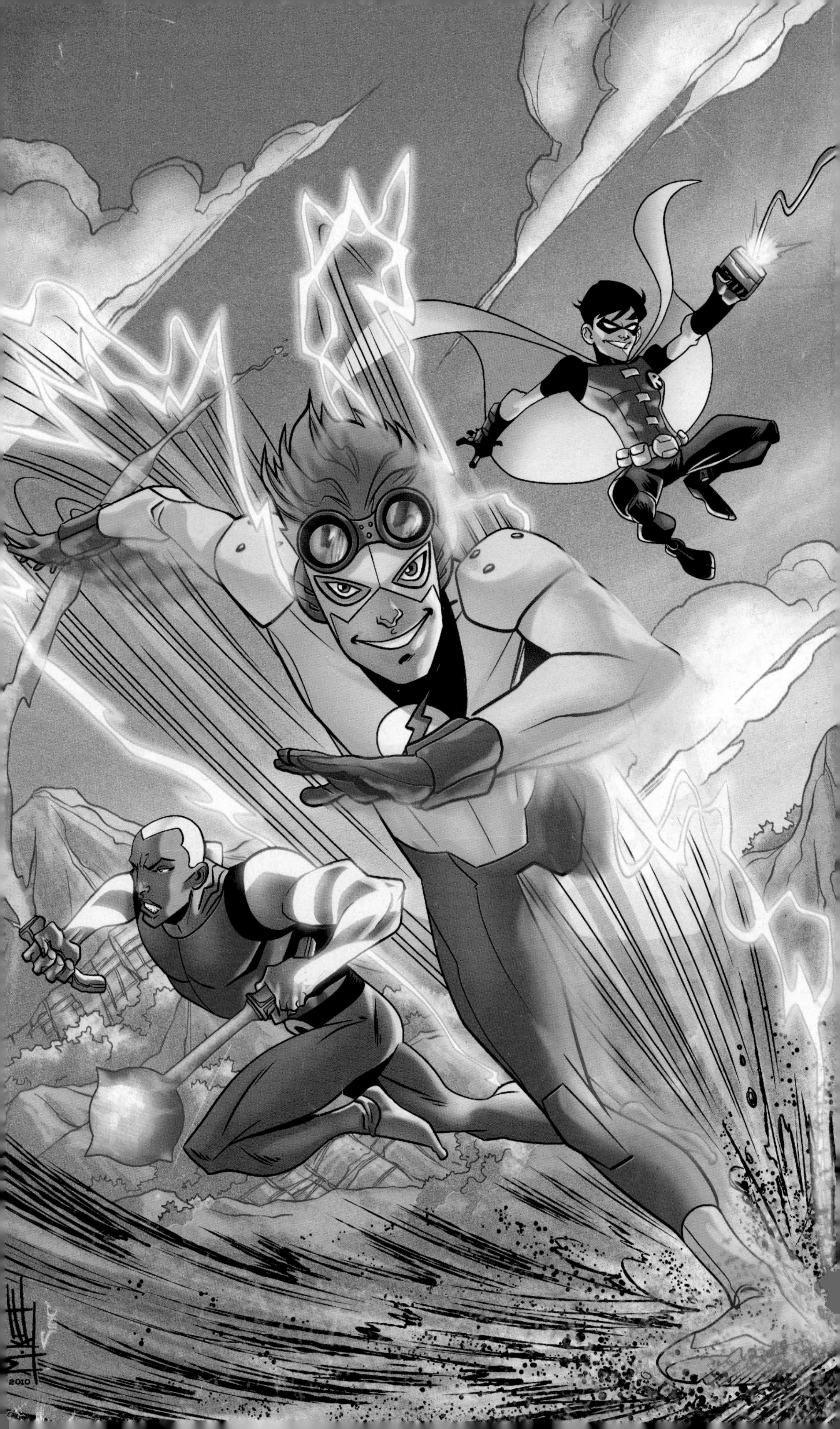

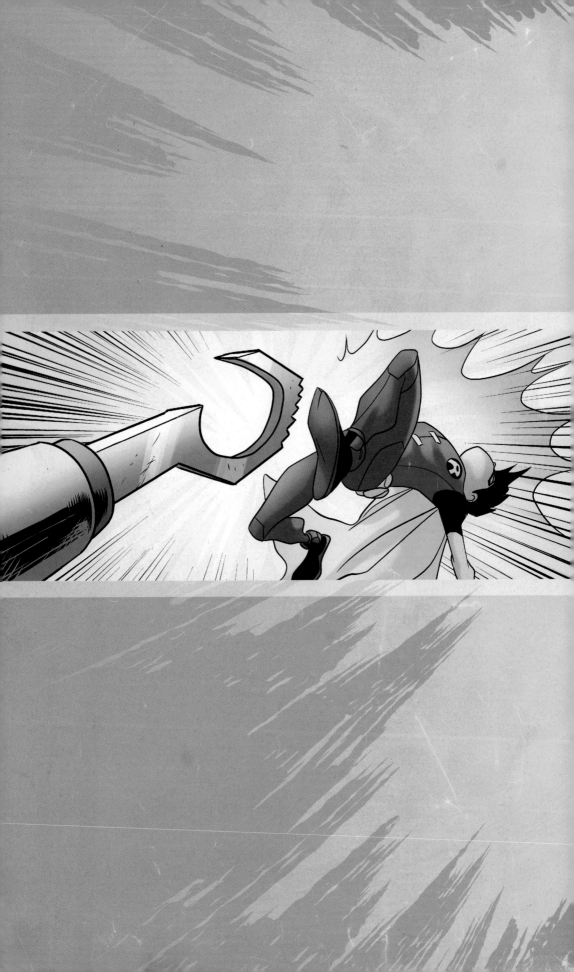

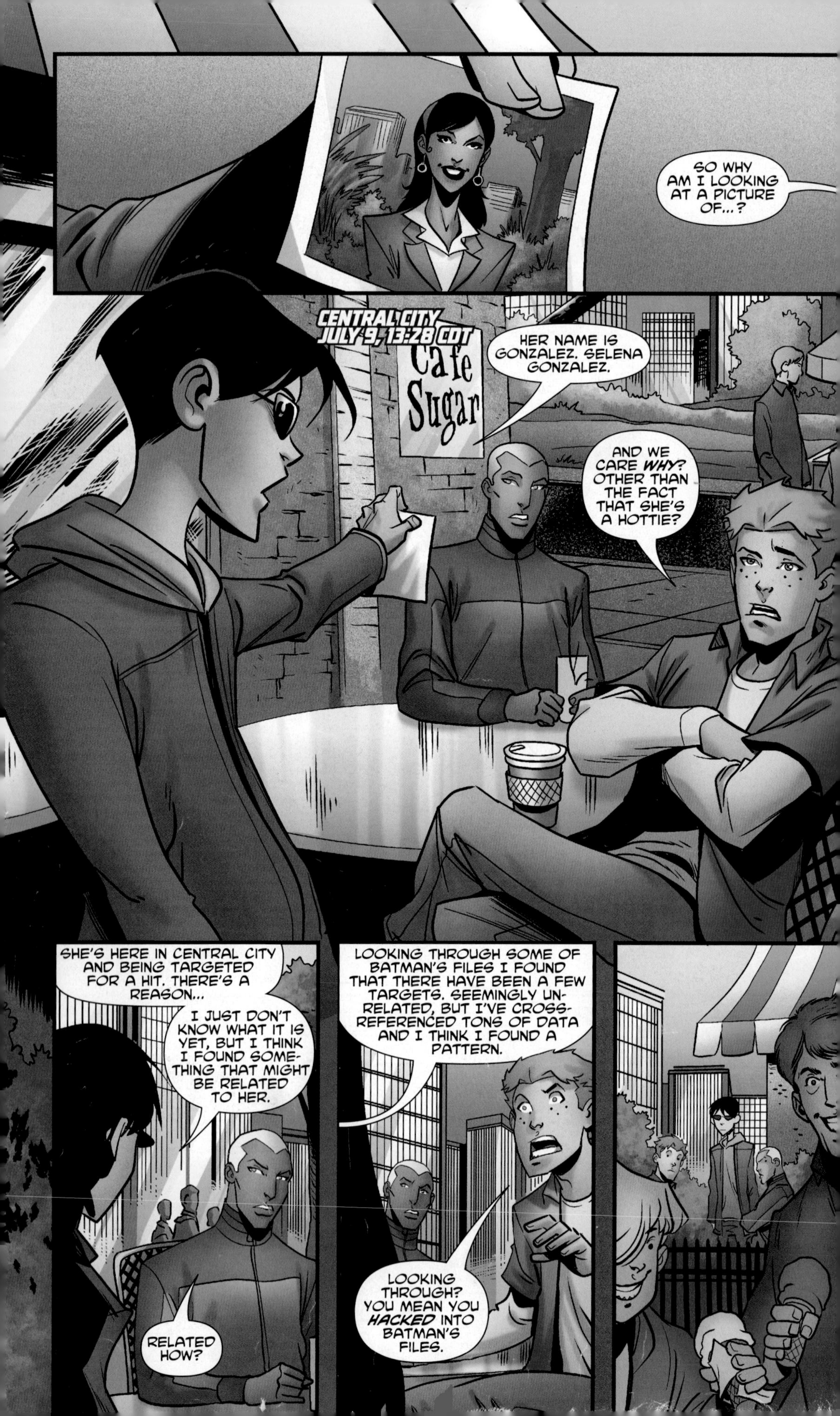
SO WHY AM I LOOKING AT A PICTURE OF...?
CENTRAL CITY JULY 9, 13:28 CDT
Cafe Sugar
HER NAME IS GONZALEZ. SELENA GONZALEZ.
AND WE CARE *WHY*? OTHER THAN THE FACT THAT SHE'S A HOTTIE?
SHE'S HERE IN CENTRAL CITY AND BEING TARGETED FOR A HIT. THERE'S A REASON...
I JUST DON'T KNOW WHAT IT IS YET, BUT I THINK I FOUND SOMETHING THAT MIGHT BE RELATED TO HER.
RELATED HOW?
LOOKING THROUGH SOME OF BATMAN'S FILES I FOUND THAT THERE HAVE BEEN A FEW TARGETS. SEEMINGLY UNRELATED, BUT I'VE CROSS-REFERENCED TONS OF DATA AND I THINK I FOUND A PATTERN.
LOOKING THROUGH? YOU MEAN YOU *HACKED* INTO BATMAN'S FILES.

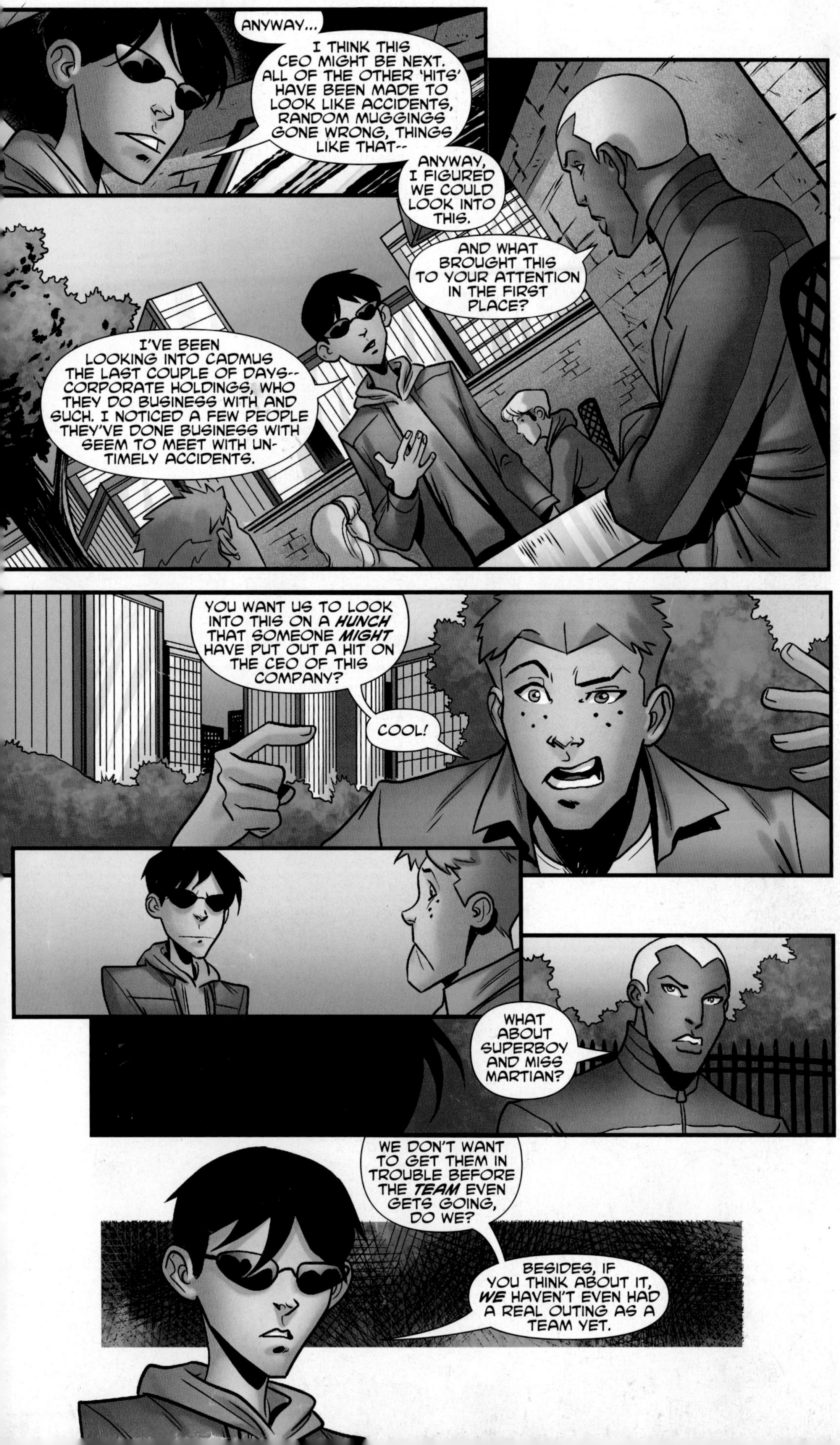
ANYWAY...
I THINK THIS CEO MIGHT BE NEXT. ALL OF THE OTHER 'HITS' HAVE BEEN MADE TO LOOK LIKE ACCIDENTS, RANDOM MUGGINGS GONE WRONG, THINGS LIKE THAT--
ANYWAY, I FIGURED WE COULD LOOK INTO THIS.
AND WHAT BROUGHT THIS TO YOUR ATTENTION IN THE FIRST PLACE?
I'VE BEEN LOOKING INTO CADMUS THE LAST COUPLE OF DAYS-- CORPORATE HOLDINGS, WHO THEY DO BUSINESS WITH AND SUCH. I NOTICED A FEW PEOPLE THEY'VE DONE BUSINESS WITH SEEM TO MEET WITH UN-TIMELY ACCIDENTS.
YOU WANT US TO LOOK INTO THIS ON A *HUNCH* THAT SOMEONE *MIGHT* HAVE PUT OUT A HIT ON THE CEO OF THIS COMPANY?
COOL!
WHAT ABOUT SUPERBOY AND MISS MARTIAN?
WE DON'T WANT TO GET THEM IN TROUBLE BEFORE THE *TEAM* EVEN GETS GOING, DO WE?
BESIDES, IF YOU THINK ABOUT IT, ***WE*** HAVEN'T EVEN HAD A REAL OUTING AS A TEAM YET.

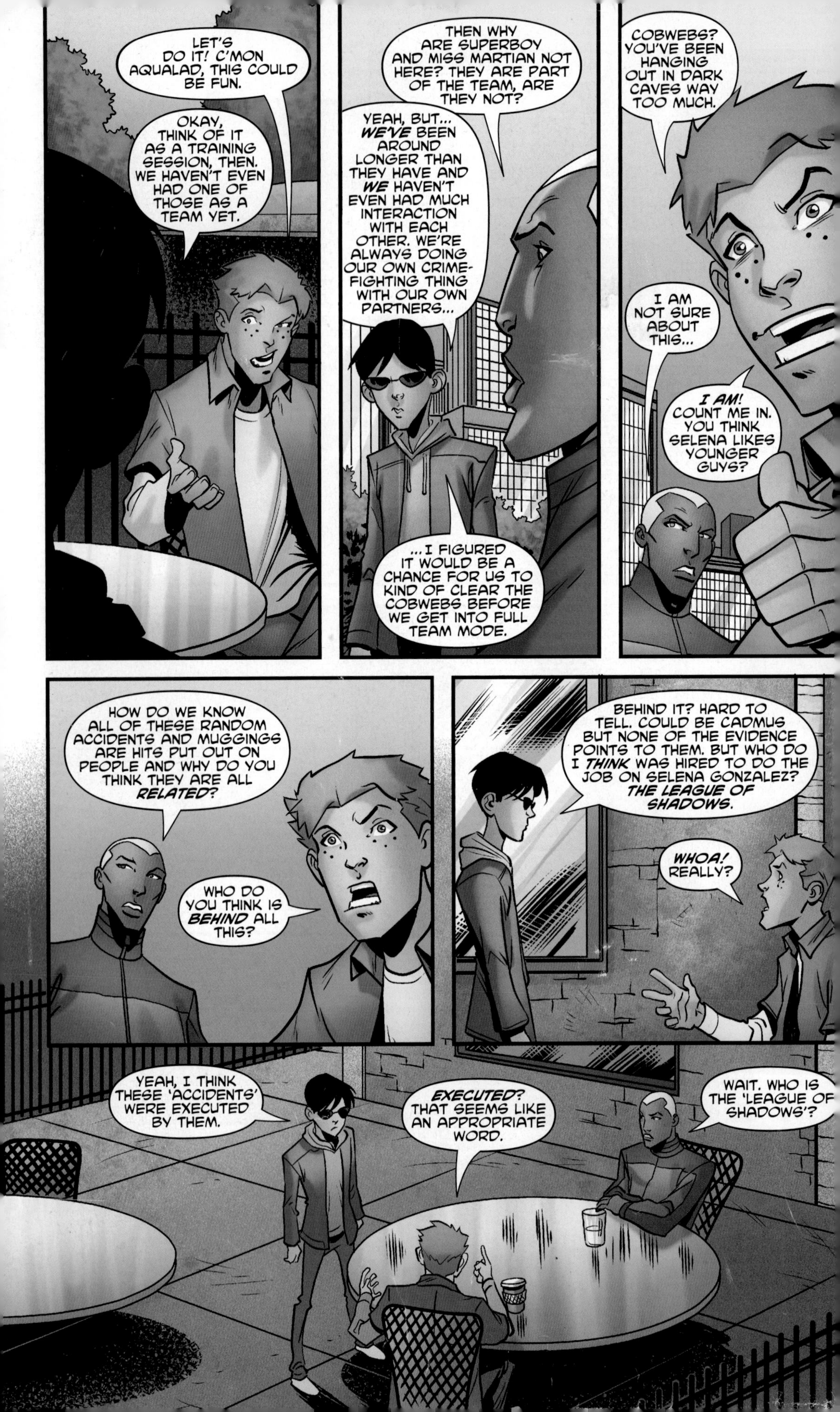
LET'S DO IT! C'MON AQUALAD, THIS COULD BE FUN.
OKAY, THINK OF IT AS A TRAINING SESSION, THEN. WE HAVEN'T EVEN HAD ONE OF THOSE AS A TEAM YET.
THEN WHY ARE SUPERBOY AND MISS MARTIAN NOT HERE? THEY ARE PART OF THE TEAM, ARE THEY NOT?
YEAH, BUT... WE'VE BEEN AROUND LONGER THAN THEY HAVE AND WE HAVEN'T EVEN HAD MUCH INTERACTION WITH EACH OTHER. WE'RE ALWAYS DOING OUR OWN CRIME-FIGHTING THING WITH OUR OWN PARTNERS...
...I FIGURED IT WOULD BE A CHANCE FOR US TO KIND OF CLEAR THE COBWEBS BEFORE WE GET INTO FULL TEAM MODE.
COBWEBS? YOU'VE BEEN HANGING OUT IN DARK CAVES WAY TOO MUCH.
I AM NOT SURE ABOUT THIS...
I AM! COUNT ME IN. YOU THINK SELENA LIKES YOUNGER GUYS?
HOW DO WE KNOW ALL OF THESE RANDOM ACCIDENTS AND MUGGINGS ARE HITS PUT OUT ON PEOPLE AND WHY DO YOU THINK THEY ARE ALL RELATED?
WHO DO YOU THINK IS BEHIND ALL THIS?
BEHIND IT? HARD TO TELL. COULD BE CADMUS BUT NONE OF THE EVIDENCE POINTS TO THEM. BUT WHO DO I THINK WAS HIRED TO DO THE JOB ON SELENA GONZALEZ? THE LEAGUE OF SHADOWS.
WHOA! REALLY?
YEAH, I THINK THESE 'ACCIDENTS' WERE EXECUTED BY THEM.
EXECUTED? THAT SEEMS LIKE AN APPROPRIATE WORD.
WAIT. WHO IS THE 'LEAGUE OF SHADOWS'?

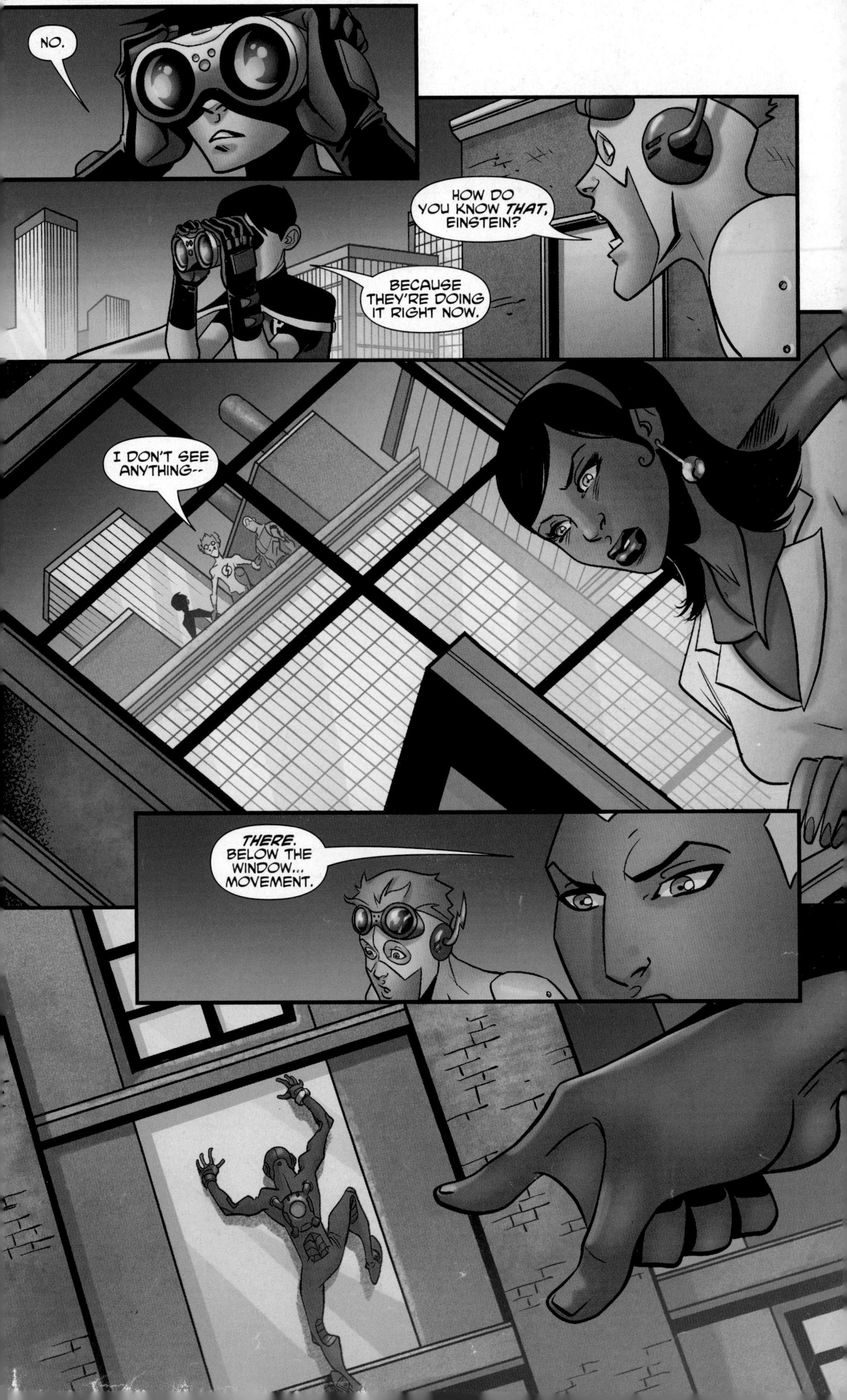
NO.
HOW DO YOU KNOW *THAT*, EINSTEIN?
BECAUSE THEY'RE DOING IT RIGHT NOW.
I DON'T SEE ANYTHING--
THERE. BELOW THE WINDOW... MOVEMENT.

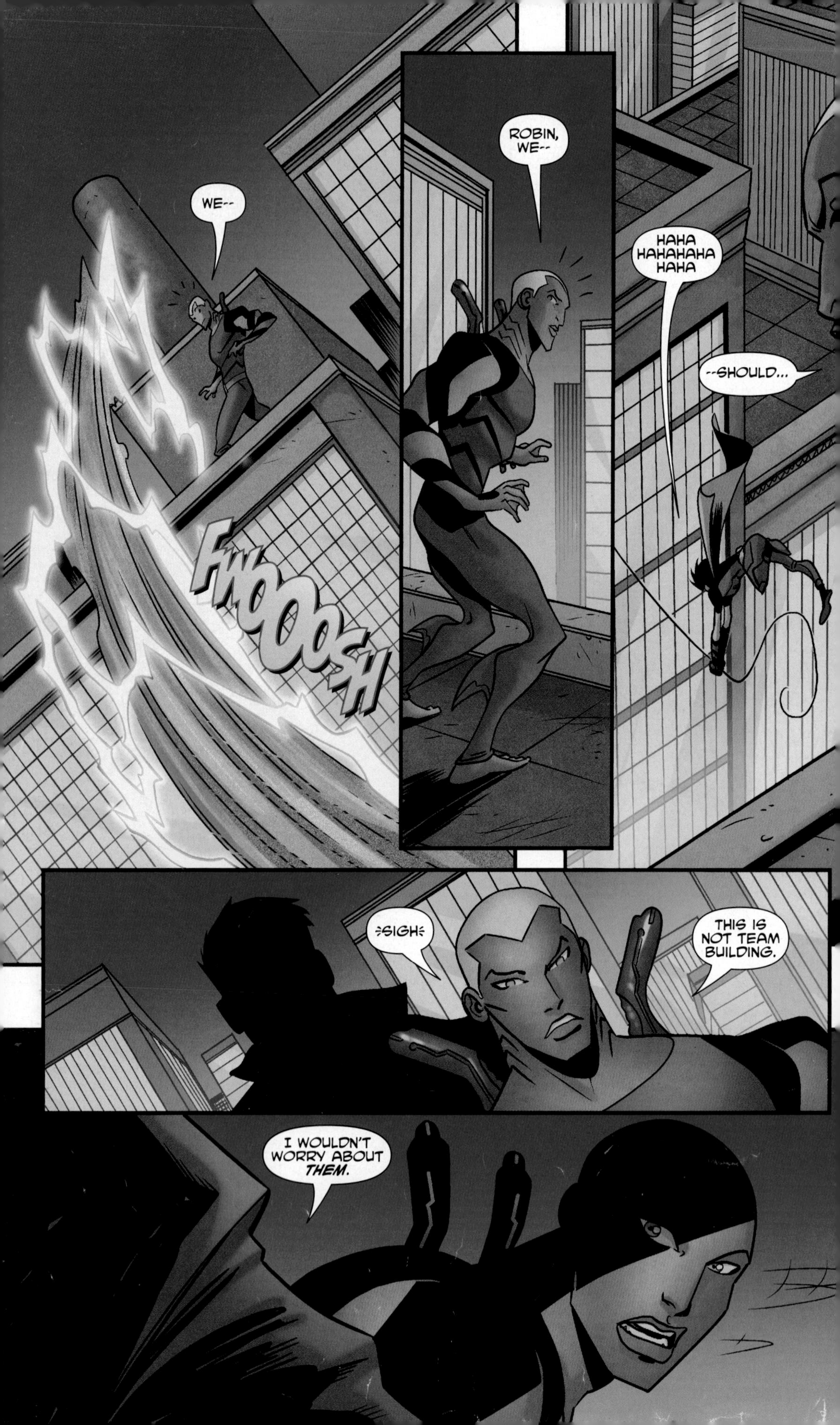
WE--
FWOOOSH
ROBIN, WE--
HAHA HAHAHAHA HAHA
--SHOULD...
SIGH
THIS IS NOT TEAM BUILDING.
I WOULDN'T WORRY ABOUT *THEM*.

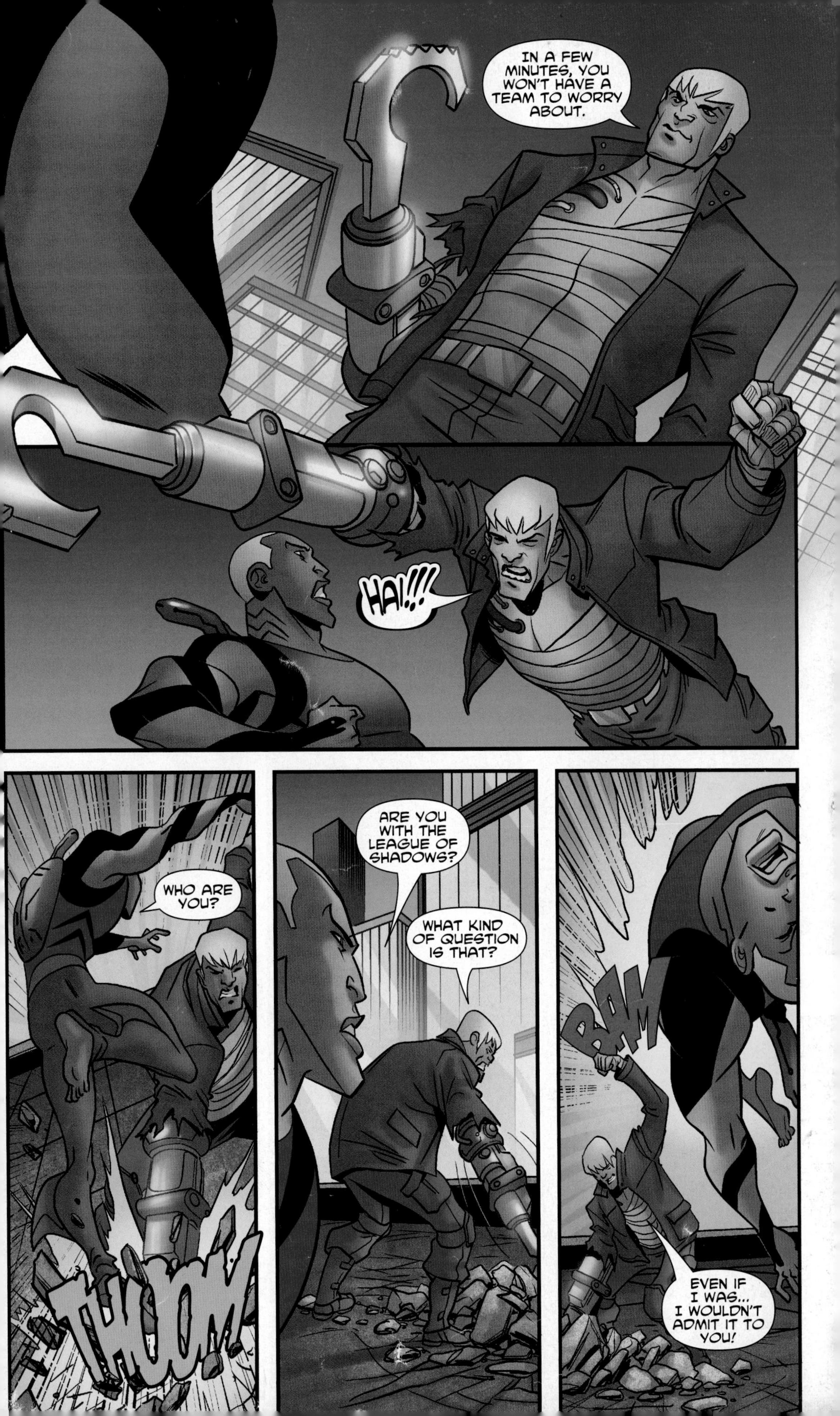
IN A FEW MINUTES, YOU WON'T HAVE A TEAM TO WORRY ABOUT.
HAI!!!
WHO ARE YOU?
THOOM!
ARE YOU WITH THE LEAGUE OF SHADOWS?
WHAT KIND OF QUESTION IS THAT?
BAM
EVEN IF I WAS... I WOULDN'T ADMIT IT TO YOU!

DOESN'T MATTER ONE WAY OR THE OTHER--

BECAUSE YOU--

SLAM

--WON'T BE ABLE TO DO--

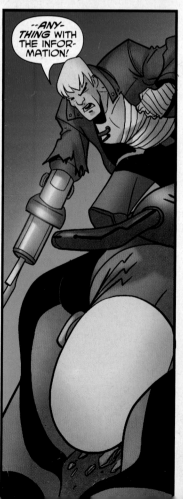

--ANY-THING WITH THE INFOR-MATION!

NOW...

...WHAT SAY WE GO FIND YOUR FRIENDS?

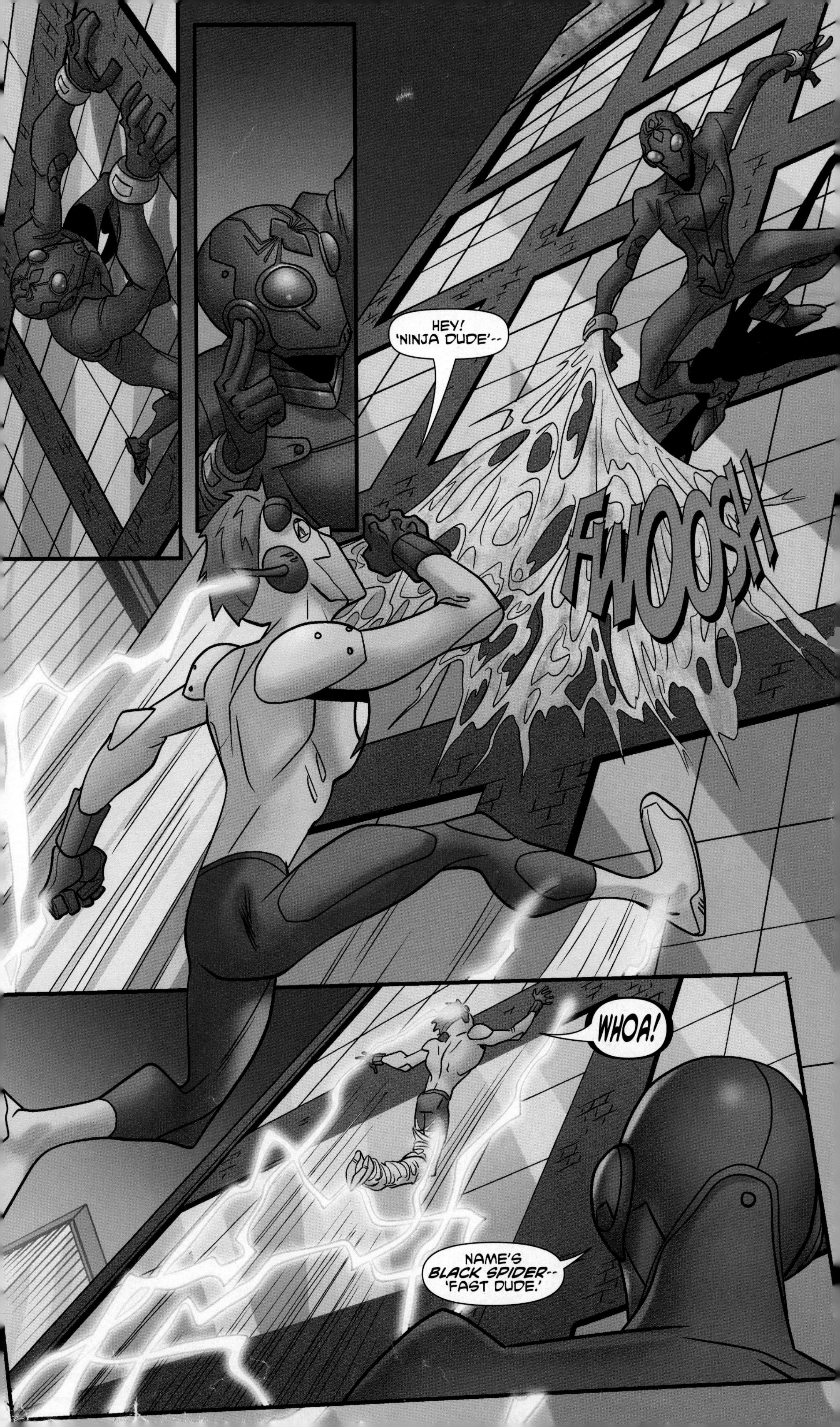
HEY! 'NINJA DUDE'--
FWOOSH
WHOA!
NAME'S *BLACK SPIDER*-- 'FAST DUDE.'

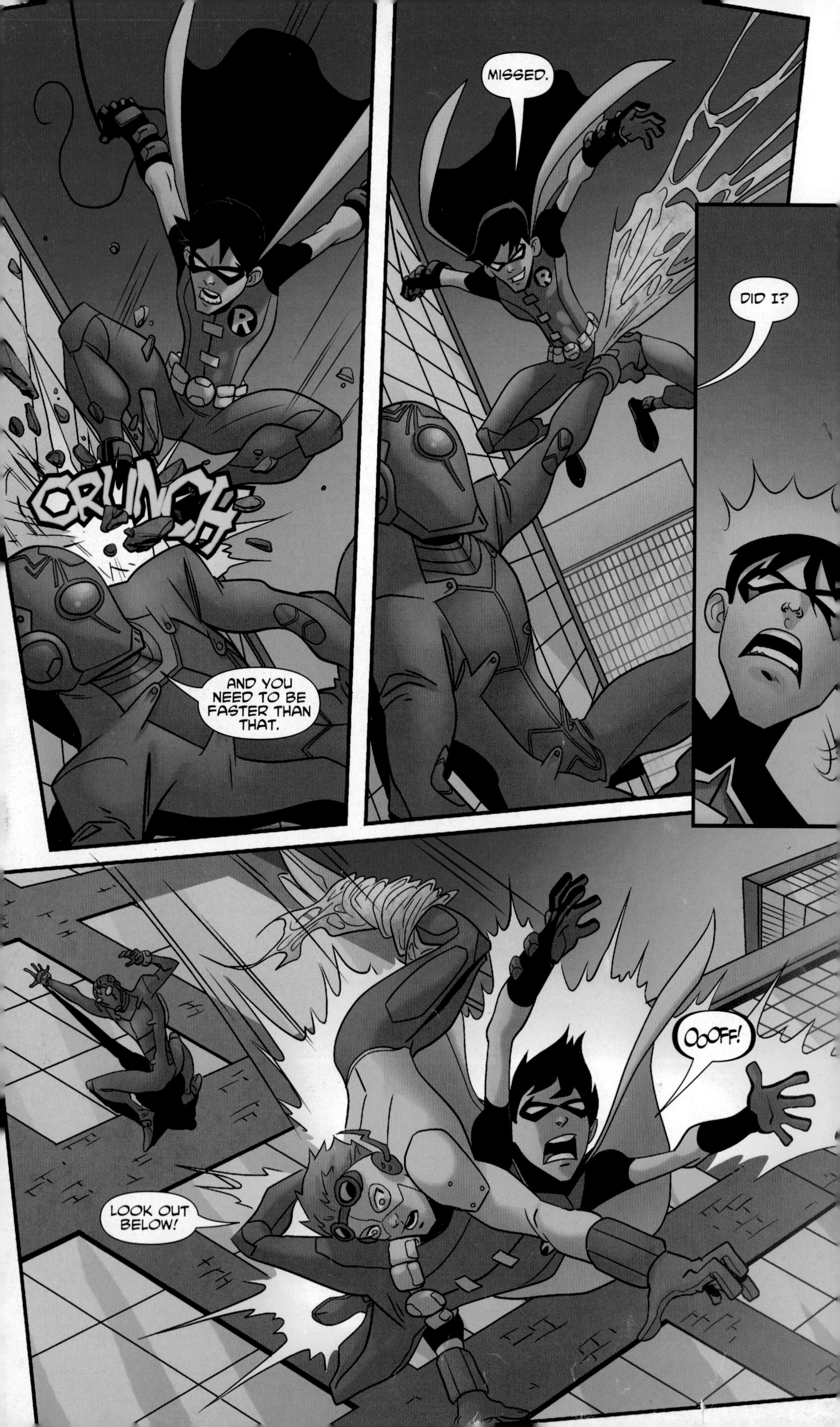
CRUNCH
AND YOU NEED TO BE FASTER THAN THAT.
MISSED.
DID I?
OOOFF!
LOOK OUT BELOW!

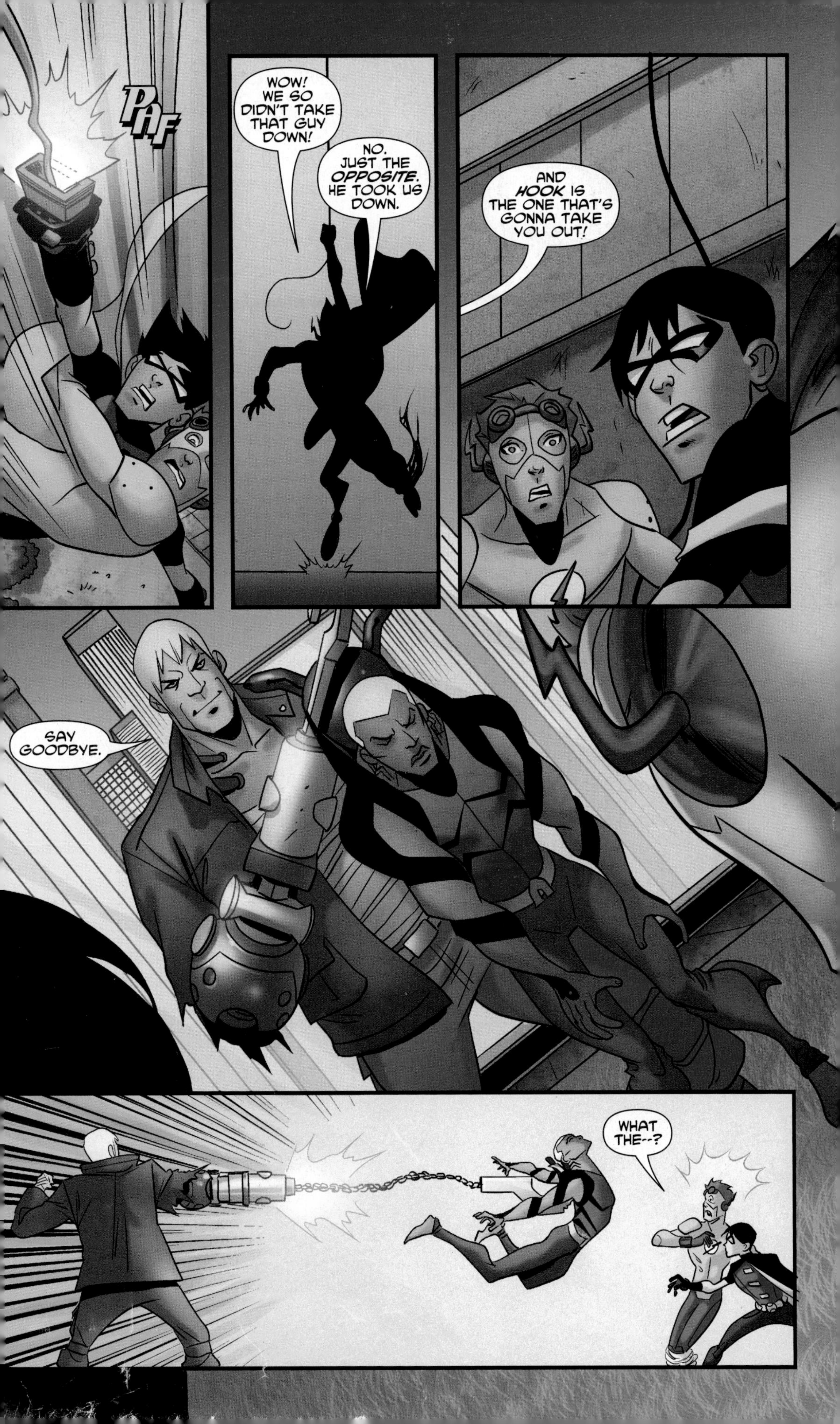
PAF
WOW! WE SO DIDN'T TAKE THAT GUY DOWN!
NO. JUST THE *OPPOSITE*. HE TOOK US DOWN.
AND *HOOK* IS THE ONE THAT'S GONNA TAKE YOU OUT!
SAY GOODBYE.
WHAT THE--?

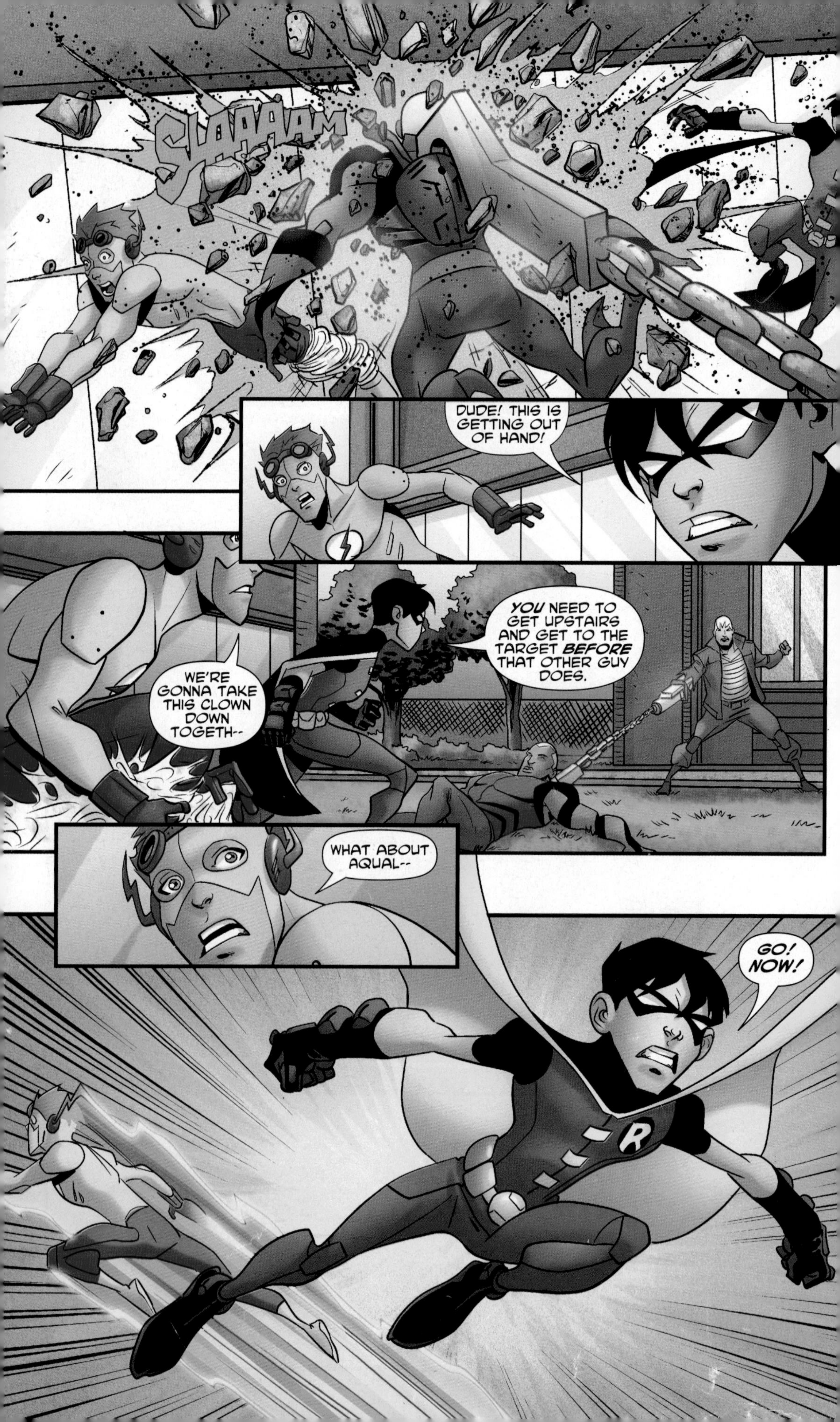
SLAAAAM
DUDE! THIS IS GETTING OUT OF HAND!
WE'RE GONNA TAKE THIS CLOWN DOWN TOGETH--
YOU NEED TO GET UPSTAIRS AND GET TO THE TARGET BEFORE THAT OTHER GUY DOES.
WHAT ABOUT AQUAL--
GO! NOW!

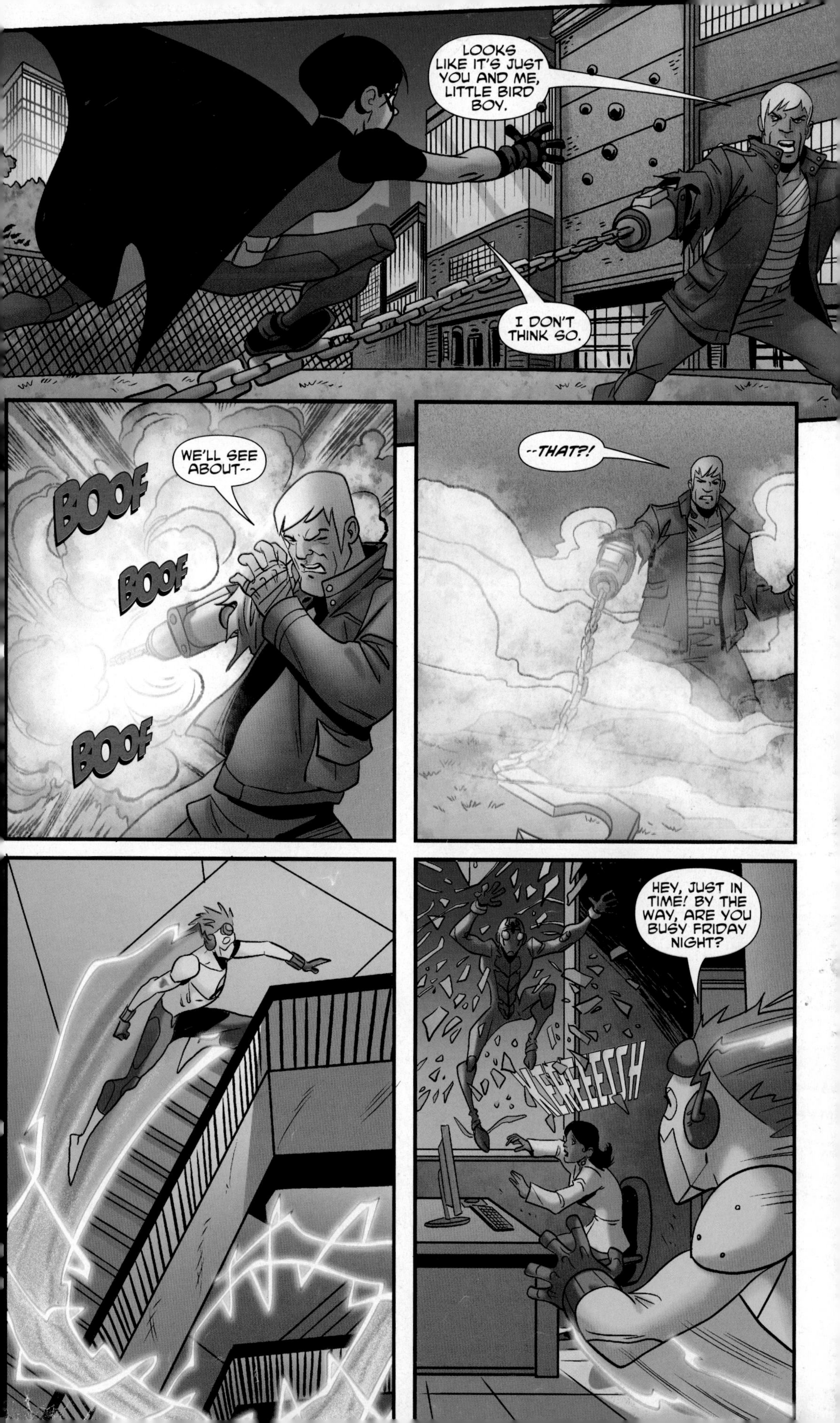
LOOKS LIKE IT'S JUST YOU AND ME, LITTLE BIRD BOY.
I DON'T THINK SO.
WE'LL SEE ABOUT--
BOOF
BOOF
BOOF
--THAT?!
HEY, JUST IN TIME! BY THE WAY, ARE YOU BUSY FRIDAY NIGHT?

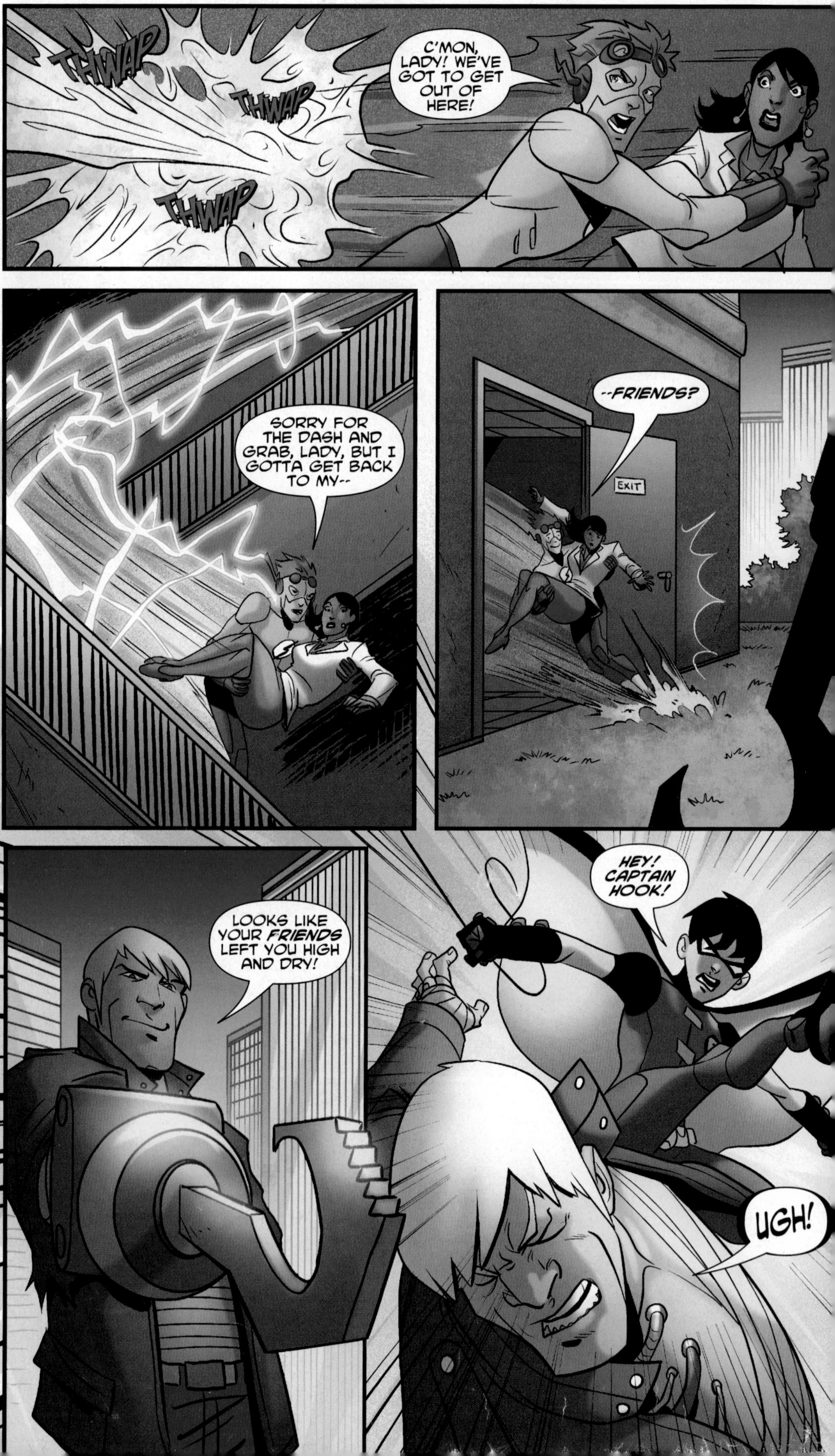
THWAP
THWAP
THWAP
C'MON, LADY! WE'VE GOT TO GET OUT OF HERE!
SORRY FOR THE DASH AND GRAB, LADY, BUT I GOTTA GET BACK TO MY--
--FRIENDS?
EXIT
LOOKS LIKE YOUR FRIENDS LEFT YOU HIGH AND DRY!
HEY! CAPTAIN HOOK!
UGH!

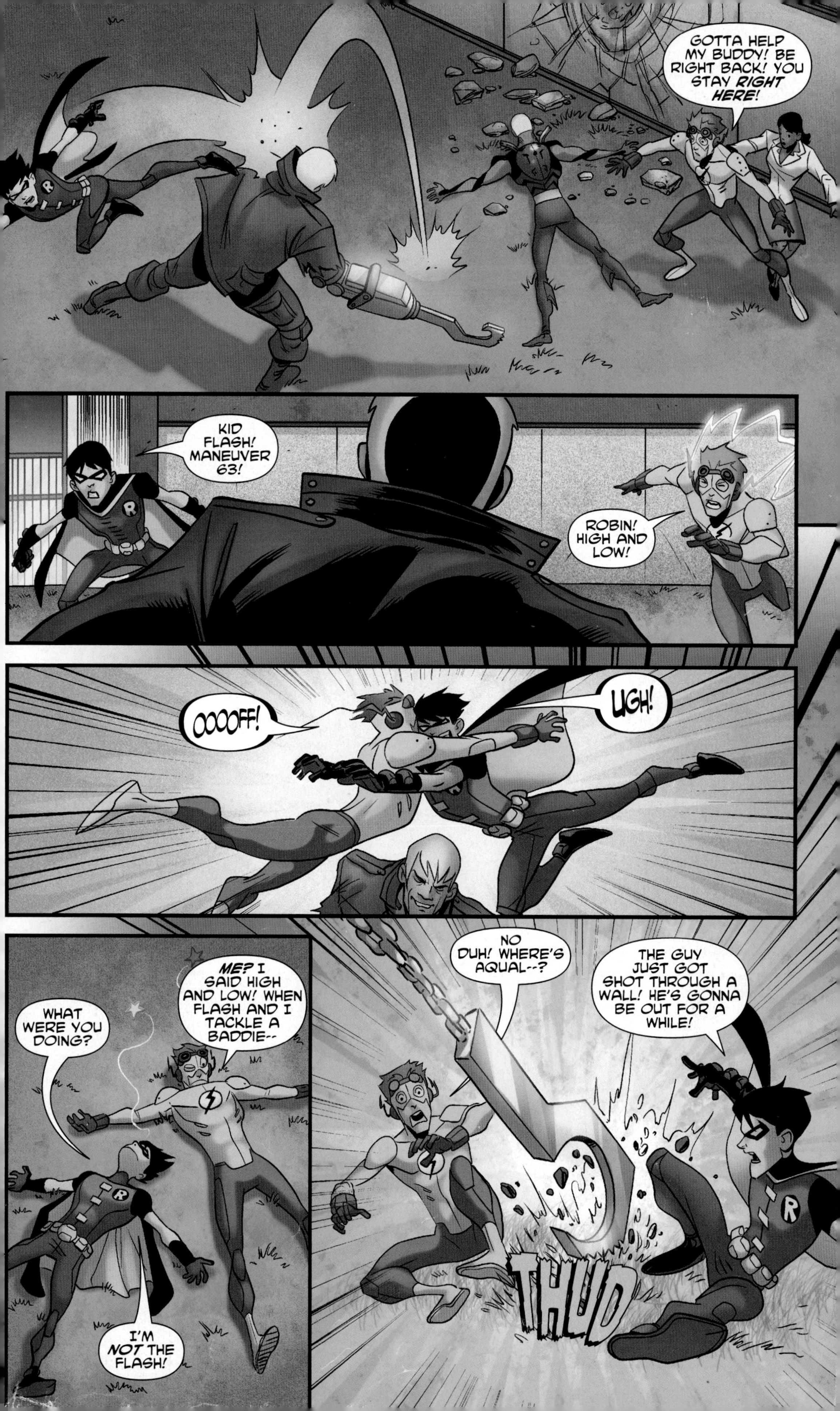
GOTTA HELP MY BUDDY! BE RIGHT BACK! YOU STAY *RIGHT HERE*!
KID FLASH! MANEUVER 63!
ROBIN! HIGH AND LOW!
OOOOFF!
UGH!
WHAT WERE YOU DOING?
ME? I SAID HIGH AND LOW! WHEN FLASH AND I TACKLE A BADDIE--
I'M *NOT* THE FLASH!
NO DUH! WHERE'S AQUAL--?
THE GUY JUST GOT SHOT THROUGH A WALL! HE'S GONNA BE OUT FOR A WHILE!
THUD

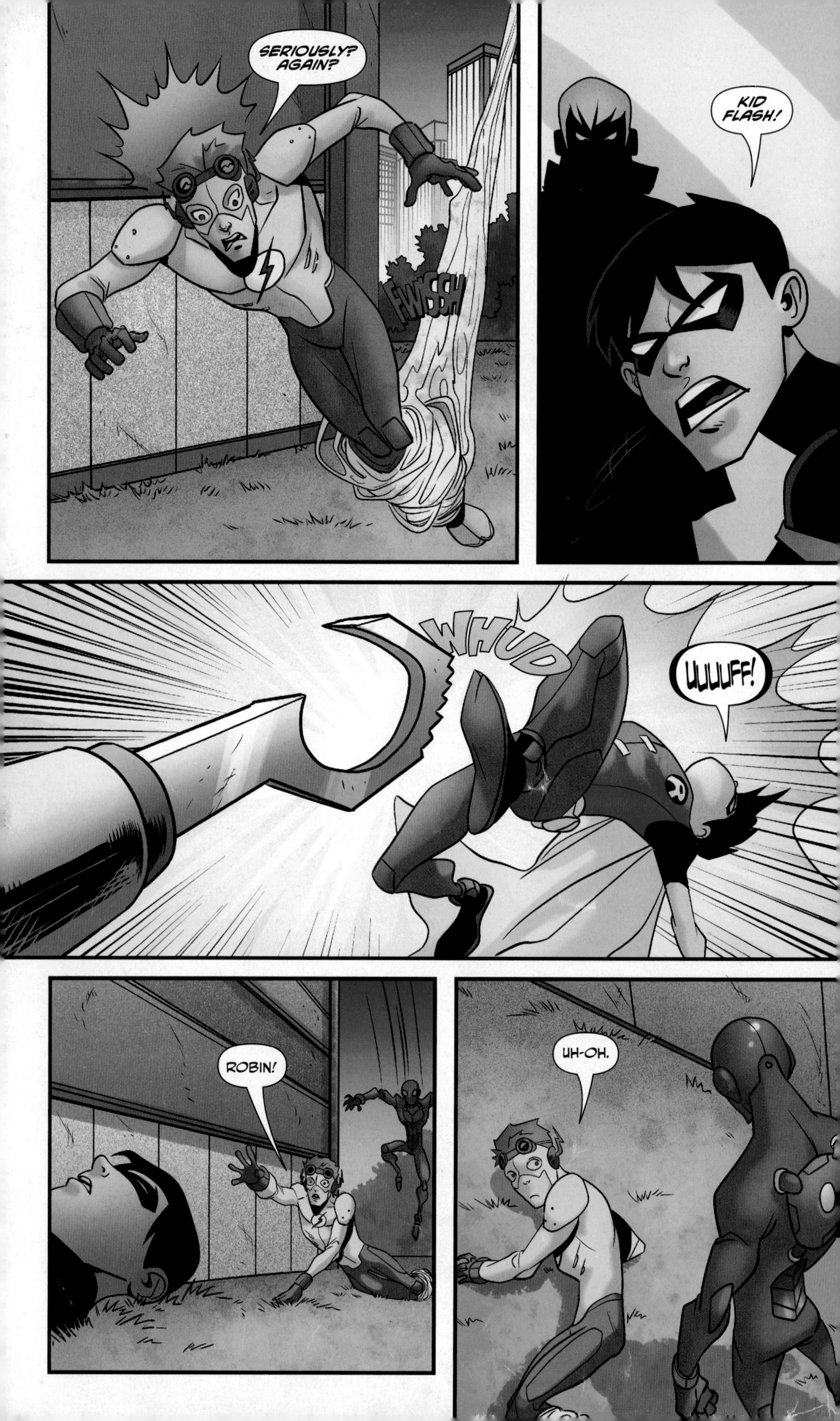
SERIOUSLY? AGAIN?
FWISSH
KID FLASH!
WHUD
UUUUFF!
ROBIN!
UH-OH.

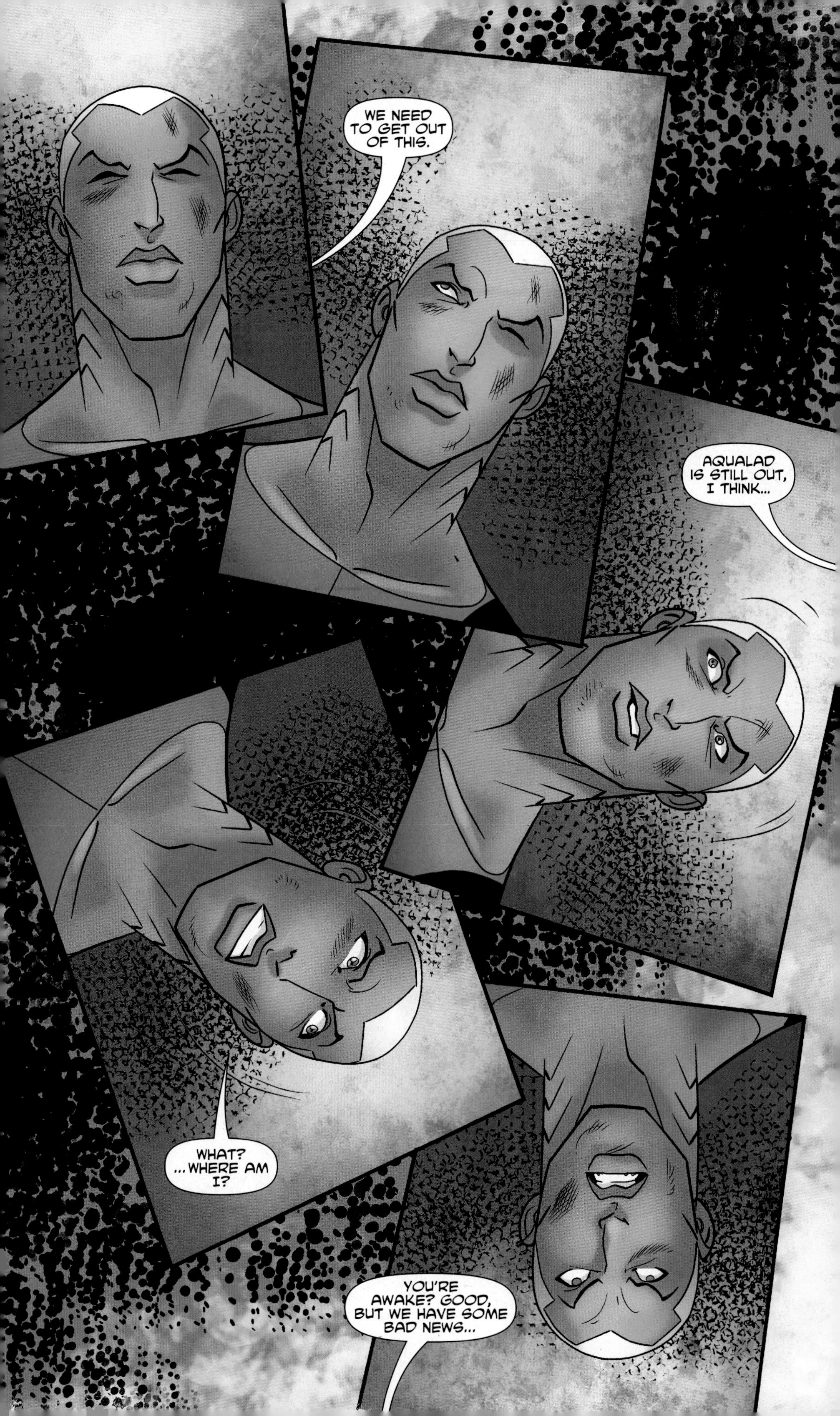
WE NEED TO GET OUT OF THIS.
AQUALAD IS STILL OUT, I THINK...
WHAT? ...WHERE AM I?
YOU'RE AWAKE? GOOD, BUT WE HAVE SOME BAD NEWS...

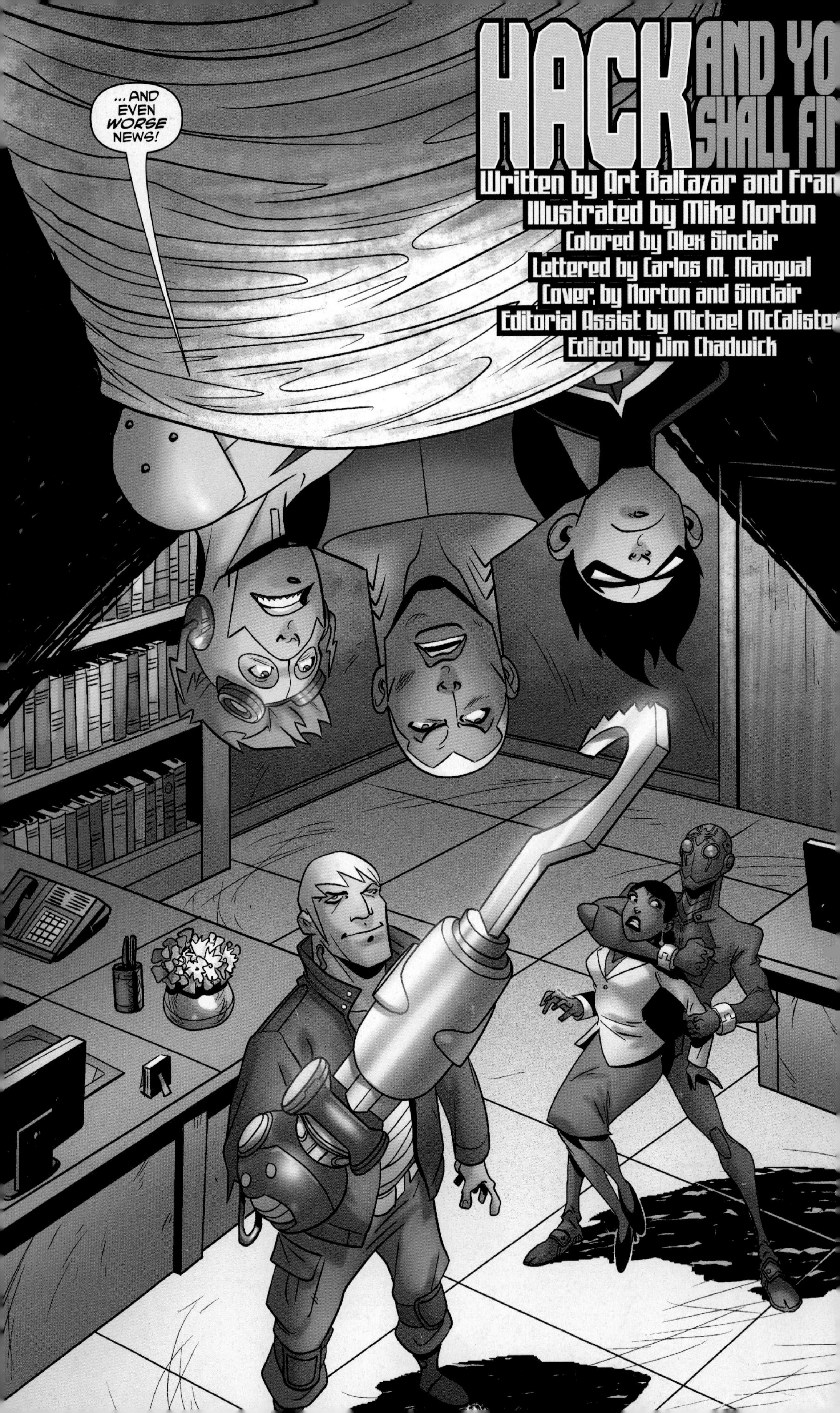

...AND EVEN WORSE NEWS!
HACK AND YO
SHALL FI
Written by Art Baltazar and Fran
Illustrated by Mike Norton
Colored by Alex Sinclair
Lettered by Carlos M. Mangual
Cover, by Norton and Sinclair
Editorial Assist by Michael McCaliste
Edited by Jim Chadwick

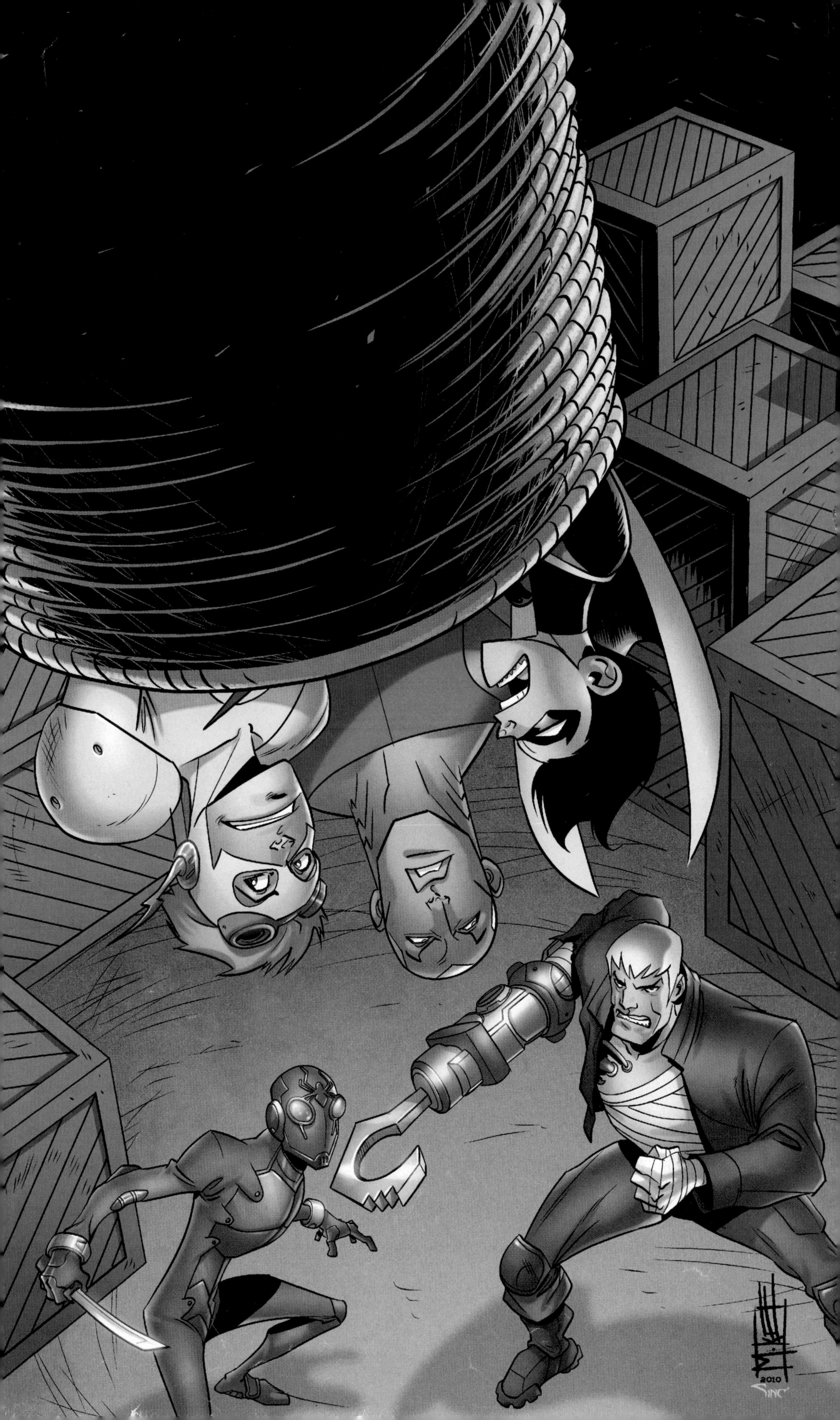

SO YOU THREE JUNIOR-GRADE GOOD GUYS THOUGHT YOU COULD STOP US?

YEAH, WHAT WERE YOU THINKING? THIS IS *HOOK* AND THE *BLACK SPIDER* YOU GOT HERE! WE'RE GOOD AT WHAT WE DO. WE'RE PROFESSIONALS.

YEAH, PROFESSIONAL HIT MEN FOR THE *LEAGUE OF SHADOWS* SENT TO KILL AN INNOCENT WOMAN!

I *WOULDN'T* GO THROWING AROUND NAMES OF DEADLY GROUPS LIKE THAT IF YOU KNOW WHAT'S GOOD FOR YOU, KID.

PLEASE... LET ME GO.

WHY ARE YOU AFTER HER? WHY IS SELENA GONZALEZ TARGETED?

YOU'RE NOT IN ANY POSITION TO ASK QUESTIONS... BUT *WE* ARE.

HOW DID YOU KNOW WE'D BE HERE?

HE ASKED YOU A QUESTION.

LIKE YOU, WE DO NOT HAVE TO ANSWER ANY QUESTIONS.

YEAH, BUT YOU'RE GOING TO 'CAUSE YOU SCREWED UP AND GOT CAUGHT! FACE IT, YOU GUYS *NEVER* EVEN HAD A CHANCE AGAINST US.

WHAT? WE CAME HERE TO *STOP* YOU FROM HURTING HER. WE *DID* THAT!

HA! ARE YOU KIDDING ME? YOU STOPPED US, YEAH, FOR LIKE *FIVE* MINUTES.

YOU SEE WHAT'S HAPPENING HERE, RIGHT? YOU LOST!

YOU DIDN'T TAKE MY UTILITY BELT.

WAIT... YOUR WHAT NOW?

YOU NEVER TOOK MY UTILITY BELT AWAY.

YOU KNOW, THE THING THAT LETS US ESCAPE.

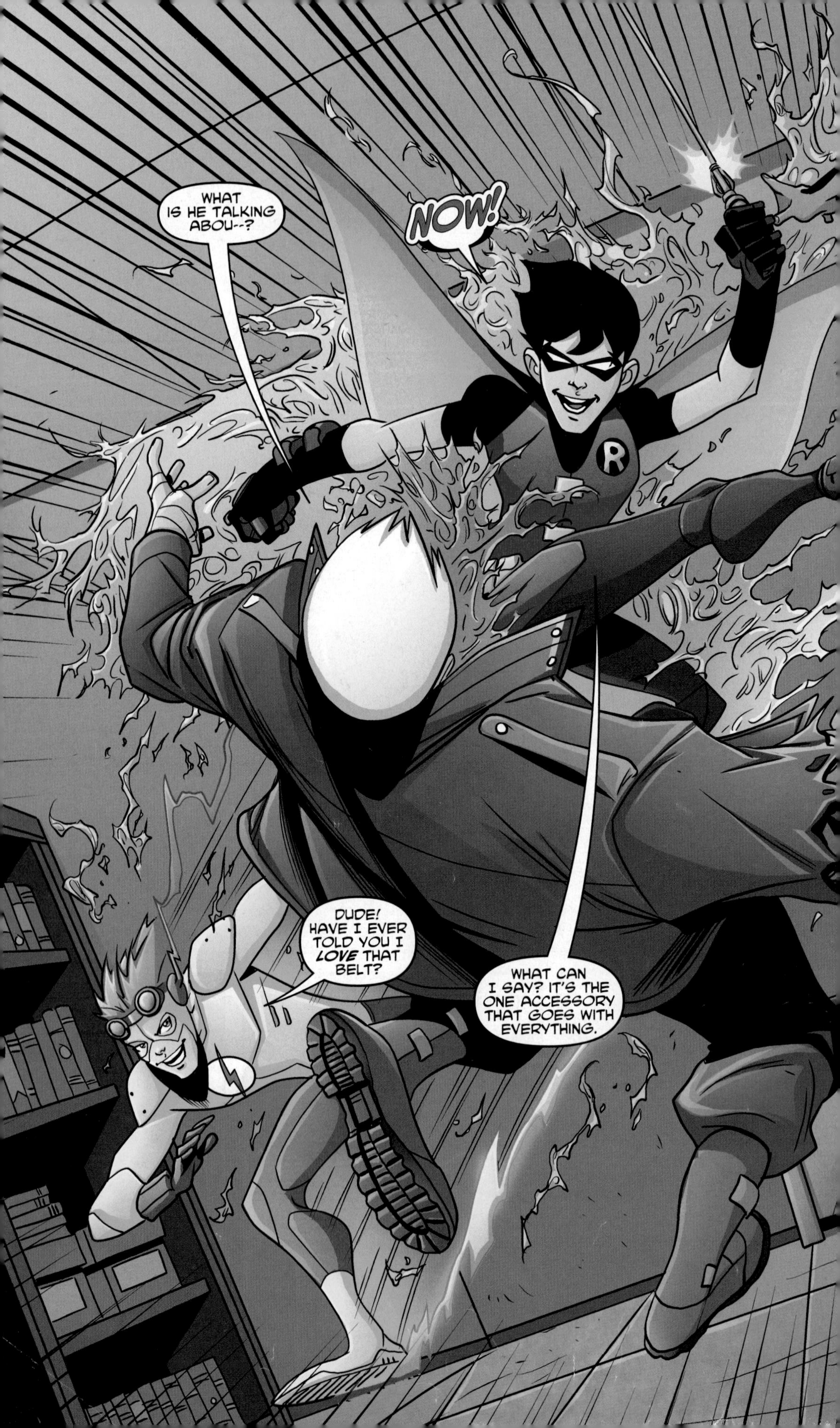
WHAT IS HE TALKING ABOU--?
NOW!
DUDE! HAVE I EVER TOLD YOU I *LOVE* THAT BELT?
WHAT CAN I SAY? IT'S THE ONE ACCESSORY THAT GOES WITH EVERYTHING.

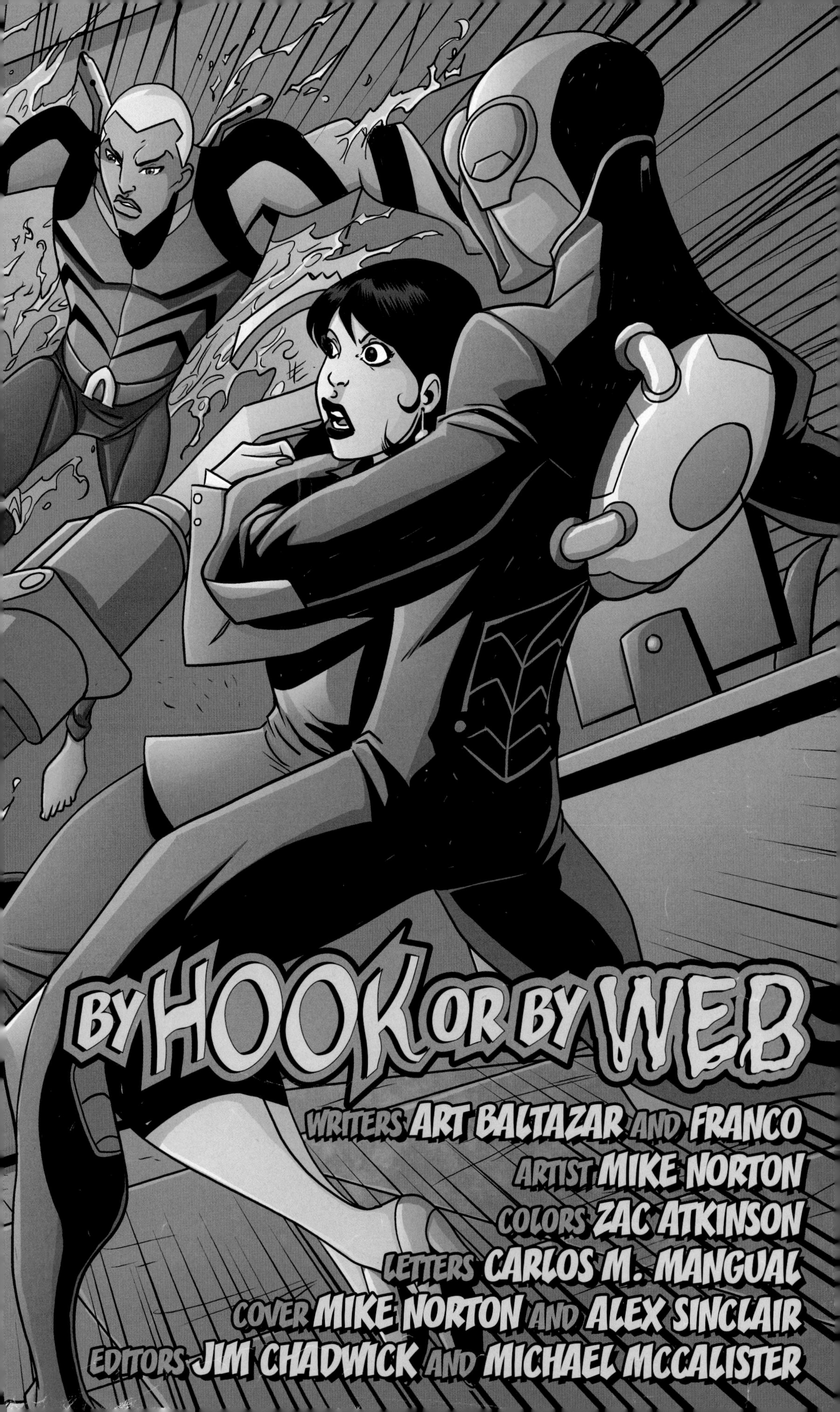
BY HOOK OR BY WEB
WRITERS ART BALTAZAR AND FRANCO
ARTIST MIKE NORTON
COLORS ZAC ATKINSON
LETTERS CARLOS M. MANGUAL
COVER MIKE NORTON AND ALEX SINCLAIR
EDITORS JIM CHADWICK AND MICHAEL MCCALISTER

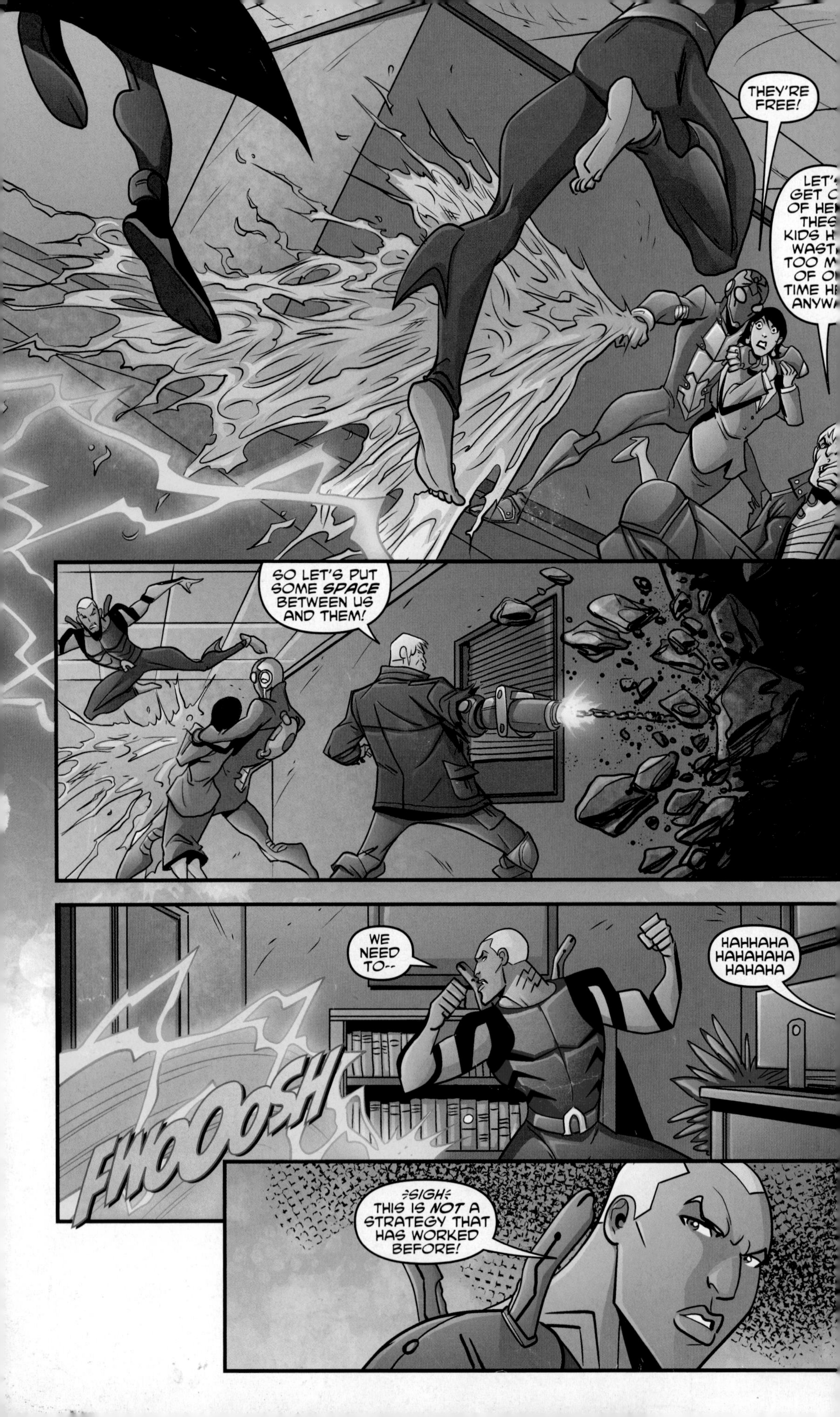
THEY'RE FREE!
SO LET'S PUT SOME SPACE BETWEEN US AND THEM!
WE NEED TO--
HAHHAHA HAHAHAHA HAHAHA
FWOOOSH
SIGH
THIS IS NOT A STRATEGY THAT HAS WORKED BEFORE!

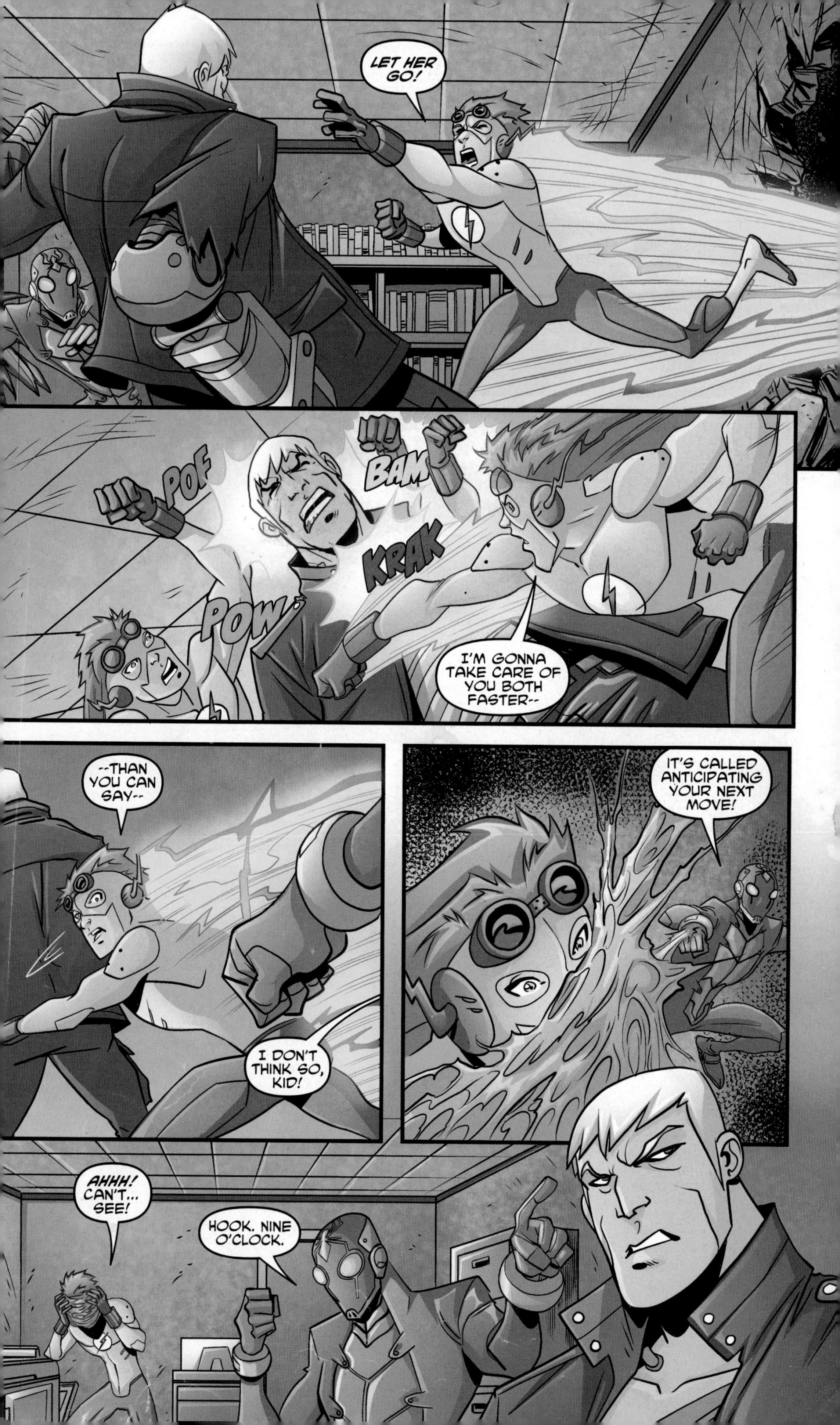
LET HER GO!
POF
BAM
KRAK
POW
I'M GONNA TAKE CARE OF YOU BOTH FASTER--
--THAN YOU CAN SAY--
I DON'T THINK SO, KID!
IT'S CALLED ANTICIPATING YOUR NEXT MOVE!
AHHH! CAN'T... SEE!
HOOK. NINE O'CLOCK.

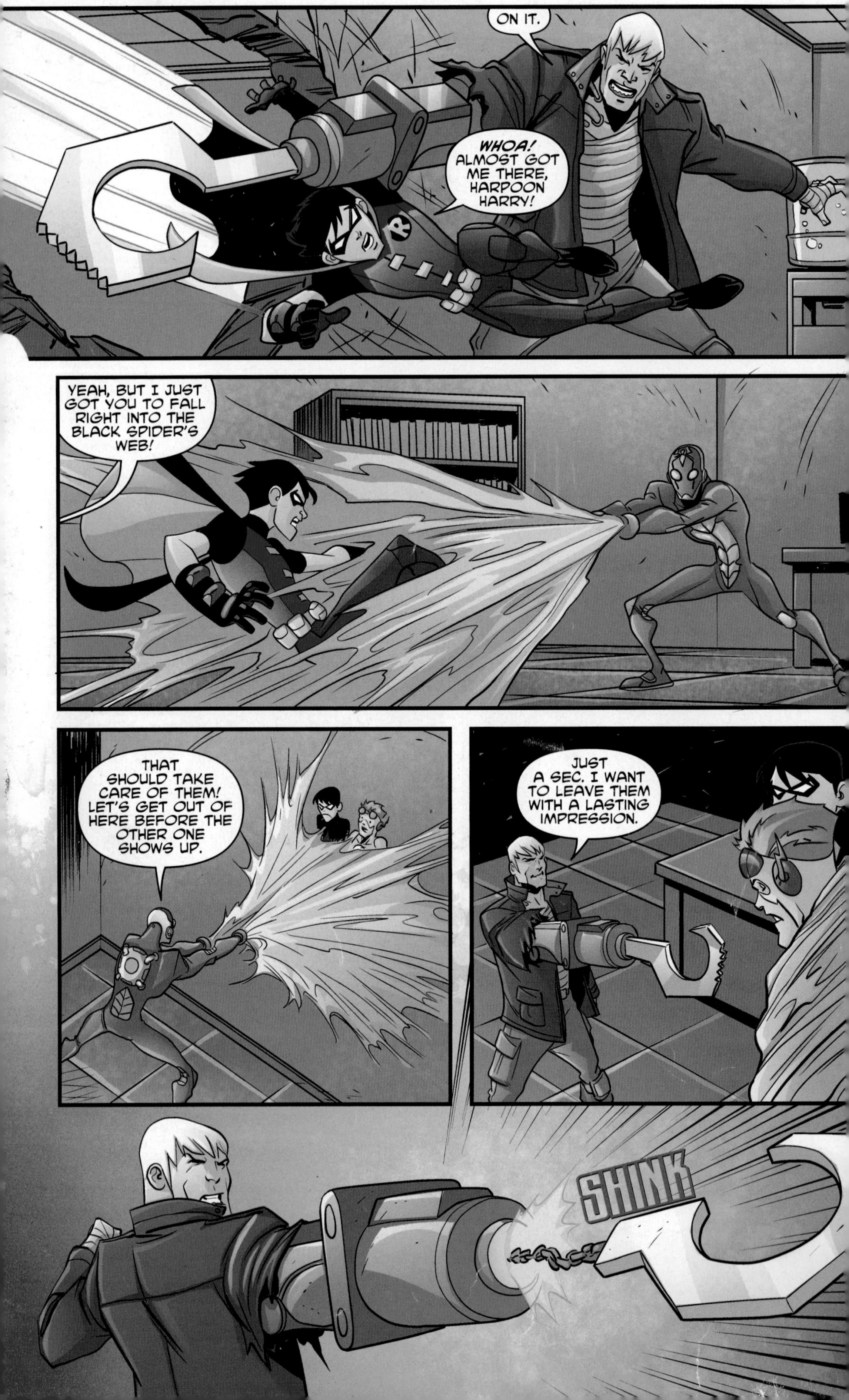
ON IT.
WHOA! ALMOST GOT ME THERE, HARPOON HARRY!
YEAH, BUT I JUST GOT YOU TO FALL RIGHT INTO THE BLACK SPIDER'S WEB!
THAT SHOULD TAKE CARE OF THEM! LET'S GET OUT OF HERE BEFORE THE OTHER ONE SHOWS UP.
JUST A SEC. I WANT TO LEAVE THEM WITH A LASTING IMPRESSION.
SHINK

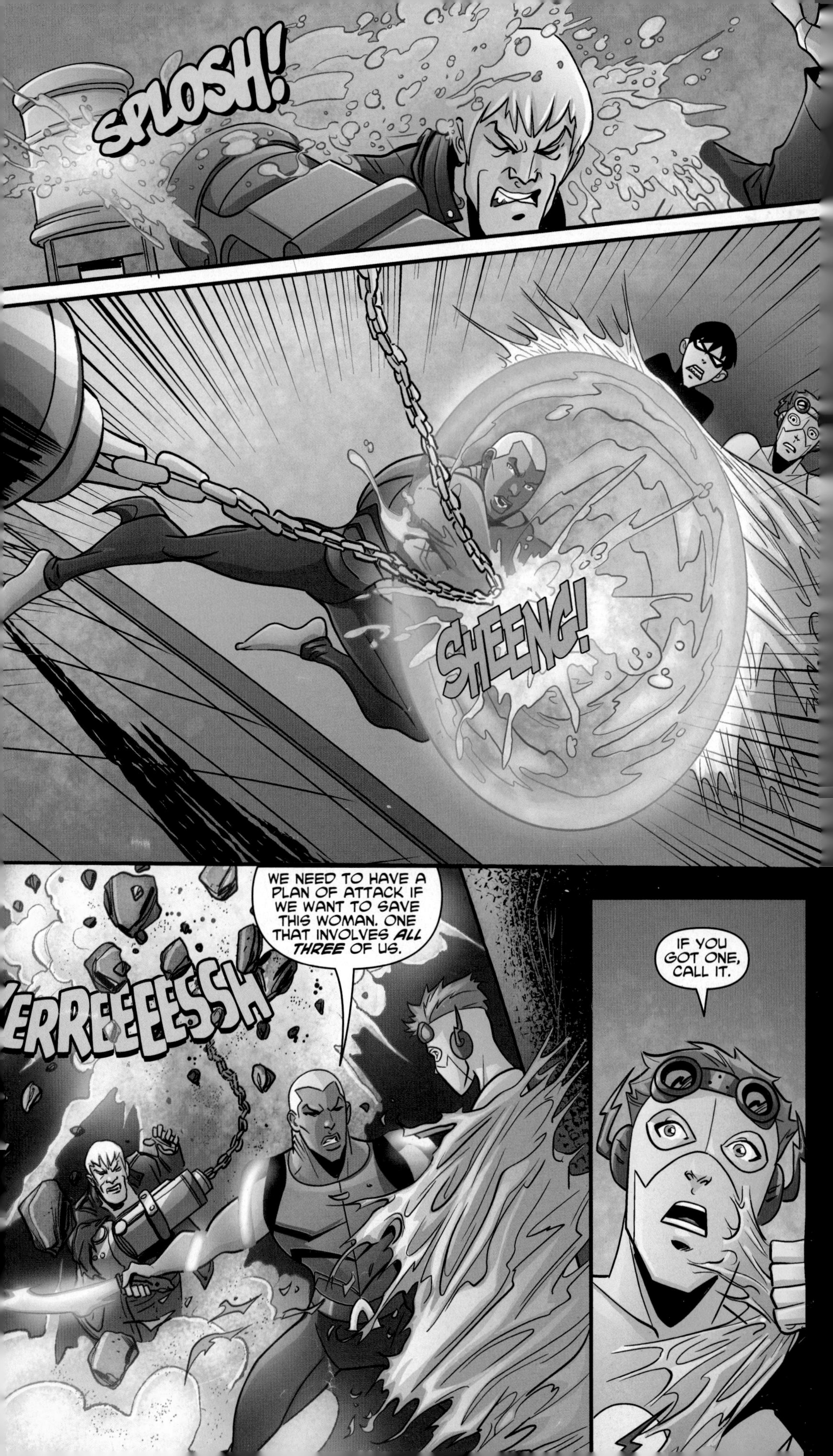
SPLOSH!
SHEENG!
KERREEEEESSH
WE NEED TO HAVE A PLAN OF ATTACK IF WE WANT TO SAVE THIS WOMAN. ONE THAT INVOLVES *ALL THREE* OF US.
IF YOU GOT ONE, CALL IT.

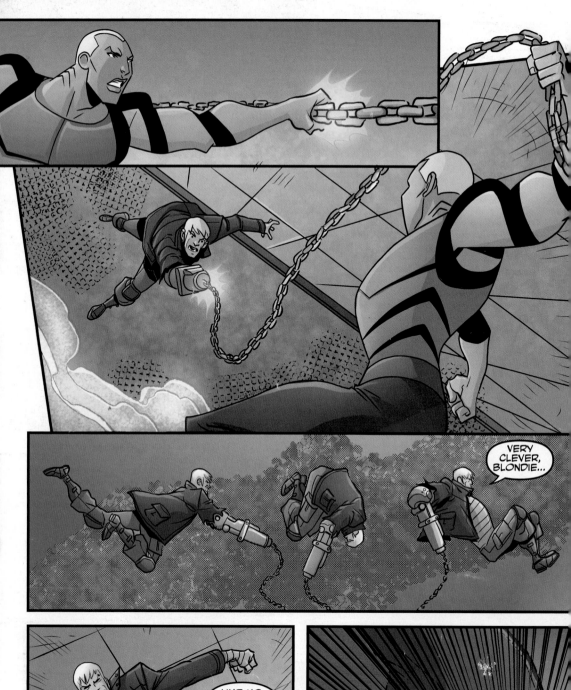

VERY CLEVER, BLONDIE...

LIKE NO ONE'S EVER TRIED THAT MOVE BEFORE.

BAW

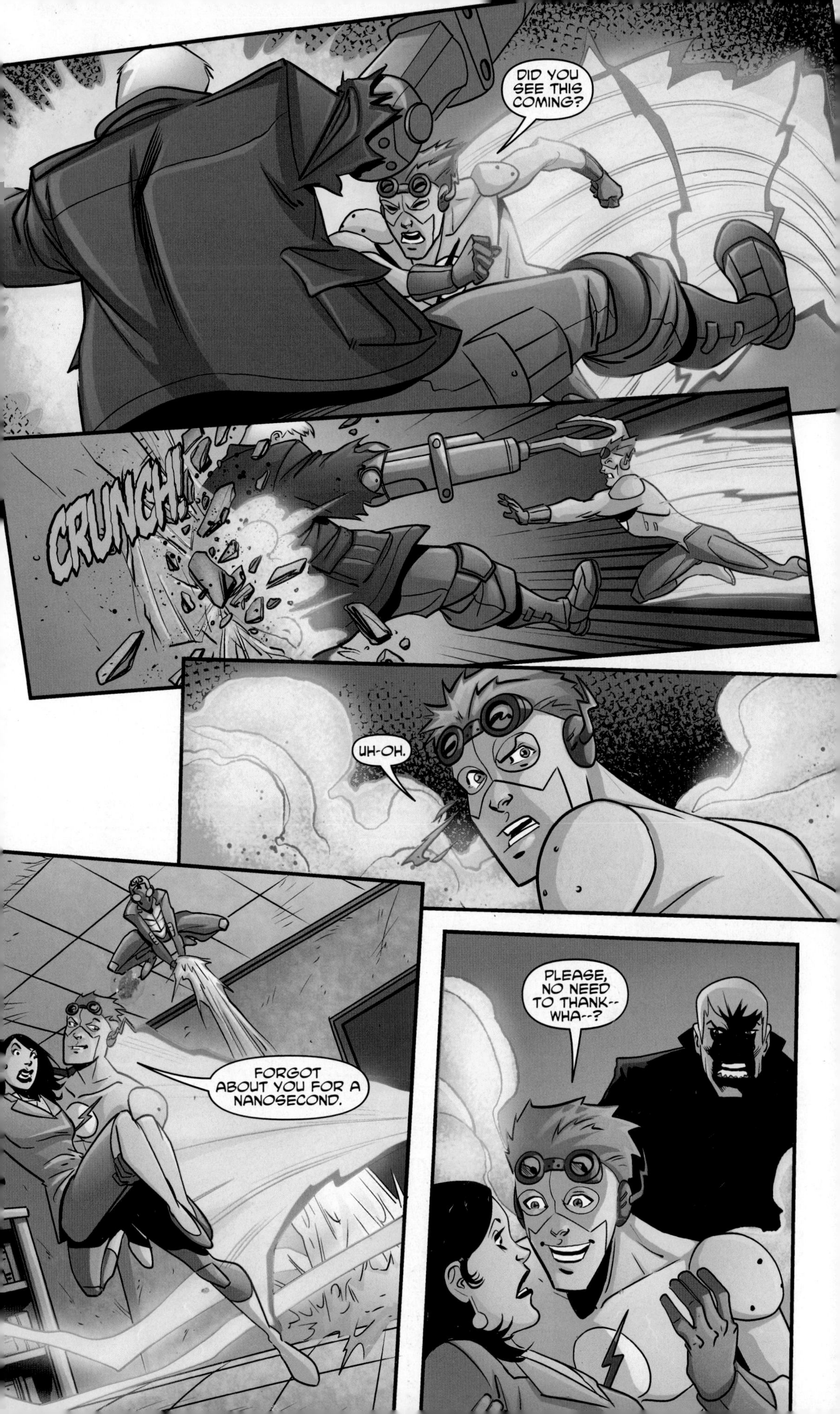
DID YOU SEE THIS COMING?
CRUNCH!
UH-OH.
FORGOT ABOUT YOU FOR A NANOSECOND.
PLEASE, NO NEED TO THANK-- WHA--?

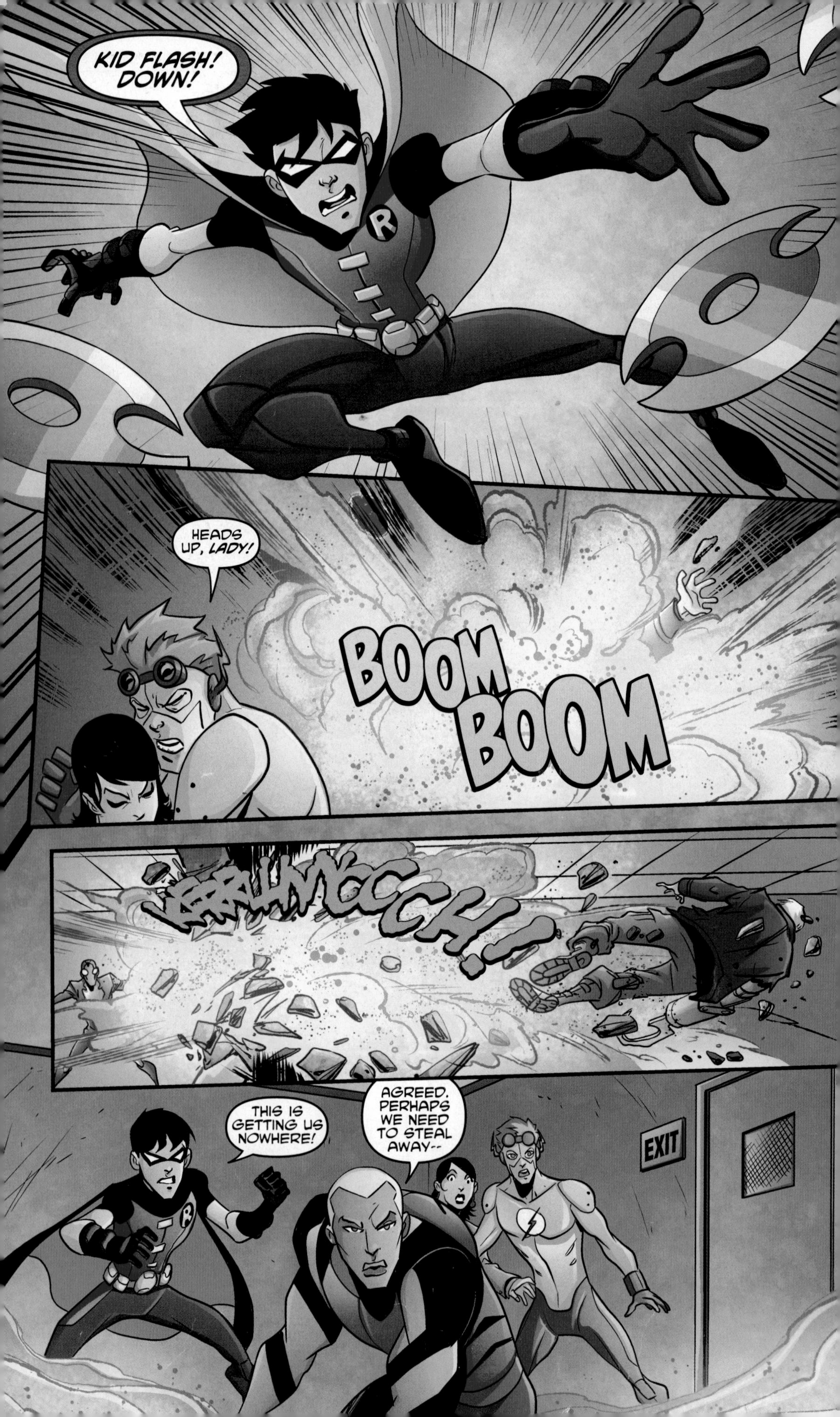
KID FLASH! DOWN!
HEADS UP, LADY!
BOOM BOOM
THIS IS GETTING US NOWHERE!
AGREED. PERHAPS WE NEED TO STEAL AWAY--
EXIT

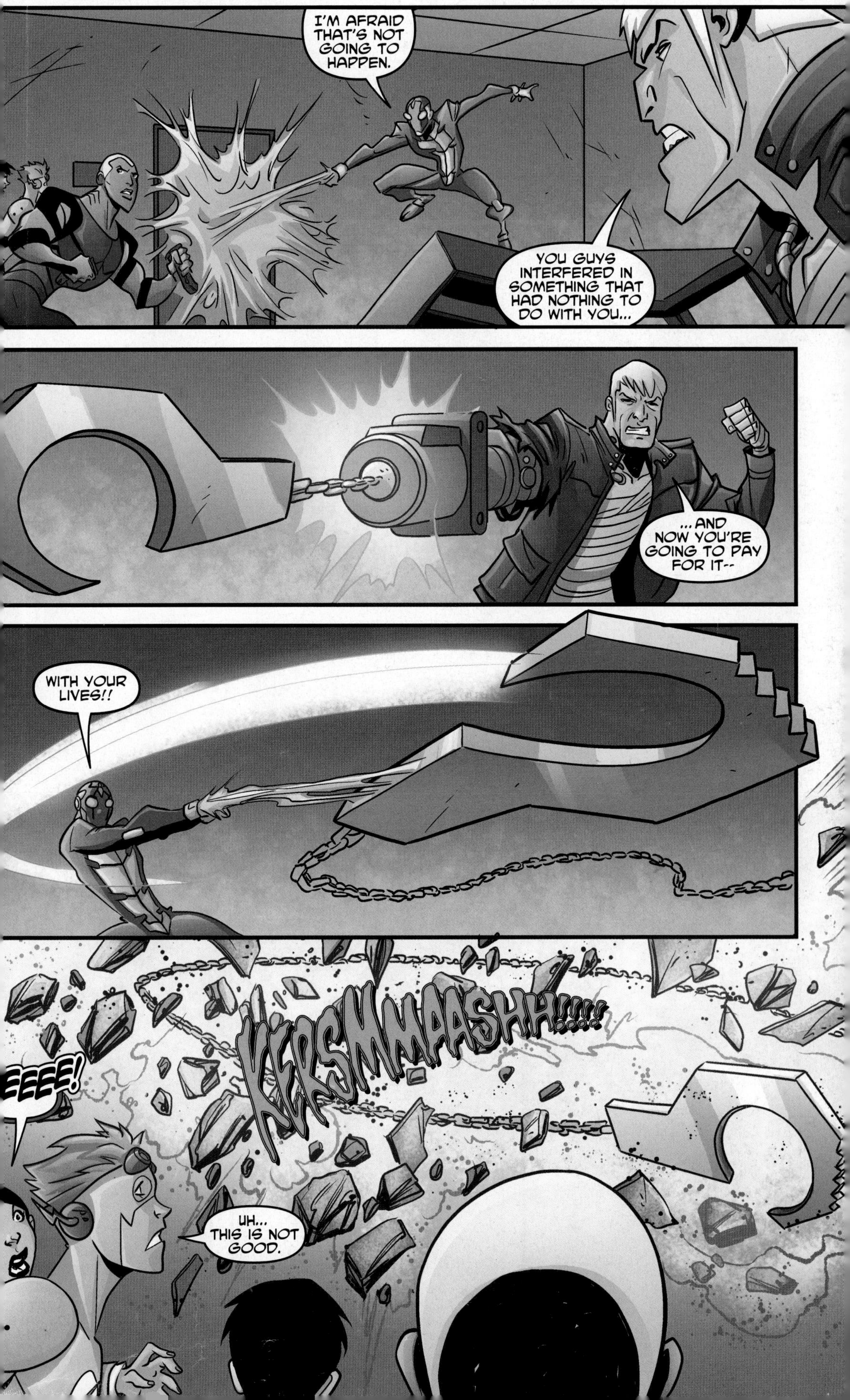
I'M AFRAID THAT'S NOT GOING TO HAPPEN.
YOU GUYS INTERFERED IN SOMETHING THAT HAD NOTHING TO DO WITH YOU...
...AND NOW YOU'RE GOING TO PAY FOR IT--
WITH YOUR LIVES!!
KERSMMAASHH!!!!!
EEEEE!
UH... THIS IS NOT GOOD.

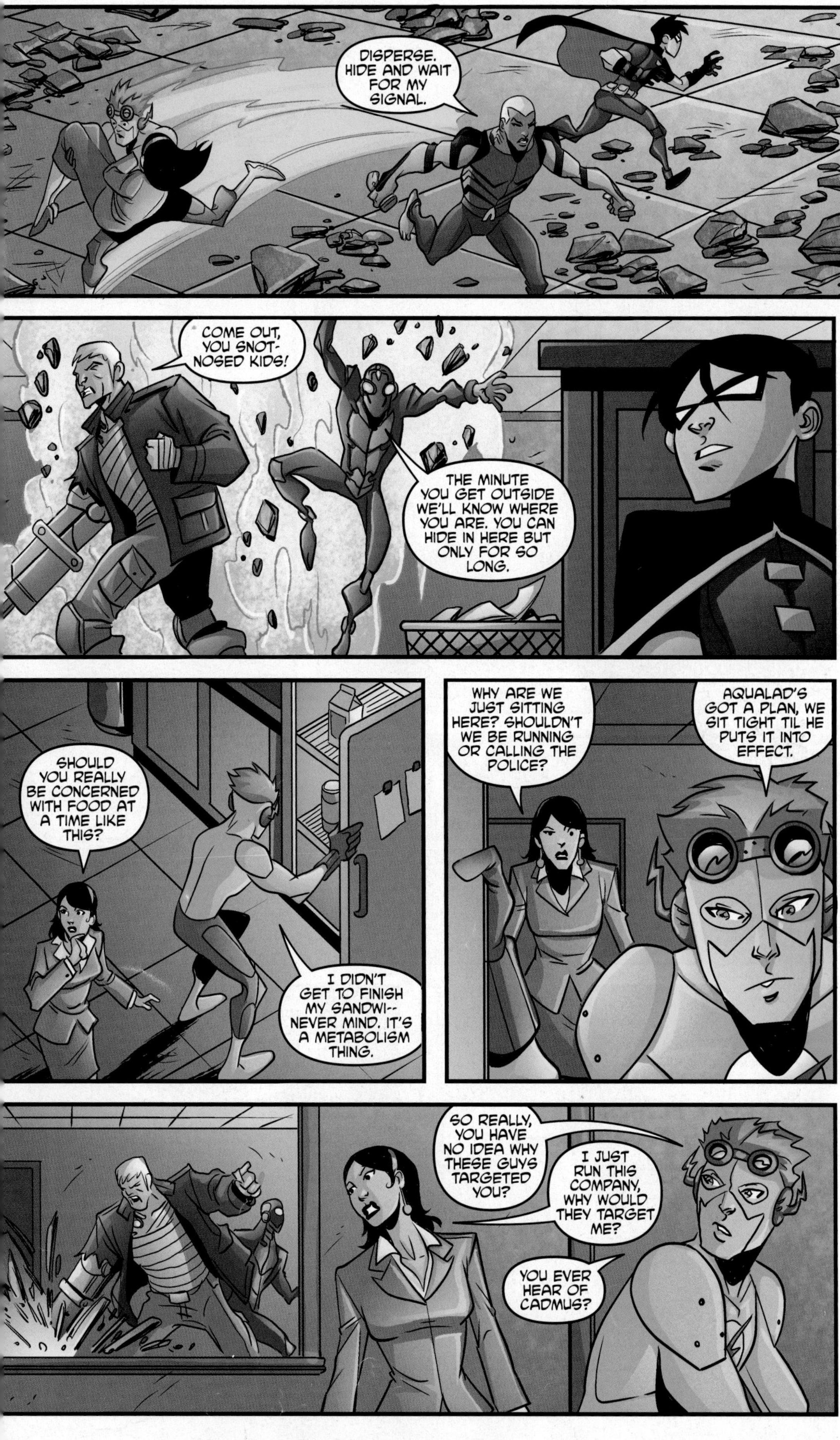
DISPERSE. HIDE AND WAIT FOR MY SIGNAL.
COME OUT, YOU SNOT-NOSED KIDS!
THE MINUTE YOU GET OUTSIDE WE'LL KNOW WHERE YOU ARE. YOU CAN HIDE IN HERE BUT ONLY FOR SO LONG.
SHOULD YOU REALLY BE CONCERNED WITH FOOD AT A TIME LIKE THIS?
I DIDN'T GET TO FINISH MY SANDWI-- NEVER MIND. IT'S A METABOLISM THING.
WHY ARE WE JUST SITTING HERE? SHOULDN'T WE BE RUNNING OR CALLING THE POLICE?
AQUALAD'S GOT A PLAN, WE SIT TIGHT TIL HE PUTS IT INTO EFFECT.
SO REALLY, YOU HAVE NO IDEA WHY THESE GUYS TARGETED YOU?
I JUST RUN THIS COMPANY, WHY WOULD THEY TARGET ME?
YOU EVER HEAR OF CADMUS?

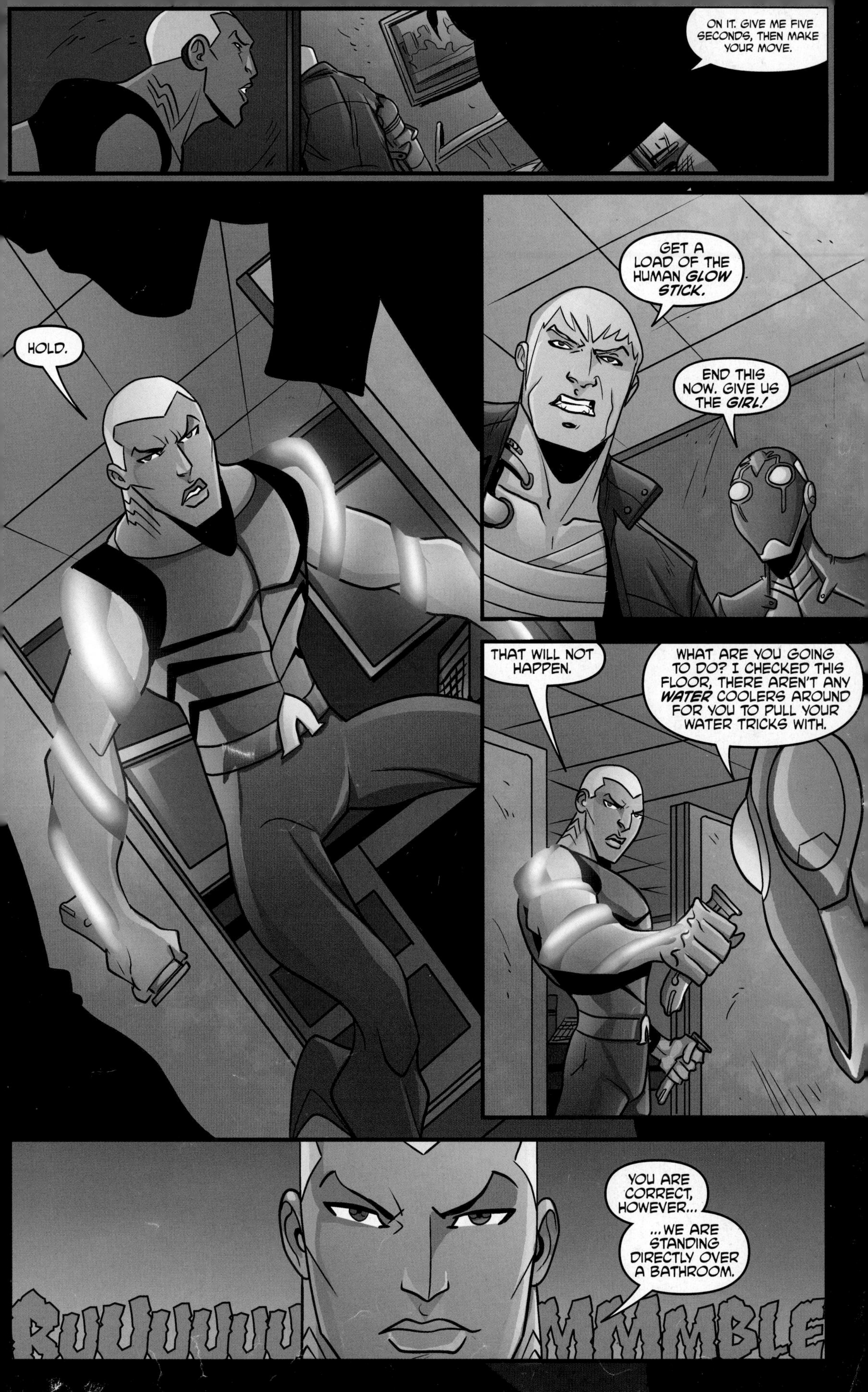
ON IT. GIVE ME FIVE SECONDS, THEN MAKE YOUR MOVE.
HOLD.
GET A LOAD OF THE HUMAN GLOW STICK.
END THIS NOW. GIVE US THE GIRL!
THAT WILL NOT HAPPEN.
WHAT ARE YOU GOING TO DO? I CHECKED THIS FLOOR, THERE AREN'T ANY WATER COOLERS AROUND FOR YOU TO PULL YOUR WATER TRICKS WITH.
YOU ARE CORRECT, HOWEVER...
...WE ARE STANDING DIRECTLY OVER A BATHROOM.
RUUUUUU...MMMBLE

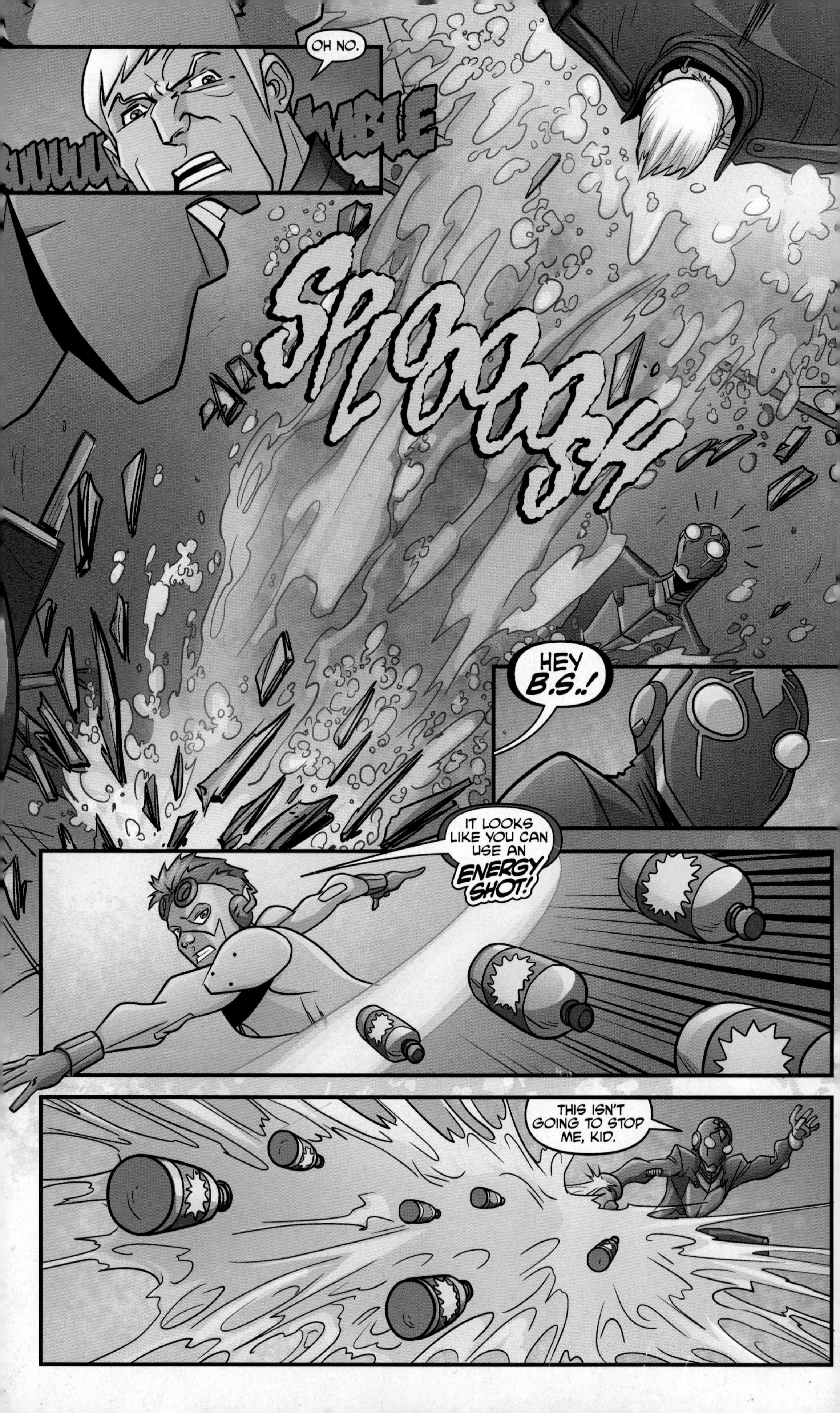

OH NO.
RUMBLE
SPLOOOOSH
HEY B.S.!
IT LOOKS LIKE YOU CAN USE AN ENERGY SHOT!
THIS ISN'T GOING TO STOP ME, KID.

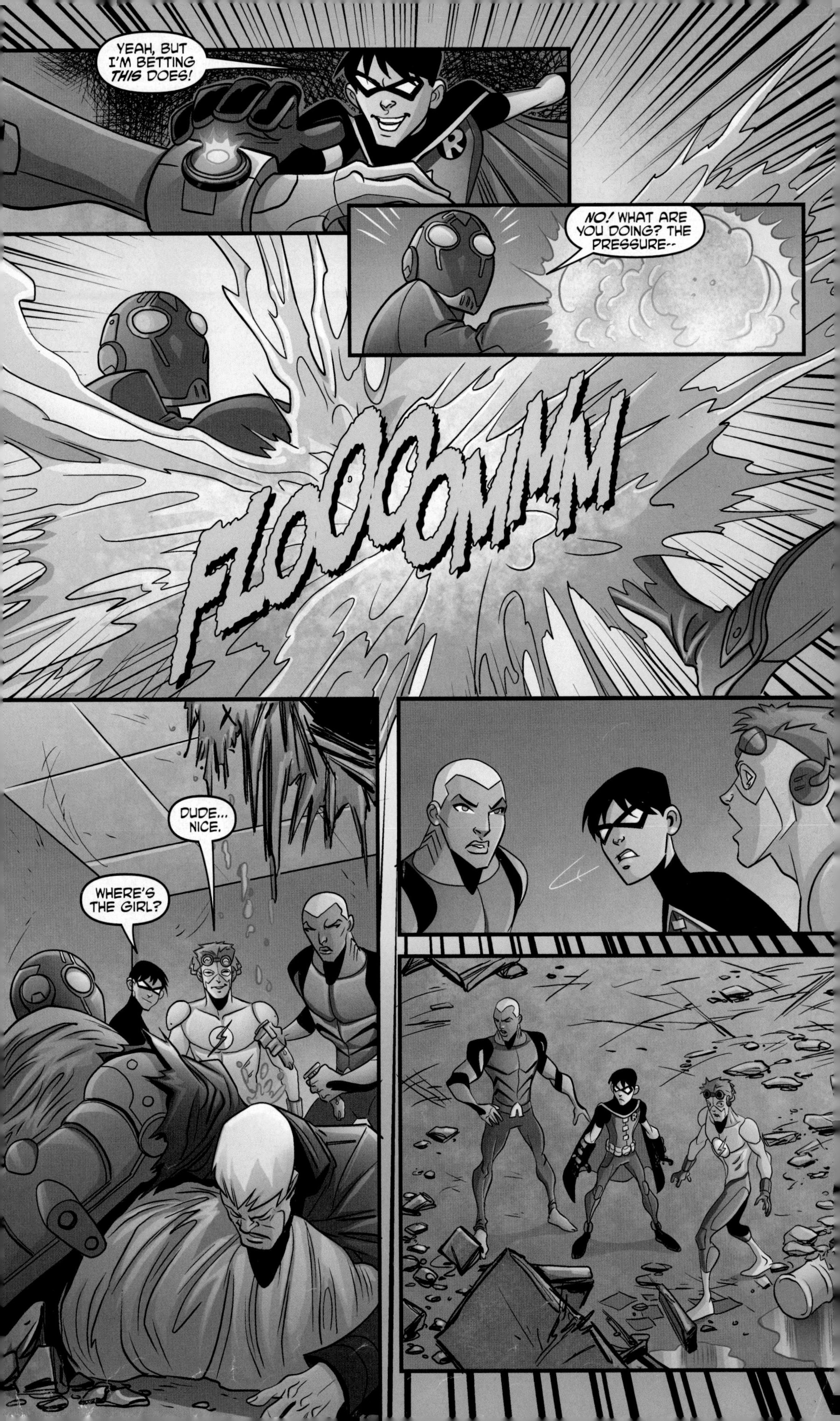
YEAH, BUT I'M BETTING *THIS* DOES!
NO! WHAT ARE YOU DOING? THE PRESSURE--
FLOOOOMMM
DUDE... NICE.
WHERE'S THE GIRL?

WE LOOKED *EVERYWHERE* FOR HER. SHE WAS PRETTY SCARED; SHE PROBABLY JUST RAN AND IS HIDING OUT SOMEWHERE.

WE CHECKED HER PREMISES, AND THOSE OF HER FAMILY. SHE IS NOWHERE TO BE FOUND.

LISTEN.

POLICE SAY IT IS TOO EARLY TO TELL IF THE DISAPPEARANCE OF FARANO ENTERPRISES CEO SELENA GONZALEZ IS IN ANYWAY CONNECTED TO WHAT HAPPENED AT THEIR CORPORATE HEADQUARTERS LAST NIGHT...

...ALTHOUGH IT IS A GOOD POSSIBILITY AS THE TWO MEN CAPTURED ON THE PREMISES AND ALLEGEDLY RESPONSIBLE FOR ALL THE PROPERTY DAMAGE HAVE THEMSELVES ESCAPED CUSTODY AS THEY WERE BEING TRANSPORTED TO A MAXIMUM HOLDING FACILITY.

HOW COULD I HAVE *NOT* SEEN IT?!!

WHEN WE WERE BACK IN THAT BUILDING, BLACK SPIDER SAID, "THE MINUTE YOU GET OUTSIDE WE'LL KNOW WHERE YOU ARE."

...THEY HAD OTHERS OUTSIDE.

THEY'RE THE *LEAGUE OF SHADOWS!* OF COURSE THEY HAD *OTHERS* OUTSIDE! WE JUST NEVER SAW THEM, BUT THEY WERE THERE!

SO YOU MEAN SELENA IS...

EN

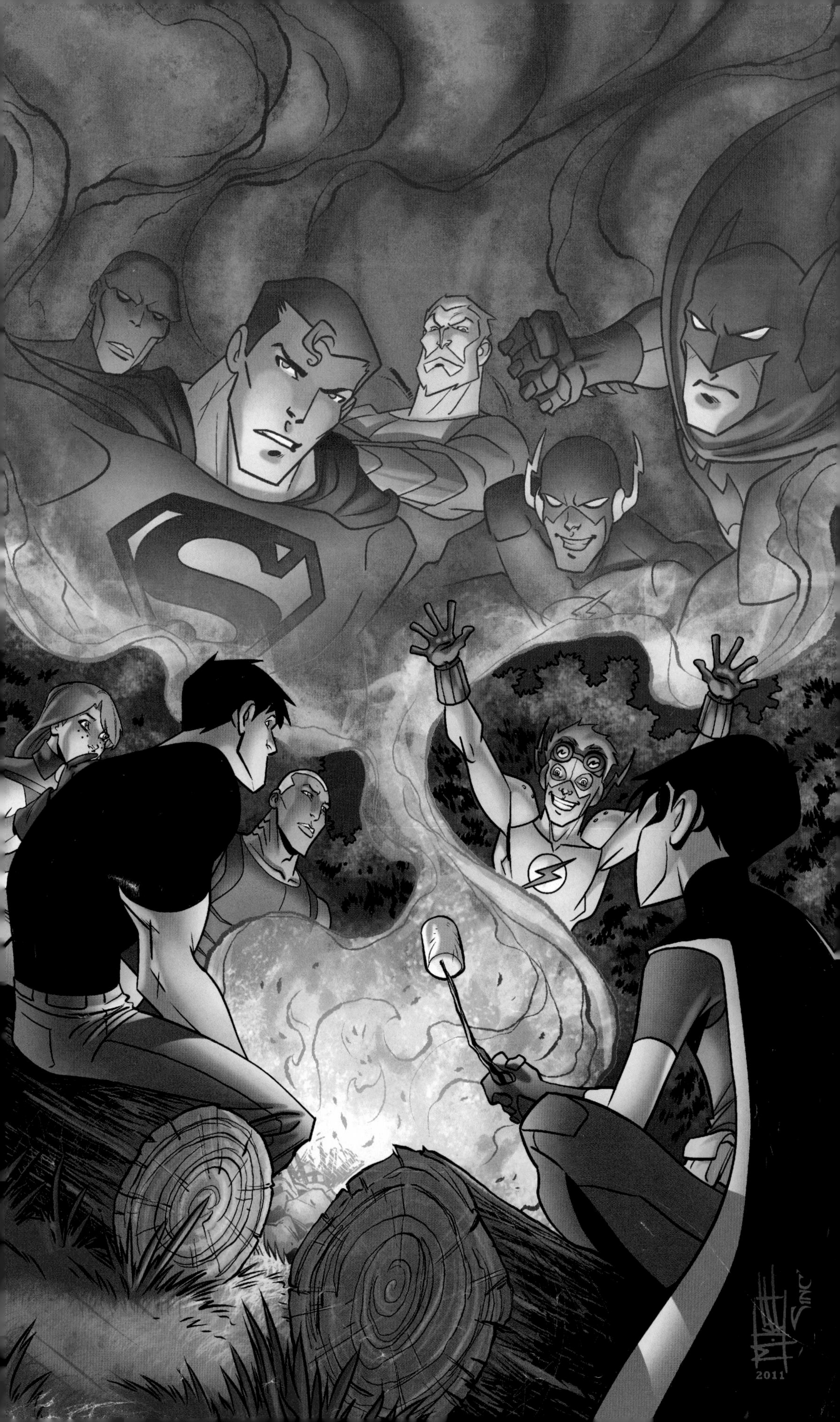

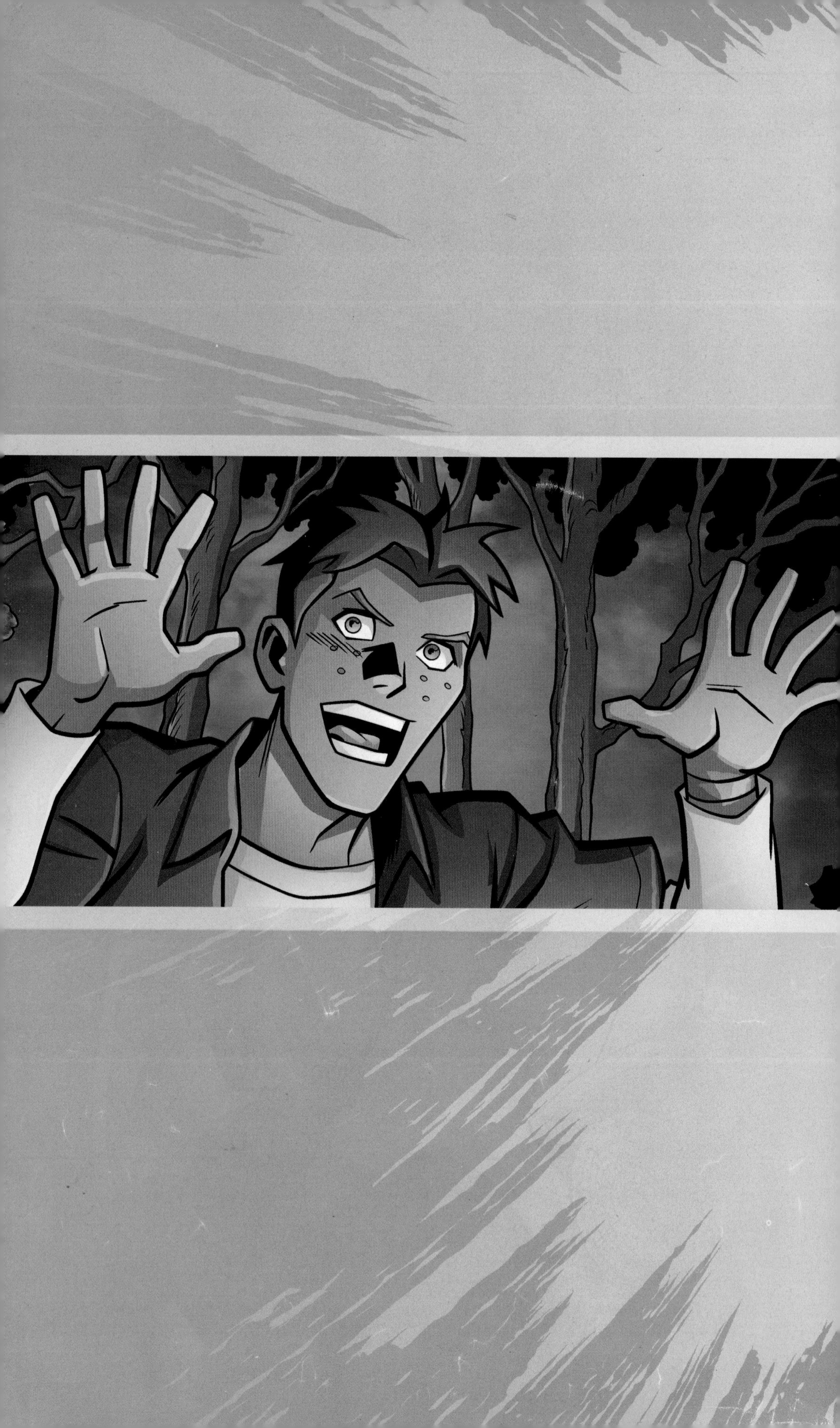

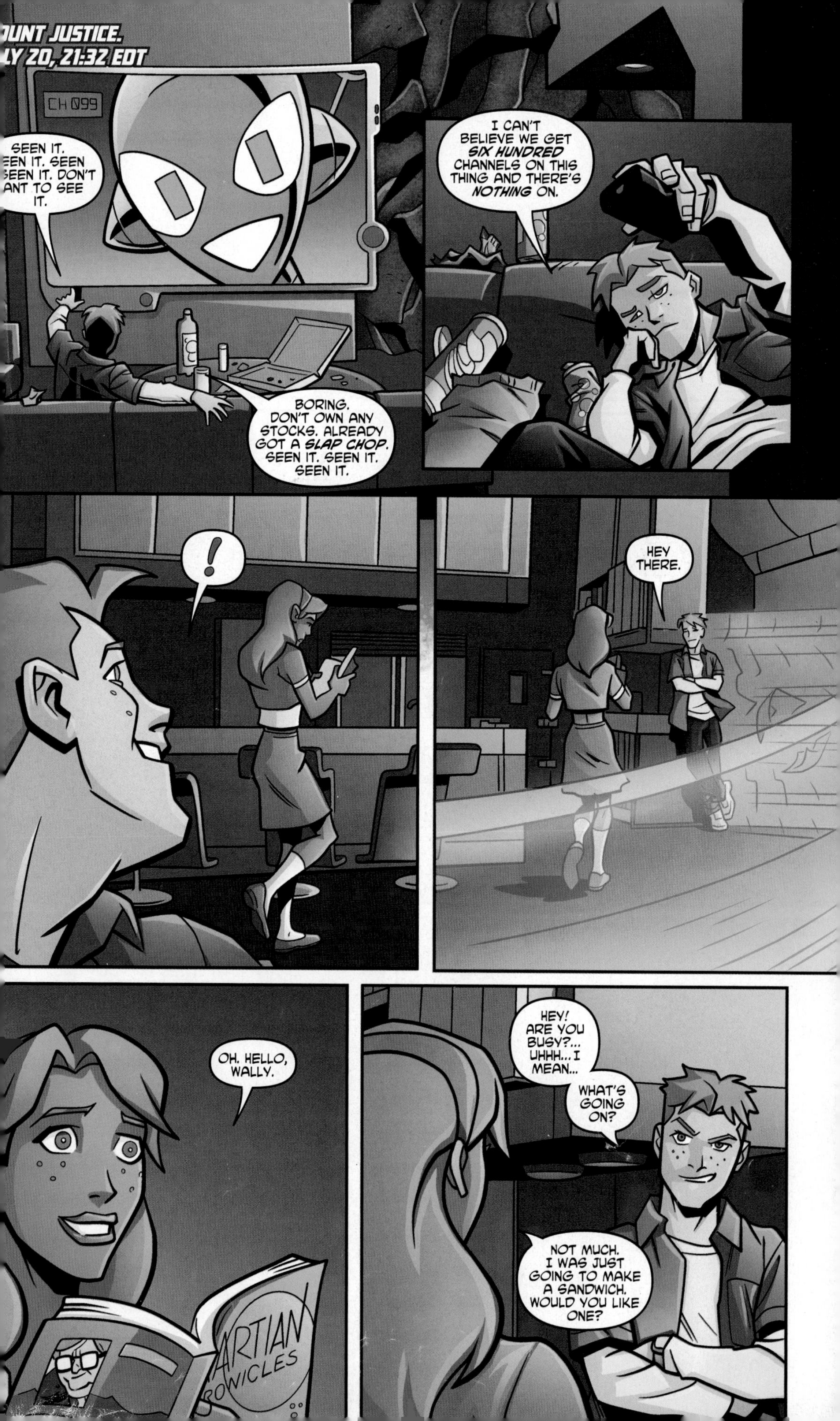

OUNT JUSTICE.
LY 20, 21:32 EDT
CH 099
SEEN IT. EEN IT. SEEN SEEN IT. DON'T ANT TO SEE IT.
BORING. DON'T OWN ANY STOCKS. ALREADY GOT A SLAP CHOP. SEEN IT. SEEN IT. SEEN IT.
I CAN'T BELIEVE WE GET SIX HUNDRED CHANNELS ON THIS THING AND THERE'S NOTHING ON.
!
HEY THERE.
OH. HELLO, WALLY.
HEY! ARE YOU BUSY?... UHHH... I MEAN...
WHAT'S GOING ON?
NOT MUCH. I WAS JUST GOING TO MAKE A SANDWICH. WOULD YOU LIKE ONE?
ARTIAN RONICLES

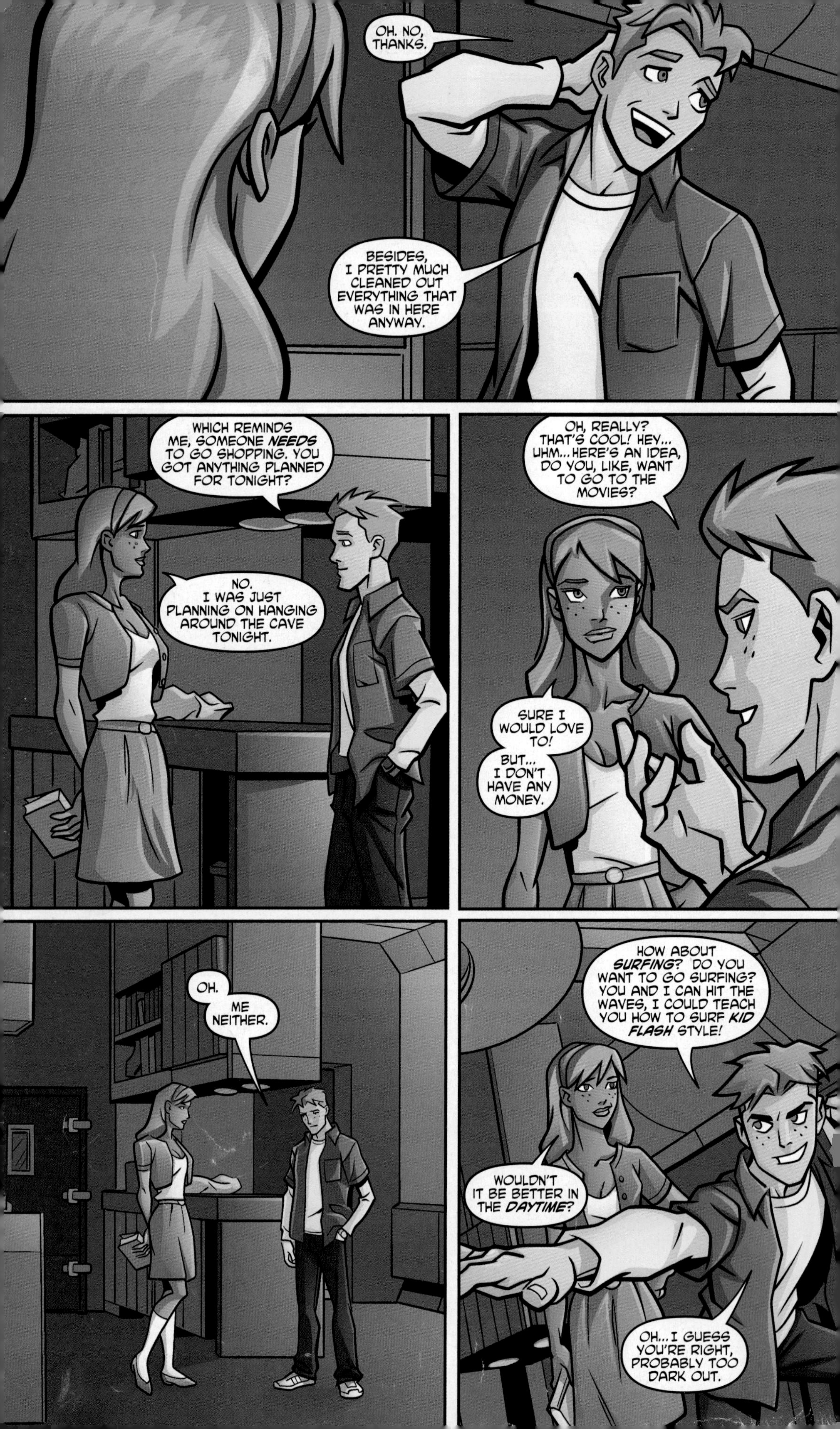
OH. NO, THANKS.
BESIDES, I PRETTY MUCH CLEANED OUT EVERYTHING THAT WAS IN HERE ANYWAY.
WHICH REMINDS ME, SOMEONE *NEEDS* TO GO SHOPPING. YOU GOT ANYTHING PLANNED FOR TONIGHT?
NO. I WAS JUST PLANNING ON HANGING AROUND THE CAVE TONIGHT.
OH, REALLY? THAT'S COOL! HEY... UHM... HERE'S AN IDEA, DO YOU, LIKE, WANT TO GO TO THE MOVIES?
SURE I WOULD LOVE TO!
BUT... I DON'T HAVE ANY MONEY.
OH.
ME NEITHER.
HOW ABOUT *SURFING*? DO YOU WANT TO GO SURFING? YOU AND I CAN HIT THE WAVES, I COULD TEACH YOU HOW TO SURF *KID FLASH* STYLE!
WOULDN'T IT BE BETTER IN THE *DAYTIME*?
OH... I GUESS YOU'RE RIGHT, PROBABLY TOO DARK OUT.

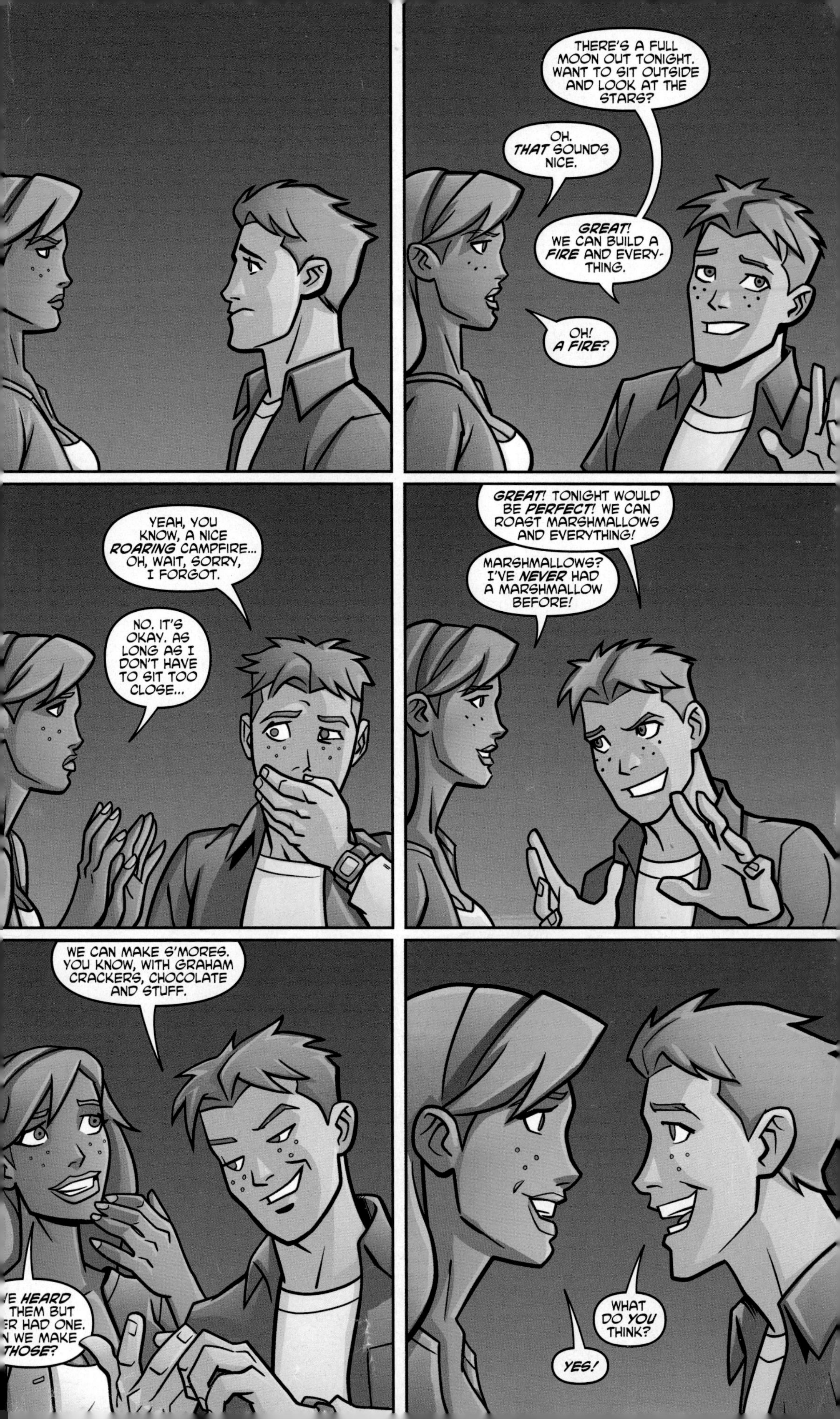
THERE'S A FULL MOON OUT TONIGHT. WANT TO SIT OUTSIDE AND LOOK AT THE STARS?
OH. THAT SOUNDS NICE.
GREAT! WE CAN BUILD A FIRE AND EVERYTHING.
OH! A FIRE?
YEAH, YOU KNOW, A NICE ROARING CAMPFIRE... OH, WAIT, SORRY, I FORGOT.
NO. IT'S OKAY. AS LONG AS I DON'T HAVE TO SIT TOO CLOSE...
GREAT! TONIGHT WOULD BE PERFECT! WE CAN ROAST MARSHMALLOWS AND EVERYTHING!
MARSHMALLOWS? I'VE NEVER HAD A MARSHMALLOW BEFORE!
WE CAN MAKE S'MORES. YOU KNOW, WITH GRAHAM CRACKERS, CHOCOLATE AND STUFF.
HEARD THEM BUT HAD ONE. WE MAKE THOSE?
WHAT DO YOU THINK?
YES!

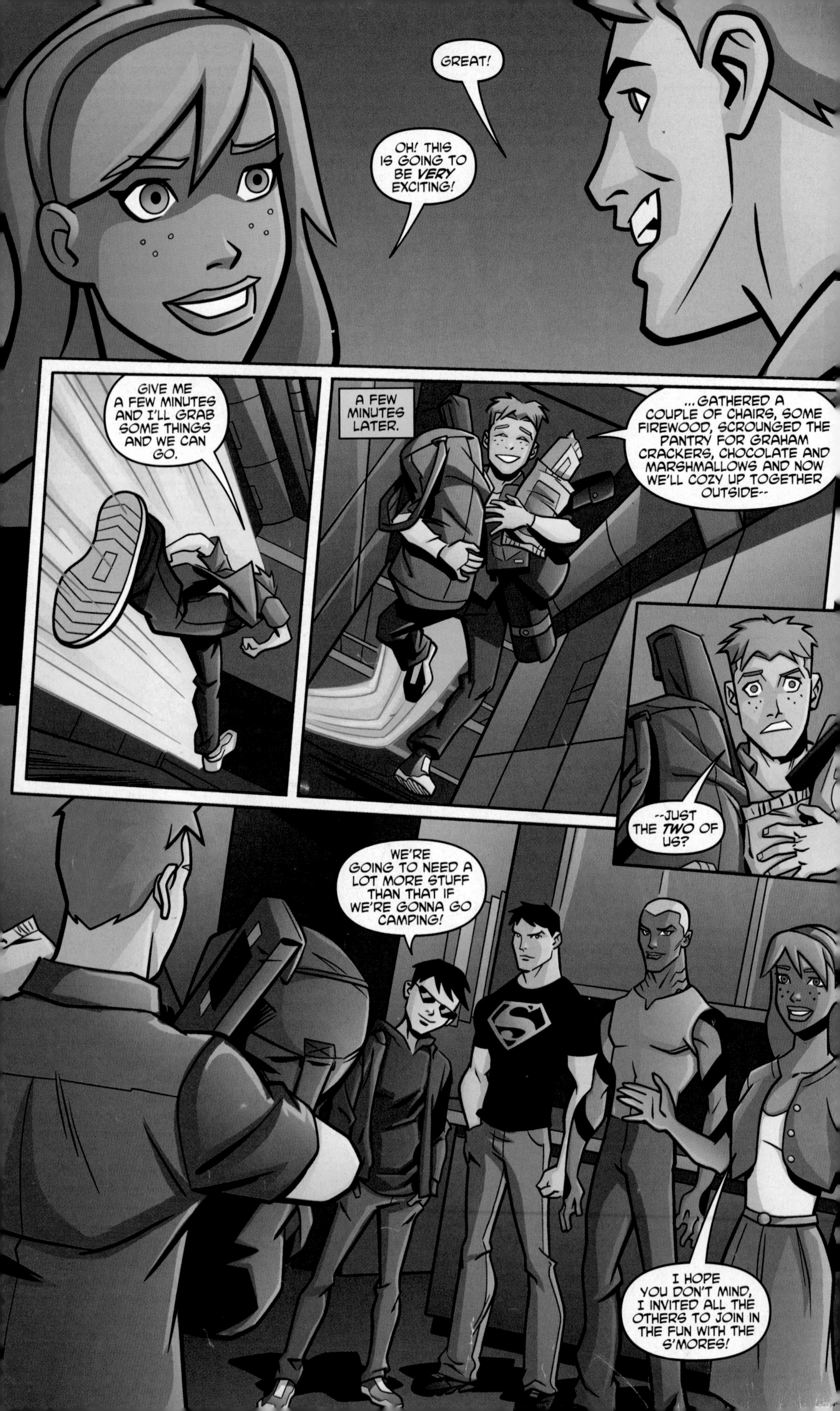
GREAT!
OH! THIS IS GOING TO BE *VERY* EXCITING!
GIVE ME A FEW MINUTES AND I'LL GRAB SOME THINGS AND WE CAN GO.
A FEW MINUTES LATER.
...GATHERED A COUPLE OF CHAIRS, SOME FIREWOOD, SCROUNGED THE PANTRY FOR GRAHAM CRACKERS, CHOCOLATE AND MARSHMALLOWS AND NOW WE'LL COZY UP TOGETHER OUTSIDE--
--JUST THE *TWO* OF US?
WE'RE GOING TO NEED A LOT MORE STUFF THAN THAT IF WE'RE GONNA GO CAMPING!
I HOPE YOU DON'T MIND, I INVITED ALL THE OTHERS TO JOIN IN THE FUN WITH THE S'MORES!

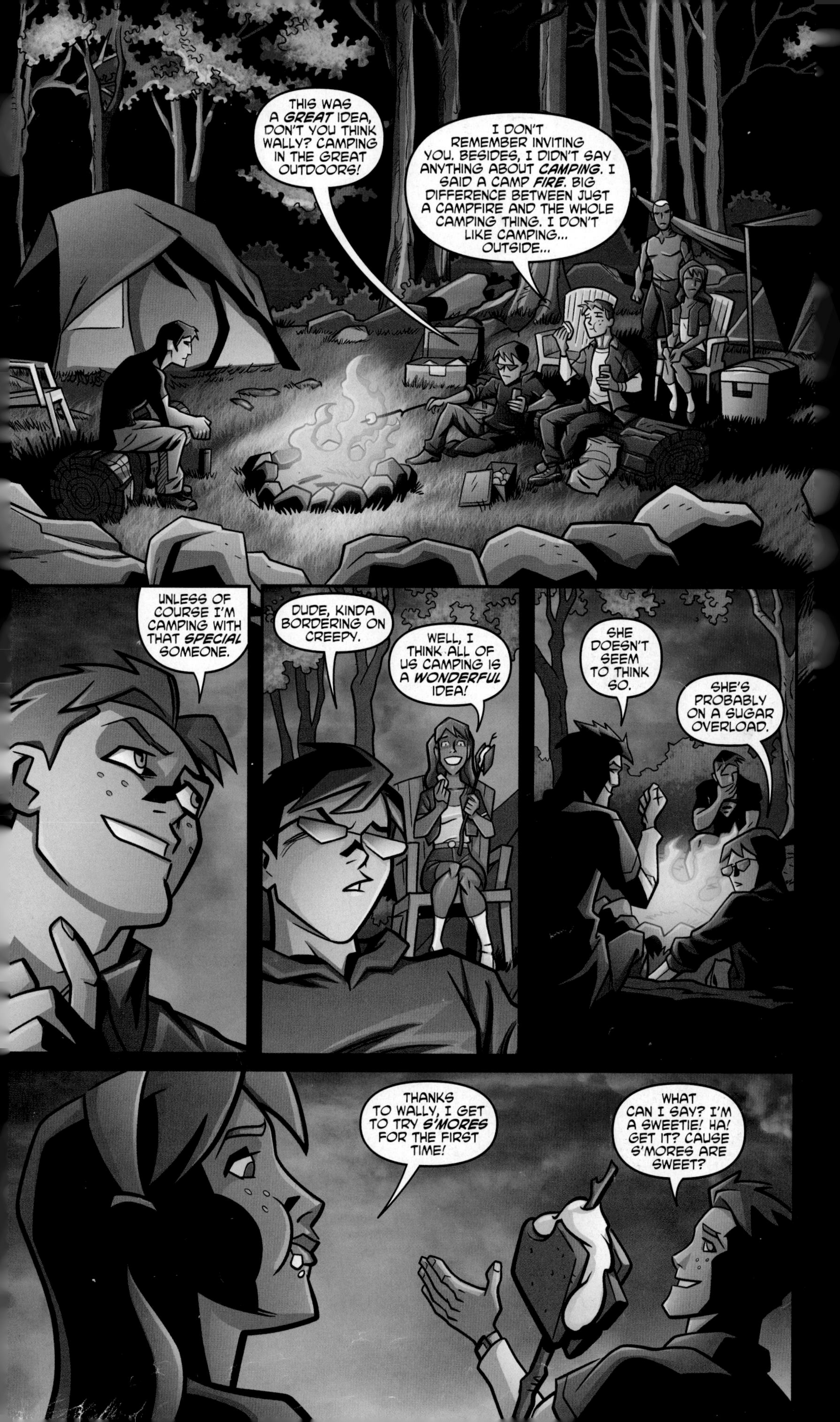
THIS WAS A GREAT IDEA, DON'T YOU THINK WALLY? CAMPING IN THE GREAT OUTDOORS!
I DON'T REMEMBER INVITING YOU. BESIDES, I DIDN'T SAY ANYTHING ABOUT CAMPING. I SAID A CAMP FIRE. BIG DIFFERENCE BETWEEN JUST A CAMPFIRE AND THE WHOLE CAMPING THING. I DON'T LIKE CAMPING... OUTSIDE...
UNLESS OF COURSE I'M CAMPING WITH THAT SPECIAL SOMEONE.
DUDE, KINDA BORDERING ON CREEPY.
WELL, I THINK ALL OF US CAMPING IS A WONDERFUL IDEA!
SHE DOESN'T SEEM TO THINK SO.
SHE'S PROBABLY ON A SUGAR OVERLOAD.
THANKS TO WALLY, I GET TO TRY S'MORES FOR THE FIRST TIME!
WHAT CAN I SAY? I'M A SWEETIE! HA! GET IT? CAUSE S'MORES ARE SWEET?

"OCEAN MASTER HAD GAINED THE UPPER HAND AND NEARLY DEFEATED AQUAMAN.

"CORRECTION.

"AQUAMAN *WAS* DEFEATED.

"GARTH, A FELLOW STUDENT, AND I INTERVENED ON THE KING'S BEHALF.

"IT WAS THE ONLY THING WE COULD THINK OF DOIN
THE DANGER DID NOT OC
TO US, THE ONLY THING TH
MATTERED TO US AT TH
TIME WAS THAT OUR KIN
WAS IN TROUBLE.

"WE HAD NO HOPE OF DEFEATING HIM WHATSOEVER, BUT THE TIME WE SPENT ENGAGED IN BATTLE AGAINST THE OCEAN MASTER WAS TIME ENOUGH FOR OUR KING TO RECOVER.

"IT MAY HAVE BEEN ONE OF THE MOST FOOLISH THINGS GARTH AND I HAD EVER DONE, AS WE NEARLY MET OUR OWN END.

"THAT WAS ALL HE NEEDED AS AQUAMAN FINALLY *TRIUMPHED* OVER OCEAN MASTER!

"HE WAS ABLE TO DRIVE HIM AWAY FROM THE CITY AND SAVE US ALL!"

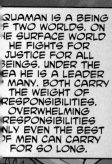

QUAMAN IS A BEING
F TWO WORLDS. ON
HE SURFACE WORLD
HE FIGHTS FOR
JUSTICE FOR ALL
BEINGS. UNDER THE
EA HE IS A LEADER
 MANY. BOTH CARRY
 THE WEIGHT OF
 RESPONSIBILITIES.
 OVERWHELMING
 RESPONSIBILITIES
 NLY EVEN THE BEST
 F MEN CAN CARRY
 FOR SO LONG.

"EVEN AQUAMAN
CANNOT DO BOTH
FOREVER.

"REALIZING THAT ON THE
SURFACE BOTH BATMAN
AND GREEN ARROW HAD
TAKEN ON *APPRENTICES*
HAT COULD ONE DAY TAKE
OVER THEIR RESPECTIVE
MANTELS, KING ORIN HAD
BEEN CONTEMPLATING
THE SAME IDEA.

"WITH THIS IN MIND, HE
APPROACHED BOTH GARTH
AND MYSELF WITH THE
POSSIBILITY OF BECOMING
HIS PROTÉGÉS.

 MUST ADMIT
E POSSIBILITY
TRIGUED ME
MEDIATELY.

"I HAD NEVER BEEN TO THE
SURFACE WORLD. AND I AM THE
FIRST TO ADMIT THAT I AM A BIT
OF AN ADVENTURER. MANY IS THE
DAY IN CLASS THAT I WOULD
DREAM OF VISITING DISTANT
OCEANS AND POSSIBLY ONE DAY
EVEN THE SURFACE WORLD.

"BOTH GARTH
AND I *SERIOUSLY*
CONSIDERED THE
KING'S OFFER.

"GARTH ULTIMATELY
CHOSE TO CONTINUE
HIS STUDIES WITH
QUEEN MERA AT THE
CONSERVATORY OF
SORCERY.

"FOR ME, HOWEVER,
THE CHANCE TO VISIT
THE SURFACE WORLD
WAS A DREAM
COME TRUE."

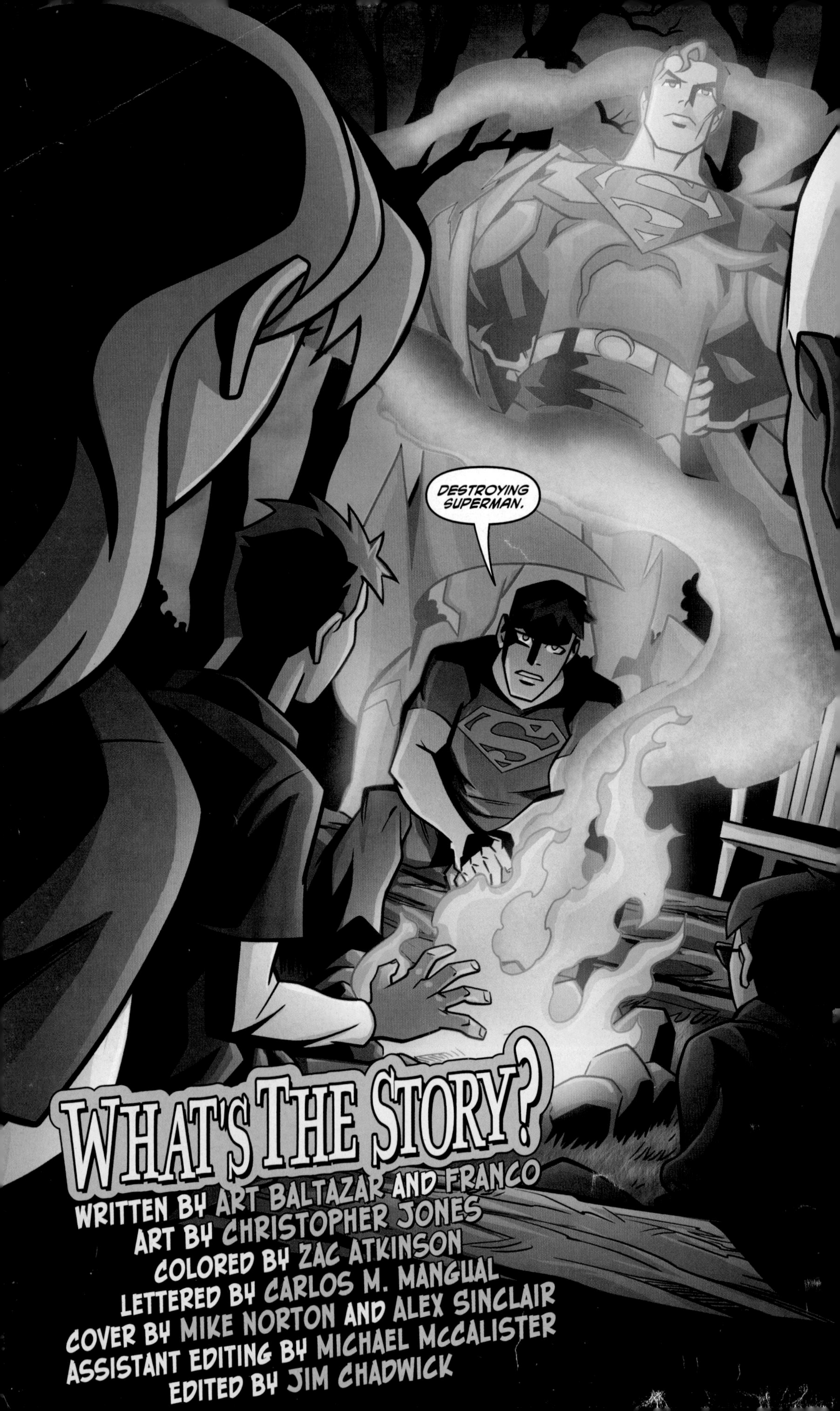
DESTROYING SUPERMAN.
WHAT'S THE STORY?
WRITTEN BY ART BALTAZAR AND FRANCO
ART BY CHRISTOPHER JONES
COLORED BY ZAC ATKINSON
LETTERED BY CARLOS M. MANGUAL
COVER BY MIKE NORTON AND ALEX SINCLAIR
ASSISTANT EDITING BY MICHAEL McCALISTER
EDITED BY JIM CHADWICK

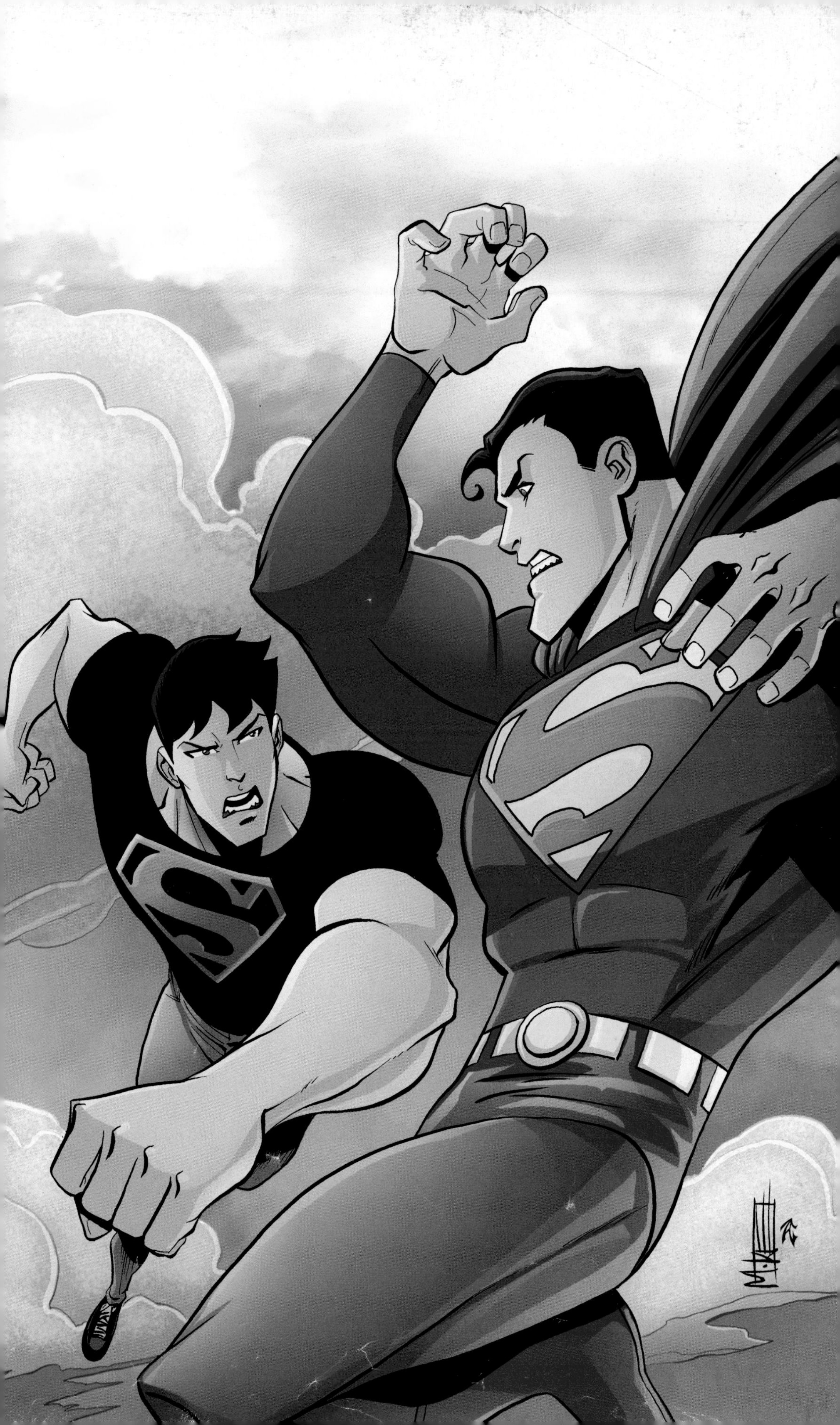

THE FLYING GRAYSONS

FOUR YEARS AGO.

"WE WERE A FAMILY... IN EVERY SENSE OF THE WORD.

THERE WAS MOM AND DAD, MY UNCLE, AUNT, MY COUSIN JOHN GRAYSON AND NINE-YEAR-OLD ME... RICHARD...DICK GRAYSON

"WE WERE THE ONES THE AUDIENCE WERE COMING TO SEE. THEY WOULD BE THRILLED WITH THE SOARING SPECTACLE OF THE HIGH-FLYING TRAPEZE ACT OF THE THE FLYING GRAYSONS!

"THE REASON THE AUDIENCE CAME TO SEE US WAS BECAUSE WE DID THE DANGEROUS STUFF.

"WE WORKED AT JACK HALY'S CIRCUS."

FEARS

HALY'S CIRCUS

WRITTEN BY: ART BALTAZAR AND FRANCO
PENCILLED BY: CHRISTOPHER JONES
INKS BY: DAN DAVIS (PAGES 1, 2, 4, 10, 11)
AND JOHN STANISCI (PAGES 3, 5-9, 12-20)
COLORED BY: ZAC ATKINSON
LETTERED BY: DEZI SIENTY
COVER BY: MIKE NORTON AND ZAC ATKINSON
ASSISTANT EDITING BY: MICHAEL MCCALISTER
EDITED BY: JIM CHADWICK

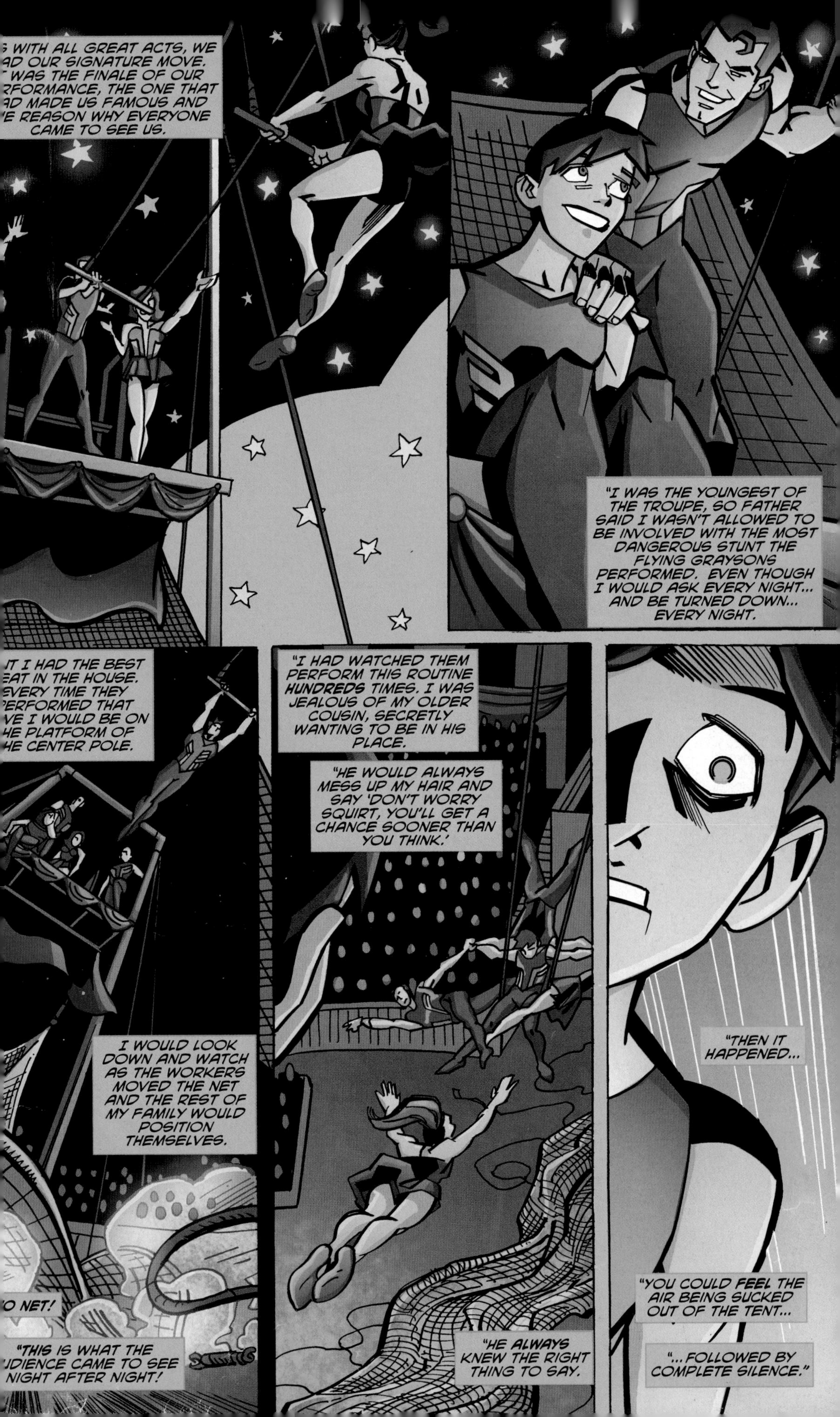
S WITH ALL GREAT ACTS, WE AD OUR SIGNATURE MOVE. T WAS THE FINALE OF OUR RFORMANCE, THE ONE THAT AD MADE US FAMOUS AND E REASON WHY EVERYONE CAME TO SEE US.
"I WAS THE YOUNGEST OF THE TROUPE, SO FATHER SAID I WASN'T ALLOWED TO BE INVOLVED WITH THE MOST DANGEROUS STUNT THE FLYING GRAYSONS PERFORMED. EVEN THOUGH I WOULD ASK EVERY NIGHT... AND BE TURNED DOWN... EVERY NIGHT.
T I HAD THE BEST EAT IN THE HOUSE. EVERY TIME THEY PERFORMED THAT VE I WOULD BE ON HE PLATFORM OF HE CENTER POLE.
I WOULD LOOK DOWN AND WATCH AS THE WORKERS MOVED THE NET AND THE REST OF MY FAMILY WOULD POSITION THEMSELVES.
O NET!
"THIS IS WHAT THE UDIENCE CAME TO SEE NIGHT AFTER NIGHT!
"I HAD WATCHED THEM PERFORM THIS ROUTINE HUNDREDS TIMES. I WAS JEALOUS OF MY OLDER COUSIN, SECRETLY WANTING TO BE IN HIS PLACE.
"HE WOULD ALWAYS MESS UP MY HAIR AND SAY 'DON'T WORRY SQUIRT, YOU'LL GET A CHANCE SOONER THAN YOU THINK.'
"HE ALWAYS KNEW THE RIGHT THING TO SAY.
"THEN IT HAPPENED...
"YOU COULD FEEL THE AIR BEING SUCKED OUT OF THE TENT...
"...FOLLOWED BY COMPLETE SILENCE."

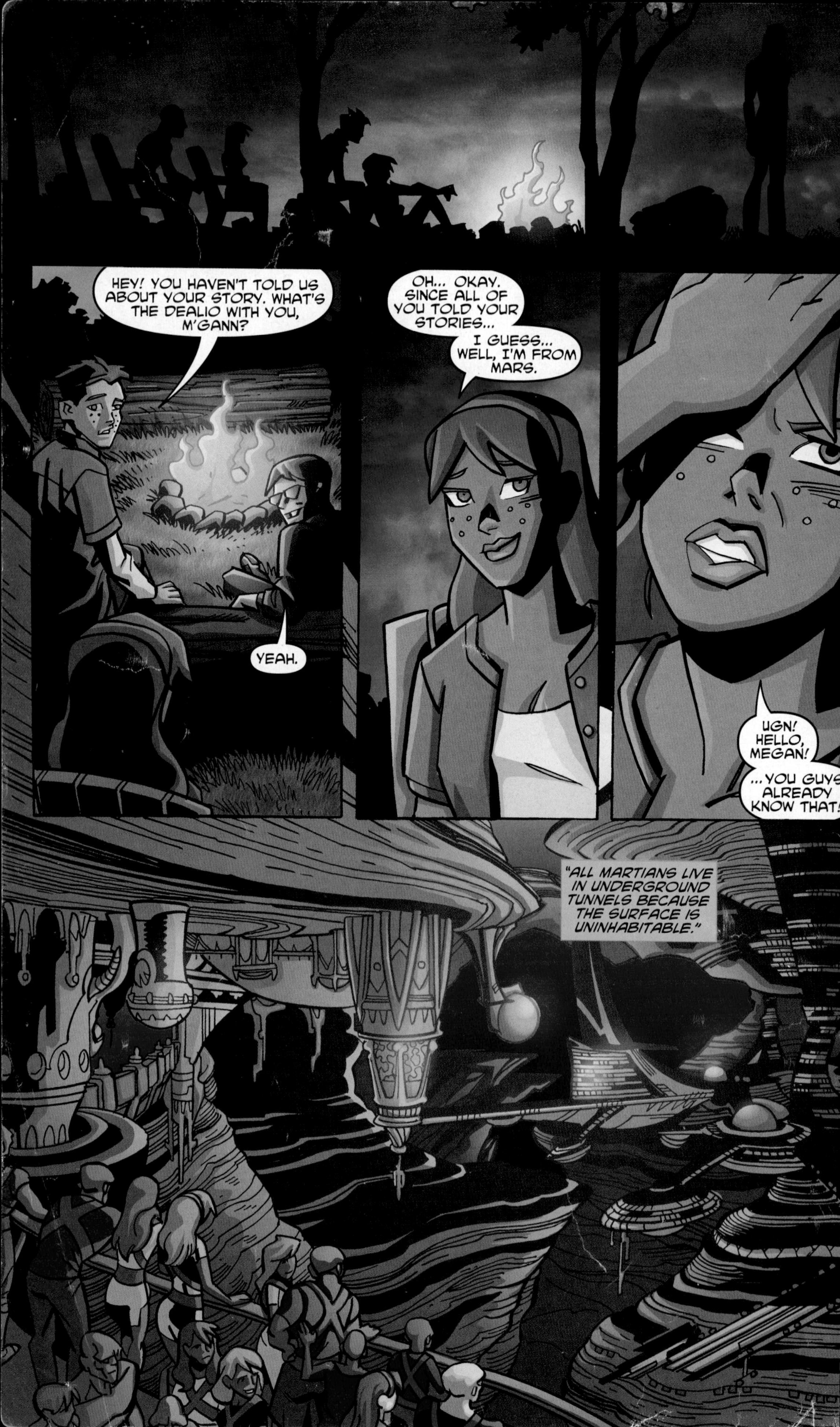
HEY! YOU HAVEN'T TOLD US ABOUT YOUR STORY. WHAT'S THE DEALIO WITH YOU, M'GANN?
YEAH.
OH... OKAY. SINCE ALL OF YOU TOLD YOUR STORIES...
I GUESS... WELL, I'M FROM MARS.
UGN! HELLO, MEGAN!
...YOU GUYS ALREADY KNOW THAT!
"ALL MARTIANS LIVE IN UNDERGROUND TUNNELS BECAUSE THE SURFACE IS UNINHABITABLE."

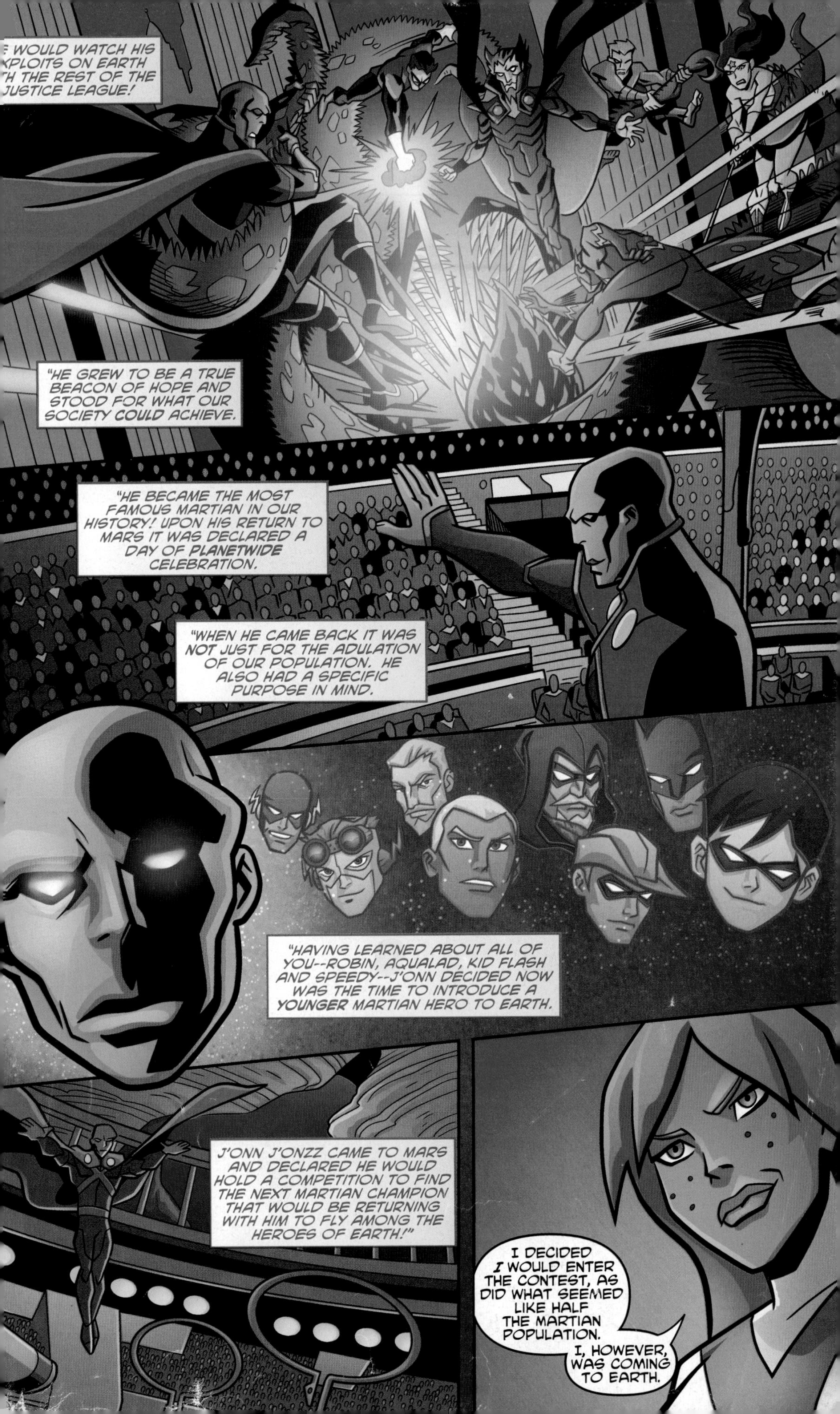
E WOULD WATCH HIS XPLOITS ON EARTH TH THE REST OF THE JUSTICE LEAGUE!
"HE GREW TO BE A TRUE BEACON OF HOPE AND STOOD FOR WHAT OUR SOCIETY COULD ACHIEVE.
"HE BECAME THE MOST FAMOUS MARTIAN IN OUR HISTORY! UPON HIS RETURN TO MARS IT WAS DECLARED A DAY OF PLANETWIDE CELEBRATION.
"WHEN HE CAME BACK IT WAS NOT JUST FOR THE ADULATION OF OUR POPULATION. HE ALSO HAD A SPECIFIC PURPOSE IN MIND.
"HAVING LEARNED ABOUT ALL OF YOU--ROBIN, AQUALAD, KID FLASH AND SPEEDY--J'ONN DECIDED NOW WAS THE TIME TO INTRODUCE A YOUNGER MARTIAN HERO TO EARTH.
J'ONN J'ONZZ CAME TO MARS AND DECLARED HE WOULD HOLD A COMPETITION TO FIND THE NEXT MARTIAN CHAMPION THAT WOULD BE RETURNING WITH HIM TO FLY AMONG THE HEROES OF EARTH!"
I DECIDED I WOULD ENTER THE CONTEST, AS DID WHAT SEEMED LIKE HALF THE MARTIAN POPULATION.
I, HOWEVER, WAS COMING TO EARTH.

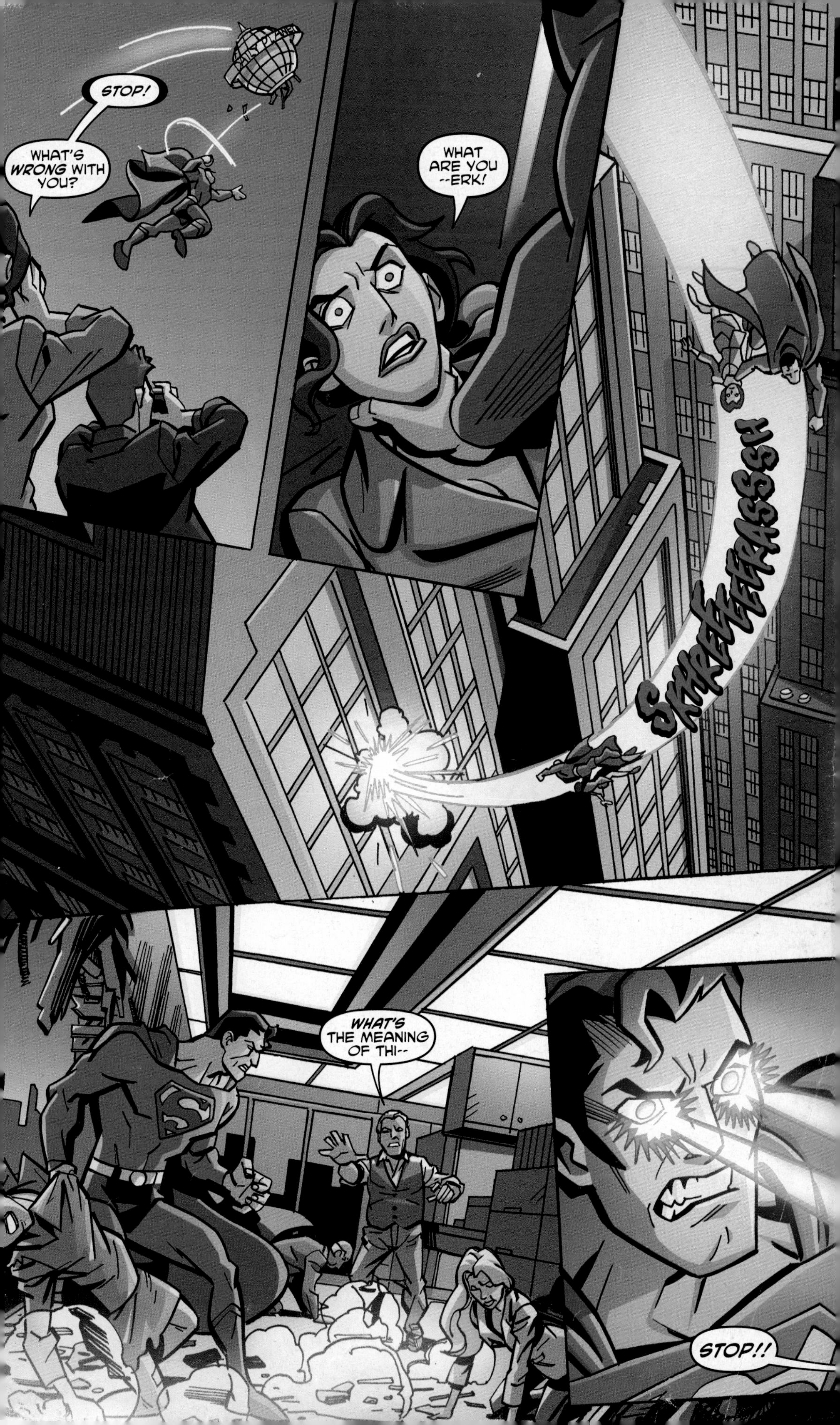
STOP!
WHAT'S *WRONG* WITH YOU?
WHAT ARE YOU --ERK!
SKREEEEFRASSSH
WHAT'S THE MEANING OF THI--
STOP!!

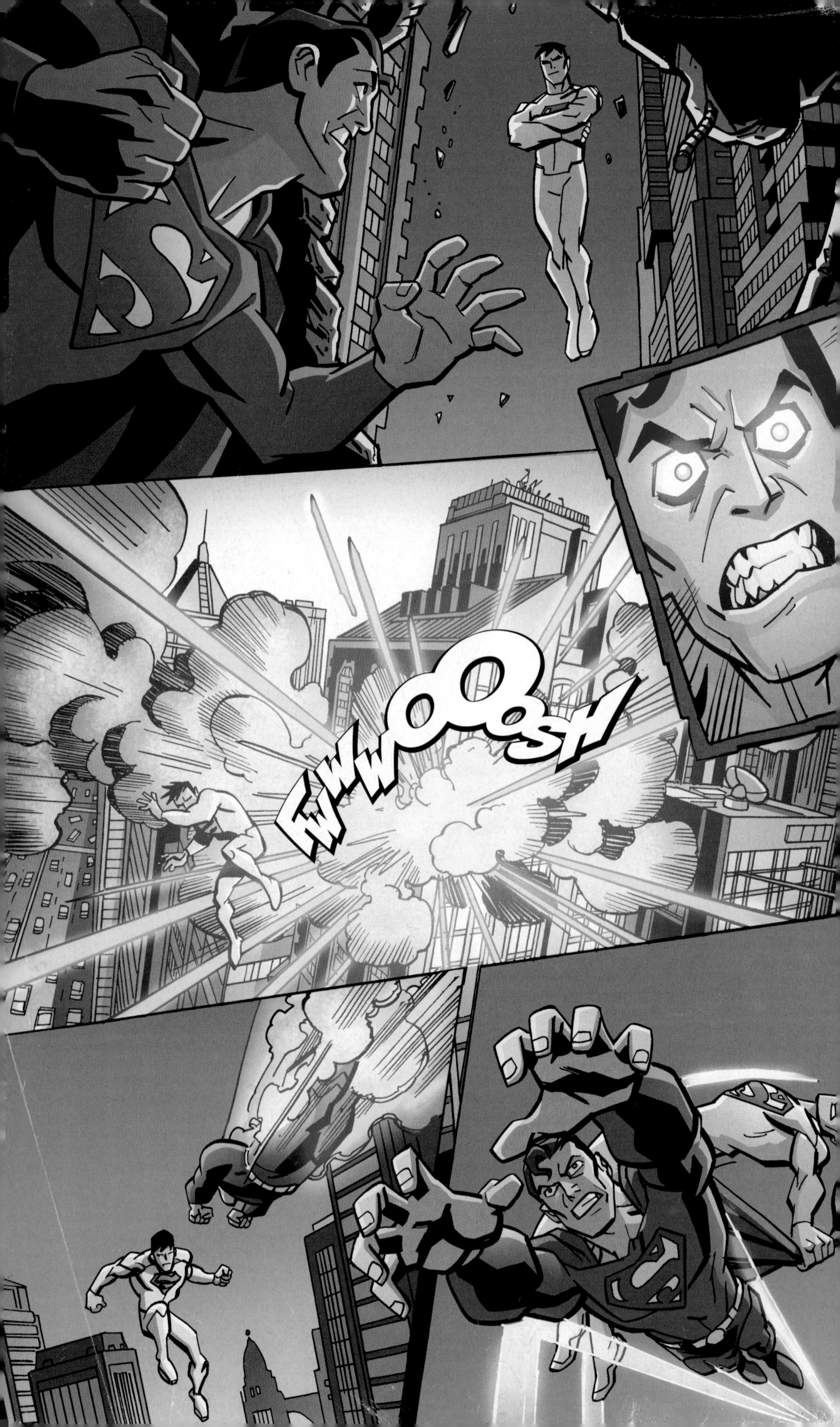
FWWWOOOSH

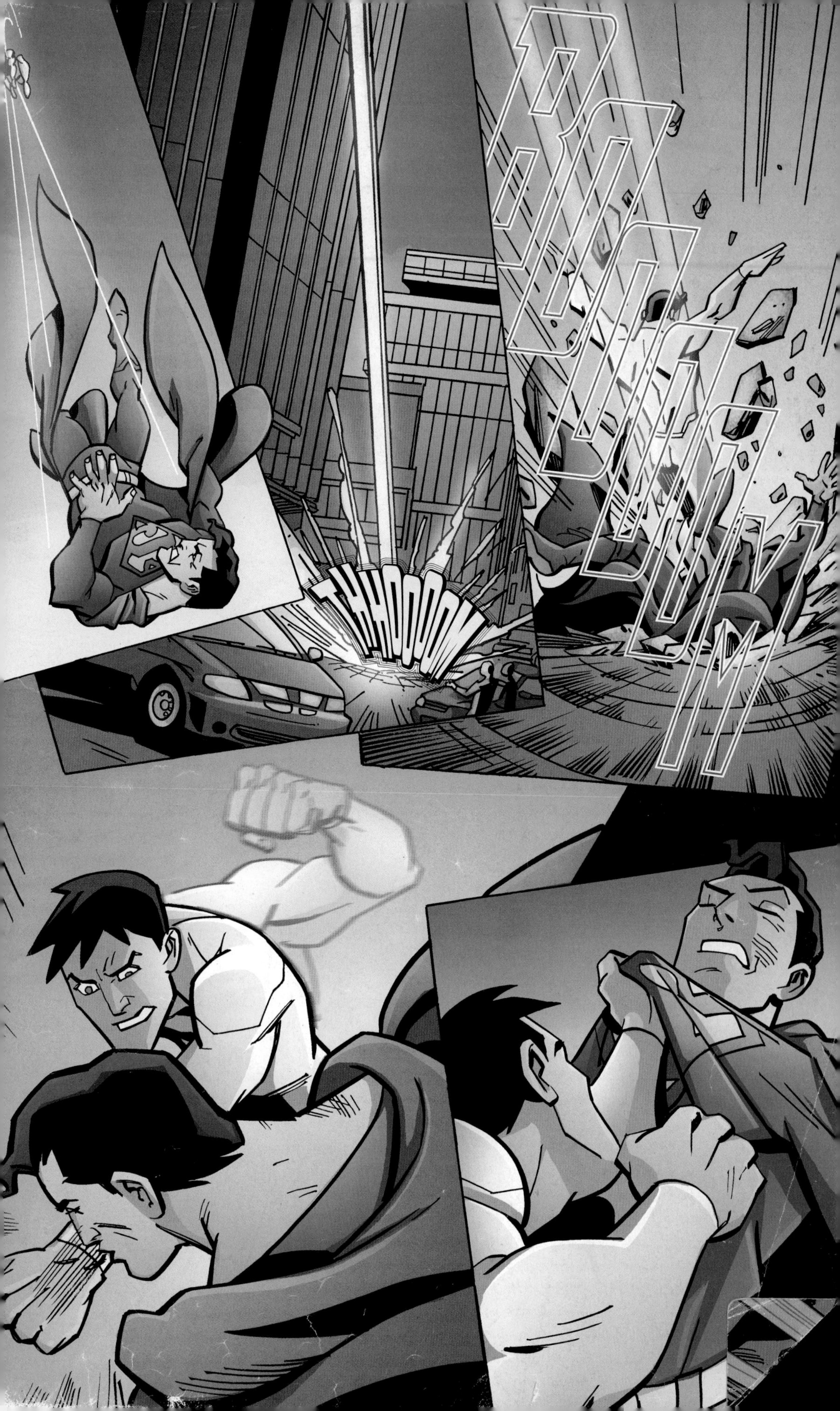
THHOOOOM
BOOOOM

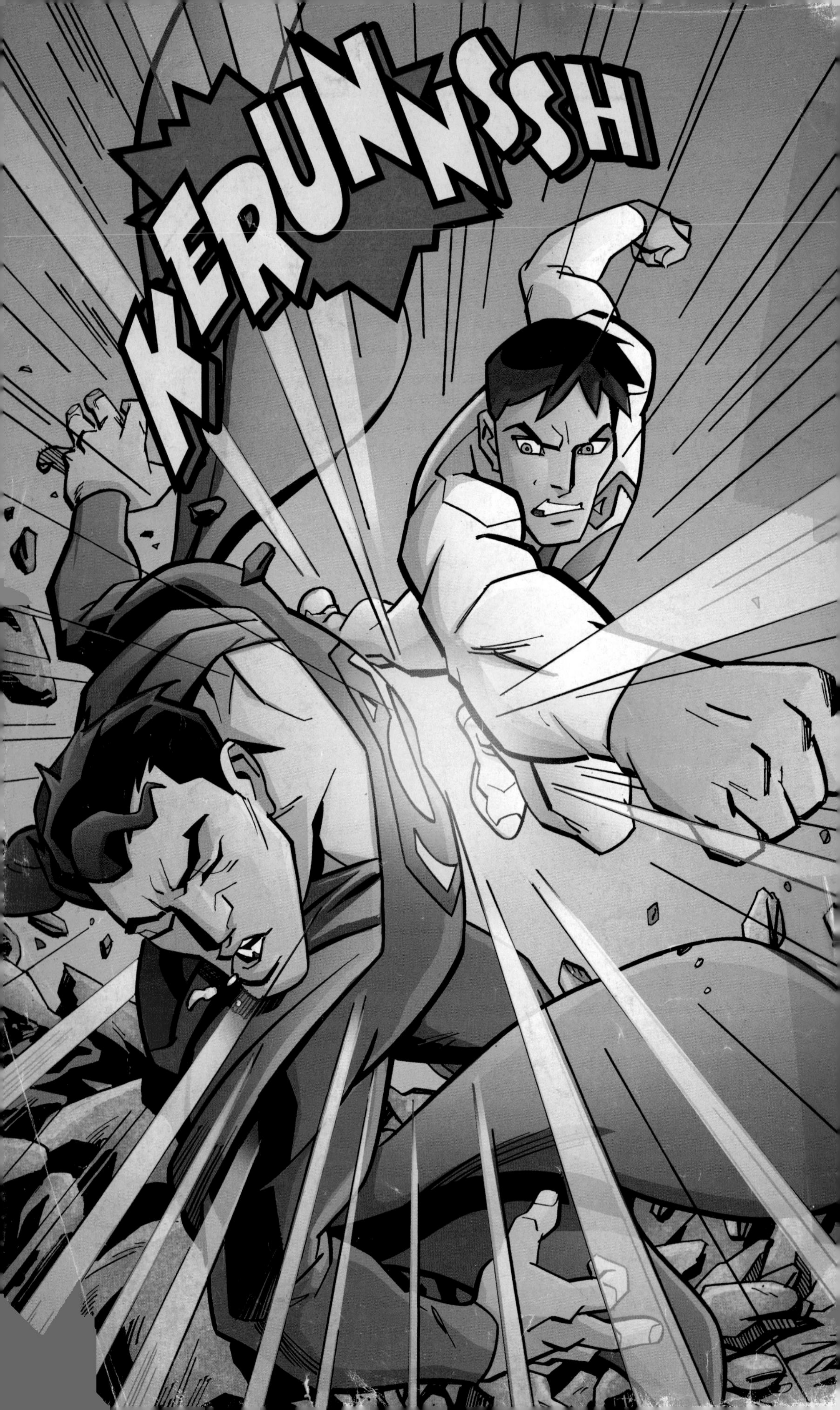
KERUNSSH